EVEN OUR FANTASIES

EVEN OUR FANTASIES
A Compendium
of Gay Erotica

Credits:
Mark of the Wolf, Copyright © by Derek Adams, 1996. *Miles Diamond and the Demon of Death*, Copyright © by Derek Adams, 1995. *Guy Traynor*, Copyright © by Torsten Barring, 1997. *Peter Thornwell*, Copyright © by Torsten Barring, 1993. "Roadie" by Michael Chelsea originally appeared in *Come Quickly: For Boys on the Go*, Copyright © by Julian Anthony Guerra, 1996. *The Mad Man*, Copyright © by Samuel R. Delany, 1994. "Rent-Boy" by Byron Esmond originally appeared in *Come Quickly: For Boys on the Go*, Copyright © by Julian Anthony Guerra, 1996. *Reunion in Florence*, Copyright © by Sonny Ford, 1992. "Christmas Gift" by Dylan Gamble originally appeared in *Come Quickly: For Boys on the Go*, Copyright © by Julian Anthony Guerra, 1996. *The Slave Prince*, Copyright © by Vince Gilman, 1994. *Islands of Desire*, Copyright © by Peter Heister, 1997. "F Train" by Cory Jackson originally appeared in *Come Quickly: For Boys on the Go*, Copyright © by Julian Anthony Guerra, 1996. "Skipper" by Paris Kincaid originally appeared in *Come Quickly: For Boys on the Go*, Copyright © by Julian Anthony Guerra, 1996. *A Secret Life*, Copyright © by Masquerade Books, 1992. *The Scarlet Pansy*, Copyright © by Masquerade Books, 1992. *Sins of the Cities of the Plain*, Copyright © by Masquerade Books, 1992. *Ambidextrous*, Copyright © by Felice Picano, 1985, 1995.

Credits continue on page 567

Even Our Fantasies: A Compendium of Gay Erotica
Copyright © 1997 by Masquerade Books
"Pornography: The Explication of the Pleasure Principle"
Copyright © 1997 by Michael Bronski

All Rights Reserved

Cover Photograph by Charles Hovland
Cover Design by Alana Lesiger

No part of this book may be reproduced, stored in a retrieval system, or transmitted in any form, by any means, including mechanical, electronic, photocopying, recording or otherwise, without prior written permission of the publishers.

First Printing November 1997

Manufactured in the United States of America
Published by Masquerade Books, Inc.
801 Second Avenue
New York, N.Y. 10017

"Gay novelists must bear witness to what they really lived through, not what revisionists and moralists would have preferred. Even our fantasies must be reported accurately—and fantasies, as Freud knew, are the most difficult part of our mental lives to censor."
—Edmund White, "The Joy of Gay Lit"

EVEN OUR FANTASIES

Pornography: The Explication of the Pleasure Principle   1
Michael Bronski

The Gay Adventures of Captain Goose   5
Larry Townsend

Christmas Gift   15
Dylan Gamble

Ambidextrous   21
Felice Picano

The Faustus Contract   33
Larry Townsend

Elliott   45
Sloan Ryder

F Train   49
Cory Jackson

Man Sword   53
Larry Townsend

Mark of the Wolf   79
Derek Adams

Rent-Boy   107
Byron Esmond

Run No More   113
Larry Townsend

Mr. Benson   127
John Preston

Chains   149
Larry Townsend

A Secret Life   175
Anonymous

Hustling: A Gentleman's Guide to the   191
Fine Art of Homosexual Prostitution
John Preston

Mind Master   207
Larry Townsend

Sins of the Cities of the Plain   229
Anonymous

The Mad Man   237
Samuel R. Delany

The Leatherman's Handbook	269
Larry Townsend	
Peter Thornwell	281
Torsten Barring	
The Scarlet Pansy	293
Anonymous	
Solidly Built	307
Matt Townsend	
The Mission of Alex Kane: Golden Years	329
John Preston	
Skipper	349
Paris Kincaid	
Roadie	355
Michael Chelsea	
Tour Guide	361
Thom Spencer	
The Construction Worker	367
Larry Townsend	
Guy Traynor	389
Torsten Barring	
Leather Ad: S	411
Larry Townsend	
Islands of Desire	423
Peter Heister	
Miles Diamond and the Demon of Death	439
Derek Adams	
Kiss of Leather	461
Larry Townsend	
Reunion in Florence	485
Sonny Ford	
The Initiation of PB 500	499
Kyle Stone	
Beware the God Who Smiles	517
Larry Townsend	
Slave Prince	537
Vince Gilman	
Rituals	551
Kyle Stone	

INTRODUCTION:

PORNOGRAPHY: THE EXPLICATION OF THE PLEASURE PRINCIPLE

MICHAEL BRONSKI

In his classic *Civilization and its Discontents* Freud postulates that humankind is in a perplexing position. We are, on one hand, driven by instinct to pursue pleasure, or what Freud calls Eros. We want to feel good, we want to enjoy our body, we want to experience the erotic fullness of life. This is not simply about sex, but about the full engagement of the imagination, emotions and body. This desire is aptly termed the Pleasure Principle.

On the other hand, the pure pursuit of pleasure would not allow us time, or energy, for things like finding food, building shelter, and putting together some form of social organization, or what Freud calls Civilization. This need is called the Reality Principle.

In the world according to Freud civilization, by its very nature, engenders discontents; they come with the territory, they are the unavoidable downside of having the world "work." Civilization, after all, is the foundation for all human endeavor, it is how we order the world, it is the bedrock upon which we build our daily lives, and upon which rests our most deeply-held beliefs. But lets not forget about the *discontents* we acquire in our trade-off for civilization. On the top of the list is sexual repression, the oil that makes the machinery of civilization run smoothly. And, of course, under sexual repression we also get men's enormous fear and mistrust of female sexuality and hatred of all homosexuality. These have led to the wholesale oppression—often resulting in physical harm—perpetrated on women and gay people. Along with sexual repression we humans have divided up the earth into arbitrary groups of nations and countries which, as they squabble over which "civilization" is better, have killed millions upon millions in wars and their ensuant famines and disasters. And, of course, there is slavery and...well, you get the idea.

Are these *discontents*—the word itself sounds so inconsequential, like not getting a seat on a crowded bus—the price we have to pay to have "civilization?" By positing one principle against another—pleasure against reality—Freud set up a paradigm in which Eros and civilization are constantly at odds. What would happen, he asks, if we all sought pleasure at the expense of sustaining life? What would happen if we pursued Eros at the expense of civilization? Good questions.

What would happen if—in some fabulous collective effort—human beings decided to to pursue a little more pleasure and a little less civilization? Well, maybe we could all enjoy sex a bit more, and maybe women could have some more freedom in their lives, and homosexuals wouldn't have to worry about being murdered for holding hands in the street. Then maybe we could get a grip on that war thing—what ever happened to that lovely 1960s notion of "make love, not war?"—and begin to deal with just getting along.

This is, obviously, a utopian fantasy. The reality is that human beings are constantly attempting to balance pleasure with reality, Eros with civilization. The problem is that for centuries and centuries we have been advised, urged, and forced to prioritize reality over pleasure, civilization over Eros. The very idea that the pursuit of pleasure— and sexuality is at the root of all pleasure— is a noble human activity has been labeled as degrading and unworthy, relegated to the crime report, confessional, and "substandard" genres of art like pornography.

Pornography was created as a place where Eros, unfettered by civilization, could run wild. If "real" literature did not discuss sexuality in explicit terms because it was too civilized, pornography existed as a realm in which the Pleasure Principle reigned. Pornography not only allowed but encouraged the sexual imagination—it was a wildlife preserve of imaginative pleasure that afforded refuge from the restrictions of reality, of civilization.

This is particularly true of gay pornography because homosexuality suffers a double repression—once for being about sex, and again for not being about heterosexuality. Gay pornography opens worlds to us that are forbidden by civilization. It creates a world of the imagination in which the constraints of civilization—the reality principle—fade and are replaced by the boundless Eros of the pleasure principle. At its core, pornography provides us with an alternative vision of life, of pleasure, or Eros.

While pornography functions as imagination—as does all literature—this is not to say that it does not have effects on the material world. First of all, it excites us sexually, it turns us on, it gives us a hard-on. Pornography—well, good pornography—brings that inner world of pleasure-seeking into the realm of everyday life: the Pleasure Principle becomes reality.

But pornography can do more than this. Like all imaginative writing, pornography is a map, a chart of the mind and imagination. It tells us where we have been, where we are now, and where we might be going. By guiding us to and granting us entree into worlds where Pleasure has replaced Repression as a guiding principle, pornography allows us to simply imagine a world in which sexual desire is provident and Eros is not at odds with civilization. This simple act of imagining is so at odds with how the material world—the "real" world—is organized that it is a radical re-thinking of how our lives are ordered. Pornography is a map to the Pleasure Principle.

Maps can be dangerous writing, for they tell us not only where we are but how we can get out, change, relocate our lives and desires. Traditionally maps from the thirteenth and fourteenth centuries charted a circumscribed known world—Europe, North Africa, the near "Orient"—and carefully marked the regions beyond these territories with the phrase "there be dragons." The maps of pornography usher us into those extreme, uncharted territories where danger and pleasure lurk. They show us who we might be, what we might do, what is possible if only we accept the the fact that this is a land ruled by pleasure not repression, Eros, not civilization. Simply by showing us these imaginative alternatives, pornography opens the possibility that actions in the material world might be different as well. By stirring sexual desire in our souls and our groins pornography makes us look at how we live our civilized lives and, at the very least, makes us understand the distance between our urge for pleasure and our ability to pleasure ourselves in the world in which we live our everyday lives.

Michael Bronski is the author of *Culture Clash: the Making of Gay Sensibility*. He has edited *Flashpoint: Gay Male Sexual Writing* and *Taking Liberties: Gay Men's Essays on Politics, Culture and Sex* for which he was awarded the 1997 Lambda Literary Award for Best Nonfiction Anthology.

THE GAY ADVENTURES OF CAPTAIN GOOSE

Larry Townsend

Late one evening a few days later, Captain Goose carried on the outskirts of a small village near Provincetown. His arrival was silent as his horse had thrown a shoe a mile out of town, forcing Jerry to approach on foot. Leading his mount along the shoulder of the road, he paused near a cluster of buildings not far from the central plaza. From the arrangement of the houses he realized he must have entered one of the old-fashioned Puritan communities that were still fairly common to the region. At this hour of night, lighted windows were few and far between. The burning of unnecessary beeswax would be considered a sinful waste by these people, as would be the disgraceful crime of lying abed once the first light of dawn appeared in the eastern sky.

Jerry tethered his mount and explored a bit between the buildings, assuring himself that everyone, including the watchman, was indeed sleep. He found the elderly gentleman who should have been safe-guarding the sleeping citizens snoozing gently in his shack behind the meeting hall. Stealthily, the highwayman continued on through a darkened alley between two rows of houses. A thin sliver of moon was just rising to the south, casting a slight glimmer on the ground. Knowing he would be severely punished if he were caught prowling about, Jerry carefully moved away from the larger dwellings where he might encounter a barking dog. He was hungry, but soon gave up hope of finding an unlocked smokehouse or some outdoor oven.

The entire village was silent, locked and retired for the night. The highwayman continued into the very center of town, stopping at the edge of the square. Since he had started thinking about it, he was hungrier than ever. Desperation was about to propel him in the direction of a darkened inn when he was startled by a muffled groan. As icy fear gripped his spine, Jerry pulled a pistol from his waistband and took a few steps toward the sound. The groan came again, followed by a little grunt, as of a tired man straining to move his body.

Once in the shadows from whence the sounds had come, Jerry was able to see the stocks, the cruel wooden frames in which the righteous Puritans punished those whose transgressions did not merit a more severe form of chastisement. The present prisoner had been placed in a standing position with his head and hands protruding through holes in the wooden block. The rest of his body was free but unsupported, causing a terrible strain from standing after being held in place for some length of time. The fellow groaned again as Jerry stepped quietly up beside him.

"Are you all right?" asked the highwayman. It was a useless question, but Jerry did not know what else to say.

The man rolled his eyes upward in an expression of agony. Jerry stepped around and fingered the lock. It was solid brass and much too strong for him to break.

"Can I do anything to help you?" he asked.

"Y-yes...er...perhaps you could, sir," replied the young prisoner, uncertainly. "You see, it's a little embarrassing, sir, but to tell the truth the watchman forgot about me on his last round, and...well, I gotta piss so bad I can't stand it much longer, and there ain't any way to get the watchman here until morning."

Jerry grinned, at first to himself and then quite broadly. He was a sturdily built youngster, not much past eighteen. Even dressed as he was in the heavy homespun of the puritans, the muscular angularity of his body was apparent.

"If you don't mind my being somewhat...personal," laughed Jerry. He reached under the edge of the prisoner's jacket, fumbling but a moment before his fingers closed about the upper button of his breeches. Quickly Jerry's hands undid the fasteners and his palm snaked inside to grasp the handsome prisoner's cock. The boy moaned again, this time in relief instead of pain. As the heavy torrent streamed from his body, he tilted his head back, causing the meager moonlight to fall upon his features. It was now Jerry's turn to gasp, for the face beneath the tousled blond hair was nothing short of angelic. Without stopping to think, his hand still grasping the prisoner's penis, Jerry leaned forward and kissed the young man full upon the lips.

The highwayman felt a response at both points where his body was in contact with the youngster. After an initial start of surprise, the lips returned the pressure, while below there was a definite lengthening of the young man's heavy-hanging cock.

When their mouths parted, the prisoner sighed, opened his eyes and smiled. "I didn't expect that," he said. "I'm surprised it...well, if you could finish getting me back, sir...it...Oh!" he sighed, as Jerry continued to hold his gradually swelling cock, and kissed him once again upon the lips.

As he kissed the sweet, pliant mouth, Jerry continued to hold the supple flesh in his hand, gently gripping it, releasing, gripping again. The cock continued to expand, to grow larger and warmer. Then it stood straight out, requiring no support from Jerry.

The young man in the stocks was breathing hard, tiny beads of sweat breaking out on his forehead. But he made no effort to conceal his enjoyment of Jerry's manipulations, in fact he would have been hard put to hide it. Finally, however, he tried to back away from the highwayman's touch, as far as the restraining stocks would permit.

"Don't you like what I'm doing?" whispered Jerry. He tried to read an expression on the lad's eyes, but the prisoner's face now hung forward, concealed in the deep shadows.

Without relaxing his grip on the youngster's cock, Jerry twisted his neck around, to press his lips once more upon the boy's. This time the lad resisted him for several heartbeats, until the fierce throbbing of his rock-hard cock expressed the desire his puritanical upbringing forbade him to show. Jerry's tongue flicked between the prisoner's lips; after a moment's hesitation, it was able to make its way between the teeth.

Jerry's free hand encircled the prisoner's waist, pulling their bodies together as the boy now answered him with all the enthusiasm his awkward position permitted. Then he was making little whining sounds, moaning deep in his throat. It was the only sound he was capable of making, while his mouth was so completely possessed by the highwayman. Taking the cue, Jerry disengaged himself and fell to his knees before the prisoner. Quickly he encircled the upthrusting cockhead with his lips. Slowly he inched along the magnificent, rigid smoothness, nearly strangling on the tremendous bulk before his nose touched against the patch of golden hair at its base. His pressed tightly against the prisoner's rounded buttocks, pulling the hard slender hips and thighs against his shoulders. For a long while he rocked back and forth, propelling the swollen shaft into his eager mouth, then out almost to the end, and back again in a rush of frantic, consuming moisture. He felt the violent shudder and heard the ecstatic gasp as the young prisoner began to come. The hips moved of themselves, unable to press close enough or hard enough against the compelling lips or the eagerly receiving mouth.

Then came a hot spurt of sweet, fiery liquid, as the lad released his pent-up desires, rearing and pounding like a stallion in his paddock. He rocked from left to right, forcing his cock to press against one side, then the other, of Jerry's throat. At last no more spurted from the tip and the highwayman reluctantly began to pull himself away, sliding his lips down the still-bulging manhood.

"No, no," whispered the lad. "Please, sir, don't stop!"

Jerry needed no further encouragement. Keeping one hand firmly against the lad's solid, constantly-flexing butt, the highwayman continued with a gentle caressing. His lips moved back and forth, traveling the full glorious length of the prisoner's hardened penis. As his own passion had been straining within his crotch, Jerry reached down his other hand, feeling the outline of his own enormous erection. Shifting his position a bit, but still kneeling before the captive figure, Jerry brought his own shaft out of his trousers. Then he stood up. Holding the two cocks against each other, he squeezed them in ecstatic pressure, sliding his own great length along the moistened surface of the other.

He kissed the boy again, wishing there were some more practical way to use his sizable rod. The boy's hot breath matched Jerry's in demand and welcome. As the moaning sounds began again, deep in the youngster's throat. Jerry fell swiftly to his knees. He took the second discharge as he had the first, while his own seed shot in milky profusion upon the ground.

When all was finished, Jerry stood up and started to return the youth's still swollen member to its proper position. As he struggled to force the hard, resisting cock back into its covering of homespun, he glanced up to meet the youngster's eyes. The boy was looking at him intently, with more than an expression of curiosity or idle admiration.

"I think I know who you are," he whispered.

"Really?" said Jerry.

"You're Captain Goose, aren't you?" said the boy, a note of awe in his voice.

"Some call me that," Jerry admitted.

"You ought to help me, then," asserted the boy. "I'm all against the Tories too. Some day I hope we can get rid of them all."

"What did you do to get put in here?" the highwayman asked.

"They think I was trying to steal a pig from old man Williams' farm," he said. "That's what I told them when I got caught sneaking out of his barn. Actually I'd been doing something like you did to me with the old bastard's kid."

"Kid?"

"Yeah...his son...not a, not a girl!" he protested.

Jerry smiled. "Let's see what I can do," he said.

With that, he slipped back to the shack where the watchman still slept soundly in his chair. A ring of keys hung from the fat little man's waist, and Jerry tried to slip them loose. When they would not come, he stepped around behind the watchman and shook him awake. As the red-rimmed eyes came open, the first thing they saw was the business end of Captain Goose's pistol.

"One sound and you're a dead man," said Jerry. "Now stand up!"

Quickly, he bound the quaking little mound of flesh to a peg set high in the wall. Once the watchman was secure, Jerry removed his pants and drawers, laughing at the tiny penis that dangled between the rolls of fat. Taking a quill from the table, he dipped it in the inkwell and etched a goose on the rounded belly, drawing the neck extended downward so the tiny jiggling penis would form the beak. Then he stuffed a handkerchief in the little man's mouth and tied it in place with a piece of rope. Merrily jingling the ring of keys, the highwayman sauntered back to the youth in the stocks.

"If I release you, will you return the favor?" asked Jerry. He said this lightly, thinking with pleasure of a further session of sex.

However, the boy took it to mean he wanted help, or maybe

money. "I'll be your slave," he said, "though I haven't any gold to give you."

"The only gold I want is here," said Jerry, running his hand across the ample crotch.

He unlocked the stocks and lifted the bar to release the boy, who promptly introduced himself as Michael. Together they slipped out of town, and Michael led Jerry to a farm a couple of miles distant. The property belonged to a friend of Michael's, and as it turned out, an intimate friend, indeed. After giving the boys a cold but hearty meal, the farmer asked them to spend the night. The offer was accepted gladly, especially when their host also promised to put a new shoe on Jerry's horse in the morning.

The farmer, a spare, balding man in his late thirties, was named Zekial. His face, deeply tanned by the sun, had about it a handsome youthfulness that belied his years, and his jovial personality made Jerry immediately like him. Even clothed, the sinewy, corded muscles gave promise of a sensuality many a younger man might envy. Once in the huge bedstead, Jerry discovered how right his initial impression had been. As was Michael, the youth's rapid recovery of sexual vigor was nothing short of miraculous. His passion, after twice ejaculating in the square, was wilder than Jerry's. Nor were the highwayman's unexpressed wishes during their affair in the center of town to remain unfulfilled. They had been in bed but a short time before Jerry had the pleasure of that powerful shaft, inserted full length in his lower orifice. The muscular highwayman contracted his sphincter about this eater, plunging pole of love, at first nearly paralyzed by the magnificent sensation. Following the lead of the younger man, Jerry was lying on his stomach while the slender farm boy's cock invaded his receptive ass. All the while the strongly corded muscles of the farmer continued to squeeze and rub against his upper back and shoulders, until he caused Jerry's desire to flame into such a craving it was difficult to restrain his final climax. Just the very thought of what was happening to him sent his wildest emotions flying.

As Michael remained ensconced upon the deliciously rounded saddle, Jerry felt himself pulled slightly forward, his upper chest raised so it rested against the farmer's thighs. In this position the highwayman was staring straight at their host's unusually shaped erection. Zekial's cock poked its beckoning shaft upward toward the rough hewn beams of the ceiling. While its length was extraordinary to begin with, easily equally to Jerry's, it was unique configuration that immediately fascinated the robber. The shaft was extremely slender through its entire extension, stretching hard and rigid between the silky pubic hairs to the underside of the cockhead. But the tip was truly magnificent, a breathtaking work of art. Like the crown of a bursting-tip mushroom, the farmer's cock terminated in the largest head Jerry had ever found. He doubted, even, if Jonathan could quite equal its rounded glory.

Nor was Zekial unskilled in using his marvelous appendage. Holding Jerry's head in place, he plunged his cock in deeply, demanding the full passage of Jerry's mouth and throat. His urgency was well matched to the quick, steady, fully-rammed strokes the highwayman was receiving from Michael. The boy remained astride the flexing, tightening ass, his hands holding firmly against the hollows at Jerry's hips, while the highwayman was helpless to do other than enjoy the double penetration. A tremendous climax was achieved when Jerry felt his own sperm begin to spurt in violent, frantic spasms. He increased his stroke on the farmer's cock, and Michael, who had been ready for several minutes, released his third enormous discharge of fluid. In fact, the boy came so hard it made Jerry wince as the tantalizing bursts flooded into his body.

CHRISTMAS GIFT
Dylan Gamble

There was Christmas music playing when I got home, even though no one was supposed to be there. It was cats meowing "Silent Night." I'd never heard anything so funny.

I kind of knew who it was before I even opened the door. Randy. It had to be.

To say the least, Randy was a flake. I don't know how I hooked up with him in the first place. It was one of those things that just happened.

Yes, there he was when I opened the door, smiling, shirtless, dancing around my apartment to the sound of cats and dogs singing a rousing medley of "What Child Is This?" and "Hava Nagila," of all things. He was decorating a Christmas tree. He had hooked glass ornaments to his nipple piercings.

"You look festive. Who let you in?"

"Landlady, Kevin. Lighten up, man, it's Christmas."

I shook my head. He came closer, holding some mistletoe over my head. He looked at me, then up at the mistletoe. "Oh, all right!" He kissed me chastely on the cheek.

I placed a hand on his chest, running my fingers along the muscles cording his ribs, passing over the nipples extending over the piercings. He always looked so damned good. So "Randy."

Randy dropped the mistletoe and stepped in closer. He threaded his fingers through my hair and slashed his lips across mine, probing deeply with his tongue. He tasted vaguely of eggnog.

"You still make me hard for you," he said, taking my hand and pressing it against the bulge in his surfer shorts. He slipped my suit jacket off my shoulders, and it pooled on the floor behind me. Then he undid the zipper on my trousers and dropped them as well. Finally, my underwear.

Randy smiled. "No one but you could look sexy in socks," he said as he sank to his knees.

All at once, my cock was in his mouth. He ran his tongue up and down the shaft, taking it in so deep that the head touched the back of his throat. He applied pressure with his lips on the way out, and tongued his way down the shaft to take my balls one by one into his mouth, where he licked and nibbled his way from one to the other.

He licked his way down the line that divides the sacs and back toward my asshole. His hands kneaded the cheeks of my ass. I felt myself getting painfully hard. My legs were getting weak. I grasped Randy's shoulders.

He came up for air and drew me down onto the floor. Sitting up, he drew down his shorts. He wasn't wearing anything underneath. His eight-inch cock was sticking straight out at attention. He lowered himself to kiss me again, licking his way down. I pulled him off.

Shrugging, he raised one of my legs and, guiding himself with one hand, he entered me swiftly and completely. The ornaments brushed against my chest.

He stroked in and out, setting a languorous rhythm completely at odds with the singing cats. His monster cock filling me completely, I rose to meet his every thrust. As he pistoned in and out, his washboard stomach grated against the small of my back.

Finally, on his last thrust, he sheathed himself to the hilt, clenched the muscles of his ass and shot violently, rivers of cum deluging my bowels with heat. As I felt his seed within me, I felt my own balls spasm, shooting liquid heat up the shaft to explode against our connected bodies.

Covered with sweat and sperm, Randy rolled to one side and propped himself up on an elbow. He brushed a stray hair from my damp forehead. "Merry Christmas, dude!" he said.

AMBIDEXTROUS
Felice Picano

I think that in everyone's early life there exists one neighborhood boy who stands out from all others by sheer dint of his troublemaking capacity; the boy whom children only mention with awe and fear and parents with anger and annoyance. Such a boy was Junior Cook. He came from an otherwise unexceptional Irish-American middle class family which boasted several other children of perfect mediocrity. But—as Mendel showed in the last century with his sweetpea experiments—sometimes out of four offspring, one gets all the dominant genes, leaving little to the third child (like myself) and a first son (unlike myself) which could have meant he was overly pampered as an infant and young child; or conversely that he was saddled with expectations he could never live up to.

That might explain his psychology, it didn't really account for Junior Cook's charisma or his natural talent for meanness and mischief. He wore his butterscotch hair in a tough year 'round flat-top crewcut. Already at fifteen, he had a tattoo on his left shoulder. He had been in fights with boys two and three years older than himself and, rumor had it, once with an adult. he swore, smoked cigarettes, had been in reform school six months for a particularly loathsome store robbery where a clerk had been nicked with a switchblade knife, and he remained unchastened by the experience—indeed, he was proud of it.

Not much taller than I, Junior Cook was slender, but wiry and already as well-muscled as a grown man. he could have become a superb athlete—runner, wrestler, boxer, decathlon star—with his strength and agility. But it was clear that he would never get beyond the ninth grade or his seventeenth birthday, whichever came first. He openly, actively hated school, parents, authority of any kind. Apart from his unexpected shortness, he was physically compelling; enough so to attract and mistreat many teenage girls. He had a squarish face, accented by a set jaw, long lips, eyebrows like horizontal brackets, a short almost snub nose with wide nostrils, all of it topped by the closed lid of his crewcut, with a small widow's peak that gave the only hint of angularity to his features. His eyes were long, but half shut most of the time as though clamped down to deliberately keep out the good things of life. Yet, when open, they were a startling Caribbean blue, specked with tiny yellow and whit dots that made them look filled with stars. He dressed "tough": black body-fitting Camels, tight fitting blue denims (the first I'd seen on someone who wasn't a workman), a wide, black garrison belt with a large buckle depicting a charging bull and black motorcycle boots.

I quailed upon entering the hideout, despite Ricky shoving me forward with a whispered assurance that it was "Okay."

Inside, the ganghouse wasn't much to look at, but as it had the aura of a fabled, forbidden place, I observed as much as I could without seeming to be nosy. A green metal shaded lamp hung from the ceiling illuminating a cramped single room with more or less vertical walls, but an oddly-angled ceiling. Loose plants of differing sized and varieties of wood had been hammered together as a floor, but one could still make out the dirt ground below through a few large knots and ill-fitting joins. The furniture was sparse and worn—three old windsor chairs with torn upholstery and cracked springs had their legs sawn off so they sat almost flat. Two black painted milk Boxes held a variety of objects I couldn't quite make out as they were in the darkest part of the room. In another corner, on the floor, was a tattered, half-rolled up sleeping bag. Most fascinating was their primitive alarm system, devised of tin cans on a string, that wound from inside the hideout to outside and would be set clanking—and warning—if one didn't know exactly where the strings attaching them crossed.

Junior cook was sitting in one chair, his feet almost straight out in front of him, as we entered. He was reading *Argosy* magazine, on its cover a lurid illustration of a bloody-chested adventurer beating to death a ferociously snarling Bengal tiger with blows of his huge rifle butt. Slightly behind them, a blood-spattered, breasty blond shrink back into the jungle foliage. When Junior Cook deigned to look up, he greeted Ricky offhandedly, looked at me for an instant, and seemingly unable to place who I was ignored me. He popped open a Rheingold, told Ricky to share it with me, gave an unopened can of beer to Bayley, who perched on one of the milk boxes and began chugging. Junior Cook drank beer and told Ricky and I to "take a load off your feet." We sat in the two remaining chairs, while Junior Cook continued to read whatever article or story had captured his attention. When he was done with it, he rolled up the magazine as though about to use it as a weapon, but threw it harmlessly over his shoulder. Still ignoring me, he asked Ricky how he'd been.

If I had been astonished by our destination that afternoon, I was even more amazed that Ricky knew Junior Cook; that they had friends somehow in common seemed so unlikely. I hadn't lost a jot of my nervousness of defensiveness, even though I did share the beer with Ricky and tried to seem as relaxed as he was. Only when—out of nowhere—Junior Cook asked, "Who's this?" and Ricky answered back, "My buddy. He's okay," and Junior Cook stared me up and down for a very long two minutes, did I begin to feel uncomfortable again.

"He sniff?" Junior Cook asked and when Ricky said I did, Junior pulled out the biggest tube of airplane glue I'd ever seen, squirted a large gob of it into a plastic bag and handed it to me. I inhaled deeply, passed it on, and quickly realized that they were going to act as though nothing unusual was happening. I too would have to act "cool", even if I was already reeling from a single deep inhalation. Junior even pulled out a cigarette, offered the pack around and he and Bayley smoked between sniffs.

"So what brings you here?" Junior Cook asked Ricky and reached forward to put a hand on my friend's upper thigh. "You getting any?" he asked, before Ricky had a chance to answer his first question. Ricky nodded at me, and Junior Cook again looked me up and down, then said, "Yeah, but it ain't the same, is it?" When Ricky didn't respond, Junior Cook went on. "I thought you said your uncle promised to whip you good if you ever saw me again?" Ricky said that didn't bother him, no one would tell. "Oh, yeah?" Cook asked, "Not even this little boy?" and he reached over and took my upper thigh in his strong grip.

In addition to my fear and nervousness and surprise, I now had to deal with a new fact, not all the subtly revealed through their exchange—Junior Cook and Ricky had once been buddies, buddies perhaps as intimate as Ricky and I, and somehow or other had been forced apart by Ricky's family. I felt if not exactly jealous, then very much like it—and confused. I wished we would leave and turned to get Ricky's attention.

He was leaning forward, grasping Junior Cook's leg back, and he said in that slightly slurred voice I knew so well from our glue-sniffing sessions, "Got another cigarette?" When Junior Cook shook out a Camel, Ricky said, "Put it in, will ya?" When that had been done, Ricky made Junior Cook light it, and made a big show of blowing out the match. For a minute I thought they would kiss, their faces were so close, the air between them so thick with beer and cigarette and glue fumes, and I felt really uncomfortable. But Bayley began to laugh, and Junior Cook leaned back and turned to Bayley to bark out, "Shut it, or I'll shut it for you." Bayley got quiet really fast, and Junior Cook repeated his first question, "So what brings you back here today?"

Ricky puffed on his cigarette then slowly said, "I told him about Bayley's big dick, but he didn't believe me. Wants to see it for himself."

Now I'd seen Ricky Hersch in many situations in the months of our friendship: as a child among schoolchildren, with his family, with his friends, with grown-ups; I'd seen him compassionate, angry, merry; I'd seen him with come dripping out of the sides of his mouth he was so sensual. But I'd never seen him like this: cool, hard, manipulative, challenging, playful yet dangerous too. Evidently he considered himself at least Junior Cook's equal—probably his superior—to toy with him as he was doing. It calmed me a bit, not much.

"Yeah? Is that *all* you came here for?" Junior cook said back, and took Ricky's cigarette out of his mouth, puffed on it, handed it back.

"Why else would I come here?" Ricky answered, and stamped the cigarette on the floor without putting it to his lips again.

Annoyed, Junior Cook said, "You heard him, Bayley. Whip out your meat for pretty boy here."

Bayley jumped down from the milk boxes to stand right between us. He unzipped his pants reached into his slightly yellow-stained jockey shorts and extracted an almost erect monster of length, girth and redness.

"You like that?" Junior Cook asked me. "Go on touch it, see for yourself. Go on. It won't bite. Though it may spit at ya. Go on," he prompted. I looked at Ricky to see what I should do, but he wasn't paying us any mind. He was slumped back in his chair sniffing glue again.

I touched Bayley's cock and it got stone hard, veins quivering all over in length.

"Go on," Junior Cook insisted, "Jerk it," and I did, although not much as I couldn't get a purchase on its smooth thickness. "Use two hands," Junior Cook instructed, and I did. "Ain't nothing Bayley likes better than having a pretty boy jerk his meat," he added, "unless it's having someone with a ten dollar bill jerk it. Ain't that right Bayley? Or even better, having a pretty boy suck on it. Go on. Put it in your mouth. Go on."

I wouldn't. I let go of it, embarrassed, frightened, not by Bayley's cock, but by Junior Cook's words, his insidious tone of voice—and the situation altogether. Ricky was now slumped even more deeply in his chair, the glue sniffing bag over his face. I felt alone.

It could be dangerous. I remembered hearing about people—children mostly—who'd smothered to death with plastic bags over their faces. I reached for the bag, pretending I wanted to sniff more, and Ricky came to a bit, looking at me, at us, as though from far away.

Junior Cook had leaned forward again, and begun caressing Bayley's cock, still erect between our faces. He began going "ooh" and "aah" as he jerked it, then make a big show of licking its length, then offering it to me, and when I nodded no, of taking the big red tip of it in his mouth, and slurping a lot as though it were a lollipop, taking it out again and rubbing it all over his face, lifting his eyebrows and following his eyes whenever he put it in or took it out of his mouth, continually offering it to me, once even saying, "Mmmmm. Better than a lollipop, dontcha' think?" until I couldn't take my eyes off him.

He must have seen it was as fascinating as it was repulsive to me, but that I would not give in to his blandishments, because suddenly

Junior Cook said, "Hey, Ricky baby. Why don't you show this little boy here how to do it. You was always an ace cocksucker." He pulled Ricky up from the cushions of the chair, at which Ricky became more aware of what was going on, although not by a hell of a lot. Bayley began moaning and groaning, and Junior Cook, still jerking him, said, "C'mon boys. Get ready for your freshly made egg creams when this fucker shoots." He almost didn't finish. Bayley groaned once more and splattered against the wall two, three, four, five, six times! before almost falling over, trying to get Junior Cook's pumping hand off him. When Junior Cook did release him, Bayley stumbled back a few steps and fell onto the sleeping bag. Junior was already on his feet. He unzipped himself and grabbing Ricky's head, pushed his cock into Ricky's mouth, where Ricky sucked him to a quick, noisy orgasm. Junior Cook fell back into his chair, his still hard cock sticking out of his fly, saying "You always was the best head, Ricky. Never got any better, even at the Home. I really miss it, you know."

Nothing much happened after that. Bayley went back to drinking his beer. Junior Cook lit another cigarette, but didn't put his cock back inside his pants, and Ricky looked sort of sheepish and very stoned. So I finally said in a small voice that I had to get going, and when I nudged Ricky, he sort of shook himself and stood up. Since no one stopped us, we left the ganghouse. Before we closed the hideout door behind us, Junior Cook said in his most insinuating tone. "Now don't be such a stranger Rick. And you too, pretty boy. You both come visit any time you want to' chew on Bayley's flank steak."

We didn't answer back, but got on our bikes and rode back home. As we passed through the now chilled, dank streets, I began to get more an more angry and upset over what had happened. Without my meaning to, tears started to my eyes and began to flow so copiously they began to blind me. I had to stop the bike and wipe them away, hoping Ricky wouldn't notice.

"What's got into you?" Ricky asked. He'd circled back to where I'd stopped.

"I don't know," I said, then I blurted out, "I wish you hadn't taken me there."

"C'mon. It wasn't that bad. You crying?"

"No." But it was evident I had been. "I don't like what he did to you. And you let him!"

"C'mon. Don't be like that. It wasn't anything special." Ricky took my shoulder, trying to comfort me. "It didn't *mean* anything, you know," he insisted.

"I know." I dried my eyes. "But he made it seem so nasty, so *dirty*. Both of them did. I don't see how you could have ever let him be your buddy."

"Well, I'm not now. I'm your buddy. I got smart, see?" He hugged me and I was beginning to fee that what I'd intuited, felt, behind all of Junior Cook's carryings-on had been exaggerated, when Ricky added, "I don't mind, see, because, well, because it's not true that my uncle said I had to stop being his friend."

"It's not?"

"Nah. I mean, he acts all tough and everything, but I got sick and tired of him. I only went there today because of you. I wanted to show you off to him. Swear on it!" he declared. "He's a tough act with his beer and his cigarettes, but he's just a jerk like all the rest of them!" Ricky went on as though talking to himself. "I mean, you know, I like sucking and jerking as much as the next guy. But the real reason I stopped seeing him was that he began to get all mushy and huffy about my other friends. Acted like I *belonged* to him, for Chrissakes! Can you believe it?"

In the dark, he couldn't see the look on my face that would have told him to stop right there, to not go on. But he didn't, and what he said next stunned me at the time and would come back to haunt me.

"I don't belong to anyone!" Ricky said, as though I were arguing the point. "Not to Junior Cook. Not to anyone! And I never will. I'm my own person. I belong to me, myself and I."

I didn't know what to say, which gave Ricky the time to add, "Hell! You're just a kid compared to Junior Cook, and even you know that. Right? *Right*?" he insisted when I didn't immediately respond.

"Right," I finally said, less than enthusiastically, hating to have to say it at all. Then I slid out from under his hand on my shoulder, got on my bike and rode off, so fast Ricky had to call out twice for me to wait up for him.

At the time, even though I'd clearly heard Ricky's declaration that he didn't belong to anyone and never would, and even though I realized that it was a warning as much as a statement of self, it didn't really sink in. After all, we were still buddies, weren't we? Ricky had affirmed that at the same time he'd declared his independence, hadn't he?

Perhaps so, but after the clubhouse incident I began to feel a new uneasiness whenever Ricky and I were together. I knew that keeping that uneasiness from him was the worst thing I could do to our friendship, but I couldn't bring myself to mention it to him, couldn't bear to hear him say, "And I don't belong to *you*, either. Never did. Never will." Which I was sure would happen if I pressed him.

That wedge so lightly hammered in, I would stare at Ricky whenever we were together and I was certain he wasn't noticing me looking at him, and I would attempt to see what other personalities I'd never seen in him before would emerge: as awful as the one Junior Cook had elicited. No more did, and I'd almost forgotten the ganghouse and its implicit warning to me, almost relaxed back into the old security of our friendship—the most important thing in my life at the time—when another, altogether unrelated incident occurred in my class at school which showed me how in love I really was with Ricky Hersch, how little real reciprocation I might expect from him, and most important, what a dreadful thing love could be.

THE FAUSTUS CONTRACT
LARRY TOWNSEND

Ed, counterman at the Cup and Saucer, leaned his flabby bulk across the partition, staring angrily at the young men in the back booth. "All right, girls," he growled sarcastically, "you've each had your cup of coffee—paid for one and each got three, and you got your asses parked over an hour. Now may I suggest you either order some food so we can make a little on you, or..."

"Burgers all around!" said Gino grandly. "Make it a double for my two hungry friends here," he added, pointing at the two boys who had joined Billy and him at the table. He laughed heartily, patting his companion on the back. "The pros got the bread tonight, don't we, Billy-boy?"

"Shit!" snarled the counterman. He lumbered back toward the serving bar. "Faggots!" he mumbled. "All the pretty ones in the back, where nobody ken see 'em!" He glanced out toward Hollywood Boulevard. A pair of foot patrolmen were just passing the front window, swinging their nightsticks and watching the crowds. Saturday night, and the place was loaded with bums up in the front, empty tables and booths in the middle, and the attractive ones...shit!

He slung a half dozen patties onto the grill and started setting up the rolls. Gino watched him from the booth, laughing as he continued recounting his tales of "gory glory" (Gino's term).

"Well, after the old fart that wanted us to give him enemas, and the guy that wanted to watch Billy jack off, we got calls from another couple of photographers," he said.

"How many does that make?" asked Rudy. This was a red-headed kid who always wore a totally black cowboy outfit, complete with chaps, leather vest and high-heeled boots. His pale skin and raw-boned frame had become a fixture on the Boulevard.

"You mean how many photographers?" asked Billy.

"Ah, counting the one before the ad broke, it's...what? Six?" He looked at Gino for confirmation.

"Seven if you count the one that took pictures of us through his glory hole," said Gino. "Only two of them wanted model releases, though," he added. "The rest were 'private collectors.'"

All the young men were laughing as Gino spoke, and a newcomer to the trade—a small, handsome youngster they called "Vet" (because he had arrived in Los Angeles with an old, very beat-up Corvette)—was asking about the photographers with more than casual interest.

"Well, it's like having a cherry," Gino explained. "See, if you never been photographed before you're worth more money. So the first guy that gets you should pay for it."

"That's if he asks for a release," added Billy.

"Yeah," Rudy agreed. "If they don't ask you to sign nothin', they can't put the pix in a book, and they ain't supposed ta sell 'em."

"Only trouble is," Billy explained, "the first time a stud poses for one of 'em, he's too green ta know the score and he goes for maybe ten, fifteen bucks."

"And after that," said Gino, "he maybe knows better, but his face has been around, so they don't want..."

Ed slipped the plates of hamburgers across the table, noisily setting the ketchup bottle in the center. "Listen, you guys," he mumbled, "if you want to hang around here, move up front where the customers can see you."

"Free dessert and coffee?" asked Gino quickly. He grinned innocently at the counterman, who glared back in feigned ill-temper. Then he smiled, too.

"Okay," he agreed. "Free pie and coffee."

"Make mine apple...à la mode!" said Vet, as the group of hustlers moved to an empty table by the window.

Outside, crowds of movie-goers were streaming out of the surrounding theaters. The boys watched as several dozen high-spirited teenagers mingled with the moving columns of older people, running through the slowly ambling flock, playing tag across the intersection. As always, the Saturday-nighters formed a completely heterogeneous group—couples of young adults; a scattering of older, well-dressed three and four...sometimes a few young girls, always in pairs; and, of course, the cruising johns.

The young men observed them all, commenting to each other on the physical attributes of the chicks, noting the potential customers among the men. Ed's strategy began to pay off as a number of single males began filing into the Cup and Saucer. The boys observed them without seeming to have any interest.

"We're still waiting to hear how you made the big score," said Rudy. "How'd ya get all that bread?"

"There was this big party in the hills—on the Valley side," Gino began.

"And the guy that gave it called to see if we'd park cars for him," Billy explained.

"At first I said no, 'cause I figured they'd pay a buck an hour and we'd be there mosta the night," said Gino, "and it was last night—

Friday. But the stud explained it was a gay party, and he said if we'd maybe be interested in earning a little extra coin, we'd have the chance. He even says he'll pick us up aheada time, if we don't have transportation.

"So, I says okay, and sure enough, the stud shows up in a big-ass Cadillac convertible, right on time. He takes us up to this house, man, that's like a castle on the top of a great big hill."

"And the guy...tell 'em about the guy!" said Billy.

"Yeah, this stud that picks us up. He's dressed like leather's the only thing, man. He's got black leather pants, leather boots, leather belt, leather shirt..."

"And leather skivvies, too!" added Billy, smiling. "We found that out later."

"Yeah, and those leather pants, see, they're not like regular pants with a zipper in the front. They got a pouch that snaps at the top, and if it gets unsnapped, the thing falls down and he's wide open—ready for business!"

"Maybe I oughta get a pair," Rudy remarked.

"And all these other cats that come up, they're all dressed pretty much the same," said Billy. "Some of 'em got zippers in the back, too. That's so they can get fucked standing up. One guy says he gets it in a crowded bar all the time like that...up in Frisco, though... don't go for that shit in LA."

"They all come in cars?" asked Vet. "I thought the leather bunch rode bikes."

Gino and Billy both laughed, hooting and hammering on the table. "Man, listen," said Gino at length, "you see them studs all in leather and chains and the whole fuckin' bit, and man, they're standin' on the corner, waitin' for the fuckin' bus!"

"Some of 'em came on bikes," said Billy, "but most of 'em had cars...Cadillacs an' Buicks, Jaguars...groovy wheels!"

"So, anyhow," Gino continued, "we parked cars until about midnight, and then the stud that's giving the party, he comes out and tells us we can knock off and come inside. Some of the guests like us, he says, and maybe we can do all right. He gives each of us fifteen bucks for parking the cars, and we go in. Man, it was wild! There's this big room upstairs where they got the bar, and a stairway that goes down into like a patio down below. And all around there's black lights and psychedelic posters of studs with big cocks, dressed in leather with bikes, or cowboy hats and nothin' else, some of them tied with chains an' stuff. And mosta the guys were naked. They're all layin' around drinkin' beer, and a few are blowing pot—and *poppers*, man! That place smelled like a fuckin' hospital...*all them poppers!*

"And all over the floor, these guys were fuckin' and suckin' an' up on the end they got a kinda rack—that's what they called it—and this stud's just hangin' there, man. His hands are strapped to a post up by the ceiling, and his feet're chained on a frame—like a crossbeam. An' he's got chains all wrapped about his hips so just his nuts and his cock're hangin' out. An' there's this strobe, see, and it keeps flashin' right on him, and he's groaning and twisting around like he's really hurt. 'Course, he's not. Guy musta really dug that shit, man!"

"Yeah but that's not the half of it," added Billy. "I got up close to him, and I almost puked. Shit! Somebody'd sewed the skin shut over the enda his cock. And they'd sewed through his tits, too, so the string looped across the front of him, and they'd hung weights on it!"

"And they'd whipped his ass good," said Gino. "Welts all over him! Man, I started ta get a little scared, you know? Some of them fuckers were pretty stout, and I wouldn'ta let nobody do somethin' like that to me, not for a million bucks!"

"Wow! I'd a gotten my ass outta there right now, man!" said Vet. "Them studs musta been fuckin' maniacs!"

"Yeah, but they was rich maniacs," said Gino laughing. "You wanna make bread in this business, kid, ya gotta play the game. You don't have ta let 'em cut your nuts off, but ya gotta play it cool and give the customer what he wants, or maybe whatcha make him *think* he wants.

"So anyhow, we both get a beer, and we go down into the patio. There's more naked guys out here, only they're not so high, an' the stud that's givin' the party's with 'em. 'Here's the kids I told you about,' he says, and he introduces us to about seven or eight of 'em. Real blast man! Like, here we are—Billy and me—and we're dressed in Levi's and a shirt, and everything. And these guys are all bare-assed except for maybe a leather jock-strap or a pair of boots. An' we're all shakin' hands and sayin' 'Nice ta meetcha,' like we was at a ladies' tea party.

"And they got this post set up out there—like a short telephone pole, maybe eight or nine feet high. It's got a metal ring in the top, and they got a stud tied to that, with his hands laced up above his head with rawhide, onto the ring. He's got a leather hood over his head so he can't see nothin', and when we come down the stairs there's a guy there bustin' his ass with a leather belt. But when the host introduces us, this stud that's whippin' the other guy's ass—he turns around and shakes hands like all the rest.

"Then, on the back side of the pole, there's another ring, about as high as your waist, and they got another naked stud tied up to that. He's on his knees, with his hands in back of him with handcuffs, an' a dog collar around his neck—the same kind they use on police dogs—and the stud's chained to the ring by that, with a big-ass padlock, man!"

"And this guy's gettin' what they call the 'water treatment.'" Billy explained. "See, all these guys is drinkin' beer, so they gotta piss all the time. And this stud that's all chained up, he likes beer second hand, so they give it to him!"

"I heard about that," said Vet disgustedly.

"Golden shower," mumbled Rudy. "That's how you get the yellow jaundice."

"I heard that too," said Gino sagely. "So, after the host makes all the fancy introductions, he says 'Why don't you fellows take some of those clothes off and join us?' And I kinda rub my fingers, and he says 'Don't worry about that.' So I take my clothes off, and Billy does too, only he's not too happy about it." Gino paused, eyeing his friend slyly. "Billy ain't always too sure about some of these things. So, we get outa our jeans, and one of the big studs walks around to the guy that's on his knees, and he grabs him by the hair and pulls his head back. 'If either of you guys gotta take a piss,' he says, 'this slave here is ready for you. Aren't you, slave?' he says real mean! He pulls the guy's head back harder, and the guy's kinda moaning, and his eyes are half closed—good lookin' stud, too. Got a nice, tight body, and good arms, man—like he works out.

"'You thirsty, slave?' the cat asks him, an' the guy's moanin' again, and he says sorta breathy-like, 'Yes sir, please sir, I'm thirsty, sir,' he says. 'Please, sir, gimme some more beer, sir!'

"I ain't shittin' man! That fucker musta been like that for hours! And everybody's pissin' all over him, and he's drinkin' the stuff, like man it's champagne!"

"Did you piss on him?" asked Vet anxiously.

Gino observed the boy with amusement. Despite the careful display of revulsion, the youngster's eyes sparkled with interest, and his excitement was evident from the tense posture of his hands and body.

"Sure," Gino told him. "I hadn't gone for three, maybe four hours, so I gave him a good shot! Let him have it right in the face, and man, he loved it!"

"You too, Billy?" asked the youngster.

Billy looked down at his hands. "Not right off," he said.

"Nah, Billy had ta warm up to it," said Gino. "Me? I got right into the act, soon's they said 'Bread', I said 'Go'! First, they took the guy down from the post—not the one we're pissin' on, the other one that was tied to the ring on top. They take the same rawhide, and they tie his hands in back of him, and then they put some irons on his ankles—like old-fashioned leg-irons. They make a loop around the center of the chain, and they tie that to his balls so he can't stand up. He's gotta crawl like a fuckin' dog.

"And they put a leather collar around his neck, with studs on it. Only the studs're on the inside, so they poke him if he don't obey. They got a leash on the collar, and they lead him around the patio, makin' him crawl on the stones and on the gravel that's along the sides. An' every time he slows down, they let him have that belt across the ass or on his back. Sometimes they let him have it on the chest or belly—even on the legs once in a while. See! He's still got that leather hood over his eyes, so he can't tell where it's gonna land, and the cat that's hittin' him, he says a big thrill for the slave is not to know where he's gonna get hit.

"Then every once in a while, one of the guys that's workin' him over will stand in front of him and make the slave eat his cock, and he took 'em all the way, man, or pow, man, right across the ass! A couple of those studs were hung like fuckin' horses, but it didn't make no difference. All the way, man, or pow!

"Then the guy gives me the leash, and says I should take the dog for a walk. 'You gotta feed him once in a while,' the guy tells me, 'but he needs a lotta discipline.' So, I gave it to him. I gave it to him good! And that stud called me sir—better believe it! I made him suck me until I almost came. Then I pulled away and let him have it again with the belt, 'cause I told him he didn't do a good enough job. One time I cracked him across the legs, and the edge musta hit him on the balls, 'cause he screams, and he falls on his side, and he's rollin' around on the ground. I was scared for a minute, 'cause I thought maybe I'd killed him, but the other studs, they says he loves it, and not to worry.

"Well, after a while, man, I am gettin' kinda horny, and the guys can see it 'cause I'm not gettin' soft in between times. And one of 'em says I should 'Fuck the slave.' And I tells him 'Okay, get some of the chains off so I can get to him.' And the guy says I can do it, all right, just shove the slave forward on his face, and his ass'll be up in the air, just right for me. See, the cat can't move any other way, 'cause of the chains around his ankles bein' attached to his balls.

"So, I do like the guy says. I shove him down so his forehead's on the ground, and he's still got the hood on, so he can't see what's coming. He's all bent double, 'cause of the chain, and his ass is up there real nice, man...real nice. I spit on old One-Eye, and *man!*"

"All those fuckers standing around cheering!" added Billy enthusiastically. "Man, what a scene! 'Ride 'im!' they're yellin'; and 'You got a stud hustler on you, slave!'—stuff like that!"

"How 'bout you?" asked Vet. "I bet you coulda rode 'im good, too."

"Ah!" Billy curled his lip. "I don't really like to hurt nobody," he said, "even if they want to get hurt. It's...I dunno...just isn't my bag."

"You musta done something!" Vet insisted.

"He did!" said Gino proudly. "This big bastard—musta been six-eight or nine—he keeps givin' Billy pot and beer, pot and beer, until finally he says he wants ta get tied up and fucked. Ol' Billy did a good job on him, didn't you, Billy-boy?"

"Yeah, I took care of him," admitted Billy reluctantly. "Only, I didn't whip his ass or anything. Just tied him up with ropes and belts, and fucked him!"

"And the stud's hollerin' for someone to take a picture of him gettin' it," Gino added. "So, after a while, this mother comes out with a Polaroid, and he starts taking pix. Hey, Billy—show 'em. The guy gave one to Billy for a souvenir," Gino explained.

Billy pulled the stiff pasteboard from his shirt pocket, and with an unhappy glance at Gino for unveiling his secret, he passed it around for the others to see. Rudy whistled softly between his teeth. "He is a big stud!"

"Lemme see!" said Vet impatiently. "Wow! Billy, you got a ass on you like that guy in *Flesh!* Jeez!"

"I wouldn't mind that myself," said a voice above them.

Startled, the young men looked up to see a tall, slender man in his early forties standing beside the table. He was greying at the temples and rather distinguished-looking, despite the wide-striped shirt-jac and flare hip-huggers. "Why don't you come over and have a cup of coffee with me," he suggested to Billy. "Maybe we could find some common interests." He smiled encouragingly, and after a moment's hesitation Billy shrugged.

"Okay, man," he said.

"He's expensive," Gino mumbled.

The man laughed. "And I'm rich," he assured the hustler.

Billy went to the man's table, where they were talking only a few minutes. The man left a dollar bill on the counter and they went out together. "See you tomorrow," Billy called to Gino.

"Man, that Billy's a real stud!" said Vet in obvious admiration.

"Yeah, and he's doing better since he's been with me," said Gino. "He's afraid to ask for what he oughta get. Now that cat just took him out. The guy should lay fifty, maybe sixty bucks on him, especially if he wants like what's in the pic. He would, too, if I was with 'em. But you watch, Billy'll come back tomorrow with twenty. Just 'cause I wasn't there."

"He's right," said Rudy wisely. "First thing you gotta learn, kid. Know what you're worth and get it. Don't be afraid to ask for it. These faggots, they got nothin' else to spend it on, man...nothin' else."

"As long as you're young," Gino added, "you got it knocked! What they're buyin' is youth and beauty, man, youth and beauty!"

"And the less they got of it themselves," Rudy concluded, "the more they'll pay. But you gotta arrange it aheada time. Like a contract, everybody knows what he's gonna get."

ELLIOTT
SLOAN RYDER

I put my hand on Elliott's T-shirt and ripped it off his body. He gasped, but the dirtbag wasn't afraid. I ran a dirty finger along his narrow chest, passing it over his nipples, up to the hollow at the base of his throat. He shivered. My cock twitched. I didn't know the little guy had it in him.

I put my hand around his skinny throat; fingers touching at nape of his neck. I brought my mouth down onto his, my hair shading our faces. My free hand roamed his body, feeling his ribs, rubbing his belly and the waistband of his pants.

I wanted to ram the hard-on in my leathers right up this dirtbag's bony ass. I moved in on him, covering his body against the wall with my own. I could feel his cock straining against his pants and simply pulled at his zipper. Keeping my hand at his throat, I said, "Take 'em off."

He kicked out of his pants and underwear while I undid my own leathers and revealed myself in front of him.

He nearly came when he saw me—ten thick, long inches of prime beef standing at attention. He reached out a hand to touch it. His fingers were cool and oddly soft against my skin. Between the excitement of taking Elliott and the feel of his hand on my cock, I was getting so hard that I felt like I was made of steel.

"Don't do that!" I breathed.

He pulled his hand away immediately. I pushed him—hard—against the wall and looked down. He wasn't nearly as big as I am. But he was hard, and his little dick stood straight out in front of him.

Pulling him away, I turned him around and pressed his face up against the wall. He grunted at the force I used.

Without bothering to prime the way, I took him hard from behind and rammed my huge cock up his tight little ass. He was so aroused that he screamed as he felt me coming in. I plunged in and out roughly. He was so tight. He didn't even seem to care that his face kept hitting the wall every time I entered him. A guy could get to like this.

He was so tiny that I doubted I'd even feel him if I let him inside me. He was a great fuck, though.

His small cock was slapping against the wall and I lowered a hand to feel it. He seemed bigger now. I played with him for a bit. I could hear his grunts and moans of pleasure as I reamed out his tight hole. He came screaming in my hand, sticky, warm and more plentifully than I'd have thought possible.

It was enough. I exploded inside of him, torrents of my hot cum firing within him. It backed up as I pulled out, leaking down Elliott's thighs and dripping off my dick. He turned real fast, knelt, and sucked the cum from my cock, taking in the last few jets. I didn't care how dirty and pungent my big dick must have been. I was too spent to begin again, but he probably could have done it, all right. He may have been ugly, but he was a prime lay.

Leaning against the bar, I passed a hand over my face, feeling the stubble of my beard and my leathery skin from too much time on the road. Elliott looked well-fucked. I liked that. I reached for my leathers and put them on.

I left without saying good-bye. Maybe I'd be back.

F TRAIN
CORY JACKSON

I'm hanging onto the pole, facing the door, trapped into an unnatural position by the crush of riders on the Manhattan-bound F train. This guy gets on the train at Roosevelt Avenue and stands behind me, his front touching my back. I'm annoyed. I don't know this guy, but I get the powerful sense that he's copping a feel!

Well, the doors close with that irritating electronic bing-bong, and we pull out of the station. I'm minding my own business, trying to keep my balance, shifting my weight from one foot to the other. But with every shift of my body, with every movement of the train on the tracks, this guy's rubbing his dick across my ass. I can feel it; from the right cheek past the crack, to the left cheek, and back again. The swaying of the train is helping him do this. I'm shifting to get him to stop, but he doesn't. I'm bored anyway, so I close my eyes and go with a fantasy.

I still can't see him, but I know we aren't on the train anymore. I'm still hanging onto a pole, but only because my wrists are tied to it with some kind of rope; soft, but strong. He's behind me. I can feel him. He's got my jeans down around my ankles, and I see his hand coming from behind me, wrapping itself around my dick. His fingernails rake gently up and down the length of my cock, the tip of one finger playing with the head. The palm of his hand cups my balls and rolls them around like those Chinese health balls. I'm thinking this is really weird, but I'm also getting hard, and wonder what's coming next.

He's still rubbing his cock against my ass, but now there's no fabric between our skin. And, his cock is huge, uncut (I just know it is), and bucking and rearing against my butthole as if it had a life of its own. A phantom finger runs down my back, taps the left cheek of my ass twice, as if he was thinking about something. His hand leaves my cock alone, disappearing around back. Suddenly he's spreading my asscheeks and ramming himself home.

I am filled with him, gasping. His hands reappear. He's stroking my cock again, while his other hand caresses my belly, tweaking my nipples, sticking his fingers into my mouth. I can feel him moving within me, slow spirals to a reggae beat.

The tempo picks up and the hand job goes faster, priming my cock in time to the pistoning of his dick in my ass. I can feel the slap of his hips against my ass, louder and faster as he gets closer to cumming.

His fist closes around my cock and I cum like wildfire, white jets of sperm squirting out into the dark. As he feels it, his cock spasms hard and thick in my ass and it erupts, hot and sticky, overflowing as his cock slips out...

My eyes open as the "F" train stops at Queens Plaza. I turn around —I don't know whether to punch the guy or kiss him, but he runs off and is lost in the crowd transferring to the "G" train. The doors close.

MAN SWORD
LARRY TOWNSEND

Cracow: Winter 1574–5
Paris: Spring 1575

Peter remained in Henri's service for as long as we were in Poland. I became very fond of the boy, and by the end of December I think I was close to being in love. Only the foolish confusion I maintained over Anatole prevented my taking this prize for my own. Even Henri noticed, and he indicated he would have no objections. "She's a lovely trick, dear Louis, but the peace of your soul is worth more to me," the king assured me. I was so very young, and so very, very foolish!

In other areas of my life, however, I was receiving highly professional instruction, which resulted in exceptionally rapid maturation. On the day following our exhibition with Peter, for instance, the king ordered me to arrest Kurbsky. I talked him out of it, which later earned me considerable praise from some of

Queen Catherine's functionaries. The Poles in Henri's circle of advisors were particularly relieved to learn the king had changed his mind, as the possibility of further alienating this powerful Russian prince frightened them. I had been reading a French translation of a book by Machiavelli—gift from the Black Queen just prior to my departure. I discovered how perceptive the man was by applying his principles to the current situation. I allowed Kurbsky to learn how close he had come to disaster. It was the last trouble we had from him.

Hindered by the snows, messengers between Paris and Cracow were few and far between. Of course, these highways did not begin to receive the tremendous falls which blanketed the northland and Russia, but it was enough to limit the flow of information between Henri and his brother, King Charles. The Black Queen, as usual, managed to keep a closer touch, sending envoys when the roads were covered to the height of a man's hips. One of those who came through shortly after Christmas was Cavalcanti.

The dark, wiry Italian seemed none the worse for his travel, and he never voiced a word of complaint. I will credit him with this, for never—in all the time I knew him as a servant of the queen—did he ever say anything that could be taken as critical of her. Naturally, Cavalcanti reported first to Henri; after they had conferred for over an hour, he came to me.

"The queen sends you her personal greeting," said the Florentine. "I am glad to see you looking so well. Her Majesty seems to have a special regard for you."

"Her Majesty does me great honor," I replied guardedly. I could not help disliking the man, and his suave manner made me distrust him—maybe fear him. I know I was far more cautious in what I said to him than I have ever been with anyone else, even the queen.

Cavalcanti glanced about, obviously wondering if we were alone. "Can I speak freely?" he said.

I laughed softly. "Unlike some palaces, this one has no secret passages," I told him. "At least, I haven't been able to find them."

"That is not exactly reassuring," he mumbled.

I shrugged. "Few of these Polish peasants speak French," I added deprecatingly.

The queen's envoy nodded. "It has been my unpleasant duty to inform His Majesty," he said in oily tones, "that his brother, our king, seems in failing health." He stopped, watching my expression.

I thought back on the angry conversation I had with Anatole. "The queen will poison her own son, if need be," he had told me. I shuddered, at which Cavalcanti lifted an eyebrow.

"It's so drafty in this rock pile," I remarked. "Henri is always cold."

"So I noted," said the Florentine. "But, as I was saying, King Charles had been in rather frail health for several months. The doctors are at a loss to cure his condition."

"He is in danger of...death?" I asked.

Gravely, Cavalcanti nodded. "I was not so blunt in speaking to His Majesty," he added. "I wished to spare him any unnecessary concern."

"We are all homesick for Paris," I replied," but the death of King Charles would be a terrible price to pay for such a...reprieve."

The queen's envoy almost smiled. "You are learning Louis," he said.

"I have been well instructed," I replied.

"Now, it had occurred to us...in Paris...that if this tragedy were to befall us, and Henri inherit the throne...it would not do for the king of France to expose himself to the types of insult he was forced to endure on his trip to Poland. Naturally, I did not feel it proper to discuss this with him now. However, Her Majesty is quite concerned that when...and if...the time should come, Henri be persuaded to return home via some southern route."

"Through Catholic territory," I added.

"Right! Now, we are all aware of His Majesty's faith in your judgment, and we would like to leave it in your hands."

"You may assure Her Majesty that I shall do my best," I told him. When he left a few minutes later, I was still wondering how much Henri knew. Did he suspect his mother was seeking the throne for him by murdering her own son? There was little doubt in my mind that she was doing just that; but, naturally, I had no more than suspicion. Maybe I was being unfair to her. I could not believe Henri was devious enough to be a party to such a thing, if the Black Queen really were guilty. But the blood of the Medici...I'll never know, I thought.

Less than a month later, word arrived that King Charles IX of France was dead. By then, I had steeled myself to the possibility, and I refused to think about the implications. Later, I was too involved with other activities to worry about it.

Henri, maintaining a sufficiently somber expression to impress those about him, called his council into session and announced his abdication: "It grieves me greatly," he told the assembly, "that I must lay down the crown of Poland and return to govern my homeland."

Then, to the consternation of us all, the Poles refused to let him go! A contingent of the royal army surrounded the place, and the king of Poland suddenly found himself imprisoned in his own keep.

"What can they be thinking of?" he stormed. "Do they expect me to rule France from Cracow? Maybe I am supposed to annex the realm to Poland!" He was furious, and in his anger he momentarily forgot to be a woman.

While the king paced his apartments in impotent fury, I set about trying to solve his dilemma. So far, no one was restricted to the palace except Henri himself. How long this would go on, I could not guess; but I did not like the turn of political climate—nor the apparent allegiances being formed among the Polish nobility.

It was obvious Henri could not be kept prisoner forever; already, his supporters must be aligning themselves with whichever candidate they expected to succeed him. Without the protection of his Polish faction, I wondered how long King Henri would be safe.

The arrangements I made were quite simple, really. I had two good horses saddled and kept in readiness at a tavern some distance from the palace. No one would expect the king to flee his realm on horseback, with only a single guard to assure his safety. Once the details were taken care of, my one remaining problem was to convince the king.

"Oh, my dear!" he protested. "On horseback, all the way to Vienna? Oh, Louis; you must be playing with me!"

"Henri, do you realize what may happen if they elect a new king of Poland, and you're still here?" I asked harshly.

His face drained of color, and he stared at me. Fear caused his eyes to bulge until he reminded me of his mother, and again the feminine quality left his voice. "You mean...you think...?"

"I think you'll be much better off with a pair of buttocks that ache from a few days in the saddle, than sitting on a dungeon bench," I said.

"Oh dear, oh dear! But, you will come with me?"

"Of course," I assured him. "I couldn't turn a lady loose alone in this barbaric country, could I?"

He laughed with relief, and threw his arms about my neck. He kissed me gently on the lips, and set about at once to change his clothes. I had brought him an outfit of trader's clothing, which I ordered his tailor to line with silk, as Henri was terribly sensitive to any rough fabric. With a sigh of resignation, he put on his disguise, and together we slipped out of the palace without attracting attention. "Duke" Francine was to remain in Henri's rooms, keep the doors closed, and pretend to be the king for as long as he could get away with it. I hoped for a sufficient head start to elude whoever came after us.

Fortunately, the weather was not overly cold, nor did we encounter rain or snow the first night or following day. Henri had looked sadly at his great Russian shuba when he left, but there was no way for us to smuggle the sables out of the palace. Francine had promised to see it came through with the rest of Henri's possessions when they were sent to Paris.

We had left Cracow after dark, riding with hardly a pause until evening of the following day. By then we were both exhausted, as were the horses. We had to lay over for a few hours' sleep. I found a barn located quite a distance from its farmhouse, bordering a narrow field which separated it from a dense woods. We hid the horses and crept into the barn, where we burrowed deep into the hay. Despite Henri's discomfort, I did not dare seek other accommodations. Stopping at a farmhouse would present danger, as neither of us spoke Polish, and we would be sure to attract attention.

The only mishap occurred in the morning, when Henri was relieving himself back of the building. The farmer came around the corner, and for a moment both of them stared at each other in surprise. The king had turned at the man's approach, and now stood facing him, holding his dripping penis in his hand. The farmer regained his presence first, and started yelling something in Polish.

Quickly, the king shoved himself together, by which time the farmer's cries had attracted several men from the house. I came up behind Henri. Grabbing his arm, I propelled him across the field and into the woods. The farmer, fortunately, did not pursue us, and we were able to disappear into the foliage. We rode hastily away, the king complaining all the while about the streams of urine running down his leg.

Our second night was spent at the foot of the Carpath-ian mountains, which we started across the following morning. The pass was covered by several feet of snow, and the trail was icy. Still, we crossed the Polish border into Moravia before nightfall and found lodging at an inn outside Ostrava. Sitting before the fire, Henri relaxed and both of us drank a huge quantity of wine. The king's identity was still a secret, for neither of us knew what attitude to expect of the local residents. However, we were now in Austrian territory, well outside the borders of Poland. We could draw breath at last, without fear of either Protestant or Polack.

After sitting and drinking for several hours in front of the fire in a private dining alcove, we staggered upstairs to sleep. As was common in these crowded county inns, we had been given a room with one large bed. I expected Henri would occupy this by himself, and I was prepared to sleep on the boards with my back against the door, but the king had other ideas.

"No, no, Louis," he muttered drunkenly, "not only will I enjoy sharing the bed with you, I shall most likely freeze to death if you are not there to keep me warm."

So I went to bed with Henri III, king of France, ex-king of Poland, Duke Anjou, scion of the d'Medici, and last in the line of Valois. He surprised me by removing all his clothes before slipping between the rough, coarse-woven sheets. I was still undressing, while he watched me through half-closed lids. Strangely, he seemed happier than I had ever known him to be. Without needing to maintain the facade he had created about the court, he behaved in quite a manly way. When I, too, had stripped completely naked, I slid in beside my king. Then I learned how really manly Henri could be.

He came to me in the darkness, encircling my chest with his arms, his legs about mine as he eased himself on top of me. The king was a fairly tall man by any standards, and in comparison to me he was nearly a giant. The outwardly soft appearance of his body belied his actual strength. He held me so tightly I could hardly draw breath, and could never have pulled away. His full, moist lips pressed on mine, and I felt his cock shoving hot and rigid against my belly.

I returned his kisses with the same drunken abandon as he gave them, and I thrilled as I never expected I would to the gentle touch of his hands upon me. Slowly, he turned himself onto his side, where he lay facing me. His fingers traced the outline of my entire body and each time I started to move, he eased me back, never ceasing the motion of his hands across my skin. Wave after wave of tangling sensation gripped me, and I was driven nearly frantic by this contact that was neither caress not tickle, but something in between. For moments at a time I almost wanted to laugh, but I was also aroused, and my penis reached, swollen and granite, across my groin.

The king's fingers closed about my nipples, kneading, squeezing them; he slipped his head beneath the covers and chewed first one and then the other until I could no longer bear it. I tried to push his face away, and he slipped farther down, his tongue leaving a trail of moisture across my chest, into the navel and below to the fine path of hair where my cockhead stretched forth to meet him.

His lips encircled the tip, and his tongue slid around beneath the foreskin, soaking it, exciting the solid flesh to an even greater tumescence. Slowly, he descended, drawing me completely inside him, forcing my bulk of manhood far into the depths of his throat. He alternated then, between periods of rapid motion up and down my shaft, and long minutes when he lay still, setting me aflame with the light, heated touch.

Whether it was the wine or the excitement we both felt at successfully escaping Poland—the prospect of going home—I cannot say. But suddenly we were again in each other's arms, sharing a spiritual closeness more than simply a passing moment of sexual pleasure. Henri actually spoke words of love to me, and strangely enough, I found myself returning a powerful surge of feeling. Before this, I had never been physically attracted by the king—had never fantasized him as a sexual object. During his stay in Poland, however, he had fretted off much of his excess weight, until the body pressing against me felt firm and muscular. My passions rose, I forgot his rank and all the myriad responses I had previously made to his femininity. Nor would I have cause to be reminded of his undesirable mannerism that night! As he held me in his arms, he became very much the man.

I felt myself pushed gently onto my back, while Henri slipped on top of me. He rubbed his body against mine, arms and legs gripping me once again while his manhood pressed relentlessly upon the tightened flesh of my midsection. Gradually, he raised himself, sliding upward until his man-thing probed my lips. He pressed it into me, and I took it, savoring it, wishing a worshipful love upon it. Henri was endowed with a nicely formed cock that was barely long enough to penetrate the throat, but its great beauty was its unusual width and the exceptional hardness of its core. Crowned with a loose, heavy foreskin, Henri's penis seemed to slide within a cover of velvet as he rammed the powerful member, time and again, deep within me.

Later, oblivious to the chill, he cast aside the coverlet and twisted his naked body to take my erection into himself. He lay atop me, thrusting downward over me, while he pulled my trembling flesh deep into his own being. The heat of his body on top of mine, the lingering odor of horse and leather about his groin, produced a frantic desire. I threw my arms around his waist and reached out to grasp the skin about his back and shoulders. I crushed myself against him.

I thought we would find fulfillment in this position, but Henri had still another surprise that night. When the waves of sensation were peaking toward a final release, and the sparkling lights of passion were about to overwhelm us both, he gently disengaged himself. He knelt astride me and leaned over to kiss my lips. His tongue probed fully into me before he slowly eased one shoulder off the bed. He raised his body high above, touching me only where his knees pressed on the sides of my hips. I felt his large, strong hands seize upon my arms, as he began turning me onto my belly! Never had I known him to do this, not with any man or boy he had possessed in all the time I served him. Yet neither had I seen him behave as he had since fleeing the capital of Poland.

I made no resistance, turning onto my stomach and lying with my arms curled above my head. His hands began their tantalizing motion across my back, lightly passing over my shoulders and down my sides. They were warm, seeming to burn in contrast to the coolness of the room. Across the small of my back and onto my ass they traveled as Henri fondly stroked the rounded curves of my buttocks. His fingers finally came to rest just under me, to either side of my hips. He held gently upon those twin spots where the pulse beats in the crease which marks the joining of leg to loin. Then his lips caressed the cleft between my cheeks and his tongue explored the darkness, traveling downward until he found the opening. For a long while he probed and explored the area, seeming to revel in the newness of his experience. His tongue entered me many times, hotly licking the walls of my canal, moistening it, loosening it, making me desire what he had to give.

When he finally straightened up, I was nearly spent from the flames of desperate craving he had kindled. My entire body quivered in expectation as Henri centered his great, wide crown against me.

"Are you ready?" he whispered.

"Yes," I gasped. "God, yes!"

"Do you want it?" he asked.

"Yes, yes, give it to me," I begged.

He pressed a little harder against me. "Tell me how much you want it," he said.

"I want it all the way," I groaned, "... all of it...in me..."

Henri shoved down, and I felt the sharp pain of his initial entry. The wide shaft split me like a searing wedge, and I gasped at the wonderful agony it brought. Slowly he continued, possessing me, filling me with the hard yet gentle force of his descending column.

"Tonight, I am the king," he whispered.

x x x

We had another two days of hard riding ahead of us, and we started early the following morning. I must admit to some discomfort in the saddle following the royal use of my person. But that night we had forged a bond which would last many years, and we both knew the words we had spoken in our wine-induced moment together had been something more than expressions of a momentary passion. Foolish and irresponsible as Henri might appear, and inept as he was yet to prove himself, I had discovered a core of manhood which few who knew him ever realized he possessed. What I felt was not the love I had lavished on Anatole, nor the passion attraction I had held for Peter. But I felt a warm and almost brotherly comradeship with my king, and in the days to come, Henri indicated a like regard for me.

In Vienna, Henri was finally feted as the king of France. The emperor received him like a long-lost son, and together they hosted an enormous banquet after our arrival. Naturally, there was a large and well-staffed em-bassy in the city so the king had no further need to travel in the guise of a merchant. Still, I think both of us felt a sense of loss at this end to our adventure and the intimacy it had brought us.

Once rested, the king of France proceeded in an elegant gilded coach, surrounded by an Austrian guard of honor. Because I had no French soldiers to command, I rode with the king and acted as his personal companion. I now wore the uniform of a captain, and everywhere I was regarded as the man to see by those who sought favors of the king. What may have been whispered behind my back regarding the relationship I enjoyed with His Majesty was a matter of little concern. I soon grew used to it, and I soon realized that I was envied by most of those who secretly derided me.

From Vienna, we proceeded south, avoiding the Protestant areas of the Cantons. Because of the mountains, we went all the way to Venice, then across Lombardy to Milan. Here, we were in

French territory, and the reception of the king was tumultuous. We crossed Piedmont and traveled through the Cenis Pass at Susa into the lush green meadows of Savoy. Spring had already come to southern France, but with it came the rains, which slowed our progress. I was grateful to be inside the coach as torrents of water pounded on the roof, sluicing across the windows and obstructing our view of all that lay beyond.

At Lyon, we were met by most of Henri's court—or rather the members of his brother's former court. Among these was the duke of Guise. Taller and grayer than I remembered him, the duke greeted Henri as if he were welcoming a foreign dignitary to his realm. A great banquet had been arranged for the king, and Henri soon found himself surrounded by flocks of old acquaintances who now pushed and maneuvered to place themselves ever closer to him.

I, of course, was shoved into the background. I did not resent this, except it saddened me to realize the moments of intimacy I had shared with Henri must now become a thing of the past—or at least assume a very different tone. Neither was I the ranking officer of his personal guard— at least, not yet. What I did retain was a highly increased loyalty to the king as a person, this despite the greater distance at which circumstances placed me.

Anatole was with the group of men who served the duke of Guise. I saw him first at a distance, fawning over his master until the sight nearly made me sick. Everyone knew the only way to rise in the duke's service, however, was, to be a total supplicant, a boot-licker to the most degrading degree. I spoke with him later that evening. Both of us had been excluded from the festivities, and we met quite by accident in an antechamber to the great hall. I was pained to see the changes time and service with the duke had worked upon my former lover. He had grown heavier, and while he still seemed a handsome man, there was a hardness about his lips and eyes. His manner was restrained until we had taken several goblets of wine together. Then his tongue loosened, and he began extol-ling the virtues of his master.

While Anatole did not speak openly against the king, I detected a note of scornful contempt, and his conversation made it clear he considered Henri of Guirse by far the more suitable candidate for the throne. What I missed, and what a more experienced mind than mine should have noticed, was the sincere devotion he had for the duke. But this was so submerged beneath the flotsam of his overstated servitude, it would be years before I perceived it. And then...well, then it almost destroyed both our souls.

Anatole wanted me to sleep with him, almost begging me. I made an excuse, although his nearness and the wine combined to fire my loins. But there was something about him I could no longer love.

"I must remain on duty tonight," I told him. "I am responsible for the king's safety, and I dare not leave it to someone else.

"Perhaps some other time," said Anatole coldly. He was obviously offended.

"In Paris," I said, "there will be less danger."

We parted with an outward aspect of good will, but the love we had known was gone. In its place was a lingering attraction, buried beneath a mantle of distrust and a knowledge that either might try to use the other for the advantage of his lord. After this, I avoided Anatole, and we did not speak again until Henri was crowned.

On the trip to Paris, it became apparent that France was in a shattered state. The religious wars had devastated many towns, and we passed through entire areas where the fields lay fallow, unprepared for spring planting. Farmhouses stood empty, many of them gutted by fire. The crowds that gathered along our path seemed to force their cries of greeting from mouths set too long in somber lines. Our last few days on the road, the sky was overcast and gloomy, reflecting the mood of both the king and his people.

I no longer rode in the coach with Henri, for there were too many men of rank about him. Instead, I led a guard contingent on horseback, riding ahead of the royal carriage and seeing the king only at night when he retired to his apartment. Here, I still basked in his favor, for he frequently called me to him and took a glass of wine with me before he went to bed. We did not sleep together, but the ties of our friendship seemed firmer than ever.

Henri's coronation ceremonies were dismal, lacking the spontaneous joy they should have engendered. The crowds were there, and all the regal trappings were paraded with the proper pomp and elegance. Yet the people seemed tired and afraid. The regency of Queen Catherine had done much to bring this atmosphere about.

She had summoned me almost as soon as we arrived, and the questioned me at great length about Henri's activities in Poland. She was also particularly interested in who seemed closest to him during his travels home. I answered her honestly, for I could see no harm in her knowing. However, I realized after I left her that my true loyalty by now with the king. Had there been anything I felt would injure him, I would not have told his mother. As it was, I had omitted mention of our night together, nor did I tell her of the way I felt about the king.

Henri's reciprocal regard for me was made public immediately after he was crowned King of France. One of his first acts was to elevate me to the rank of chevalier and to formally invest me with the lands and titles which had belonged to my father. I would have liked my mother to be present for these ceremonies, but the messenger I sent to fetch her returned to tell me she was too ill to make the journey. As I had not seen her since first coming to Paris, I asked the king's permission to visit my estates. After a brief hesitation, he agreed.

On the eve of my departure, I was again summoned by the Black

Queen; she seemed annoyed that I had not consulted her before deciding to leave the city. "But it will give you an opportunity," she said, "to observe what is hidden from you when you travel in the company of the king. See all you can," she added, "and look behind the pictures which are erected for your benefit."

"What, especially, should I seek to learn?" I asked her.

"Our land is in an unhappy condition," she answered finally. "Many say it is because of me. I know this, and I expect it. I am still 'the Foreign Woman,' and nothing I do is seen in its proper light. Still, Louis, you must remember that it is my son—my last son—who sits on the throne of France. I have been queen of this same France for so many years I no longer think of myself as belonging to any other nation. When I act, it is only for the benefit of my child, and hence for the good of the land he rules.

"But there are others who do not seek the welfare of the king."

So I traveled to Tours, which lies south of Paris, in the very heart of France. I went through Orleans and followed the river Loire through Blois, to my home in the Touraine. I talked to a great many people along the way, both wealthy landholders and poor peasants who tilled their fields along the highway. I had dressed in respect-able but unremarkable attire, and I rode with but a single attendant. We traveled by horse, stopping at public inns and taverns.

The picture which formed in my mind was not encouraging. The greatest problem, I felt, was the lack of one single power to pull together all of France. There was still the loyalty of the simple man, who sought nothing more than to support the winning side. And after all is said and done, what more is a leader's power than his ability to convince a majority of his people that, if they support him, he will in turn have the strength to protect them from the others who also seek his loyalty. But such a one was not to be found.

The royal treasury was low; hence, the armies of the king were not as large as they should have been. His power rested in the feudal oaths of the nobles, and among these was a sharp, bitter division. The duke of Guise had indeed been active, and I know of many who openly supported the king but secretly favored the duke as the stronger potential ruler. They saw in him the virility and masculinity Henri lacked.

To further complicate this struggle for the hearts of the common man, the king of Navarre stood as head of the Protestant faction. While he never openly opposed Henri nor expressed any intention of seeking the crown of France, he had a tremendous following among those of his own religion. However, he was passionately hated by everyone else. Our Catholic majority regarded the Bourbon king of Navarre as an earthly representative of heathen disloyalty.

The further I traveled from Paris, the more hostile I found the regional religious groups. Armed conflicts were frequent, and a man took his life in his hands if he journeyed outside the immediate area of his home village. Being young and foolish, I refused to be intimidated by these threats of violence and I continued on my way, accompanied by Matthew, my single man-at-arms. I must have been watched over by heaven. I reached home safely, although we did have one fright when a band of armed men appeared in the road behind us and gave chase. We outdistanced them, but it was a sobering experience.

I arrived home just in time for my mother's funeral. I was especially saddened by this, for I knew I had not given her the attention she deserved during her latter years. I mourned her deeply, but circumstances forced me to cut short my time of sorrow. She had been a good woman and had done much with the estate while it was under her management. Now she was gone, and I would be forced to find a man I could trust to take over during my absence. I looked on this search as a final tribute to her, for she had loved the farms and the village. Mother had looked on the people as her children, and they had felt an almost familial loyalty toward her.

There were many experienced men I could have picked, but when I made a tour of inspection, I noticed the highly superior management of the small tenant farm on the western side of my chateau. I inquired and found it was now being run by Gene, my old friend from childhood. His parents had died some time before, and he had taken over. I also learned he had become an especial favorite of my mother's.

I rode across the edge of the land allotted to him and saw Gene in the distance. He was stripped to the waist, struggling to guide a team of oxen which was tugging a stump from a newly cleared section. Watching the animal grace with which he carried himself and the magnificent movement of hardened muscles beneath the tan of his skin, I thought back to our former association. As children we had played together, and later, as we approached the time of manhood, we had experimented with one another's bodies. Gene was still unmarried, though having reached his nineteenth year, as had I. It gave me hope my visit might not prove as futile as I had expected.

A week after my mother's funeral, I sent a servant to fetch Gene from the fields. It was late afternoon and nearly time for him to cease his labors. He came into the garden covered with sweat and dirt from the planting he had been doing. Embarrassed at his appearance, he stood uncomfortably before me, twisting his cap in his hands, fearful lest he had done something to offend me. I reassured him at once and offered him a cup of wine. He sat on one of the marble benches, and we talked together of our childhood for some time.

Gene had developed into a most attractive man. His hair was dark, almost black, but his eyes were blue, like a Northman's. He was taller than I by at least a head, and his slender, well-proportioned body was hard as oak from his daily labors in the fields.

EVEN OUR FANTASIES

Watching him, his huge fingers wrapped about my mother's dainty stemware, I recalled the flaming attraction I had felt for him when we were little more than boys.

At last, when both of us were glowing from the warmth of wine, I broached the subject of our earlier experiences. "I have thought of you many times," I told him, "and wondered if you still remembered the afternoons we spent in the loft."

He blushed beneath his tan, but he smiled in pleasure at the memory. "I hope our behavior has not been a source of concern," he said lightly.

"Only of occasional frustration," I replied, "on certain cold, lonely nights."

He grinned broadly, wiping back a twist of hair which fell across his forehead. "Let us hope there will be no long, empty evenings here in the Touraine," he laughed.

"Need there be?" I asked.

He shrugged. "One never knows," he answered teasingly.

I watched him intently, feeling myself growing hard beneath the velvet of my breeches. His beauty was compelling, enhanced rather than depreciated by his rags and his dirt-streaked face. I wanted him then and there. "Let's walk back to the old barn," I suggested softly.

He continued to regard me with his knowing grin, but he rose when I did, and together we walked to the building where I had first discovered the exquisite essence of another man. We stood behind the deserted barn for several minutes, watching the workers in the distance as they left their fields for home. The sun had dropped below the horizon, and its final, brilliant rays made long yellow lines across the sky.

"Maybe I should wash this grime off me," Gene said casually. He strode over to the pump, where he quickly stripped off his clothes and sloshed his body with water. He shouted as the chilly fluid coursed across his shoulders, jumping about in the fading light, wiping off the layers of dirt with the sides of his hands. He knew I was watching him, and he took pleasure in this display of his physical maturation. The clean limbs and body were hairless, except for a patch of black in the center of his chest and another above his long, slender penis. He held this under the water spout and rubbed it well to remove all the soil and grit. He turned his back and allowed the water to rush down the cavity between his cheeks, cleaning that, too, should it be subjected to my inspection.

There was a box of rags inside the barn, and I found a clean one for him to use. He thanked me, drying himself carefully, working the cloth between his legs and about the other sensitive parts of him.

The sunlight faded completely then, giving way to the silvery glow of moon and stars. Watching him, I noticed an unmistakable increase, a definite swelling of his penis. He had dried it for a considerably longer time than necessary, so it now hung in a soft arch, stretching outward from his groin. As he moved, it swayed with a springy bounce against the solid roundness of his tightly updrawn sac.

At last he stood before me naked, his legs apart, his hands resting easily on his hips. Moonlight reflected off his broad expanse of shoulder and caused the crisply curling hairs on his chest to shine as if dipped in silver. Hanging darkly in the shadow of his legs, his cock had ceased to be in light. Only the vaguest outline defined its alert and waiting presence. I knew he was aroused, but holding back, awaiting my first advance. He was so magnificent—so truly a thing of beauty. Standing exactly as he was, I hated to disturb the perfection by causing him to move. I wished I were a painter and could have captured that pose forever.

We were standing on straw which had been tumbled from the loft above us. Without another word, I dropped onto my knees before him. Worshipful, I took his long, expanding penis into my hands. Admiringly, I fondled it, watching it increase in size until it stood out hard and straight. It seemed to reach for me, projecting its flaring head toward my lips. I took it then, and felt the slender shaft slide into me, questing toward the back of my throat. My lips pressed his groin where the scent of sweat and grass still clung to him. He pulled my head against him and groaned at the long-forgotten sensations I created. A long while I worked upon him, my hands clasped about his buttocks, his damp, work-hardened legs leaning upon the shoulders of my satin doublet.

We could have climbed into the loft where as boys we had know the naked contact of our beings. He would have reciprocated, I knew, but I wanted him just this way. This first time we came together as men, though, I wanted to kneel before him and take him and let his seed flow down my throat without him doing a thing for me. There was some inexplicable thrill for me, as a finely dressed officer, to drop to my knees before this beautiful youth. So I held him where he stood when he would have pulled away to preserve his store of energy. I looked up the naked ridges of power outlined and softly glowing in the light of heaven. I saw the firm underside of his chin, the tousled halo of hair above it. His eyes were closed, his teeth clenched by the pressure of his impending release.

I slid my hand slowly up his sides, across his narrow waist, and onto the wide, smooth planes of his chest. I found his nipples in the darkness, and I pinched them, twisting the pointed tips until I felt the muscles of his belly tighten and heard the sudden rush of pent-up breath from his lungs. Then he came, bending slightly at the waist, grappling roughly at the back of my head as he plunged his manhood in short, rapid strokes against me I felt his heated flow begin, the salty sweetness of it as it coursed across my tongue, filling me with himself, dominating me, possessing me in the moment of his triumph. He trembled now, his whole body shaking from the power of his discharge. My lips tightened about his shaft, and I traveled several times from base to tip, drawing out the last of him, wanting it all. Even then, I remained fastened upon him as his erection slowly faded, and I held just a swollen softness.

Finally I stood up and brushed the dust from my clothing. I smiled at him, and I heard him sigh in relief. "I was afraid you would be angry," he muttered softly

"Angry?" I laughed. "Why should I be angry?"

He shrugged. "You are the master here," he said. "I...well, I am only a tenant farmer."

"You're more than that to me," I assured him. "I have always looked upon you as my friend." I placed my arm about his naked shoulder, pulling him against me. I kissed him, gently at first, and then with increasing depth and passion. He returned it after only a slight hesitation. I felt his hard body, smooth as the silk that touched it, pressing warm and solidly upon me.

"I should go," he whispered as our lips parted. "It would not do for someone to see me here this late."

"Nonsense!" I told him. "It is my land, and I shall entertain whomever I like. You will stay and dine with me, Gene, because I have some important business to discuss."

"But my clothes..." he began.

"If it will make you more comfortable," I suggested, "go on home and change. But come back as soon as you can."

He did as I asked, and I was standing in the doorway of the salon when he tapped softly on the front door. One of my mother's servants opened it, sniffing significantly as Gene came in. This angered me, and my first impulse was to have the fellow thrashed. Instead, I called Gene to me, and I told the servant to have the entire staff assemble immediately in the hall. He looked puzzled, but he obeyed without question.

When they were all present—house servants, cooks, maids, gardeners, laundry girls—I stood in front of them with Gene at my side. He was as confused and expectant as they, and he watched me with evident concern.

"This is the first time I have spoken to all of you as a group," I said to them, "and I want to assure you I intend making no changes in the staff at this time. Each of you seems loyal and capable, and I have no desire to disturb the efficiency of the household."

There seemed a sigh of relief at this, and one of the girls mumbled a "Thank you, sir."

"As you know," I continued, "it will be impossible for me to remain here for any extended period. I have duties which require my return to Paris and it may be years before I can finally come home to stay. So, the only place that is vacant is that of overseer on this estate.

"The gentleman standing beside me is known to all of you, I am sure. He is M. Eugene Maras. He has been a close friend of mine since we were children. If M. Maras agrees, I hope to place him in total charge. He will have full authority to make any changes he feels necessary, and in my absence, he will speak for me."

Gene's mouth opened, and he stared in disbelief. A couple of the girls tittered, and the servant who had admitted him eyed his new master unhappily. "All right," I said, "you may return to your duties. M. Maras and I will be dining in a few minutes," I added to the cook.

I knew I had surprised them all, for Gene was young and inexperienced in the management of anything bigger than his small tract of land. But I, too, was young, and while my choice of manager might have lacked the years of background I would have liked, he was bright, and I was certain I could trust him. I told him this while we ate, and I assured him of my total faith. "If I can arrange it," I told him, "I shall have my banker send a man to advise you for your first few months. He should be able to teach you how to keep the accountings. I have looked over my mother's records, and you will have no trouble following the calendar she has planned."

That night Gene slept in the chateau, occupying the room next to mine, where he would live on a permanent basis. He agreed to my offer, for I was more than generous, and he could not afford to pass up the opportunity. I think both of us were fortunate. As it turned out, the arrangement could not have been more satisfactory from either standpoint. In fact, I had made the most significant and wisest decision of my life—a decision which resulted in far more than either of us could have predicted at the time.

I had already arranged for Matthew, my man-at-arms and companion on the trip from Paris, to act as valet, or "upstairs gentleman" during my stay. I had done this because I was still a little shaken from our experience on the road and apprehensive over the general lawlessness which seemed to be getting worse instead of better. I slept more easily knowing Matthew was close at hand. My mother, of course, had employed a maid to awaken her in the morning and tend to the other upstairs housekeeping duties.

In anticipation of guests, I had only the big guardsman upstairs at night. Matthew was completely aware of many things. As he was also a man of some discretion, I found the new household arrangements particularly convenient this first night with Gene. Matthew, I might add, was an older fellow, who had been but a boy when he served my father. I had come across him in another regiment and requested him for my own retinue. Physically a large, almost ugly man, his look was enough to keep most people at a distance. He was also a little dull, but extremely loyal, and grateful for the advancement I had accorded him. I was learning fast, you see, that personal loyalty can best be obtained by elevating one who does not expect the position.

I slid into bed beside Gene, and in the darkness we came into each other's arms for the fulfillment we had only sampled in the stable yard. I suppose love comes more easily in youth, and looking back, I realize I have already spoken of being in love more than once. But with Gene, I had returned to my original passion, to my first awakening of sexuality. He was something more than a casual encounter, and to him I represented a memory no less vivid.

EVEN OUR FANTASIES

Our exchange of sex was memorable and full, but more important than this was the warm devotion that possessed us both. On this first night, and all the remaining nights of my stay, we slept with our bodies entwined, our flesh seeking to close more tightly then physically it could. We found a completeness and peace which neither had known before. The quiet countryside contributed to this, and the days I spent with Gene left me filled with a tender, gentle love I might otherwise never have known.

MARK OF THE WOLF

Derek Adams

I was shown to my cabin by an obsequious young steward with an ass that pushed back against his tight pants like a pair of ripe melons. Had he stayed for a moment longer in my cabin, I would have jumped him, but he bid me a good day and left before I pinned him to the floor.

I sat in the tasteful luxury of my private sitting room, reflecting on the changes that were taking place in me. My depression was indeed gone, replaced by a sexual euphoria that gave me no peace. I had never behaved like this in my life. Even at boarding school, where privacy was virtually nonexistent and sex was at the forefront of every adolescent mind, I had been shy and furtive, carefully guarding the secret of my sexuality.

At college, it had been much the same. I had encountered men like myself, but I had always held myself in check, intimidated by the size of my own genitals. Even my affair with Marcus had been initiated by him and marked by a rather tentative approach to the act of sex, on my part at least. Prior to my bout with depression,

I'd had several affairs, but they had been restrained and civilized—too much so, judging by the fact that all had been terminated by my partners, not by me.

Now, however, all of that had changed and changed radically. I had become a sexual predator, obsessed with the idea of sex—and with the act itself. This newfound sexual athleticism aroused me greatly, but I feared that it might become dangerous. I had, after all, brutalized my personal trainer. Rex had been proud and arrogant—although ultimately willing to experiment, however reluctantly—but he had not deserved what I had subjected him to up in the ballroom that afternoon. I had punished him for my own pleasure, and that fact frightened me very much.

I brooded over this state of affairs for the remainder of the afternoon, ignoring the embarkation festivities offered to all the passengers. I would have remained secluded for the remainder of the day, but hunger eventually drove me out to mingle with my fellow travelers. I could have ordered room service, but I needed to escape my morbid thoughts. I did not, after all, wish to return to my former state of mind, regardless of the dangers inherent in this metamorphosis I appeared to be undergoing.

My luggage had been delivered and unpacked, the cases stowed away long before I set foot in my rooms. Marcus had, as usual, managed everything perfectly. The closet was filled with the appropriate clothing for an ocean crossing made in high style. I disliked playing dress-up, as I had rather caustically referred to it when Marcus had explained the details of my birthday gift, but it was expected of me and the only convention I had defied during my life had nothing to do with matters of dress. With that in mind, I laid out white shirt, tux pants, and dinner jacket, located my father's sapphire studs and cuff links, black silk socks and highly polished, soft leather dress shoes. That accomplished, I showered, shaved, and made myself ready to face the world.

"Damn!" I pounded my fist on the marble top of the lavatory

and scowled darkly at my reflection in the mirror. I was dressed, but I was unable to master the intricacies of my bow tie. I had often told Marcus that a simple clip-on tie would work as well, but he had always merely laughed and tied the damned thing for me. Now, Marcus was miles away and the little strips of black silk hung down uncooperatively on the snowy white expanse of my heavily starched, pleated shirtfront. It was already five past eight and late arrivals for the second seating at dinner were probably frowned upon. I locked my cabin and made my way toward the dining salon, keeping an eye out for a steward who might have the dexterity to help me out.

"Sir? Excuse me." I turned to the source of the pleasant tenor voice, my left eyebrow cocked in expectation.

"May I help you?" The man who was speaking to me was very young, his fine features still resolving into their chiseled maturity. His auburn hair was thick, combed back from a high forehead, the ends barely brushing his tight white collar. His eyes flickered to the ends of my tie. I shrugged, he smiled, and I felt a tightening in my chest.

"You seem to have forgotten to tie your tie, sir."

"Not forgotten, I'm afraid. It defeated me soundly in a set battle in my cabin." The young man's laugh was soft, musical. He smiled at me again and the hallway suddenly seemed quite warm.

"I can take care of it in a flash, sir."

"I'm afraid I'll make you late for dinner as well. From the looks of you, you're on your way to the eight o'clock seating."

"I'm always late," he replied, shrugging his shoulders. "It won't take a minute."

"Thanks."

The young man came and stood in front of me, close enough for me to smell the faint citrus of his after-shave, although his cheeks looked too soft to need much in the way of shaving. He took the ends of the tie in hand and stared at them intently.

"This won't work."

"Not a problem. I'll scare up a steward. You better go on in to dinner."

"Sorry?" He shot me a puzzled glance. "Oh. I just meant that I can't get it from this angle. Come over here." He motioned me toward the staircase that led to the next deck. "Stand here." He indicated a position at the foot of the stairs. I stood. He slipped behind me and stood on the first stair. "This will work," he said. He draped his arms over my shoulders and seized the ends of my tie. I cast my eyes down and watched his long fingers gather the ends of the silk and miraculously transform it into a perfect bow. The backs of his hands were sprinkled with freckles and, when they caught the light at certain angles, a dusting of fine down was visible, barely stained with the coppery hues of his lustrous hair.

"Perfect." I felt his hands on my shoulders as he surveyed his handiwork in a mirror across from where we stood. The hands were pale against the dark fabric of my dinner jacket. His handsome young face hovered directly behind me, so close that his breath tickled my ear. Our eyes locked for an instant in the mirror and he smiled sweetly. I shrugged his hands away and moved to a safer distance. Being alone with this young beauty was leading my thoughts in dangerous directions.

"Thanks very much...uh, I don't even know your name."

"Gavin, sir. Gavin Huntingdon."

"Jeffrey Ashford."

"Pleased to meet you, Mr. Ashford."

"Jeffrey, please."

"Jeffrey." He rolled my name off his tongue as though he were savoring a fine wine. "Maybe I'll see you at dinner, Jeffrey." With that, he turned and vaulted along the hall, disappearing through a doorway at the far end.

I stayed where I was until my hard-on stopped tenting out the front of my trousers. Gavin had disturbed me—as almost all men seemed to do these days. His hands had felt so good, heating my skin, even through shirt and jacket. He had left his hands on me for a long time—an unconscious gesture, surely. I shook my head in an effort to banish inappropriate thoughts and made my way to the dining salon.

The room was full when I entered and I couldn't help but notice the number of people who turned their heads to stare as I waited for the steward to lead me to my place. I heard my name whispered at a number of tables as I followed the steward's tapered back across the room. I recognized none of the whisperers, but they obviously had seen enough of my face in the society pages of newspapers and magazines over the years to know who I was. The advantages of my father's wealth obviously did not include anonymity. Marcus would have thoroughly approved. I, on the other hand, was distinctly uncomfortable at this pointless recognition, not of me, but of my bank account.

I was seated at the captain's table—Marcus hadn't overlooked a single detail—between a rather florid matron and a younger woman who was, I soon discovered, her unmarried daughter. I was impervious to the mother's rather pointed remarks regarding her only child's marital and financial status, primarily because the person seated across from me absorbed my interest so completely.

"I hoped I'd see you at dinner, and here you are." Gavin grinned disarmingly and introduced me to his parents, a rather stiff couple who appeared to have spent most of their lives in dim drawing rooms presiding over well-stocked bars. They registered my name with obvious approval, then turned their attentions back to the consumption of a steady stream of cocktails.

I ate to the accompaniment of Gavin's excited descriptions of the places he planned to visit in Europe, occasionally punctuated by a remark from the anxious mother seated to my right. For my part, I could think of little to say. I was strongly attracted to Gavin, but I had resolved not to act upon my feelings. He was so young and innocent, and I felt so jaded at the moment that seducing him was out of the question—if not out of my fantasies.

I finished my meal and waited for the earliest opportunity to decently slip away and go back to my cabin. Immediately after dessert, the captain rose from his chair, bid us all a good voyage, and returned to the bridge. I followed him out of the dining room before Gavin could extract himself from an exchange with another passenger.

I slept fitfully that night. My dreams were all intensely sexual, prominently featuring a handsome young man with auburn hair and gorgeous eyes the color of cornflowers. In the dreams, I pursued him through the passageways of the ship, finally running him to ground in the dining salon. He offered to tie my tie, but instead he took off my clothes and I carried him to the captain's table, deposited him face down on the snowy cloth, and mounted him in full view of his parents and the mother whose daughter was in danger of becoming a professional spinster. I fucked him straight through all the dinner courses, including the dessert. When I finally came, I pulled my cock out of Gavin's ass and spouted jism like a fountain for minutes on end while the ship's orchestra played a rousing tune and the passengers all cheered and danced around us. My geyser of come only abated when Gavin mounted me again in a valiant attempt to protect the passengers from imminent danger of drowning in my slippery balljuice. He sat on my cock, flexing his tight ass until my jism began bubbling out of his mouth, flecking his pink lips with white. I finally pulled him off to save him from drowning, then sat on the banquet table, dazedly watching my spouting prick until I dissolved completely in a funky lake of creamy white jism.

I woke up the next morning with a dry crust of sperm on my belly, the sheets of the bed stiff with my discharge. I hadn't had a wet dream in a number of years, yet Gavin had excited me to the point of orgasm, even in my sleep. I jerked off in the shower, trying not to think of anyone even remotely like him, drank the juice and coffee my steward delivered to me, then went in search of the gymnasium which the ship's promotional literature vaunted as "world-class."

The big room was empty, all its gleaming equipment idle. I put my clothes into a locker, pulled on gray jersey shorts, white socks and shoes, then walked back into the gym and began to stretch.

I was pumping iron furiously, the sweat streaming down my torso, when the door to the gym opened. I looked up and felt the tightness in my chest again. It was Gavin, dressed in shorts and T-shirt, a small black gym bag clutched in his right hand. He scanned the room and when he saw me his handsome face lit up with pleasure.

"Good morning, Jeffrey," he called out heartily.

"Good morning, Gavin," I replied, continuing to curl the barbell, savoring the burn in my quivering biceps.

"Looking good," he enthused, his eyes sweeping me, head to toe. I felt suddenly exposed, wished that I had chosen to wear sweats for my workout instead of the skimpy shorts that clung to my ass and held my genitals front and center, concealing nothing from view. "Would you be willing to offer me some pointers?"

"Pointers?"

"Yeah, you know, tell me how you got your body to look the way it does. That physique is obviously no accident."

"Just good genes," I muttered uncomfortably, dropping the barbell noisily into the rack and walking to the bench press.

"Not to mention hours a day in the gym, right?"

"Right." I wanted him to go away, but that was obviously not a part of his plan. He just stood there, smiling longingly, waiting for me to offer to help him out. "Get changed, Gavin. I'll see if I can come up with a few exercises for you." His eyes lit up and he was off like a shot.

When he returned, I showed him a few basic stretches and floor exercises, then sat at one of the leg machines and began to work my thighs. Gavin stood near me, chattering away as he limbered up his lithe muscles. He was lean and tight, his physique already showing promise. I had no doubt that he would be able to sculpt a heart-stopping body if he was willing to make the effort. It was apparent that he had already worked to pump his biceps, and his pecs suggested that he was no stranger to push-ups.

"Now what?" Gavin popped up in front of me, hands on hips, chest heaving.

"That all depends on what you want to achieve," I replied, eyes fixed on the muscles in my thighs as I strained to squeeze out the final reps.

"Well, this for starters." He put his palm against my chest and stroked the hard curve of my pecs. I stiffened at his touch and the muscles jumped under his hand. "And I want arms like yours." His hand strayed to my biceps, his fingers hot against my skin.

"Come on then," I barked gruffly. I stood up abruptly and marched over to the weight rack. I yanked two twenty-pound hand weights down, turned, and thrust them at him. He took them from me, slightly abashed by my manner, and listened intently as I told him what to do. I then demonstrated a few simple arm and chest exercises and went back to my own workout, thoroughly disconcerted by his presence.

Gavin interrupted me every few minutes, always eager for a new suggestion. He worked at everything like a demon, obviously impatient for results. I knew he would be very sore later on, but I didn't restrain him. If his muscles ached, then perhaps he wouldn't come to the gym the next day.

When I had finally exhausted myself and went to the locker room, Gavin followed me. Fortunately, we were not alone. Another man was sitting in the Jacuzzi next to the communal showers. He nodded and I began talking to him, desperate to get rid of Gavin before I lost control of myself.

I stripped out of my workout gear, rinsed off before Gavin could follow me into the showers, and joined the man in the Jacuzzi. It was a small tub, barely big enough for two. I sat with my back to Gavin, arms stretched along the sides, leaving no room for a third. I nodded at the man across from me and he introduced himself. I was aware of Gavin behind me, watching me, but I didn't turn to him, barely acknowledged his mumbled good-bye when he stalked sulkily out of the room.

The man in the tub was attractive in a rough-and-tumble way. His nose had been flattened like a prizefighter's and his chin receded slightly, but his eyes glowed with an animal vitality. His body was firm, but not remarkable except for the development of his pecs. They were obviously his fetish, puffed out almost to the point of absurdity, totally overbalancing the symmetry of his upper body. His nipples were enormous, the dark areolas the size of silver dollars, the points in the center jutting out like tiny fingertips. The right was pierced by a thick gold hoop, the left by a stud with two gold balls anchoring it. He saw me looking and flexed, puffing the muscles to amazing proportions.

I winked at the man and he popped up out of the tub, strode across to the door, locked it, and returned. "Just so we won't be disturbed," he explained leering at me hungrily.

"Fine," I muttered, rising from the tub and facing him. He eyed my hard-on hungrily and made a grab for it. I caught his wrist and spun him around, wrenching his arm up along his spine till his fingers were splayed out at the level of his shoulder blades.

"Hey, knock it off!" he yelped, his voice rising in pitch to a shrill whine. "I was just gonna touch it."

"You'll do more than that," I growled, shoving him roughly up against the wall. I heard the gold hoop that adorned his tit clack against the tiles. I reached up and latched on to the distended tab of flesh, at the same time wedging his thighs apart with my knee.

I began pinching his tit at the same instant that I crammed my prick up into him. He let out a moan of pleasure, punctuated by a sharp cry of pain as I breached him. I drove in up to the hilt and began fucking, hard mechanical thrusts geared to reach orgasm as quickly as possible. As I played with the man's swollen tits, his cries turned to soft moans and he began to jerk himself off.

I came violently, slamming the man against the wall, battering him mercilessly. He snorted and bucked, his asshole spasming as he climaxed. I yanked my cock out of him and he dropped to his knees, still pulling on his pud. I saw his jism pool on the black marble surrounding the Jacuzzi as I stalked into the showers to clean his smell off my body. As I stepped under the cascading water, I heard him unlock the door and skulk away.

I was angry with myself. I hadn't really even desired the man, had only used him because he was convenient. If Gavin had stayed with me and we had been alone, would I have treated him the same way? The thought frightened me so much that I determined to avoid him for the remainder of the voyage, even if I had to lock myself in my cabin until the boat docked.

True to my convictions, I holed up in my cabin for the remainder of the crossing, taking meals in my room, ignoring Gavin's messages asking for my help with his exercise program. The steward brought me books from the ship's library and I managed to pass the time, working on a series of lectures on ancient Greek civilization that I had agreed to present at the University in the autumn. I had no official position at the school—taking a professorship away from someone who needed the money and security seemed impertinent to me—but my classes were well attended and the Board of Regents seemed pleased to humor my wishes. My grandfather Ashford had, after all, endowed the school with millions of dollars in his will. For my part, I looked forward to a resumption of my duties as a way of celebrating my return to life.

My lectures took shape and I managed to pass my days in relative peace, but I couldn't control my dreams. Once asleep, I was totally at the mercy of erotic fantasies so vivid they were palpable. And then I made a discovery that was truly disturbing—one which made me begin to doubt my sanity.

It all began innocently enough, nothing more than a dream—or so I thought. I was prowling deep in the bowels of the mighty ship. It was late—no crew was about—and no sounds rose above the monotonous droning of the huge diesel engines that powered the vessel. The gray metal plates of the floor were cool against the soles of my feet. I looked down and discovered to my mild surprise that I was naked, yet this exhilarated rather than alarmed me. The vibrations of the engines rose through my body. My cock swelled and twitched, lengthening and thickening, not yet erect, but incredibly sensitized. It slapped against my thighs with every step, promising unlimited pleasure at the first touch.

I was aware of the heat increasing as I went deeper into the oily gloom. And then I saw him—an engineer by the looks of his grease-streaked arms and hands. He was leaning against the railing of a catwalk, stained white T-shirt pulled up into his armpits, his dungarees around his knees.

The bared torso was hot—flat belly split by a line of dark curls that gleamed in the light cast by the bare bulb over his head; swell of pecs partially exposed, more dark curls, fat, succulent nipples like candy kisses. The line of belly hair thickened as it approached his crotch, got longer, thicker, burgeoned around the base of his prick like soft black moss.

The man was jerking off—the scent of his raunchy musk wafted to my nostrils over the distance that separated us. I pulled back into the shadows, gripped my own prick, stiff now, began pulling myself, mirroring his stroke and speed. He was intent on his pleasure, head thrown back, eyes closed, mouth gaping as he ran a finger around his helmeted knob, teasing the juice out and smearing it up and down the shaft.

He leaned forward, pursed his lips, drooled a gobbet of white, frothy spit into his collared fingers, stroked himself faster. I mimicked him, tugged my foreskin up, stretched it wide with my fingers, spit in it, quivered at the feel of hot spittle bathing my burning cockknob. I spit again, held it, then slowly dragged my hand down, squeezing tight. An intense body rush shook me and I groaned softly.

The man's eyes flew open, his hand frozen in mid-stroke. His eyes were dark, flashing sparks of reflected light as he looked all around attempting to penetrate the gloom. I held my breath, not moving, conscious of the turbine-heated air on my bare flesh, aware of every hair on my body, the sweat trickling down my sides, the dull, tingling ache of pleasure in my balls.

At last, satisfied that he was alone, the man continued, gripped his cock around the hilt, squeezed, puffing veins flaring the rim of the crown. I did the same, felt the lube leak out of me, drip down the inside of my leg, splatter on the metal floor. He began to rub his belly, fingers climbing higher, reaching the rise of his pecs, groping for his tits. When he made contact, his shoulders jerked, his balls bounced and jiggled. He pinched it, pulled, drew it out from the mound of muscle, held it there, his other hand pumping faster and faster.

The smell of the man was intoxicating, so intense it made my nostrils quiver. Sweat, ball musk, the heady funk of sex—all combined to drive me wild with desire. I crept out of the shadows, moving silently, pumping my prick as I drew closer. I could see the sweat sheening his belly, the prick honey glistening on the shaft and head of his prick. I wanted to touch it, taste it, feel it against my skin.

I was close now, so close I could hear his hand slipping against his cock flesh, so close I could see the veins pulsing in his forearms and his neck. The tingling in my gut intensified as the jism began to pump, propelled by the spasmodic contractions of the muscles in my groin. I pulled my fist up, dragging my balls onto the shaft, bunching the skin up over the head of my dick. I held it there, fingers flexing, teasing the tortured bundle of nerves massed at the tip of my hard-on until I could hold back no longer.

I shot a high, arcing streamer of balljuice that cut across the man's arm and shoulder like the mark of a whip. His eyes opened wide, cock abandoned now, flexing wildly, shooting seed up along the ridges of his gut. I reached out to him, tried to speak, to reassure him. His mouth gaped in horror as he jumped back, screamed, then toppled over the rail of the catwalk, arms and legs flailing wildly.

I woke up with a start, sat up in bed, chest heaving, heart pounding. I was alone, in my cabin, safe in my bed. I reached out shakily for the glass of water I had placed on my nightstand. It was empty. I turned on the light, got out of bed and walked into the bathroom. When I returned, what I saw on the plush pale carpets stopped me cold. Footprints. Dark footprints leading from the bed to where I stood. I knelt and touched one of the spots. Dirty oil. I examined the soles of my feet. They were black with it. I sat down on the floor and leaned against the wall, staring hopelessly into the darkness. Head pounding, chest constricted by fear, I remained there until the gray light of dawn smudged the windows of my cabin.

I scrubbed my feet and did my best to remove the stains from the carpeting, unwilling—or afraid?—to explain the footprints to the cleaning crews. When the steward brought me my coffee the next morning, I mentioned as casually as I could manage that I had heard that there had been an accident on board the ship. He looked at me strangely, then smiled wryly.

"I don't know how you could have heard of it, sir."

"I was on the promenade earlier," I lied. "I overheard members of the crew talking about it. I hope it wasn't anything serious."

"It was one of the crew down in the engine rooms. He could have been a hell of a lot worse off. Just a couple of cracked ribs and a mild concussion." The steward lowered his voice and winked confidentially. "Silly bugger was having himself off and lost his balance. Fell right off a catwalk in the engine room. He could have broken his bloody neck. Claimed he saw a ghost. Can you top that?"

I was so relieved that I laughed out loud. "I'm glad to hear it wasn't serious. I always whack off in bed myself. Much safer."

"Indeed, sir."

"We arrive early tomorrow morning?"

"That's correct, sir. Passenger disembarkation will begin at seven o'clock in the morning. It's been a pleasure to serve you, sir." I gave the man an extravagant tip and he left me, all smiles and wishes for my good health and happiness. I asked him to arrange for the packing of my luggage and he assured me that he would handle it personally.

That evening, long after I had dined alone in my cabin, I heard a knock at the door. Had I not thought that it was my steward returning to deal with my clothes, I would never have answered it. I was lying on my bed, reading a book. I was naked and merely wrapped the towel around my hips that I had used to dry myself after my shower.

"Gavin!" I opened the door and he was through it like a shot, ducking under my arm and pushing it closed behind him.

"You've been avoiding me, Jeffrey," he said, his green eyes flashing with indignation. "Why?"

"I...I haven't been avoiding anyone," I retorted defensively. His charms hadn't lessened in the days that had intervened since I had helped him out in the gymnasium. If anything, he was even more delectable. His auburn hair was tousled, as though he had been in bed when my perceived injustice had driven him out to confront me. He was wearing a thin white cotton robe that had slipped off one shoulder, baring his flawless, creamy skin and a pale pink nipple. The lamp light caught the coppery hairs on his bare legs, making them glisten. I suddenly felt very vulnerable.

"You were so nice to me when we met. Did I do something to offend you?" The muscles in his neck and shoulders tensed, almost as though he expected me to strike him with my fist. I saw for the first time the tawny flecks imbedded in the blue irises of his eyes, catching the light, flashing fire back at me.

"You certainly didn't do anything to offend me," I assured him, uncomfortably aware of a stirring in my loins.

"Do you think I'm ugly?" There was a slight quaver in his voice now, as though he had bared his worst fear to me.

"You're very handsome, Gavin. It's just that..."

"Make love to me, then." He wriggled free of the robe and stood in front of me, naked and dangerous.

"I can't, Gavin."

"Why? Because I don't have rings and pins piercing my tits?" Just exactly how much had he seen in the shower room that day? Obviously enough to send his imagination into overdrive. "I saw you looking at that man, Jeffrey. If that's what you want, I'll get a needle and do it right now."

"For chrissakes, Gavin. Don't be ridiculous. You have a beautiful body. I...I'm...it's just that I'm not interested." I looked at him angrily, trying not to see the full curves of calves and thighs, the lush rise of his buttocks, his belly, the flame-colored bush that looked like silk. "You're really not my type."

"Maybe not," he replied, his voice soft. "But I seem to be his type." His hand shot out and I felt his fingers wrapping around the shaft of my rigid prick. It had betrayed me again, jutting out from under the towel wrapped around my hips. "Make love to me, Jeffrey. I'll do anything you want. Anything."

I could still have thrown him out of the room if he hadn't suddenly stepped forward and wrapped his arms around me. My cock pressed up against his belly and I felt the heat of his hard-on against my thigh. His face was against my chest, his hot tongue lapping at the deep valley cut between my bulging pecs. I put my hands on his shoulders, intending to keep them there. Instead, they slipped down his back to the smooth mounds of his ass flesh, and I was lost.

I lifted him and his long, lean legs twined around my waist. His mouth pressed against my throat, my chin, against my mouth. My tongue wedged between his full lips and I tasted his sweetness. He pulled his head back slightly, eyes wide, staring into mine. Triumph and trepidation were mingled in his expression as he smiled at me.

"Jeffrey?"

"What?"

"I-I...please show me what to do. I want to do everything with you. You will teach me, won't you? Please say yes."

I looked at him solemnly, felt his heart pounding against my chest, the warmth and smoothness of his skin, the insistent, pulsing stiffness of his cock. I searched my mind, but could conjure up nothing but the utmost tenderness when I looked at him. I felt confident that I would be unable to hurt him. He was so beautiful. Instead of answering, I kissed him and he melted against me.

I carried him to the bed and knelt amidst the tangled sheets. His arms and legs untwined and he sprawled back where I had lain while I was reading. I crouched between his outspread legs while he played with my cock, stroking it gently, tugging my foreskin. I had the distinct feeling that he had never touched a man's cock other than his own.

"Do you like that?" He was smoothing my overhang against his palm, stroking it then removing his hand to watch my knob emerge from its hood. Every time he touched my hard-on, the hot, fat cylinder of his own dick jerked against his belly.

"It's beautiful," he sighed. "It feels like silk." He glanced down at his own dick and scowled. "Mine got cut off."

"It doesn't matter, Gavin," I assured him. "It doesn't change what you feel and it doesn't make your prick one bit less attractive to men. Don't worry about it."

"But it feels so good," he protested, tugging on it again.

"Do you want to try it on?"

"Try it on?"

"Well, temporarily." He looked puzzled, but he nodded enthusiastically. "Up on your knees." He scrambled into position. "Hold your dick steady." He gripped his stiffer with both hands to keep it from jumping around with every beat of his heart.

"Ready?" He shook his head eagerly. I thrust my hips forward, pressed the tip of my cock to his and shucked my foreskin up over his glans. His shoulders hunched forward and his eyes fluttered shut. I stretched it up as far as I could—one inch, then two—tugging on myself until I was in pain. I smoothed it on his shaft and held it in place, joining our cocks securely.

"Fuck it," I said softly. He looked at me, his cheeks reddening. Then his slender hips began to move, back and forth, back and forth. He pressed his fingers against the insides of my wrists, began tracing the thick veins up my forearms to my biceps. He kneaded the thick muscles, rubbed my shoulders, tracing collarbones, deltoids, neck. From there, down the center of my torso, across the full, hard rise of my pecs and over my belly, always humping, mashing cock-knob to cock-knob as he quickly discovered the primal rhythms of sex.

"Jeffrey?" He was looking up at me again, hips still twitching, his innocent expression belied by our actions.

"Gavin?"

"Can I suck your cock?" I smiled and nodded. He pulled his dick free from my skin and crouched between my thighs. He eyed my hard-on warily, then lunged forward. I yelped with pain and pushed his head away.

"What?" He looked up at me in horror.

"Too many teeth," I said, rubbing the end of my prick. "You

have to…" I winked at him and shrugged. "I'll show you. It's easier than trying to explain it." I pushed him back on the bed and put my head down between his legs. I nuzzled in tight between his thighs and licked his balls. They were hot and tasted sweet, like honey. I drew the fat orbs into my mouth and pressed them against the insides of my cheeks. Gavin whimpered and his fingers twined in my hair. I sucked them till they began to draw up on their cords, then released them and began to lick at his shaft, starting with the swollen ridge between his balls and asshole, then moving gradually up along the bulging juicetube to his crimson knob.

I kissed the tip, let it slide between my lips, going down slowly, savoring the taste of the juice that had begun to leak out of him, the silken texture of his skin. His prick was long and slender, arcing slightly to the left, the entire surface networked with delicate blue veins. I drew my lips back over my teeth, curled my tongue to fit the rigid contours and began to give him head, relishing his throaty moans of carnal pleasure.

I didn't suck him long, knowing that he would all too soon erupt in a torrent of sticky jism. I could have let that happen, let it be over sooner rather than later, but I didn't want to cheat him. Or was it that I didn't want it to end for more selfish reasons? Because I couldn't get enough of his taste, or his warmth, or the texture of his skin and hair and the intoxicating scent of him? Whatever the reason, I didn't make him come. Instead, I let him push me away and experiment with the techniques I had just demonstrated.

It was obvious that he had been paying strict attention during my little lesson. His teeth remained cushioned by his lips as he managed to engulf the head and the first few inches of my shaft. His lips stretched tight around my girth, spittle oozing out and dripping on my balls as he strove manfully to give me head.

"We can both do this at the same time," I said, pulling him up onto my body and spinning him around till his cock, balls, and asshole were all at my disposal. I went down on him and he lunged for my throbbing spike, sucking with a vengeance.

Gavin came barely a heartbeat later, his hips thrusting forward as his prick began shooting off gobbets of come faster than I could swallow them. His juice was salty, pungent, and copious, overflowing my mouth and streaking my cheeks. When he was drained, he squirmed around to face me, straddling my belly. His expression was sheepish.

"I'm sorry."

"Nothing to be sorry for, Gavin. You came because you had no choice. Sex can be like that."

"I don't want to stop, Jeffrey."

"Somehow that doesn't surprise me, Gavin." I pinched the tip of his dick. It was still flying high, curving up against his belly.

"I'm not boring you, am I? I mean because I'm such a…a…" He blushed crimson and lowered his eyes.

"Such a virgin?" He shot me a look of protest, then chuckled softly, shrugging his shoulders in acknowledgment of the truth of my statement. "No, Gavin, I'm not bored." I pulled his hand behind him to my erection. "Do I feel bored?" He shook his head and licked his lips.

"Jeffrey?" Gavin wriggled around on the bed beside me and propped himself on his elbows, his sweet body pressed close against my feverish skin.

"What?"

"Will you fuck me? When I dream about you, I always dream that you put your cock up my ass and hold me down and fuck me. And your body gets hotter and hotter on top of me, and you start to sweat, and your prick hurts me at first, then it starts to feeling really good. Then, when you shoot, I can feel it pumping up into me and it makes me so hot I come right then, with you. Then you lie there on top of me and kiss my neck and stay that way all night, fucking me again and again, every time your cock gets hard. Then you fall asleep on top of me and I lie there and listen to your breathing."

He leaned over and pressed his lips against the swollen point of my left tit. The barest pressure of his full, soft lips pinned me to the bed, put me totally at his mercy. My sex-swollen cock throbbed against my belly. Gavin saw it, reached down, began stroking it with a fingertip. "Please fuck me, Jeffrey. Put your big prick up my ass and screw me, nice and hard."

"Do you know what you're asking for?"

"I just know what I've dreamed about, Jeffrey. Please." I sat up, rolled Gavin onto his back, spread his long legs, knelt between them. He smiled nervously, tongue flickering against his upper lip. He put out his hand to me, traced the ridges of my abs with his fingers, tangled them in my damp pubes, stroked along the sides of my rigid cockshaft. I growled softly, baring my teeth. My meat slapped up against my gut, then slowly lowered till it was pointing at his asshole like a loaded gun.

I put my hands on the swell of muscle in his calves and stroked up along his legs till my thumbs were pressed against his moist, hot asspucker. His eyes fluttered shut and his dick flopped against his belly like a grounded fish. I pressed against the ring of muscle, savoring the resistance of his clenched sphincter, imagining the ecstasy of punching my dick through it and savoring the hidden delights of his virginal man channel.

I rubbed his asshole, applying more and more pressure until my thumbs disappeared up to the first joint. Gavin dropped back flat onto the bed, his chest heaving, fingers curved against the silken skin of his belly. I wiggled my thumbs around in the heat, stretching the little muscle, feeling it tighten down like a rubber band.

"Uh huh. Uh huh. Oh, Jeffrey, yes. Yes!" I kept my thumbs in him and began stroking his balls, rubbing the firm surface, gently stretching the cords they dangled from. His dick was rigid, swollen, flushed pink. I leaned forward, sinking my thumbs into him up to the webbing. He looked up at me, eyes glazed, lips parted, his breath hot on my face.

"You are so hot, Jeffrey," he mumbled, his long, sandy lashes fluttering seductively. He put his hands on my shoulders and squeezed the knotted muscles. "I want to be just like you." I smiled enigmatically and lowered my head to his chest. I kissed his swollen nipples, then sank my teeth into the fleshy point capping his left pec. The muscle beneath swelled, pushed against my lips. I increased the pressure of the bite, at the same time pulling my thumbs apart, stretching his sphincter. I heard his sharp intake of breath and his fingers dug tighter into my shoulders.

I raised my head slightly, pulling the tender nub of his tit until his shoulders rose off the bed. I rubbed my tongue across the captive point one last time, then released it and bent back down to torment its twin. I slowly pulled my thumbs out of him and guided my prick to its burrow. The little ring of muscle pulsed against the tip, sending sensually charged sparks along the shaft that exploded in my belly and balls, raising my level of arousal to critical levels.

The juice was pumping out of me in a steady stream, slicking his hole and running down his crack. I pressed my dick firmly against him and milked it, drooling goo into his ass channel. Then I gripped Gavin's ankles, pulled his legs straight up and scissored them roughly apart. The globes of his ass flexed, then spread apart, baring his crack and the lube-slicked pucker at its base.

"Help me," I demanded, staring down at him. My cock was hovering above his ass, leaking steadily. Gavin gripped it and looked up at me questioningly.

"Like this?" he asked, pulling it down, mashing my knob against his quivering anus.

"Yes!" I stabbed at him roughly. My knob caught in the slot, hesitated, then drove through into the moist channel.

"Aieee!" Gavin wailed piteously, tears misting his eyes. He

splayed his hands on my belly, pushing against me. I felt the muscles in his legs contract as he tried to bring them together, tried to close himself up. I held him, splaying his legs wider, no longer the gentle suitor to his virginity. I wanted him, wanted to penetrate him, stretch his bowels, make them conform to the rigid straightness of my tool.

"Jeffrey! Please! Aaahhh! So big. So big! Unhhh!" His fists pounded futilely at me, striking my chest and belly. I grabbed his flailing hands, ready to pin them to the bed and spear him to the hilt. Then I looked at him, saw the fear in his eyes, the tears rolling down his smooth cheeks. I pulled his hands to my lips, kissed the palms, withdrew my prick from his heat, looked down at him, nostrils flaring.

"I'm...I'm sorry, Gavin." My heart was pounding with an intense passion for him, tinged with a dark, unnameable fear.

"No, no. Please. I don't want you to stop, Jeffrey. Just give me a little more time. Please. Oh, Jeffrey, I want you." I released his hands and he scrambled to his knees, threw himself against me, his tears hot against my shoulder. I held him, stroked him, cupped his sleek ass in my hands until he had stopped trembling. How could I have thought to hurt this tender, untried man? He was offering his innocence to me. I owed him more than pain.

I fought back the powerful urges that drove me to tear into him, calmed myself, brought myself back under control. I cupped his chin in my hand and tilted his face up to mine. I kissed away his tears, pressed my lips to his, kissed him tenderly.

"I'm ready, Jeffrey," he whispered, his randy prick still stiff against my belly. "Thank you for your kindness and patience. I won't be such a silly twit now."

"It was my fault, Gavin." I smiled at him. "You turned me on too much. You made me lose control."

"I did?" He sounded surprised, distinctly pleased at this newfound power over me.

"You did. I think it would be better if you took this at your own speed."

"How?"

"Like this." I leaned back, braced my hands behind my back on the bed. My dick rose up like a vein-gnarled pole, pulsing strongly, knob bared, gleaming honey oozing out, streaming down the shaft and over the bloated orbs of my balls. Gavin eyed it hungrily, then looked at me.

"Please, Jeffrey. Tell me what I should do."

"Straddle my hips." He obeyed quickly, balls against my belly, my dick pressed against his spine. "Now, raise that pretty little ass of yours up in the air and sit on me. Take your time with it, Gavin. As long as I have you to look at, I can keep it hard."

"I think I believe you," he said, looking at me intently.

"How could you doubt it?" I retorted, pumping my hips, rubbing my cock knob against his backside.

Gavin kissed me, then set to work popping his own cherry on the fleshy spike of my libido. He set about his work seriously, one hand on my shoulder, the other wrapped around my cock, guiding it up into him.

I slipped my hands under his ass to steady him. He wedged my snout against his sphincter and flexed his legs. I felt my knob slip in, then pop back out as his asshole clenched. Gavin grunted, tried again. This time he sank down further, bounced up a bit, but remained impaled, his sphincter pulsing rapidly against my steely meat.

He looked at me and I smiled encouragement, holding him steady. He breathed deeply, expanding his chest. My eyes alighted on the nipples I had so recently mauled. They were still swollen taut, still glistening with spit. I pursed my lips, dragged them across the tender flesh.

"Oh, yes," Gavin sighed, his body opening a bit more to me. I kissed both his nipples, then began nibbling, my bites gentler, more restrained. Gavin groaned, crouched lower, his heat engulfing yet more of my shaft.

"Aaahhhh!" His body tensed and his cock vibrated like a tuning fork. I pulled back, looked at him curiously.

"What is it, Gavin?" I asked. "Am I hurting you again?"

"No. No, Jeffrey. I feel something. Something really incredible."

"This?" I flexed the muscles of my groin, flared my cock-knob against the hard knot of his prostate.

"Yes!" I flexed again, saw his eyes open wide, then flutter shut as a wave of intense physical pleasure washed over him.

"Prostate," I cooed, nuzzling his throat. "Does that make up for the pain?"

"Yeah, it sure does." He threw his head back and began to twitch around, struggling to keep the point of contact between my dick and his pleasure spot solidly bridged. In the process, he sank down several more inches on my piece, sheathing well over half of my length.

"Oh wow," he gasped, "I'm...I'm coming!" The spunk gushed, splattering my chest and belly. Gavin twitched and writhed, trembled violently, then fell forward against me. "That was wild," he panted. "Like getting jacked off from the inside. I want to do it again."

"You are a horny little bastard," I chuckled, stroking his sweat-streaked back. "Are you sure you want to go on?"

"Don't you?" he retorted, grinding his ass around my hard-on, shooting waves of pleasure through me. "I think I'm ready for it now. Ready to have you on top. Ready to be fucked like a real man this time."

I laid him back on the bed and crouched over him, my dick buried deep in his clutching manhole. I pumped my hips experimentally and Gavin moaned lustily. I drew out till I was in the clear then slid back in deep. I repeated the stroke again, then again, each time driving just a bit farther. At last I had him opened deep enough to accommodate my entire aching length. I pushed it in tight, grinding my pubic bone against his crack.

Gavin bucked lustily under me, a purring growl escaping him as he stroked the swirls of fur around my nipples. He pinched the swollen points of flesh and I flexed my pecs, knotting the muscle like rocks beneath his fingers.

"Suck on them, Gavin," I urged, jabbing him with my dick. He raised his head and pressed his face to my chest. I felt his teeth on me and howled, bucking my hips, head thrown back as the nerves connecting tit to groin throbbed to life. He sank his teeth into the swollen point and began to suckle me, the rhythmic movement of his lips quickly becoming the underlying rhythm of the fuck.

I kept up a steady, deep humping, plunging into him up to my balls, drawing out, then riding it home again. The heat and tightness of him was intoxicating, his springy ring dragging tight along my cock on every stroke. I felt him shudder in my arms every two or three minutes, felt his jism, knew he had blown yet another load. I waited for some signal from him that we should stop, that his battered ass channel couldn't take another stroke, but if I did slow my strokes, he'd simply buck impatiently, grab my hips and drive my spike back deep into his steamy sluice.

I was gasping for air, my heart pounding as though I had run uphill for ten miles. Sweat was pouring off of me, plastering my hair against my skull, splashing onto Gavin's face and neck. His jism glued us together, the spicy scent of it tickling my nostrils. I heard his breath catch in his throat, felt his ring flex, knew that he was coming yet again.

"Wait for me, Gavin," I moaned, humping him frantically.

"I...I can't, Jeffrey," he cried, trembling uncontrollably. "I can't wait. Come in me, please. Shoot your load up my ass. I want to feel it in me. Aaaahhhh!" His body began to convulse against me as yet another load began to spew. I tensed every muscle, willed myself to climax. I felt the force of it gathering in my loins, the pleasure curling my toes, knotting the muscles in my belly and neck. My hips rose and fell, rose and fell, my prick flexed, my balls snapped up tight between my legs and I felt the unmistakable thrill of pleasure at the tip of my cock that signaled imminent release.

I held my breath, went rigid, felt Gavin beneath me, his body rising and falling, spearing himself on my hard-on in a frenzy of passion. I drove my hips down, pinned him to the bed, roared my relief as the jism pumped along the length of my prick and began to spew into him.

"Oh!" His eyes flew open and his arms locked around my neck. My body shook violently as the first gush pumped out of me. "I feel it!" he cried, tears springing to his eyes. "I feel your come, Jeffrey. I can feel it filling me up." I slipped my arms under him and held him tightly against me. His spewing jism heated my belly yet again as the last of my spunk squirted into him.

"I guess I'm not a virgin any more, huh?" We lay, limbs entwined, my cock draped limp against my thigh, his head against my shoulder.

"I guess not," I replied, tousling his damp hair.

"Thanks for being so patient with me. Some other guy might have hurt me, but not you."

"No, Gavin," I muttered, stroking his lean flank. "Some other man—but not me."

I fell asleep, then awoke with a start several hours later. Gavin was beside me, his breathing deep and steady. I sniffed at him, nose pressed close to his smooth flesh. I could smell his innocent sweetness, not quite masked by the reek of dried spit and come and sweat. I settled myself against him, arms encircling him protectively, my tongue lolling out of my mouth as I licked his tender, vulnerable neck.

RENT-BOY
BYRON ESMOND

He stood on the corner, thin, hungry-looking, cold. When I pulled up in the car, he leaned into the window. He seemed frightened; I hadn't seen him on the streets before. Despite myself I let him in.

We drove to a motel. He stood silently near the bed. I went to him, lifted his chin with a finger, and kissed him gently on the lips. He flinched away. I stepped back. "Are you sure you want to do this?" I asked him.

He nodded quickly. "Sorry, mister," he said. "I never done this before."

His accent was Southern, making me wonder what he was doing this far up north. "How old are you, boy?"

"Twenty-one." He came to stand in front of me.

Shaking my head, I took out a condom. I unbuttoned the fly of his jeans and unwrapped him like a prize package. I liked what I found inside.

The boy looked at me, a flicker of interest in the depths of his eyes. "Before we start," I asked, "how much is this going to cost me?"

"Fifty dollars."

Nodding, I took his hand and placed it on the cock I pulled out of my fly. His fingers were warm, slightly moist. He began to slowly draw them up and down my shaft. Sometimes he held it too loosely; sometimes he squeezed it till it hurt. For a minute or two at a time, he got it so sweet, I'd have closed my eyes if I'd trusted him better. More than a hand job and less than a hustler's professionalism, it seemed more investigatory, as if to explore the texture, length, and breadth of the organ. He was feeling his way.

With the knowledge that I was his first came overwhelming arousal. My cock jumped in his hand, and he pulled back a little in surprise.

I opened the condom packet and held it to him. He took it between his fingers and rolled it over my shaft until it was snug at the base. I looked down at the kid's semihard cock. At least some part of him seemed to be enjoying the procedures.

He stood up and moved to the bed, waiting for me to tell him what to do. I positioned him on his knees at the foot of the bed, his tight ass up in the air.

There should be a bull's-eye tattooed on it, I thought. His cock was hidden by his body, but his balls lay heavy and full between his thighs. I took them and rolled them in the palm of my hand. The kid sucked in his breath and wriggled his ass in my face. I heard him groan softly. My cock was rockhard. Taking the rounded baby globes of his little ass in my hands, I spread them enough to finger the tight hole, running my thumb around the sphincter and up and down the crack. The kid wriggled his ass again and groaned a little louder. Sighing, I entered him slowly.

Pushing myself, inch by inch, in his tight asshole, I was surprised when he shot his ass back to meet my thrust. Slippery with the lube, it was a simple thing to slide my cock back and forth, moving in small circles inside him. I withdrew almost totally, then plunged back in again, my shaft embraced by the kid's tight hole. Faster and faster, each thrust was met with a grunt and a slapping of balls. I fucked him like an animal, like a dog or a lion. I fucked this virginal little hustler boy, and I liked it.

Suddenly the kid cried out and shuddered. I felt the contraction in my own balls, and the warm cum shot out to pool deeply in the reservoir at the tip of the condom.

Pulling out, I snapped off the soggy rubber and wiped my dick off with a tissue. The hooker lay there on the bed, sleeping, his cock in a puddle of cum, a slight smile on his face. I tugged a blanket over him and went to get my pants.

Fully dressed, I tugged a crisp hundred-dollar bill from my pocket and laid it on the bed next to his head. "Go home," I whispered, even though I knew he had probably done this a thousand times already.

I left him sleeping.

RUN NO MORE
LARRY TOWNSEND

We made our way through darkened back streets, leaning into the wind which whistled around every corner. I could see a light in the window as we climbed the stairs, and Kurt answered our knock immediately. His eyes widened slightly when he recognized us, but otherwise he gave no indication of surprise. With a slightly exaggerated graciousness he bowed and waved us in. "Is Edgar here?" I asked at once.

"No, he went to the city. He was just leaving when I came back from the cottage yesterday," Kurt replied.

"The city! You mean Munich?"

"Yes. He should have returned by now." Kurt glanced at his watch. "The last train came in an hour ago."

"He must have decided to stay over another night," said Jim softly.

I couldn't imagine why Edgar would suddenly have taken off for Munich, but without a phone at the cottage and with the snow as heavy as it had been it was reasonable that he might not have gotten word to us. I never thought to doubt Kurt's word, nor did Jim.

"Come in," he urged us. "Sit in front of the fire and warm yourselves." He led us into the room and took our jackets. "I'll make us a little Englischer grog."

The cold had sobered me considerably, though the fire was quickly undoing the gains. I unlaced my boots and pulled them off, extending my stocking feet toward the flames. Jim did the same, noting that his feet were wet. "Take off the socks, then," Kurt called to him. "You will get a cold from it otherwise."

His attitude was so unexpectedly attentive and friendly it totally disarmed me. In fact, it regenerated the guilt I had felt earlier. The fire reheated my blood, and with it the alcohol I had been so freely imbibing. Kurt handed a mug to each of us and settled himself cross-legged on a cushion next to Jim. "You will be staying with me the night?" he asked.

Jim and I glanced at each other. He grinned; I shrugged. "If your hospitality extends that far," I said. "It's a long, cold walk home."

"Good!" he said. "Very good!" He rested his hand on Jim's leg. "You are wet here, too," he said. "You should take those things off. It is very bad." He got up and took a blanket from the bed. "Here. Take off everything and wrap this about you." He looked over at me. "And you?" he asked. "Are you also wet?"

I felt my clothes, all of which were perfectly dry, quite warm from the fire. "No," I said, "but if you'd like to make a little nudist commune, I'll take a blanket, too."

I was just giddy enough from all the booze that I started stripping along with Jim, the two of us making a joke of it while Kurt watched silently in the background. I could sense a suggestion of amusement in his demeanor, which was the closest to levity I'd come to expect from him. But in this case, his stern expression only made us the more determined to provoke a genuine smile.

"Well, come on, stud," said Jim laughing. "What's sauce for the goose..."

Jim and I were naked by then, huddled like a pair of squaws with the blankets over our shoulders, leaning toward the warmth from the hearth. If we were going to stay, we were obviously going to play some kind of a scene. All three of us knew it. Jim, though far less tipsy than I, was also teasing Kurt. A couple of times, I think he almost cracked. "Did you want Edgar for any special reason?" asked Kurt casually. He had moved to the side, not quite between us and the fire. He was naked to the waist, standing with perfect balance on one foot as he unlaced the ski boot from the other.

"No," I answered quickly, "we just got ourselves stranded in the village and decided to try his place first." I purposely didn't look at either Kurt or Jim as I said this, and really could not have explained why I felt the need to lie. If Kurt suspected anything he didn't show it. He had both boots off and now made a little production of removing his pants. He did have a fantastic body, tall and lean with a finely molded set of muscles. His skin was a natural golden ivory, unblemished and smooth except for the barely perceptible line of an abbreviated bathing suit. His crisp black hair had broken loose from its casual arrangement, falling over his brow as he bent down to pull the black denims off his ankles. There was a small patch of silky fur in the center of his chest, and just the faintest trail from his navel to the matching triangle about his groin. His genitals hung loose and deep; I'd never seen them shrivel or draw in upon themselves. Now, completely at rest, his cock was a living sculpture of unmutilated symmetry, thick foreskin gathered to a puckered pout beneath the width of crown.

I glanced up at his face and noted the satisfied, sardonic grin. Kurt was more than a little exhibitionistic, I thought. *He enjoys being watched...and admired. Probably why he gets on so well with Alfred. Wonder what they did in bed that night? Probably nothing, but...I wonder...* The idea struck me as funny, and I started to chuckle again. Kurt regarded me curiously, but his own smile broadened...still restrained and controlled, but more perceptible than it had been till now. To cover myself, I nudged Jim. "You want to hire that stud?" I asked.

My companion nodded. "He'll do until something better turns up," he said.

Kurt reached one wide, thick-fingered hand into his crotch to adjust his balls, freed the sac where it adhered to the inside of his thigh. He remained where we was, standing over us expectantly, watchful and almost on guard. Our levity must have frustrated him a little; I had never known him to approach a scene without being dead serious about it. Laughter was the one ingredient that could shake his poise.

"Have I two chickens or one?" he asked at length.

"I'm still sore from the last time," I answered quickly. I looked at Jim, who had ceased to laugh and now stared sightlessly into the fire. I sensed his resistance to being cast as bottom man, but I knew he'd go along with the situation. Somehow, though, I knew he really...really didn't want to. He was aroused, however. That was already obvious from the tumescence that wallowed in the shadows between his thighs.

I was not anxious to play M, either; but I was just drunk enough and just turned-on enough to do about anything that was asked of me. *Except...I want to do it with Jim.* Kurt had me going, but the really warm valence that gripped my balls was for this dark-haired little guy beside me. At the very least, I wanted to share with him. "I'm game if you are," I said softly.

Jim turned to me, his face still serious, but holding a smile just below the rest. It was more of an expression of gratitude, I thought... *gratitude? To me? For what?* "I guess it's two chickens," I said evenly. "But take it easy, baby!" I added strongly. Kurt shifted his weight and moved a half-step closer. "I mean it," I warned him. "No rough stuff!"

Kurt nodded. "A light scene," he agreed.

He knelt down between us, easing us back against the cushions. I closed my eyes and felt for Jim's hand, found it and interlaced my fingers with his. Kurt's palm was gently stroking my chest and moving down onto my stomach. I moaned and let the intoxication reclaim my senses. I guess I had been mentally staving off the full effects of everything I'd consumed, because I now slipped into a pleasant euphoria. I accepted the floating envelopment and my skin tingled to the thrill of Kurt's steadily increasing motion. I felt his fingers explore the length and girth of my cock, lift my balls and fondle them, letting them drop back into the chasm of my crotch. I looked up to see him staring at me intently, but when he saw my eyes come open he gestured with his hand that I should turn onto my belly.

He used a single leather strap to bind my wrists, and did the same to Jim. He remained between us for some time after this, stroking our backs as he had the front sides of our bodies. As it always did, the sense of being bound created a hot, heavy expectancy in my nuts, made my cock press hard and full against the cushions. It was a sign, I suppose, of mental as well as physical surrender. Kurt rose up finally, stood for a moment to stretch. Experienced as he was, he knew his technique was having its proper effect. I saw him take hold of Jim and turn him around, placing him on his side, facing me. He then rolled me into a similar position and shoved us together, sliding us both across the floor as the cushions formed sleds beneath us.

My face was against the dark, silky patch of Jim's groin and I could feel the warmth of his breath against the underside of my upthrust cock. Involuntarily, I moved against him, sensed the moist pressure of his lips caress my sac at the same moment Kurt passed a heavy nylon rope around my neck. He tied it securely at the throat, pulled it between Jim's legs and anchored it to my companion's neck. From here, he repeated the process, drawing the line tightly through my crotch and up the crack of my ass so the smooth, taut length nestled hard against my asshole. He made his final knot at the back of my neck, tying it off and leaving us secured in an escape-proof "69."

My head was drawn forward by the bond, and being an inch or two taller than Jim I was not centered quite as precisely upon the apex of his cock and balls. His sex was as aroused as mine, however, so the projection canted off at an angle, just below my lips. His cockhead touched the lower edge of my jaw. Kurt stood above us, straddling both our bodies. I could feel the pressure of his ankle against my ass, the cloying motion of leather as he trailed the end of a belt across our sides and arms. "Take him!" he said hoarsely, but whether he spoke to one or both we had no way to know. I reached out with my tongue, grasped Jim's rod by curling the tip under it and sucked it into me. I could feel him do the same as white heat boiled about my shaft.

I heard the belt strike a glancing blow off my companion's hip, and I felt his head lunge harder against me. "I gave him permission, not you," Kurt growled. "You wait until I tell you!"

Jim backed off, allowing my cock to fall free of his grasp. The surge of desire, which had been drawn to a peak about my groin, receded…throbbing urgency racing in to replace it. Obeying my own impulse more than Kurt's demand, I sucked Jim's shaft inside me, forcing the swollen, pliant cockhead completely down my throat. "Now!" said Kurt. "Now, you can take him."

Again, my rod sank into the churning liquid fire. My body trembled as it had from the cold. Kurt continued to let the belt slide across us, swinging like a pendulum, striking lightly against my back and over my arm onto Jim. Back and forth, higher or lower on our bodies, sometimes a trifle faster and harder. It was precisely the proper touch, adding an element of demand that made me drive myself more furiously upon Jim's rigid sex, sent endless waves of trembling excitement up my spine and caused my hips to plunge in autonomous cadence, timed to the motions of my companion's lips and tongue.

Kurt reached down and forced us over, rolling me onto my back so Jim was lying with his full weight on top of me. His legs enveloped my face; his shaft became a plunging piston, hurling itself into the deep, constricted nether regions of my throat...withdrew and fell again, while his own heated moisture never faltered in its frantic reciprocation. A trickle of sweat fell from his groin, forming a small, steady flow of salt and heady maleness. His entire body exuded the subtle odor of manhood, tinged with the sweetness of a citrus cologne.

Kurt repositioned us again, and this time I was on top. I assumed the rhythm as Jim had done, slid the wet slickness of my cock deep within the well of grasping heat and pressure. "Faster!" Kurt commanded. His belt exploded across my butt and the sparkling energy surged outward from the point of contact. I devoured the fleshy rod and pressed my nostrils into the softness of the sac. I could feel Jim's balls draw up against the base of his cock, and I pressed down on them, separated the orbs by driving my nose between them. The rope had pulled more tightly about my neck, and the tension of its binding hold was more pronounced against my prostate and the lips of my anus. The strap around my wrists had never ceased to remind me of my dominated posture...the fact of my being a prisoner of this other man and completely subject to his command.

I rolled my hips in response to the goading blows from the leather strap, pushed down, and sank my cock to the roots. I could feel the rushing approach of climax and I wanted to warn Kurt of its imminence. But he knew. He stopped us short of fulfillment and he untied the rope which bound our bodies together. He stretched us out, side by side on our bellies, telling us how badly we had done and punishing us with his belt. His strokes were moderate, however; he was carefully observing the limits I had set.

Still, the blows produced a stinging glow, enflamed the cheeks of my ass and projected the warmth inside me...created an emotional craving which would have permitted a much heavier usage than he was giving me. Unexpectedly, he stopped, fumbled a moment with a container and deftly eased his finger into my asshole. I knew he was doing the same with Jim, applying some lubricant to us both. A few seconds later, though, I realized it was more than just the grease I had been able to feel on his digit. A burning sensation permeated my flesh; an itching heat surged inside me, a stimulus that bordered pain yet never quite passed its threshold.

Kurt wiped his hands on a towel, sitting back on his haunches to watch us. He was holding his strap again, and again he used it on us. This time he struck higher on the back...slow, well-centered blows that fell atop my spine and paralleled it to either side...snapping, leathery sounds accentuating each semi-painful impact. The searing itch in my ass grew more intense and I strained to reach my fingers down to ease it. Kurt swatted at my hands, ordered me to raise them. "Do you want something in there to stop the fire?" he taunted me. He pressed his thumb deeply into me, made me wrench and twist at the sudden penetration.

He dropped the belt and moved directly behind me. His slick, oily fingers grasped my loins from either side and he lifted me, positioning my groin above Jim's ass and placing me directly on top of him. His tightly restricted arms were crossed beneath my chest, the tips of his fingers moving against my skin. Kurt reached between my legs and grasped my cock, forced me to lift enough to permit his centering my cockhead upon the tight ring of Jim's sphincter. With his other hand, he shoved down against my ass, drove my shaft inside the glowing furnace. At first it was all slickness and heat and pressure; but within a few seconds the tingling menthol fumes began to seep inward, electrifying the contact until my cock seemed to burn with the same fire that seared the inside of my own body.

Kurt had been kneeling behind me, his knees close up against the inner surfaces of my thighs. I felt his fingers probe again, sensed the wide, thrusting pressure of his cock. I tensed, but hardly had I made this involuntary response when the flames of hell seemed to explode within me. Kurt's hard, powerful torso collapsed upon my back; his cock lay imbedded, unmoving, for the first few seconds. Gradually, then, he drew it up...dropped against me, ground his loins across my backside...withdrew again, each arc of motion a trifle more than the one before it. His hands gripped down firmly on my hips, and he forced my own pumping cadence to continue, hammered into me and drove my own shaft more deeply into the well of heat below. As his pace increased, I assumed its rhythm...lunged downward and up, plunging into Jim and impaling myself in turn on the massive strength of the master who guided my every motion. The menthol fumes had reached my nostrils, distorting my sense of smell, making me captive and reminding me of the frantic need to feel that cock inside my ass. The harder Kurt ground himself upon me, the more intensely I felt the surging need and more desperately I transmitted his lust to the man beneath me.

Kurt's hands had trailed across my balls in the course of his manipulations, and they also smarted with the glow of medicated heat. The climax I had been denied before now gathered once again. While I would have liked to prolong the wildly blissful contact, I was powerless to hold it back. In a rush of sensation that merged and mingled the weight and pressure with the artificial heat and the perception of light and color, I felt the boiling pressure build, crescendo, and erupt from my balls in an endless flood of draining heat and energy. I was riding Jim's resilient saddle, trying to enter him beyond the limits of physical possibility. My balls were striking the inside channel between his thighs, slapping moistly into the cavern and projecting back their own sensations. I could feel the weight of Kurt's testicles in the same position on myself, and I knew when he moaned and shuddered, wrapped his arms about my chest and held me, that he was also blasting loose a flood of fiery passion.

When he finally permitted our bodies to slide apart, I rolled onto my back, my hands still bound behind me. Kurt turned Jim over, running his hand across the groin. Apparently my companion had not yet shot his load. No moisture adhered to the front of his body and his shaft still rose in projecting desire above the matted hair of his groin. Kurt ordered him to stand and fastened a leather collar about his neck. This was attached by another length of leather to a hook above the mantle. Jim now stood facing us before the flames, body bound and rigid, head pulled up and slightly back by the pressure of his leash and collar. Kurt reached behind him and freed his hands, both men momentarily silhouetted by the crimson glow…all moving flesh and sinew, dark against the leaping tongues of flame.

Kurt ordered Jim to stand erect and directed him through a series of military commands, finally instructing him to make himself come. He stood to the side and slightly behind his captive, snapping Jim's butt with a belt each time he slowed or when the sensations of approaching release made him break the rigid stance. After several minutes Kurt commanded me to my knees and made me kneel in front of Jim, not allowing me to touch him, but requiring that I stay until the hot spurting stream burst out of him and cast itself across my face, onto the upper portion of my chest. He had us hold, then, remaining where we were until Jim's cock began to soften and the coating of his discharge had dried upon my skin.

Kurt turned us loose and smiled at me. "Light enough for you?" he asked.

"Yes," I told him. "Great." But there had been a barely concealed suggestion of sarcasm in his tone, and for the first time that evening I caught the glimmer of hostile arrogance. All may not have been forgiven, I realized. Within himself, Kurt would continue to nurture his resentment…and more? I had failed to read him accurately a couple of hours before. I wondered how much closer to the truth my impression might be at this moment. But he quickly slammed the door to his inner feelings, remained friendly and cordial until we went to bed and slept with Jim pressed tightly between us.

MR. BENSON
JOHN PRESTON

Of course, I had been to the Mineshaft before, but only once or twice. This was the heaviest leather bar in New York, the source of half the gossip of my circle of acquaintances. "You know what he did at the Mineshaft last night?" That was the normal prelude to bar dish among the fluff queens. Tonight, I walked with a purpose up the stairs to the second floor entrance to be tested by Mr. Benson.

A week had dragged by since last I had seen him. I called Monday to tell him my decision about the future. I told him clearly, even calmly, that I was offering myself as his slave, that I wanted to take the test he had prescribed to see if I could be good enough, obedient enough, sexy enough to pass his inspection. His response was hard and pointed. He had spent plenty of time setting his standards. There were things which Mr. Benson would not tolerate.

One of them was my job. He explained carefully that he had no intention of dealing with someone running off to clerk at an insurance company when there were things to be done in the house. He gave me an option that I accepted. I wouldn't need the job if I went to live with him; I would have to trust him to provide for me. He suggested that I take a week's vacation. If I went to live with Mr. Benson, it wouldn't matter if I returned, but the week would be a kind of second test. If I failed, I could leave his house and go back to my 9–5 ritual of humiliation-for-pay.

I would also have to give up the apartment and my few goodies from Bloomies. Mr. Benson thought I had little worth carting around.

So, I would have two tests: this Saturday night and then a whole week, after which I would have to decide again if I was ready to make a commitment so intense that it would leave no room for my friends and furniture.

The week of fantasy leading up to the climbing of these stairs bounced me through many conflicting thoughts about my trial. I looked forward to it sexually. I wanted to taste the piss flowing through Mr. Benson's long, sensuous cock, I wanted to lick his good-tasting pit sweat, I wanted to feel his fist glide up my ass again. But there was also fear. That one previous night had been the heaviest SM trip I had ever endured. What if I couldn't take any more? What if I had only gone through it because of a passing fancy for that handsome man? What if the pain overtook the pleasure and I lost it?

Doubts started through my mind as I handed the Mineshaft bouncer the entrance fee and saw him look over my clothes. He was not impressed with my Adidas sneakers, but to some they are a fetish. The rest, well, he didn't know about the rest. I eased past him into the first room, the bar of the Mineshaft. The early crowd had begun to line the walls of the room. Leather, denim, and skin alternated in the rows of bodies out for early display. I had my orders. I went to the coat check and began my obedience number, just as Mr. Benson had ordered me.

The coat check at the Mineshaft is different from any other

bar's in New York. They don't limit themselves to customers' jackets. The man behind the counter hardly blinked as I stripped off my jacket, then my pants, my shirt and, finally, even my sneakers.

I think that the sneakers were the part that had bothered me the most. The Mineshaft was not a place where I wanted my bare feet to make contact with the floor. But the orders had been explicit: at midnight I was to be standing in front of the fake wooden rail fence in the front bar, and I was to be wearing only a jockstrap.

Waiting for Mr. Benson.

The jockstrap didn't produce a second glance in a place so used to them; a sign on the wall said that the Jockstrap League of America met here once a month. A couple cowboys admired what they called my "flat golden nipples." An "Indian" liked my body with its rounded pecs. One particularly mean-looking state trooper started to come over, but a subtle shaking of my head staved him off. I leaned back against the fence and watched the game being played on the pool table. It was not pool.

The clock over the bar said that I had fifteen minutes to countdown. I debated a beer. I had been smart enough to put a couple bucks in my pouch. I was dry-mouthed with tension, waiting for a climax to a week of solitude with my thoughts, fears, and fantasies. I went over and got a Bud, ignoring the comments and the looks as I leaned my bare ass over the counter to place my order. I took the good-tasting suds back over to the fence and put a foot up on the first rung.

Waiting for Mr. Benson.

I kept wondering what form the test would take. Why the Mineshaft? There was only one answer to that question; Mr. Benson intended to make this a public event. I had realized that from the beginning. My stomach felt light as I thought about all these eyes watching me now, and what they would see after Mr. Benson arrived. I remembered my body sprawled on his floor, sucking his toes, licking his feet, his instep crushing down on my open jaws.

Would I be doing that here tonight? With his boots? Would I be polishing them with my tongue while he lashed at me with a belt? A riding crop? A whip?

I remembered the piss-drinking, its golden flow down my throat. Would Mr. Benson repeat that here in the Mineshaft? Right in the front room? With all these people watching me gulp down his manwater?

I remembered the other deeper and darker rooms in the joint. Through that corridor was the room with the sling. A black leather sheath suspended from the ceiling. I had seen men climb up and in and open their asses to some stud standing greasy-fisted in front of them, widening the groove of their pain-fucking cheeks, forcing their limbs into the body. Was Mr. Benson going to do that to me in front of all these men? Would he let them pinch and tug at my tits while he worked his fist in and out of my butt? Would he make me suck their alien cocks?

Beyond that was a dark room, the least lit in the place, where the game was cocksucking. Was Mr. Benson going to take me in there? Would I end up spending the whole evening licking these men's pricks, drinking their come? Giving them all the pleasure they wanted?

And downstairs there was another dark room with walls slippery with ooze. Was Mr. Benson going to take me downstairs into that room and add my screams of pain to all the echoes of past beatings that had taken place there? Would they all gather around and watch him cut my backside with deep lashes from a coiled leather snake?

The second room had a bathtub in the center. Was Mr. Benson going to put me in it? Was he going to let all the anonymous bodies piss on me? Would he make me drink their gallons of urine? Would he pull me out of the place soaked, my hair carrying the stench of aggressive men?

Or the last room—another bar—would Mr. Benson drag me into the dim light on the stage in that last room? Would he auction me off to the highest bidder? Or the biggest cock? Force me to do whatever man, god or troll, climbed up on the stage with me? The pouch of my jock strained against my pulsing dick as I catalogued the possible adventures.

I should have known that Mr. Benson would have done none of them. After five years I know now that Mr. Benson is too much of an elitist to let me be used and abused by just anyone. Then there are his friends, and I was about to learn how much Mr. Benson values friendship.

The crowd at the Mineshaft must be the most jaded in New York. There is almost nothing that they haven't seen take place right there in those six rooms and the two toilets. Every trip from rubber to wingtip shoes had been celebrated in its walls, but still there was a sudden hush when The Presence came into the room. I hadn't been paying attention. I was too far gone in the fantasies of my evening to see It coming, but I heard the silence. I looked up and saw him standing there, directly in front of me.

The black doorman from that first night.

He was wearing a very different type of uniform now than last week. He had on a black motorcycle cap. A tan uniform shirt with a black belt stretched across his chest. Then black leather britches, shiny with care, and exaggerated by a strip of white leather down each thigh.

I don't know if I had appreciated his immensity before. His body towered over me, even taller than Mr. Benson's, but he had none of Mr. Benson's sleek lines, only menacing bulk in front of my face.

"Are you ready for Mr. Benson, boy?"

I was speechless except for a nod: *Yes!*

He reached up and attached a dog collar to my neck; its stiff leather felt comfortably uncomfortable from the start. Then he reached into his pockets and took out handcuffs. He joined my wrists behind my back. Then he pulled sharply on the leash and led me out down the stairs and into the waiting car. He just led me, naked and barefoot into the New York winter night.

No one in the bar dared say anything. They correctly assumed that I went willingly. And I was willing, but scared shitless. He shoved me onto the floor of the back seat of the new Mercedes, locked the door, strode to the front, and folded his bulk into the driver's seat. We sped off through the Village streets. It only took a few minutes actually, until he stopped and dragged my shivering body out into the middle of a warehouse district I couldn't recognize. South of Canal Street? North of Chelsea? Who knew?

He led me into one of the warehouse buildings through a door marked only with the smallest of signs: THE TOPMEN.

I was suddenly right under a light bulb. The black man announced my arrival. "Mr. Benson, your new pet."

As I gratefully warmed up in the well-heated room and adjusted my eyes to the third-degree glare, I found seven men lounging around on old furniture, all holding beer cans, all dressed in the same black-and-tan leather outfits as my captor.

The best of them was Mr. Benson.

I was going to see the interior of this room often; I would end up here in Mr. Benson's clubhouse many more nights than I could have predicted. This was where Mr. Benson liked to pass his rare social hours. There are seldom guests in the penthouse, and I had been correct when I had assumed that Mr. Benson and the other Topmen liked to spend their time together here in this ancient warehouse, far from the ears and cares of intruding, curious people.

Mr. Benson actually smiled as I looked at him across the room. I used to mistake actions like smiles from Mr. Benson to be things like welcomes. That was no welcome. Tom, the doorman, had unthinkingly begun a new game.

Mr. Benson played it out. He strode over to me and put a hand on my neck; turning to the other Topmen, he said, "A pet, gentlemen. My new pet."

They laughed uproariously.

"I had thought to introduce you to my new slave, but I think Tom is right. It's more accurate to think of this fine specimen of *humanus sclavus* as a pet: one who, I am sure, will bring me many hours of pleasure and companionship."

His little speech was delivered with a great dramatic flair. The audience responded appropriately by applauding the presentation.

"Mr. Benson," one called out over the applause. "What *kind* of pet is this?"

I looked up at the speaker, easily the most handsome of the group: blond, blue-eyed, clean-shaven with a squared frame that provided a fully muscled body. Yet the swastika on his armband gave rise to the greatest reaction of fear.

"A pig, Benson, that's what he is, a pig!" The second one to contribute piped in; he was just as easily the least attractive. His Hindenburg body bulged incredulously against the smart uniform that added to the others' military-sharp appearance.

"In that case, Porytko, he certainly would be willing to suck even your cock." Mr. Benson tugged hard on my leash and pulled me over to stand in front of the overweight giant. As I came closer, I realized that he wasn't really ugly. He had a different look, a Slavic bluntness that became macho good-looking when it was more closely inspected. I was learning that masculine beauty was lots more than Hollywood Handsome. His bulk was also deceptive; his size had led me to think him fat, but the force was with him as he worked his arms to pull his fat uncut cock out of his pants. Mr. Benson leaned down on my neck as the gargantuan Polack started his baiting call, "Come on, sooee, come on, little piggy, show us how much you can eat." The crowd picked up his taunts. I went to my knees and took the fat Polish sausage, its girth stretching the corners of my throat and its fleshy length striking the back of my mouth. The stranger pulled on my ears and shoved his whole

Slavic prick into me, forcing me to gag with almost every stroke. My only recourse was to open up as willingly as I could. After only a minute of ramming himself down my helpless body, he shot a thick load of salty come down my gullet. Intense. In record time.

"Now, Porytko, who's the pig?" Mr. Benson exclaimed. He watched me gulping down the hot ooze.

"Mr. Benson!" A squatly built bearded man, sitting next to the Pole, said: "I think the pig looks more like a cat, myself."

"Yeah, a cat!" The men toyed with me. With a heightening intensity, Mr. Benson asked the group, "And what is going to prove him a cat?"

"Well, Mr. Benson, I know that mine has a tongue that won't stop going. Licks me everywhere."

Mr. Benson jerked my neck up off the Polish cock, the sharp tug on the stiff collar forcing my face to look up into his. "Well, asshole, why aren't you licking me?" The humor left his face. He spit full down upon me, the viscous fluid splattering over my nose and cheeks. "You don't like me as much as Mark's cat likes him?"

I was terrified by this new game. There was none of the quiet masterfulness I had seen in Mr. Benson before. None of the underflow of caring strength that had attracted me in the beginning. This was pure cruelty, I thought. These men, their uniforms, ganging up on me. But the fear made me rub my face directly in Mr. Benson's crotch and start to lick at the bulge I knew was there. I wasn't going to fail! Neither him nor me!

"Mr. Benson." I couldn't see which one was speaking now. "My cat does more than lick; the poor thing's forever drinking out of a toilet bowl!" That raised every man's high spirits. Mr. Benson played off the perfect new cue. He got me up onto my feet. My hands bound behind me threw me off balance as I struggled to keep up with the figure moving through applause to a doorway across the room.

Luckily, the doorman's body broke my fall and his strong arm helped me on the way as I went into the bathroom behind Mr. Benson. I was surprised when the lights went on and I saw how large it was—much too large for the clubhouse; it had two urinals and two toilets. The walls and floors were immaculate white-and-black tile, freshly scrubbed. I was to see a lot more of this room in the future. The care they had put into it should have prepared me. One good toilet deserves another. It takes one to know one.

I hadn't seen the signal Mr. Benson must have given the doorman, who unlocked my handcuffs. The group had followed us into the large room and was forming a semicircle. "Hey, Mr. Benson, wait a minute." The Pole spoke out as he stepped up to the toilet in front of where we were standing. He smiled broadly as he pulled out his dripping dick and immediately started to piss in the bowl. Thick yellow streams flowed into the clear water. It was all too apparent to me what was happening. I took a deep breath just as the hands behind me forced me down on my hands and knees and pushed my head toward the white porcelain.

My face entered the cold water while the chunk of a man above me was still pissing his bladder out. He soaked my hair; piss ran down the sides of my face and into my mouth. They ordered me from above to slurp up the toilet water.

The others, or at least some of them, joined in and within seconds, streams of hot piss flowed down my back into the bowl. The different shades of their piss were mixing into the toilet bowl. It was my bowl now! I was not going to fail so early! I was going to show them. I was going to show Mr. Benson. I not only drank the water, I drank it eagerly. Two weeks before I would have fainted at the thought of the stinking fluids, but now I sought them out. My tongue lapped the different streams down the white surface. I slurped noisily.

As the whole ordeal kept going, the pride in me matched my defiance. I was not going to let them win over me so easily. I was going to prove myself to Mr. Benson. I would find manly nobility at the bottom.

When he finally pulled up on the leash, I was bloated. The stink of all the men filled my nose. The slurping had left trails of water and piss streaking down my chest, drenching my elastic jockstrap.

There was a quieter sense to the laughter as they put their cocks back into the uniform pants. A cat? Okay, a cat! I remembered the first story and went back with my mouth to Mr. Benson's crotch, pulling my tongue over the slick leather of his uniform, burying my nose in the full curve of his flesh. His hand petted the back of my head.

"Hey, Mr. Benson!"

"Now, what?" Mr. Benson was less raucous as he continued to pet me.

"Well, Mr. Benson, since this is sort of a universal kind of pet, why don't you show him? You know, like at those Madison Square Garden fancy dog shows?"

Laughter.

Without further words, Mr. Benson pulled up on the leash and led me back into the first room. The doorman pulled out a stand; it was the size of a small dining room table. "Up, boy!" Mr. Benson slammed his fist on its surface.

I climbed on and knelt up on my knees. Mr. Benson came to the side of the table as the group returned to their seats in obvious anticipation of this next primal act. Mr. Benson picked up some of his showmanship again. "Gentlemen, this fine specimen is a blue-ribbon without doubt." He reached over and ran a hard hand down my side, emphasizing each point in his monologue. "Notice the smooth lines, the full chest, slimming into a tight waist, and filling out again into fine, rounded hips." Whistles greeted his hand's progress around to my ass.

"Yeah, but, Mr. Benson!" It was the sturdy dark man again.

"When you have an animal that has lines as fine as those, well, you should be doing something to bring them out. You know, they shouldn't be covered with all that unnatural cloth."

Mr. Benson agreed and jerked down my jock to expose my half-hard-on and my balls, pulled up with fear and excitement. There was low moan of approval. Mr. Benson put up his hand to calm their dripping lust. "Now, of course, our good brother here is correct, there should be nothing to interfere with such obviously championship qualities."

"But, Mr. Benson, he has hair!"

"Never fear! You should certainly know that hair never lasts long in my household." New laughter clued me that the last's remark was a bow to Mr. Benson's own special tastes. Obviously this was the opening for something Mr. Benson had planned all along. The black doorman brought over a simple bag, a doctor's black house-call case. Mr. Benson opened it on the table and placed a can of shaving cream, a deadly straight-edged razor and a long, wide razor strop on the top. Accompanied by the appreciative noises of his audience, he went over to a nearby wall and attached the strop to a ring screwed directly into the brick. With his most dramatic gesture yet, he sharpened the straight edge with long graceful strokes. For my pleasure? The group's? Or his own?

The appearance I was putting in on the table was almost a relief. Whether it was the sudden realization that this had more in common with a fraternity hazing than anything else, or whether it was the sudden surge of pride and resolve on my part, or whether it was the sudden pride in Mr. Benson's compliments on my body, I'm not sure. It may also have been the fascination with which I watched him sharpen the instrument on the strop. I couldn't help but anticipate what was coming. I certainly knew that my crotch fur was going to go. Was any more? I looked down on my chest and saw the few strands of hair that had been so proudly growing across to join my nipples. Before that moment, I don't think that

I had ever really thought much of the hair under my armpits. Would that sweaty mat be sheared too?

Mr. Benson came back over. The room was quieter now as the men sat back to savor this next act of the show. My cock started to fill. They didn't laugh at its growing hardness; they chuckled knowingly. A cool handful of stiff suds was rubbed over my cock and balls. Then in the clump of hair over them. The wave of foam went up to my navel. Expertly, smoothly, Mr. Benson touched the cold steel to the base of my cock and scraped up, taking with the metal edge almost all of my brown bush. He repeated the long strokes with slow, deliberate care until my crotch was almost totally stripped of any covering.

Then he grabbed my now fully-hard prick and moved around to stand almost directly in front of me, pulling the sharpened edge down the length of my tool. Then he grasped my balls and stretched them to their limit; the steel cleaned off my double sac in shorter strokes. I was breathless as Mr. Benson peeled the covering from the delicate egg shapes. I dared take gulps of air only in between the runs of his steel on my flesh.

He stood aside when he had finished and wiped the blade almost carelessly on my flanks. A soft whistle came from the men in front of me as they looked over my totally sheared flesh.

"But, now..." Mr. Benson smiled as he put down the antique shaver. He manipulated my body until I had turned away from the audience and then forced my head down on the wooden surface, leaving my ass sticking in the air. He pulled my legs apart at the knees, exposing my asshole to the group. I felt the foam being applied again, its sudden chill going up and down my crack. I clenched my fists as I prepared for the rasping metal against my delicate hole. At first I had my eyes closed, waiting. When I felt the steel hardness against my thin-skinned vulnerability, I pulled up on my butthole.

It was then that I saw it. In front of me, now that I had my face away from the table. Standing over in the corner of the room where I couldn't have noticed it before. I hardly paid any attention to the rest of the shaving. I barely heard the comments on the excellence of the job being done by Mr. Benson. The new sight gripped me with fear. Could I withstand that? Would I be able to take it? I should have known that I would have no choice.

I have never found out if Mr. Benson or the others had noticed my noticing, or whether it was really planned that they would grab me. From beyond my sight, their hands reached out and took hold of my ankles and then my wrists. They pulled without questions; they stretched my body against the table, my waist cutting into its edge. Two of them must have sat on the floor in order to maintain the pressure on my legs. Two others I could see as they held my arms sharply against the corners of the top.

I could see Mr. Benson as he came back around the table, this time walking past me and over to the corner where he bent down to pick up the handle that rested over the edge of the brazier, its wooden end protected from the hot coals that had turned the metal edge red with heat.

There was no circus hint in Mr. Benson's voice now. "Men, this slave is mine. He's come here of his own free will. He's agreed to be in my service. These games have been fun, but it's time we got down to the business of establishing ownership." He had walked around to the back of me. Cold sweat ran down my forehead. My guts wrenched. I turned my face over and opened my mouth to bite my arm. I would not scream.

Mr. Benson held the branding iron for all to see.

Then he lowered it below and behind my line of sight. My butt sizzled. I smelled my body cooking, like so much meat. Tears streamed out of my eyes. A sigh of appreciation came from the men around me. I thought that I would faint from the rush of pain that tore through me, reaching out from my right buttock, now, forever, marked by Mr. Benson. They let go of me almost as soon as the act was over. I was so shocked with the glowing hurt, I stood there, bent over the table, grasping its edge even after they had released me.

A cool hand went over my ass, smoothing a salve of some kind, but shocking my skin over the wound. The sudden new wave of sensation jerked me upright. The black doorman was beside me, the strange medicine sending its smell into my nose. The sobs still heaved in my chest from my cries. I tried to hold them back, to regain myself. "Come here, boy. You aren't finished yet."

I closed my eyes in a sense close to desperation.

What more?

What more could he want?

The fire burned in my shanks as I faced him.

There it was. The Source. Mr. Benson's hard cock hung out, celebrating my pain and marking. His heavy balls hung down over the snaps of his leather codpiece. I went over to him, wincing at every movement of my butt, dragging my right leg to try to keep it stiff, but giving up when I reached him and swallowing to ready myself for the quick rage of pain as I knelt and prayerfully took his beautiful cock in my mouth.

I knelt in communion with Mr. Benson like a religious fanatic who had journeyed to a shrine. My week of abstinence, my humiliation, my trial, had all been for this. This godstick and these ripe and full nuts hanging beneath my chin. I went mad with desire for his cock. Oblivious to my branded butt, I chowed down on the pole in front of me.

Mr. Benson's cock.

His fabled virility poked down my throat. I worked my head and neck to feel his smooth surface against my inside. Before long, his shaft began to swell with come. The veins pushed against the outer layer of skin. I gulped further down at the early warning and, when he shot, the precious juice pistoled straight into me, hardly any of it even into my mouth, the taste of this man—I can say it now—went straight to my soul!

Five years ago all that happened.

I have never been allowed to grow back my manhair. The scar on my buttock, of course, has cured to a fine mark. But now the sensation of that seems so far away that I think it more pride than pain because it is Mr. Benson's mark on me: a large B in a simple circle.

The night, that first night, was not over. But the branding brought a climax to my center-stage performance. Tom took me over to the doorway of the toilet when Mr. Benson's cock was finished with me. The enormous black reapplied my handcuffs and pushed me back down on my knees, reawakening the pain in my buttocks. The last joke of the evening came from Porytko, who put a roughly lettered sign around my neck: TOILET. The Topmen went back to their drinking and smoking, ignoring me for a while except when they took the sign literally.

I drank more piss that night than I had imagined doing in my fantasies at the Mineshaft. The sharp taste burned in my mouth, relieved only by each new load that one of the club members brought over to me as the great amounts of beer flushed out his system. Twice my own water flowed unnoticed on the floor. It was the first time that I was able to watch these men as a group; I listened to them talk, trying to figure out who was who and what was going on, and trying to forget the brand that still sent shock waves through my body every time I moved.

Tom, the black doorman, was obviously an attendant to Mr. Benson. Some sort of second lieutenant. There is no doubt from the way he acted that his presence was because of my new master. His huge size and the terror he would throw in the eyes of anyone who saw his thickly sculptured African face was betrayed by the care he gave Mr. Benson's needs, and even mine. Tom was, after all, the man who applied the salve to my wound that night.

If Tom was a stereotype in any way, the other black in the group was the opposite. From the conversation, even through my pain,

I could tell that Brendan was a cop. I was startled by the thought of his tall stature in a deep blue uniform and was able to spend a lot of time wondering if it would look any better buttoned and zipped and strapped into the outfit of New York's finest than it did in the Topmen's uniform.

Brendan talked with a drawl that was almost Southern; probably at some point it was, but its edge was cut with an academic ability that showed itself whenever he and Mr. Benson talked. They were obviously the most intelligent of the group, and they enjoyed that intelligence greatly. Often, it would seem that they would have to check their conversation or risk leaving the others, more brawn than brains, behind.

More often, Porytko would stop them before they had a chance to get too far. They never seemed to mind the good-natured hulk breaking in with a joke that too often seemed funny only to him. The big guy's deep laugh would fill the room often with self-congratulatory guffaws. He was easily the least sinister of the group. But he could spit a hawker over twenty feet right on the target!

The most sinister, by far, was the German they called Hans. The others used my mouth to piss in so casually that they seemed to just want to save themselves the walk into the toilet behind me. But when Hans came over, he would reach down and take my tits between his fingernails. His vise-grip squeeze-tortured my smooth brown nipples. My gasps of pain he muffled with the heavy uncut cock he shoved in my mouth. Once Mr. Benson stopped him with a sharp call when he was reaching down to scratch at my fresh brand. I had to psych myself every time that Hans stood to approach me and get my tender nipples ready for the sharp action he sadistically loved to give them.

Mark, the man who had talked about the cat, was the most self-conscious of all, I thought. His attitude seemed a little too studied as he pulled up his belt every time he approached me. His scowl seemed more put-on than the natural curl of the lip that Hans showed. He seemed to have the least to say to the rest of the group. He seemed to want almost to change places with me.

The two most talkative, really, and the two most unlikely—and the two who would have driven my old bar friends crazy with lust—turned out to be lovers. They were two matched Italians, both well over six feet tall, both heavy-chested, hair pouring up over their collars, both rich with sweet-smelling piss and tasty cocks. Their dark black mustaches were full and regulation-clipped on their olive faces. The completion of the fantasy for all to acknowledge came when they talked of the construction company they jointly owned, and the weights they jointly worked out with. Frank and Sal were strange partners; their demeanor was so obviously masculine and their conversation with the other men regarding sex showed they were both masters, but their manly affection for one another was somehow a natural part of their being between them.

The Topmen.

They were all in that group. I'd learn later that there were bottoms that they owned. Some, though, like Mark, were loners, or like Hans, could never have expected anyone to stay around that long. Frank and Sal had little room left in their relationship for a third person to stay. Only Mr. Benson and Brendan had the strength to rule any one person as fully as Mr. Benson would rule me for the next five years.

The beer and the smoke got to them. My exhausted body lay over in the corner, but the agonies I had endured must have turned them on. The evening was drawing to a close as I watched an early morning light come in over the crack in the doorway; the Topmen would come in and take their pleasure—all except, thankfully, Hans.

Brendan the cop was the biggest. I was shocked when his huge tool had first been pulled out to piss up my ass. And I was delighted to take on the task of trying to accommodate the member when he brought it again swollen with lust over to me. This time I chewed on his long, black foreskin as it passed through my teeth that first time. He loved it. I had marveled at the pinkness of the front of his prick when I had first seen it peek out from under the folds; the contrast was sharp against the dark shaftskin.

The sexiest, most tender encounter was when Frank and Sal came over together and used my face as a hole to fuck while they made out over me. Their sloppy kisses and hard "Do it, man" slaps left me with a raging hard-on after first one, then the other, had shot into me.

Mark strode over and drove into my mouth. He like to talk dirty. His monologue describing my piss-drenched and come-saturated body seemed more for his own turn-on than for my debasement.

Tom came over almost perfunctorily. He was laughing as he stuck his stick in my bruised and bleeding mouth.

Hans glowered from where he sat. Was he angry that Mr. Benson had stopped him from inflicting too much pain on me? Had Mr. Benson stopped him from going over this last time to join everyone else in climaxing the evening? Whatever, he left abruptly, saying he was off to the Mineshaft to see if there was anyone worthwhile left for him.

The others took this as their cue and got up to leave. They departed one by one leaving the mess of beer cans and filled ashtrays. I remember I used to wonder who had the job of cleaning up. I wondered who had ever assembled this extraordinary group of Manhattan men. But the thoughts didn't go far. As soon as they had left me alone and the continual flow of piss and come into me ceased, I had given in to a burden of fatigue and slumped down, the only thing even slowing my sliding into immediate sleep being the pain as my raw wound hit the floor. But I did sleep. Or pass out.

I didn't wake until we were standing in the elevator of Mr. Benson's apartment. I wasn't standing. I was in Tom's arms. The two faces smiled down at me, ignoring my stench.

Even with the draperies nearly closed, the sun streaked into Mr. Benson's apartment. I had no sense of time left. Only a relief to be at home.

Home!

A sudden start! I understood for the first time that, after only one night, this was home.

With the least possible aid from me, Tom lowered me into a warm and soothing bath. He dried my weak body and put on more of his strange salve, covering it with a gauze bandage. The collar had left my neck stiff, the skin red from its rubbing. I chafed my wrists, which showed deep red gashes where the steel handcuffs had bruised me to the bone.

Mr. Benson played for real.

When my nude, nearly hairless body was dried, Tom took me into the living room. Mr. Benson was waiting. He had drunk and smoked noticeably less than the rest of the group. Now he sat in his favorite chair, stripped down to his leather britches, sipping out of an amber glass. He smiled a welcome to the two of us. Tom deposited me and went wordlessly on his way. I sank onto the floor, sprawling once again at his feet, desperately tired and hoping he wouldn't want more from me now.

"Well, boy, that wasn't really a test. I was sure you had firmly made up your mind." He paused while he sipped. "We'll consider it a beginning to your training."

"Yes, Sir." I could barely get the words out.

Then Mr. Benson, the tyrant of this night of nights, reached down and gathered my body into his arms. I wrapped one of my own arms around his shoulders and put my head against his chest.

"Boy."

I looked up.

Mr. Benson bent his neck down and softly, but firmly, kissed my bruised lips. That was all I remembered that night. When I woke up in my sleeping bag the next morning, I could only hope that his affection would be repeated.

Tough and tender, the kiss from Mr. Benson made me feel proud to be a man so valued by another man.

CHAINS
LARRY TOWNSEND

Frank had been working at the mill for almost a month, and was now beginning to feel very much at home with the other people. Most were Middle Westerners, like himself...either that, or people from modest middle-class backgrounds that made them earthy and basically friendly. He especially liked Shirley, a heavyset woman in her early forties who had been afflicted with polio in adulthood and was now confined to a wheelchair most of the time. On her better days she could hobble around a bit on crutches, but even these moments seemed to be growing less frequent. A genuinely compassionate, motherly type, she was accepted as confidante and advisor by most of the younger girls.

Frank's immediate affection for Shirley was natural and almost automatic, certainly in keeping with all his lifelong patterns of behavior. He had never been able to think of himself as strong or desirable, tending toward a deflated self-image which sometimes made Paul nearly blind with anger. "I'm not worth a shit," he'd say. "I'm too ugly for anyone to be interested in me. You just go out and do your thing. I'll stay home where no one has to look at me."

In the more formal, and in some ways more glamorous, atmosphere of the studio, Frank had occasionally been uncomfortable. Promotions were very political, and he had never mastered the rudiments of that particular art. At the mill, things were different. The office staff was tiny in comparison to the army of people who had been trying to push and shove their respective ways up the ladder of success in the studio. He had started as assistant to the comptroller, which placed him on a higher level—and gave him a better salary—than most of the others...certainly more than the women. Being a personal friend of Michael's eliminated many of the fears Frank had always held for "the boss," especially as the vice president who was Michael's immediate superior was a friendly, somewhat comical man, referred to by the other employees as "the penguin." But the work was not difficult, the only threatening aspect of it being the escalating importance of the computer. An undisputed genius in this field, Michael patiently introduced Frank to the complexities of the various evolving procedures.

In all, Frank's period of feeling a stranger should have been short-lived, and it was only his basic, inevitable sense of insecurity that prolonged it. Frank was a worrier, with his old chronic condition made worse as a result of the protracted trial...delay after delay while the lawyer had made every effort to inconvenience the punk to an extent where he would fail to show up. But it hadn't worked. The kid had become obsessed with his role as prosecutor...avenger; like a latter-day Javert, he clung on to the very end, defeated only by the law itself. The emotional scars which this had left on Frank's psyche were still raw and open; nor were they likely to heal very quickly. Michael did everything he could to ease the way, recognizing many of Frank's problems—doing this partially out of friendship, partially for reasons of his own.

Several other people in the office sensed Frank's tension, but knowing nothing of its causes ascribed it to his being new. Shirley, "the mother of them all," was the first to respond. At the morning and afternoon coffee breaks she made a point to leave the big, open office where the girls had their desks, halting her wheelchair in front of the door to Frank's glass-walled cubicle, asking him if he was ready to join her. She would also find an excuse from time to time, and come into Frank's office with a question or minor problem regarding their work. Some of her own emotional requirements were thus fulfilled, and Frank responded gratefully to the attention...in effect, they formed a somewhat classic example of dovetailing neurotic needs.

Shirley's attentions did not go unnoticed by Charles and Lee, who were certainly aware of Frank's status—knew that he was gay, and that he had been a friend of Michael's long before coming to work at the mill. They were, of course, the only ones who knew this...or at least the only ones who knew it as a certainty. Hungry for a husband as the other, younger women were, it was only too natural for them to suspect the truth when all the eligible bachelors in the plant seemed more interested in each other than in them. Only Charles's recent engagement served to cloud the issue.

Very aware of all this interplay, Charles was thoroughly enjoying it. If the truth be known, his short tenure in Michael's home had been a hustle—a young good-looking guy being kept by a slightly older, vastly less attractive man. Charles thought of himself as "straight," or at the very least, bisexual. Still, he enjoyed camping it up with Lee, who was older than any of the rest in their group, and had once tried the marriage scene himself. "I hope you make it," he told his friend, "but if you're smart you'll see there aren't any kids until you're sure."

"But that's why I'm doing it," Charles had told him. "I wanna be a daddy!"

When Charles repeated this remark at the coffee break, it became Frank's first entry into the back-and-forth banter of the group. "Some people produce with their minds," he said. "Some can only use other portions of their anatomy."

When the giggles died down, Charles rebutted: "Some can't even use that part."

"Now, now...one big happy family," said Shirley.

"Reminds me of the Pollock woman who suddenly realized her kids were being too quiet," Michael chimed in. "She's in the kitchen with her hands full of flour and she yells, 'Hey, vot you kids doing?'

"From way up in the attic comes a faint little voice: 'Fockink, Mudder.'

"'Dot's nice,' she says. 'No fight!'"

"No laugh, either," said Lee dryly. "If we're going to start on Pollock stories, I'm going back to work."

"If that's all it takes," replied Michael, "I'll have to tell them more often."

Slowly, then, through these continuing exchanges, Frank's tension lessened; he fell easily into the routine of work, gradually into the verbal play and sparring of the others. The pay was good, substantially more than he'd been making at the studio; Michael had seen to that, and the actual work was not as demanding. In fact, it troubled Frank a little that his actual salary was now slightly more than Paul's. That didn't seem right to him, although Paul's sales job included an expense account and full-time use of a company car. Against these additional benefits, Frank was still able to rationalize himself as being the lesser contributor.

Paul sensed a good portion of Frank's feelings, often perceiving more deeply than his friend was capable of probing in his own, limited introspections. He recognized Frank's emotional dependence, and he took it both positively—as a compliment to his own strength—and negatively...sometimes almost contemptuously, as an indication of weakness. While enjoying the noncompetitive quality of his and Frank's relationship, Paul also found it disturbing constantly to be thrust into the role of decision maker, often without Frank's even expressing an indication of his own wishes. This had happened throughout the last year, certainly, as in the decision to purchase the home they presently shared. Even Frank's new job had been partially Paul's doing, as were the decisions regarding each and every household expenditure, the priority of paying the monthly bills...down to the selection of which television program to watch or which movie they should go to see. Had Frank's responses been otherwise, Paul reasoned to himself, they would constantly have been arguing. Yet Frank's failure to assert himself was having a destructive effect on their relationship.

Sexually, Paul was distant, and it was never he who initiated whatever was supposed to pass as "sex" between them. Apparently unwilling, or unable, to perceive or admit his own part in this deteriorating situation, Frank seemed to lay the blame on Paul's increasing interest in leathersex...S&M sex, which Frank insisted he didn't like. In Paul's opinion, this was also self-deception. He was sure that Frank felt the same unbidden attraction as many others—Michael among them. It was partially curiosity, partially the need-fulfillment which the role-playing gave him. Frank could never be bottom man; Paul knew that for sure. But top? He wondered if the thought ever entered his friend's mind, how much unspoken desire lurked in dark, hidden recesses which Frank refused to acknowledge. On the few occasions when Paul had hinted at the possibility of their playing with leather, Frank had been quick to refuse...even before the incident with the punk, and now with a firmer conviction.

For Paul, this situation also had a dichotomy of desirable and undesirable aspects. He had met Frank during the early, awakening stages of his interest in leather. He had been attracted to the smaller man physically, and this initial valence had sustained their relationship just long enough for each to perceive a number of compatible qualities in the other's personality...in all, the rather usual evolution from trick to lover. Their resultant partnership was now three years old, sustained by bonds which bore little resemblance to the earlier conditions—ironically, as Paul noted, when the third anniversary is traditionally "leather."

It would be quite fair to say, then, that Frank's emotional dependence on Paul had become a major factor in holding the two men together; a "need-fulfillment" on either side. But, regardless of the other needs that were being met, their sexual relationship had deteriorated to a point of being almost nonexistent. And it was Paul who felt the lack most strongly. His basic drives were higher—at least, not as suppressed, and prior to meeting Frank his affairs had been much more numerous than his friend's had been.

From the beginning, the two men had agreed to a non-exclusive sexual arrangement, although Frank had seldom strayed from his own bed. While he made no overt effort to prevent Paul's exercising his freedom, his feelings were all too plainly displayed whenever it became apparent that Paul was "going out for a while."

On this Friday evening, almost exactly a month after Frank started working at the mill, he and Paul had been involved in one of their increasingly frequent discussions.

"...so why don't you go out and get yourself a trick?" Paul insisted. "It'd be the best thing in the world for you, and..."

"I'm tired. I've had a hard week at a new job, and I just don't feel like it. If you want to go, go on. Don't worry about me. I'll be all right." He said this with a forced conviction, but the anxious expression about his eyes and the corners of his mouth belied the statement.

"I can't go out and enjoy myself, knowing you're sitting at home moping about it," Paul returned. He sat facing his friend in the semi-darkness of the terrace, feeling guilty and almost deciding not to go, despite the burning desire that gripped his loins. But as he talked to Frank, the same seething irritation rose up in him. Frank didn't want him to go, yet lacked the ability—or willingness—to supply the release which Paul required.

"You go ahead and enjoy yourself," said Frank at length. "It's okay with me...really it is." And it was, Paul realized—even from Frank's standpoint...far better to let Paul go out and do his thing, knowing he'd return afterward...better this, than try to deny him and have the entire relationship collapse.

Paul sighed, got up and went into the house to shower and change clothes. Frank remained on the terrace, lulled by the warm evening breeze and the steady drone of traffic along the Golden State Freeway, just visible over the stone wall that marked the edge of their property. One of the Siamese—a daughter of Michael's cat—had jumped into his lap, lying there "making biscuits" by the time Paul called from the front hall: "See you later."

"Have a good time," Frank returned weakly.

Paul drove through the maze of back streets, taking his usual shortcut to Sunset, from there to Santa Monica Boulevard. He was wearing a pair of faded jeans, fitted snugly across his narrow hips and ass, worn, threadbare material shaping itself about the contour of sex against his left thigh. An unpressed blue workshirt, wide black belt and heavy construction boots completed his costume...keys hanging from a heavy brass clip, swinging now from the ignition, but to be fastened onto the belt loop on his left side as soon as he stopped. He thought about Frank for the first few minutes, trying to resolve his own mixture of feelings...annoyance mingled with deep and sincere regard, a positive residual of the passionate love he no longer possessed. Yet it remained a form of love, the same as he might have for a close member of his immediate family, a younger brother or a nephew who lived with him. Knowing how deeply his own behavior affected Frank, he had hinted at the possibility of their separating; but Frank hadn't wanted that...had become almost hysterical at the prospect. Well, maybe time would cure the problem....

Paul's thoughts were distracted as he neared his destination. Several interesting numbers were on the sidewalk, all walking in the direction of the big leatherbar. He'd probably driven closer than he should have before looking for a place to park. The proximity of the bar, with the double row of motorcycles parked in the off-street triangle of asphalt...the muted sounds of jukebox and masculine voices emanating from the open doorway...all this worked its spell until Paul's thoughts were concentrated on the present, on his quest of a sexual encounter. He lucked out on a parking place, taking a spot at the curb as soon as it was vacated by the departure of a pickup with two guys in the cab. Made out early, he thought...barely ten o'clock....

The bar was one of the largest in the city, three adjoining rooms with pool tables in one, beer being served in the other two. The pair of barrooms were connected by a wide, open doorway, hung with chains in parody of a beaded curtains. Beer cases lined the walls, piled to a height which allowed the customers to sit on them. The place was already busy, though not as packed as it would be within another hour. Paul pushed himself between a couple of men at the counter and ordered a beer, receiving a smile and wink of recognition from Terry, the attractive little bartender. The kid said something to him, but Paul couldn't hear over the blare of country-western from the jukebox. He smiled and nodded back, hoping his response was appropriate to the other's remark.

He moved to the second room, through the curtain of chain, into the darker area where he had always found it easier to connect. Despite the number of people, he had not seen anything that really turned him on. In fact, he had noticed a couple of guys in the other room who had cruised him in the past, and whom he now wished to avoid. He settled near one of the back corners, perched on a stack of beer cases. Paul had purposely placed himself outside the aura of a blacklight, but watched with some amusement—and some interest—as others moved into that particular area. Some retreated immediately, obviously distressed when every piece of white in their clothing began to glow; only a few seemed pleased with the effect and remained...one younger guy in a T-shirt and muscles...a couple of others who pretended, at least, not to be aware of the spotlight effect.

Paul, whose build and features would have been complemented by the ultraviolet illumination, had discovered by hard experience that it was not the best mode for him. This type of posturing seemed to invite other guys to make the initial approach, whereas Paul preferred to seek out his own prospective partner. The other was the cruising technique of an M, he told himself, and Paul wore his keys on the left.

Without realizing it, his thoughts had wandered into a somewhat complicated exploration of his own position on the S-to-M continuum. He had not been aware of the last few people entering the room and almost jumped when he heard someone speaking to him.

"Hey, Paul, how you doing?"

He glanced up, recognizing a guy he'd spoken to several times in the past...*Jim?...Tom?* He couldn't remember for sure. "Hi," he replied. "You just get here?"

"About ten minutes ago," replied the other, settling on the case next to Paul. The newcomer was about Paul's age, but balding and considerably heavier than he should have been. While obviously interested, he had never tried to force the issue although he always seemed to make a point of greeting Paul and spending some time with him. On this particular evening, he was joined by two others, one of whom solved Paul's dilemma by addressing his companion as "Chuck." The group was congenial and feeling no pain, joking and laughing, buying beers for each other and including Paul with every round. As a result, he found himself drinking more than he usually did while all the earlier, more serious trains of thought faded into oblivion. By midnight Paul was glowing with good spirits and alcohol, considerably less inhibited than he usually was in a bar. The place had filled with people by then, and Paul had noticed a small, long-haired blond eyeing him from the row of beer cases several paces away.

"I think it's time to get down to business," he said abruptly. "There's a number over there who obviously needs his ass whipped." With that, he slipped from the group and took the empty place next to the blond.

Even in the semi-darkness, Paul could see the kid's face color slightly and realized that his three former companions had all turned to watch. "Don't mind them, they're horny," said Paul lightly.

"How 'bout you?" asked the blond.

"I'm always horny," Paul replied. "Especially when I see something I like."

The kid seemed to blush again, but smiled and extended his hand. "My name's Alex," he said.

"And I'm Paul."

They sat together through one more beer, which Paul bought for them. Their mutual interest had been expressed even before they spoke, so that when they left the bar a little after 1:00 a.m. it was merely a matter of logistics. Alex was alone and did not drive. He lived with another guy, he said, but it would be okay to go to his place. They walked to Paul's car, each feeling a sense of arousal and expectation. The few remarks that had been dropped in the bar had assured Paul of Alex's being an M, although it was obvious he had only limited experience. That was fine with Paul, just the way he liked it.

As they pulled away from the curb, Alex directed him to an address in Echo Park, and almost immediately slipped down, onto the floor. His hands explored Paul's thigh, crept into his crotch where seeking fingers slipped between the buttons on his Levi's, touching the warm, rising flesh within. They were driving east on Sunset, when the buttons parted and fingers moved to encircle the straining mast, to ease it up and out through the opening.

Almost immediately, tongue and lips caressed the tip, surrounding it with warmth and moisture.

Paul groaned, resting his right hand on Alex's head, his own fingers entwining themselves into the silky blond hair. They were coming into the area above Alvarado, where the intersections were brightly lighted and there were still people on the street. Paul's hand exerted a little more pressure, the motion advising Alex to keep his head down. They passed a cruising black-and-white headed in the opposite direction, its presence making Paul's heart beat faster as he automatically reached for the headlight switch, twisting it to dull the glow on the instrument panel. In doing this, he had raised his left thigh to hold the wheel steady, wedging Alex's head more firmly between the curve of plastic and the upward thrust of his own groin. The kid moaned at the pressure, dropping his mouth more completely onto the rigid shaft and forcing it deeply into his throat. His lips were pressed to the opening in the cloth, nose flattened by its contact with the hard-flexed surface.

They reached the street where Alex had said he should turn, and Paul relaxed his grip. "Better sit up and tell me where to go," he said softly.

After several turns on dimly lighted side streets, Alex directed him through a driveway and into a parking place behind a small house, set back from the roadway and almost obscured by a tangle of high, untended bushes. When the lights were out and the engine was turned off, Paul pulled the kid into his arms, sliding across the seat to press the weight of his body against the smaller form as they kissed. It was a hungry, passionate exchange, mouths open and straining to possess. The young, lithe form felt exactly right… small, supple, light enough to move about easily. Even the long hair, which Paul usually didn't like, seemed in place and a complement to the other's youthful aspect. It also suggested grass, which Paul seldom used and never kept at home, yet liked to try from time to time.

"Shouldn't we go inside?" Alex whispered at length.

Paul followed the smaller man around to the front of the house, and through the front door. The place was even smaller than it appeared from outside...a living room that could not have measured more than twelve feet in length, less than that in width. A tiny bedroom opened off either end, neither of which seemed to have a door. The only light came from a single, guttering candle on a spindly table near the wall. At the far side, the suggestion of a hall led to the only bath. Paul went at once to urinate, returning to find Alex kneeling beside the one comfortable-appearing chair, waiting for him. There had been music playing when they entered, and the kid had apparently turned this up as the rock beat was louder, seeming to reach into Paul's vitals. He took the chair, where he was apparently expected to sit. He looked down at Alex, who now rested his head on Paul's knee, one hand exploring the inside of thigh, reaching upward toward the crotch.

A suggestion of movement caught Paul's eye from the bedroom directly in front of him, and in the dim light it took a moment to make out the form of a booted foot atop the mattress, which lay upon the barewood floor.

"Ah...did you know your roommate was here?" asked Paul.

Alex glanced casually over his shoulder. "Oh, that's all right," he said. "Ed will probably go out later."

Paul felt suddenly uncomfortable, but decided to let the situation develop a little further before saying more. He looked back at Alex, again responding to the smaller man's attributes and to the cloying touch between his legs.

"Do you smoke?" asked Alex. "Grass, I mean," he added quickly.

"Sometimes," Paul replied.

"Good, maybe Ed'll share a joint with us before he goes, then." With this, Alex slipped to his feet, went into the bedroom where he whispered to the other man, and returned with a plastic container of grass. He knelt down again beside the coffee table, where he carefully placed a newspaper over the surface and began shaking out grains into a piece of rollie paper.

"Ed does this much better than I do," Alex explained. He removed his shirt and sat cross-legged on the tattered carpet beside Paul's feet. A few moments later, the man who had been lying on the mattress in the bedroom came out...a bigger, slightly older version of Alex, wearing only a pair of tattered, faded jeans, with black belt and boots. He did have a bunch of keys at his left hip, however, and except for the long, darkish blond hair he looked very much the part of an S. He lifted one hand in half-hearted recognition of Paul's presence, then stood over Alex, watching his clumsy attempts to roll a joint.

"Here," said Ed. "Let me do that." He hunkered down beside the smaller man, at which Alex scooted closer to Paul.

Paul watched the skillful manipulation of Ed's fingers, his own hand idly stroking the head which lay against his knee. He was very aware of the situation, assuming that the two men were lovers and that Ed really didn't want to leave.

"Look...I don't want to...intrude..." said Paul haltingly.

"No problem, man," returned Ed. He put the joint to his lips and lighted the end of it, taking a long drag at the pungent smoke. He did not appear disturbed, although he seemed to avoid looking at Paul. Taller than Alex, hair a little shorter and a shade darker, his features were not as pretty. Still, he was symmetrical and attractive in a less innocent appearing way. There was something almost sad about his eyes, and it was this suggestion of unhappiness which had led Paul to make his comment.

Ed passed the joint to Alex, who took his hit and handed it to Paul. Everything seemed completely natural and peaceful between them, and Paul's apprehension decreased. He tried to feel some effect from the marijuana, but knew from past experience that he would not get any sensation until they were through the second... maybe the third joint. He was, however, feeling the beer and the sensual contact that Alex was making against his thigh and crotch. Ed rolled a second joint, and Paul began to wonder if he was really going to leave...was gradually persuading himself that it didn't matter. He disliked three-ways, as a rule, but he was too enflamed now to dispute the circumstances.

Ed placed the newly rolled joint on the edge of the table and proceeded to make another. When he finished, he stood up, mumbling something to Alex as he sauntered back to his bedroom. Less than a minute later, he emerged wearing a leather jacket with a loop of chain hanging from its left shoulder. He lifted his left hand in a half-hearted wave and went out the front door without another word.

"Want to use Ed's room?" asked Alex. "All our stuff's in there and...there's a hook in the ceiling."

"Get your clothes off first," said Paul. Although he had previously tried to accept the presence of the other man, he now felt a sense of relief. He also felt himself in command, again, unthreatened by the ill-defined authority of the departed roommate.

Alex knelt between Paul's legs, bent to kiss the opening at his fly, then obediently stood up to remove his boots and jeans. Naked, he stood in front of his master, head slightly bowed, arms hanging loosely at his sides, awaiting the next instruction. He was a beautiful kid, Paul realized, with smooth, unblemished skin; a natural, youthful body with an easy definition down the front of his hairless chest and belly. An almost spherical mound of dark blond hair stood out in stark contrast at his groin, cock and balls pulled up, as if trying to contract and hide within the darkness.

Paul stood up, feeling suddenly unsteady as he stripped his shirt and jeans, replacing his boots and working his belt free of the loops, buckling this around his waist. The smaller man hadn't moved, although the fingers of one hand were only a couple of inches from the drooping curve of his master's cock. Deliberately, Paul allowed the crown to graze the back of Alex's hand, at which the fingers twitched and finally fastened about the shaft. Paul allowed him to fondle it for a moment as he felt the surge of lust begin to fill the passages once again and the powerful mast rose back to its full, demanding projection.

"We can use Ed's room," Alex suggested again.

Paul nudged him toward the room, turning him and grasping the slender shoulders as he guided the smaller man toward the doorway. "What does Ed do with that ceiling hook?" he whispered. "Does he string you up to it...?" Paul allowed one hand to slide down the front of Alex's body as they reached the darkness of the bedroom. He pressed his groin and stomach against the warm smoothness of the other's backside. His fingers grazed the silky mat of pubic hair, roughly seized the rigid cock and tightly lifted balls, twisted them until he felt the trembling form tense and press more deeply into the arching curve of his body. "Does he wrap these up in rawhide and make you dance around beneath that hook?" he rasped, "...tie your hands in back of you...make you swing by your balls from the ceiling?"

"Yes, sir," Alex gasped. "Only we don't have rawhide...uses chains and locks...rope...belt, maybe...."

As his eyes grew more accustomed to the deeper gloom of the cubicle, Paul was able to distinguish various items lying on the floor beside the mattress. There were two sets of handcuffs, some chains of various lengths and thicknesses, and several lengths of white nylon rope. He grasped both of Alex's wrists, pulling them together behind the smaller man's back, holding them there with one hand while he leaned down to retrieve a set of cuffs. Quickly, he placed these and set them, securing his prisoner who moaned, now, and gasped at every touch of Paul's hands upon the trembling surface of his arms and upper chest and back.

Paul turned the captive to face him, encircled the kid with both arms, crushing the helpless form against himself, kissing him deeply. He sensed the pulse of his own and the other's straining shafts, ground between their tightly compressed groins and lower bellies. When they finally moved apart, Alex staggered slightly, bracing the top of his head against Paul's shoulder. "Sir," he whispered, "could we smoke another joint?"

Paul moved quickly into the other room, returning with the two rollies which Ed had left for them on the table. Placing one on the footlocker which served as a nightstand, he lighted the other, took a deep drag and held the butt to his captive's lips. Gradually, he eased the other down, allowing him to lie on his side to avoid the pressure of steel against the youngster's back. As the joint burned down and it became difficult to hold without burning one's lips, Paul began to feel the seeping, pleasant sense of euphoria. He snubbed the tiny patch of paper—all that remained of the joint—and returned his attention to Alex. The kid had remained exactly where Paul had placed him, and at the touch of his master's hand upon his shoulder he sank onto his belly, hands positioned in the center of his back, securely joined by the metal bands. Paul knelt astride the upper thighs, hands moving warmly, slowly across satin surface, exploring each curve and depression of flesh, his own sac resting heavily upon the crevice between the young man's legs.

He touched the rounded surfaces of the cheeks, felt the coolness of smooth white skin. "Your ass ought to be warm," he whispered. "...should be hot and glowing when I lay down on it...ought to be red and hot and waiting for me." He lifted his belt, doubled it and pressed it firmly atop the solid rounds, grasping it at either end and allowing his weight to stretch the leather tautly across the span of flesh. He paused, feeling the responses, alert to any sign of protest. When there was none after several moments, Paul sat back on his heels and brought the doubled belt down with moderate force across one cheek. Alex moaned, twisted slightly as his ass raised an inch or so higher off the mattress.

Paul delivered a second blow, a third, each striking in a different spot, all landing with a firm, flat contact that produced a sharp, resounding "crack!", the sounds echoing off the high, bare walls of the cubicle. Between every third or fourth blow, he paused, tracing the surface of Alex's butt with the flat of his palm, sensing the rise of temperature where the strap had made its contact. The warmth that touched his fingers seemed to be communicated to his own body, to center in his groin and fill his loins with a reciprocating glow. His senses, heightened and pleasantly distorted by the marijuana, responded almost frantically to each and every contact with the other's body. The ass and back and upper thighs were casting back an aura of heat which suggested the soft and subtle radiance of smoldering coals. He seemed almost to sense the shimmering waves of rising warmth.

He had paused again to stroke the taut, responding smoothness, when he heard the click of the front door latch, and glanced over his shoulder to see Ed reenter the house. For a moment, Paul expected the other to continue into the bedroom, perhaps to create some scene or at least to say something. Instead, he seated himself in the living room, where he proceeded to shake some grass into a paper. His back was turned toward them. Somewhat self-consciously, Paul returned his attention to his companion. He lowered his weight atop the warm expanse of ass and back, allowed his cock to find its own enclosure between the other's thighs. He felt the contact of steel against his belly, an uncomfortable pressure which he still found pleasant as Alex's writhing fingers toyed with the hairy surface of his abdomen. For quite a while Paul lay there, gently working his hips to drive his cock a fraction up and back, rigid core sliding within the looser surface which adhered to the walls of the other's thighs. Despite the exquisite sense of physical satisfaction, Ed's presence had an inhibiting effect…and more than this, there seemed a new and alien shadow of desire…alien, yet disturbingly familiar.

"Did you hear your friend come back?" he whispered at length.

He felt Alex nod his head in the darkness. "He'd join us if you asked him to," he whispered.

"...that what you want?"

"Whatever," returned Alex.

Paul remained in place for several minutes more, recognizing the acceleration of his own desire, the urge to make the most of the prospective situation, yet reluctant to admit the direction of his own desires. "If...I ask him in...I'd...maybe have to let him put those irons on me," he whispered finally.

He felt the smaller body contract beneath him, legs move apart to permit his balls to fall between them before they pressed together once again, imprisoning him and squeezing his nuts to the brink of pain. "He'd like that," said Alex.

"And you?" asked Paul.

"I'd do whatever I was told to do."

Slowly, Paul lifted his upper body to kneel again astride the narrow hips and ass. He realized that he was quivering as involuntary spasms of excitement coursed through his being. The arousal he had previously felt was nothing compared with the fiery lust which possessed him now...now that he'd expressed his willingness; and the prospect loomed close and real. It was an impulse he could not bring himself to admit in everyday discussion of his proclivities; yet now his body was aflame with it...here with a pair of guys who didn't know him, who could use him as they willed and not expose his secret. His cock had responded so desperately he seemed almost on the verge of climax.

"Maybe we should smoke that last joint," he suggested. His fingers were already working the key in the cuffs, allowing Alex's hands to separate.

"I think Ed just started a fresh one," Alex muttered. He slipped from the room the moment his hands were free, dropping on his knees beside the chair where his friend was sitting. As the pair of them whispered together, Paul felt the tingle of anticipation grow more intense. He was almost shaking with excitement while alternate waves of hot and cold seemed to sweep his viscera; an almost painful weight contracting into itself while his balls pulled tight against it... outwardly a manifestation of fear; yet the frantic arousal of a few moments past had not diminished. He still felt very close to coming.

Paul was kneeling on the mattress, his hands hanging loosely at his sides, as the other two moved toward him. Alex was slightly ahead, the outline of his slender musculature a silhouette against the ruddy, flickering candlelight. Ed wore his jeans and jackboots, but his jacket had been removed. Seen from Paul's present perspective, his build was larger, heavier, not as well defined as Alex, and covered down the front with a light distribution of blond, curly hair. Because of his size and the hippie length of his hair—this hanging almost to his shoulders—he would not normally have attracted Paul in a bar or on the street. Yet he now assumed the proportions of explicit desire, and Paul sat back on his heels to make more room on the mattress.

Alex sank down beside him, the two completely naked except for the boots on Paul's feet. Ed knelt on the edge of the mattress, his back to the muted glow of light. He passed the joint to Paul, whose gaze never left the front of the other's body while he sucked in the pungent smoke, watched the ruby ember reflected on the smooth, lightly tanned surface. Perhaps it resulted from his own intense excitement or perhaps it was simply the point at which his body had absorbed a sufficiency of grass; regardless of the cause, Paul felt an expanding effect before he released the lungful of smoke. The glowing halo outlining Ed's form grew more intense, became a deeper yet brighter hue. The steady beat of music in the background seemed suddenly to absorb him as the primordial fear was drained, replaced by a rush of heat and a pulsing tide of desire. His previous willingness to surrender was stripped of residual doubt, and the lump of apprehension dissolved.

Unhurriedly, Ed moved toward him, grasped Paul's wrists and brought them together behind his back. Holding them in place, he pulled Paul's body tightly against his own, ground his lips roughly onto the other man's, engulfed him with his own warmth while Alex moved around them to retrieve the cuffs and place them on his former mentor. Paul heard the ratchet click, felt the steely circles close about him, responded with another surge of arousal. He returned the pressure of Ed's lips with an almost violent desperation, leaning into him until he would have fallen forward except for the supporting hold. Slowly, then, he felt Ed loosening his grasp, gathering his legs beneath him as his body began gradually to rise. Paul's lips were held upon the pulse of the other's throat, body twisted backward and kept from toppling by the pressure of large, strong hands about his upper arms. He licked and caressed the chest, sucked at one nipple as it paused within reach, then down the center of the chest, the belly...another pause while Paul's tongue explored the navel...down, pubic hair brushing his chin and nose until he felt his face driven hard against the tangled, dark-blond patch. Ed had opened the buttons on his jeans, but left them on with the ends of his belt dangling to either side of the opening. His cock was still within, hard and risen, outlined against the faded denim.

He stood, finally, holding Paul's face upon his crotch, allowing the moving lips to trace the outline of sex, moisture soaking the material...saliva from the mouth of the kneeling figure, an oozing suggestion of fluid from the tip of his cock.

"You want it?" he asked at length.

"Yes, sir," whispered Paul.

"Then work it out...get it free and see if you can take it!"

Warm hands grasped his shoulders and the dusky scent of groin and sweat dominated his senses. The heavy beat of music seemed in time with the thunder of his own pulse, and his entire world was comprised of the shadowy area where he knelt on the mattress, body commanded by another while he strove to obey the demands being placed upon him. His lips and tongue worked to free the rigid bolt, nose straining against cloth until it slipped a trifle lower on the narrow hips. He twisted his tongue beneath the solid base, gradually eased it up and out until the entire shaft popped loose...a springy, wedge-shaped mast, gnarled contour narrowing toward the tip, where the small, round cap formed a finial to its upward projection. The balls were still inside the sagging cloth, hanging deeply, stretched to the bottom of the sac by the falling pressure of the open fly. Paul felt the hand against the back of his head, the thrusting pressure on his lips, the driving lunge which carried the cockhead past his palate, choked him until the gorge rose inside his throat and tears began to blur his vision. He was helpless, responding only to the guidance of the hands upon his head and neck, the penetrating fullness, sliding unchecked across the viscous secretions of his mouth and throat. He was forced to kneel and take it, to kiss the crown and all along the underside, to suck the testicles from their hidden recess, to pull them into him, caress them, fondle them with his tongue and lips. This action commanded his full attention, forcing every other vestige of reality from his conscious mind. All logical thought or perception had long since been suspended, and he responded with a purely sensual awareness. He felt the searing thrill which every motion evoked within his lower body, the swinging contact of his balls with the insides of his thighs. His own cock stood in full and total hardness, but he couldn't see it, and merely reacted to the frenzied desire, not caring about his own display of sexuality.

He felt himself being lifted, strong hands beneath his armpits, pulling him to his feet, face moving upward, now, across the sweat-moistened surface he had traversed in the opposite direction. He stood unsteadily, helped from behind...a touch which reminded him of Alex's presence. He'd almost forgotten, lost in the nebulous space of the other's domination. He felt a rope being wrapped about the base of his cock and balls, tied in place with a tight, upward pressure. He was vaguely aware of some motion behind him as Alex stood on something...a chair, he supposed, and passed the length of rope through a metal loop in the ceiling...ceiling, so far away, dark and distant...too far to see it clearly.... Then the rope was tied about his neck, wrapped several times around and tied against his throat. The hands...all the many hands were gone, and he found himself struggling to hold his balance on the soft, uncertain surface of mattress. His weight dragged alternately at his balls and at his neck, causing him to twist and move in a narrow circle, tethered at the end of his lead.

"Stand up straight!" Ed commanded sharply.

From the edge of his darkening vision, Paul could see him standing there, naked now and holding the loop of belt in his right hand. The constriction of rope around his neck was forcing him to breathe in a raspy rattle, while the pulse whispered loudly in his ears and the imprisonment of his balls was desperately, painfully sensual. He tried to do as he was told, but his booted feet found little purchase on the aged, sagging surface.

"I told you to stand up straight!" Ed repeated sharply; and this time he swung the belt to make it crack against Paul's ass.

The blow had not been hard, but it had been unexpected. A low moan broke from Paul's lips and he tried again to gain his footing. The belt caressed his ass again, and then his back. It fell in a steady series, striking several different places, eventually touching all of his back and ass and thighs, as well as the sides and front of his body. Ed was muttering something, making reference to Paul's use of Alex, apparently passing the belt to the smaller man and allowing him to seek his own retribution.

Paul was twisting in his bonds, trying to avoid the harder blows, yet never knowing where they'd fall, or which would be the sharp and painful contacts, which would merely be the smooth caress of leather upon the tingling heat of his skin. Despite the pain, however, and the involuntary response of avoidance, he wanted it...especially the lighter blows, and even the heavier ones, once the initial impact had receded into the warmth of his glowing flesh.

"He wanted to warm your ass, didn't he, baby?" Ed growled.

"Yeah...yes, he did...said he wanted me hot enough to fuck."

"Wanted to fuck, huh? Wonder how he's gonna like this shoved up his ass. Think it's hard enough, baby? Think it's hard enough to make him feel it?" Ed fondled his cock, standing back to watch while Alex used the belt upon their captive. Paul's eyes were watering profusely, now, and his face was perceptibly darker than the rest of his body, even in the shadowy illumination. But he was too desperately turned on to care. He was able to breathe, and beyond this the strangling pressure was only an added element of sensual possession. He heard Ed's comment, through the pounding of his own pulse and the constant crackling contacts of the belt...and he wanted it...wanted that thick, stubby wedge shoved into him. He saw Alex sink to his knees in front of Ed, take the solid projection between his lips and work it, pumping at it while the prisoner hung helplessly, rolling his eyes to watch, increasing the pressure on his throat in the effort to better observe the exchange between his captors. He wanted to ask for it, but his throat was dry and words refused to form themselves. He felt the searing aftermath of the belting, his body enclosed in an envelope of sensual warmth. As he watched Alex working on the master's cock, he seemed almost to feel it along the length of his own distended rod. The only rational thought to penetrate his senses was the hope it would not end there...that Ed would not succumb to the frantic ministrations and shoot his load before...

Then Ed was on his feet and Alex's mouth was pressed against Paul's backside. The seeking tongue now probed his anus, drove deeply into him, lubricating the passage for his master, forcing Paul to gasp and pull against his bonds as exquisite passion boiled within, threatened to erupt in response to the darting penetration.

A moment later, Ed was standing hard against him, cock sliding across the crevice between his cheeks, seeking the open, lubricated passage. Alex had moved to the front, where he tongued the tightly compressed balls, pulled and sucked at them while the cockhead found Paul's asshole and Ed's hands grasped the prisoner's hips to steady himself. The wedge-shaped bolt slipped into him, entering Paul at the same moment that Alex dropped his mouth about his shaft, drawing it into the fiery moisture of his throat, holding it deep within himself as Paul tottered in the grip of debilitating euphoria. Any pain of penetration was dulled and all but lost in the frantic storm of pleasure...the awareness of helplessness and total possession by this pair of men. He'd been subjected to their use, punished, forced to do their bidding, degraded and made the subject of their every demand.

Cool air moved against his face, which seemed to burn as if the sun were beating down on him, instead of the predawn darkness. His skin seemed to tingle, wanting to itch where it pressed against the leather seat, separated by the cloth of shirt and jeans. *Why?* he wondered. Why had he done it again? Why had he turned M in the middle of a session and responded so completely to it? *Must have been the grass*, he reasoned. *Must have been the grass, unless...opposites, or something....* He vaguely remembered a conversation in the bar one night, a couple of older, more experienced guys discussing the reason for some men to be M's, when all the other aspects of their lives were otherwise. "A need to submit," one of them had said. "A need for punishment."

Anyway, Paul thought, *I sure dug it! Wild! Just hope they didn't mark me...at least not above the waist where it's going to be hard to hide from Frank. Wonder what he'd think...never be able to understand...no way! Wonder if he ever will...if he'll ever understand any of it....*

A SECRET LIFE
Anonymous

A week or two after my first visit with Cecil, the one I was telling you about, my mother had to go into the country for a short trip to see a friend who was ill, and consequently she didn't want to take me with her. Cecil got wind of this and at once offered to put me up until my mother returned to Paris. The offer was accepted, as it put an end to the my mother's difficulties in finding someone to care for me.

The place where my mother was going was in Touraine, and she left by train in the morning. After lunch, I went for a drive with Cecil in the Bois, and when we returned we went directly to his bedroom.

I did not feel shy this time, and as he sat beside me I put my hand on his crotch and felt his cock. But he didn't seem the same as he was the time before, and I had hardly set my fingers to opening his breeches before he got up, kissed me tenderly, and gave me a peculiar look.

I wondered what the matter was and why he had changed, but

I said nothing, guessing that he would explain himself presently. And I was not far off, for after an interval he took his place beside me and putting his arm round my neck, exclaimed; "I am very much troubled to know what to do tonight, Gaston. I belong to a kind of club, which meets this evening, and as I am one of the principal members I ought to be present."

"Well, couldn't you take me?" I asked.

"Ah, no, that would be impossible. You see, it is strictly limited to members."

"Can't you bring me as a guest?" I said halfheartedly, not wanting to be left behind. He seized on the idea at once, and clapped his hands with glee. But he grew more grave afterwards, saying; "I don't know whether it could be managed. If I take you, Gaston, you must be very careful how you speak and act. I must tell you that it is a club where we—well—amuse ourselves in different ways, so you mustn't betray surprise at anything you see. Can I trust you?"

"Perfectly," I replied, foreseeing an adventure. "I will be as sober as a judge, and as careful as an ambassador."

He rang for Maurice, and when the manservant appeared, he said; "I want you to get some evening clothes for Monsieur le Comte to wear tonight: I wish to take him with me."

By dinner time I had been transformed altogether, and looking at myself in the long glass in Cecil's room I saw the reflection of what anyone would have said was a smartly-dressed young man— and not a bad-looking one, either, I think; at least, the other two men told me so.

I was much pleased by my image. Maurice had outfitted me in the height of fashion. Though I am younger than Cecil, I am nearly his size. I wore an exquisite pair of his trousers, which fit rather snugly about my hips. I had on a white silk shirt which felt wondrously sensual next to my naked skin, and over that Maurice had buttoned me into a beautiful brocade vest of the deepest burgundy color. Over the evening coat, which tapered gracefully in at the waist, Maurice presented me with a dramatic opera cape. He lightly pomaded my hair and sprayed me lightly with a very subtle cologne, one which I had smelled before on my father, and recognized as a very rare scent. I regarded myself and smiled, pleased with the reflection. My hair gleamed like black oil, and the tapered coat accentuated my hips and buttocks.

Cecil entered the room and said, "Bravo, Maurice. You've really done a splendid job of it." Then he approached the looking glass and stood behind me.

"You look ripping Gaston. Absolutely stunning!" he said, rather softly. I turned, my eyes aglow with anticipation for the unknown adventures of the evening ahead. I remarked on how splendidly turned out Cecil was, which seemed to please him greatly.

"This is an evening you shan't forget," he said to me cryptically, and by the devious look in his eyes I knew I could regard that as a promise. I shivered with erotic expectation, because instinctually I knew that our evening outing would prove to be sensually oriented.

We went downstairs and ate a light supper by the light of candles. As we ate, Cecil instructed me upon my manners when we arrived at the meeting of Society X.

He said that he was going to introduce me as his younger brother and request that I be considered as a prospective member of Society X. It seemed important for me to pose as his brother, so that if I found I was not disposed to take no part in the Society's proceedings I would not be forced to leave the meeting. Cecil took particular care to impress upon me the element of choice, though he also stipulated that if any overtures were made to me, and I felt inclined to participate, I had his blessing to include myself.

This all sounded wonderfully mysterious. I felt my cock stirring under the table at the prospect of an exciting evening in Paris with Cecil, who looked quite stunning in his evening dress. I was quite proud to be included with him and I said so.

"It is nothing, my boy," he smiled. "I will tell the members of Society X that you were reared in the country." He began to laugh convulsively at his pun. At last, wiping his eyes, he began again. "I will tell them that you have been raised in the country and that this is your first visit to Paris. That will be sufficient explanation, should you become shy or bashful. In this way you will be permitted to stay no matter what. Ordinarily at Society X, if one is not going to participate in the...ah...festivities, one is generally not allowed to stay. But in your case I am certain that they will make a concession if you simply choose to watch."

For all of Cecil's precautions, I was perhaps even more convinced than before that I wanted to accompany him to the meeting of Society X. Finally we left the house and drove off in his carriage. On the drive I was so excited about the mysterious evening ahead that I stole a few caresses. Hiding my groping hand under Cecil's opera cape, I lightly stroked his cock through his light spring trousers. He laughed and squeezed my tremulous cock with great affection. I was feeling randy and flushed by the time the carriage arrived in front of a great mansion in a district that I was not entirely familiar with. The enormous house sat back from a secluded street. The carriage entered the gates and we pulled up in front of the great doors. Inside, fires blazed and the windows glowed yellow in the night. Several porters in full livery advanced to our assistance, but Cecil lightly declined. Obviously having been here before, he gracefully stepped into the great entry hall of the mansion.

I gasped with surprise at the finery of the interior. We walked quickly up the grand spiraling staircase, which was broad and richly carpeted. Two handsome young men stood at one corner of the huge landing, and offered to take our capes. After leaving our wraps with them, we ascended yet another flight of stairs. I breathlessly took in the new surroundings: the candlelit chandeliers giving off a fine crystal glow, the rich dark paintings that hung on the walls of the great staircase. At length I gasped, "Whose house is this, Cecil?"

Cecil did not answer me, but simply looked over his shoulder and smiled cryptically at my query.

Soon we found ourselves in front of two very imposing oak doors. Cecil gave a special knock and the doors swung open to reveal a most lavish apartment. It was a room outfitted in the richest style, with a great many mirrors and painted panels on the walls. Heavily tapestried curtains covered the long windows, and rich carpets from Persia covered the floors. At one end of the huge room there was a fireplace that was big enough to step into, and within it a roaring fire gave the room a warm, sensuous glow.

There were a score or more of young men standing in a tight group talking, and as we entered they all advanced to greet Cecil. I noticed that they were all very good-looking men, and exceptionally well-dressed. They all seemed genuinely happy to see Cecil, and regarded me at first with some little reserve.

After Cecil made his initial greetings, he said, "I should like to introduce my younger brother, Gaston. Please welcome him as a prospective member of our Society."

The young men instantly relaxed in my presence and came forward, each giving me the traditional kiss of welcome on either cheek. I was surprised at all the attention and, to my embarrassment, I blushed a cherry-red color. Soon they were all teasing me about my shyness, and I could only laugh and join the group as we made our way to a long table at one end of the room, which had been spread with wines and cakes and fruits. Cecil filled my glass with claret, and I withdrew to a low divan in one corner so that I might sit down and take in my new surroundings at leisure.

I watched Cecil with pride as he amiably chatted with the other members of Society X. I could hardly contain my curiosity, for it seemed that this was a simple fete in which young men had come together to share wine and conversation. Though I did notice that many of the young men stood very close together, some even leaning familiarly against one another. Cecil at last came and joined me on the sofa, and I felt comfortable in leaning in close to him. He promptly put his hand on my upper thigh, teasingly close to my cock.

Presently Cecil called out, "Has anyone seen Sir Henry?" And almost as soon as he said that, the great oaken doors swung open and an exquisite gentleman stepped into the room. He was accompanied by a younger man, who was closest to me in age of anyone there and nearly as beautiful as the man whom he apparently served.

The members of Society X were immediately silent, and formally approached one by one to greet the newcomer. Cecil rose from the couch to follow suit, and I made to remain seated, but he bade me to stand and follow him.

"That is the President of Society X," whispered Cecil.

As he advanced he gave me a little shove forward, and said, "Sir Henry, may I introduce Gaston, my younger brother, and a prospective member of Society X." I was intoxicated by the startling handsomeness of this man, and I stupidly put out my hand in greeting.

"Ah, come now, Gaston," said Sir Henry, his blue eyes dancing. "Give us a kiss," and he leaned forward and gave me a kiss on either cheek, which I returned.

"Cecil, I didn't know that you had such a beautiful little brother. You have been hiding him from us, eh?" teased Sir Henry.

I blushed again, to my shame, as Sir Henry turned to me and said, "Gaston, we welcome you and hope that you will enjoy yourself on this very special night." His voice was deep and velvety, and it felt as though he was caressing me as he spoke. "Feel free to please yourself as you will. Drink wine, and make yourself comfortable. Welcome," Sir Henry repeated, and then made his way across the room to converse with the other members of Society X.

I was positively flaming with desire as he left our presence. He was the most striking man I had ever laid my eyes upon, with his golden hair that hung very nearly to his shoulders. He had the flaxen hair pulled back with a black leather strap. He wore tall leather riding boots and black suede riding breeches. His white shirt billowed at the sleeves, and he wore it open at the neck. The white of his shirt matched the brilliant white teeth that flashed in a ready smile. Needless to say, my cock leapt to erotic attention, and as his lips graced my cheeks I tried desperately to hide my readily-apparent desire.

The group of young men once more fell to chatting amiably, and I watched with rapt attention as Sir Henry threaded his way through each little grouping of men, smiling, laughing and lightly caressing the other men. I followed Cecil to the table, where he filled my cup with the deep red claret once again.

"I see you've taken a liking to Sir Henry," he said, half-teasingly. I think that at the time I might've detected a little jealousy in his voice, but only in retrospect have I realized that. Nevertheless, he reached down and gave my cock a squeeze. I smiled in acquiescence, but made no response. I secretly stole another glance at the gallant figure of Sir Henry as he stood surrounded by a small group of young men, and my heart raced as I found his laughing eyes returning my gaze, looking at me appreciatively.

Presently the young men began to disappear in twos and threes through a small door which presumably led to a smaller antechamber to the large apartment.

Cecil turned to me and said, "I will return shortly. Drink and make yourself comfortable." And with that he gave my bottom a light pat, made his way to the door, and vanished into the interior. Soon I was the only person left in the room, and I felt the keenest desire to know what was going on in the other room, but I distinctly felt that it was secret, otherwise Cecil would've invited me. I could hear soft music issuing from the antechamber, and now and again there were bursts of laughter.

I passed the time drinking the delicious red wine and tasting the array of sweets that were spread on the table. In about a quarter of an hour Sir Henry's handsome manservant returned, and I was momentarily shocked to find him quite naked as he entered the room. As he proceeded to circle the room, dousing the candles, I sat back to enjoy watching his fine form in the low light. When his task was finished the only light in the room came from the great fireplace, where the blaze crackled brightly. Soon after that, the young men began to slowly reenter the room in pairs, some in groups of three. When I tell you that each and every member of Society X reentered the room completely naked, you can fancy the state of my feelings. My heart started to beat like a hammer and my legs were all a-tremble as I watched the parade of their naked forms before me, silhouetted by the firelight. I had the opportunity to compare the merits of their muscular buttocks, and the sizes and lengths of their cocks. I wondered at all the variations of shapes and sizes, not to mention the many different colors of hair that surrounded their members. All this was revealed to my astonished but delighted gaze.

Cecil came over and lazily sat beside me, amongst the pillows of the couch where I had ensconced myself. He whispered, "If you wish to remove your clothes, you may, Gaston." With that he gave me a meaningful smile, and reached between my legs and gave my swelling cock a tight love squeeze.

"Why was I not allowed to join you in the other room?" I asked, and was immediately embarrassed at the boyish plaintiveness in my voice.

"Oh, Gaston," laughed Cecil. "Someday, when you are a full member of Society X, you shall learn. But, for tonight, you should just partake of those things that please you, and ask no questions."

"Of course," I stammered. I was thankful to have Cecil so close by, especially when a moment later we were joined on the couch by a young man who introduced himself to me as Scott.

"He's too beautiful, Cecil," said Scott, nodding towards me. "Really, where did you find him?"

"I am a friend of his parents," replied Cecil.

As they spoke I noticed that Scott had moved closer to Cecil, and was caressing his prick with utter familiarity. I sat next to the men as they began to embrace and slowly explore each part of one another's anatomy with lazy abandon. Scott soon took my hand and placed it on his cock, saying, "You're silly not to join us!"

As soon as I felt his erect member in my hand, I immediately began to stroke it. His cock was of considerable thickness and was surrounded by a copse of red curling hair. I looked to Cecil for assistance, and he smiled deviously.

I turned to Scott and said pettishly, "Well, if I'm to join the fun, I will need some assistance in removing all these constraints." I then gestured at my evening finery. I was definitely feeling overdressed for the occasion at that moment.

"Glad to help!" exclaimed Scott, who immediately set about his task with zeal. He leaned over me and, to my great surprise, he began to unbutton my brocade vest with his teeth.

Cecil laughed huskily and stroked my cheek. Then, as Scott made his leisurely way down towards the front of my trousers with his deft mouth, Cecil leaned towards me and began to kiss me on the mouth. He pressed open my lips and began to flick the tip of his tongue around the tip of my own, sending fiery chills down my spine. Scott had succeeded in unclasping my trousers with his teeth. As Cecil and I continued to kiss, Scott released my cock from its prison of cloth. Wasting no time, he pulled back the skin and began to tickle the head with his tongue. I was already erect, and Scott's lascivious kisses almost made me spend instantly.

"I say, Cecil," Scott said, looking up from between my legs. "What a cock this boy's got on him!" Cecil stopped kissing me for a moment, and laughed. "Yes, I know!"

"Well, it seems someone has taught your little brother well," said

Scott, gesturing to my hand, which was working on Cecil's balls and cock.

"Yes, yes," was all Cecil could say.

I was soon transported by further tonguing from Cecil and Scott on my mouth and cock respectively. I was so bewildered and excited by their seductions that I would have shot my burning come into Scott's mouth presently; but suddenly, almost at the moment of my climax, he ceased his tantalizing oral stimulation.

"Don't let him come yet," Cecil said. "We want to teach him how to prolong his pleasure." I sat up, not a little dazed, my balls aching dangerously. I slowly stood and removed the remainder of my clothes, and as I did this Scott and Cecil fell once again to stroking one another where they reclined on the divan.

I lay back to reexamine my immediate surroundings. I could see the couplings of men in pairs, and also those locked in the delicious contortions of ménage à trois. Scattered on the lush carpets and large cushions of the room, I saw men fucking in various positions, their bodies glowing in the dim light of the room. I found myself involuntarily searching, and at last I saw him. Sir Henry stood, holding a sandy-haired fellow's head at his cock, and the kneeling man was giving him a zestful sucking. I could see from where I lay, that Sir Henry's cock was thrusting deeply into the other young man's throat. My own cock lurched longingly at the sight. The man kneeling in front of Sir Henry had his arms wrapped around Sir Henry's hips, and his fingers seemed to be gently teasing open his tight rear opening and tickling the sensitive flesh surrounding his asshole. I was concentrating so intensely on what the kneeling man was doing to Sir Henry that I nearly jumped off the couch when I realized that Sir Henry was smiling directly at me.

He gently removed his cock from the kneeling man's hungry mouth. The sandy-haired gentleman looked up at Sir Henry, said something, and then quite blithely made his way into another grouping of bodies on the carpet. And then my heart really started to pound, as Sir Henry was walking directly towards me.

Once he was close enough, he said in a low voice, "Gaston, I am so happy to see that you have decided to join us. Come let me have a real look at you." I let myself be guided away from the divan where Scott and Cecil were in the beginnings of a rousing fuck. I hungrily devoured Sir Henry's body with my eyes, and when I let my gaze at last rest on his cock I let out a muffled yelp of surprise.

Through the tip of his penis he had a golden ring, which clearly ran through the head!

Sir Henry laughed at my astonishment as I stared at his pierced cock. I had never even heard of such a thing, much less seen anything like it. But I have to admit that it gave me a strange, thrilling sensation when I first saw it that I cannot directly explain.

"Ah!" he laughed. "I see you have discovered my ring. We call this a Prince Albert ring. Perhaps someday you, too, shall wear one."

"But does it not give you a great deal of pain?" I asked.

"On the contrary. It affords me greater pleasure, just as it might do for you!" And he laughed again, with meaning.

The thought terrified me and yet exhilarated me in a way that I had never previously known. As we were talking, he was smoothly guiding me to a couch in a far corner of the grand apartment.

At last he said, "Sit down, Gaston."

I complied immediately. He lay down beside me and I soon fell to exploring his smooth honey-colored flesh, his hands guiding me at the start in order to encourage me. He, too, began to touch my body, seeking those areas of greatest pleasure. At length he gently turned me on my side, so that he could take my cock from the front, while teasing my asshole from behind. I could feel his large member rubbing in between the cheeks of my ass, and in my erotic vexation at being seduced by so striking a gentleman, I whispered fiercely, "Fuck me Sir Henry. I want you to fuck me up the ass."

Sir Henry gave a low moan, and then he did something which quite surprised me. He slowly kissed his way down my spine and then, arriving at my bottom, he continued with his kisses until his mouth was directly upon my anus. He delicately licked and sucked the little puckered hole, lightly lubricating it and giving me the most delicious pleasure. I don't know how I kept myself from coming right then, but somehow I controlled myself, eager to feel his cock enter me so that we might come simultaneously. I had never done that, but Cecil had told me that it was the best feeling of all.

Sir Henry slowly rose and told me to get on all fours on the couch, which I did without hesitation. He mounted me from behind, taking hold of my throbbing cock with one hand and with the other spreading my ass cheeks wide. Suddenly, and with a violent thrust, he shoved his prick into my anus. The golden ring on the tip of his cock added to the friction tickling the insides of my hole. With his second thrust he entered me completely, and a powerful jolt it was, nearly making me cry out with painful pleasure. He continued to stroke my cock, at first more slowly to match the pace of his thrusts, and then more and more quickly as he pumped his well-muscled body against my own. A low, animal rumble was growing from within my depths, and every inch of my skin was aflame with desire. I raised my buttocks to meet his thrusts.

"I'm coming!" I gasped. "Oh, Sir Henry, I'm coming!" Almost in a state of delirium, I let out a great yell, and the sound of that was mingled with Sir Henry's own cry of passion. I believe that I passed out for a few moments from sheer pleasure, falling forward onto the cushions of the couch.

When I came to I found that a pair of hands were lightly stroking my cock and balls, which felt wonderfully soothing, though it was too soon for me to become erect after such a passionate spending. I assumed that the caresses were from Sir Henry, but suddenly I found myself face to face with him. He lay next to me, and he began to kiss me on the lips, searching the interior of my mouth with the tip of his devilish tongue. I gave myself up to his luxurious kisses, nearly forgetting that the hands that were lightly toying with my balls did not belong to Sir Henry. I gave myself so completely to the pleasure of our mouths' meeting, that it seemed that all my sensual nerves were resting in the tip of my tongue. Suddenly Sir Henry pulled away from me.

"Gaston," he said, looking at me very seriously, "I want you to fuck John, my man. It would give me great pleasure to watch you fuck him. Will you do that for me?" He looked at me with charming earnestness, as though I might refuse him. His voice had a hypnotic effect upon me, and I felt completely willing to do anything to please him. Besides which, I had not yet had the pleasure of fucking another man. The thought of taking his handsome blond haired servant from behind immediately sent the blood rushing from my head and straight down to my cock.

On turning, I found that the faceless hands that were softly stroking my body as I kissed Sir Henry were those of John. I turned to look at the handsome boy and reached down to find his fine cock standing.

"Let me suck your cock, to wet it," John said huskily, and with that he leaned before me and put his mouth to work on my nearly erect member. Meanwhile, Sir Henry continued to caress me, lingering on my nipples, which he pinched hard, sending painful little thrills down my spine. John was very proficient at his task. As he licked the shaft of my cock, and even took my balls in his mouth and sucked them hungrily. I reached out to caress his flaxen hair, which was silky to my touch, as his head bobbed up and down between my open thighs. I began to gently pump my hips to meet his mouth, but soon he stopped and rolled onto his belly, offering his tight pink hole up to me. I lightly teased the outer edges of his anus with my finger, and John groaned softly and writhed a little on the couch. I shoved my finger in his hole, and felt his muscles contract with pleasure. My cock was once again throbbing and ready for entry.

I mounted him from behind and prolonged my own pleasurable agony, and his, by teasing him. I rubbed my cock up and down between his ass cheeks, causing him to sigh and writhe more, rubbing his cock on the couch. When I felt that I could no longer stand it, I put the tip of my cock to his hole. And then, with all my might, I gave a shove forward and pressed in with all the strength in my hips.

This new sensation was inexplicably pleasurable. His asshole closed tightly around my cock, and the heat of his body and the snug fit of my organ caused me to begin to thrust as though I were acting mechanically. I had no other thought in my head at this point but that of satisfying my burning thirst for pleasure. As John moaned under my pounding cock, I clutched his narrow buttocks and forced my cock in till my hair was rubbing against the delicate flesh of his ass cheeks. I slowed my pace, and John lifted his ass to urge me on. I leaned forward and gave his balls a squeeze, and then I felt a fire burning in me from head to toe. Needles of anticipatory anxiety were pricking me all over, and I began fucking John mercilessly. I shot my burning load deep inside him, feeling as though I might combust then and there, perhaps burning John's internal organs with my molten spunk.

HUSTLING:
A GENTLEMAN'S GUIDE TO THE FINE ART OF HOMOSEXUAL PROSTITUTION

JOHN PRESTON

I discovered Park Square in Boston when I was fourteen. I would take the hour-long bus trip into the Greyhound terminal from my hometown. Family and friends thought I was visiting museums or going to lectures. Actually, I was hustling.

I had been something of a prodigy as a student. My parents, unsure what to do with an exceptional child, decided that they shouldn't stifle me or my mind. That specifically meant that they shouldn't censor what I read or wrote and that I shouldn't be subject to the same rules as other kids—at least, not any that might limit my academic and intellectual potential.

One result was that I was able to read some of the most exciting literature that was available. It was the end of the 1950s and the new writing that was coming out of Paris and New York was exciting precisely because it was so sexual. After years of Eisenhower repression, the country was finally beginning to talk about sex. There were a number of literary journals that were leading the way. A favorite cousin, a brilliant student at nearby

Boston College, was my guide in discovering some of this work.

One of my favorites was the magazine called *Evergreen Review*, which was published by Grove Press. One of the writers I discovered in its pages was John Rechy, the author of *The Sexual Outlaw*, chapters of which were printed in the *Review* as early as 1958. Rechy put out the first hints as to how I might go about being gay. There were young men who sold themselves in certain places, and there were men who would pay for it, he told me. The paying part wasn't nearly so exciting as the idea of doing it, and Rechy gave some specific pointers on how to find out where men met one another in any given city.

A major locus was the Greyhound bus station; in Boston, back then, it was on St. James Street in the Back Bay. That's where I went. I had a wonderful first experience with a salesman from Hartford, Connecticut. He gave me the courage to return, and he also gave me my first fee.

I was so inept that I really hadn't been doing anything right as I tried to find someone in Park Square. He probably picked me up only because he had a champagne glow, having just been to hear the Boston Pops, where he told me he had a bit more to drink than usual. He came right up to me on St. James and offered to take me to his room in the Statler (now the Park Plaza, very often the site of gay rights conferences and fund-raisers, a fact that has always amused me).

When we got to his room, he immediately started to undress. This was a business transaction to him, not a whole lot more. I was very hesitant, which soon annoyed him. I had only managed to take off my shoes and one sock when I finally told him I had never had sex before.

He thought I was trying to lead him on. I would later learn that lying about their sexual experience is a common ploy for street hustlers who use it to increase their fee. They market themselves as perpetual virgins, trying to extract a premium each time their miraculously renewed cherry is taken. Eventually I convinced my salesman that I was telling the truth. He was delighted. I didn't understand that gleam in his eye then, but now I know he was just ecstatic over the idea of plucking my adolescent purity.

He quickly got me undressed. He wasn't a dream man, but he had a decent body. His belly was a bit large, but it was solid. He had a very substantial cock. He was particularly impressed that I was uncut and, back then, had very little body hair. He proceeded to put our bodies into position for sixty-nine. I went over the edge when we had each other's cock in our mouths. I had only dreamed that it could feel so good. He then went on to fuck me, then have me fuck him. He rimmed me; I rimmed him. We had more orgasms than I could count. I tried to leave a couple times, but he always held me back. He wasn't finished yet!

I truly hadn't been looking to do anything more than have sex, but when we finally were done and I was dressed to leave, the salesman put a twenty-dollar bill in my pocket and sighed with great pleasure as he saw me out the door. I was amazed. Twenty dollars was a lot of money for a kid in 1958.

I went back to the Greyhound terminal often and walked around the neighborhood of the terminal long enough for a man to proposition me. Those men assumed that any adolescent they found in that area must be selling it. When the sucking and fucking were done and I had showered and dressed, I would always find money tastefully tucked into one of my pockets or artfully left on the hotel room bed by a departed "friend."

The money never became the reason I would go to Park Square. I kept on going back because it was the only way I knew to get sex. That's still true for many of the youths who hustle on the streets of major cities; they are not there for the cash, they are there because there are only a few other options for them sexually. I also spent countless weekends hitchhiking aimlessly over the back roads of New England. I would wait for a driver's hand to rest on my thigh, something that occurred so often that I knew it was a way many other young men were finding sex. Get on a road to nowhere and wait for a tarnished Prince Charming to come along and kiss you out of the slumber of repression; that was what many of us did back in the fifties.

In fact, I did so very well as a hustler in those early days in Boston that I nearly got into trouble with my ever-observant parents. I had much too much cash to be explained by my one part-time job. I had no pressing need for the money. I had no way to save it: Massachusetts didn't allow banks to open accounts for a minor. Besides, my obsession with hiding my homosexual activities from my family was much more pressing than any desire to accumulate savings.

So I devised a plan. As I was returning home from each trip into the city I would take any excess money and put it in a preaddressed stamped envelope and mail off the package. I calculate that I sent something over $2,000 in anonymous cash donations to the Museum of Fine Arts and other charities in those years of innocence.

Park Square and I got along very well for the years before I went on to college in Chicago. There, I also matriculated into cruising my peers in gay bars. Sex was still the goal, but it didn't need the cover of money anymore.

As I got older and more comfortable with sex, my days as a whore always made a very amusing conversation piece. But when I turned thirty and discovered myself living on unemployment in San Francisco after having quit my job as editor of The Advocate, the idea of fucking for money became a crucial issue. Could I do it? Could I live off it? What would it be like?

Of course I could do it. I had made a full-time living at it for two years. It wasn't all that bad. In a lot of ways, it was fun.

I had a guide for this new chapter in my mercenary life. I was walking down a street in San Francisco one day when a man drove by on a motorcycle. He was in full leather, even in the afternoon sun that was so warm I'd taken off my shirt. When I smiled at him, the motorcyclist made a U-turn and drove up onto the sidewalk where I was standing. I loved the overt moves he made. Of course I'd be interested in a ride on his bike, I told him, knowing full well that we were headed back to his house and an afternoon trick.

We drove back to the Castro, the neighborhood where it turned out we both lived, and went into his house. While we were clearly seducing one another, we also went through small talk. As I recall, the house was full of stained glass. Typical of gay men in San Francisco, so many of whom were into handicrafts, it was his hobby to make the stuff. The glass helped create a homey feeling to the house, not at all like the apartments of the younger men I knew who were more interested in au courant styles.

This man was at least forty. He was pleasant looking, and he wore his leather well, but he also had a belly on him. I was sexually intrigued, even though we both made it obvious that we were each interested in being on top. There was a definite role conflict present. I was still interested, though, especially when he told me that there was something I might want to know about him. What? That he was a hustler.

I was dumbfounded. To me, hustling was something that attractive young men did—in fact, men who were very attractive and very young. This guy was simply too old. Except for one thing: he was a leather top. He wasn't selling his body the way a younger man would, he explained; he was putting a charge on his expertise, not his appearance. He also told me it helped that he had a playroom, a dungeon where he had the props for sex that so many men were willing to pay for.

When I assured him that I wasn't turned off by his occupation, he offered me a demonstration. Why not? I was an adventurer in a city of adventure. He led me downstairs to the basement. It was a wonderfully decorated theatrical space, dominated by a rack in the center and with rough wooden walls on which he displayed a wide range of whips and other implements.

I stripped. He stretched me out carefully on his rack. It was an ingenious device. There were chains that ran from ceiling to floor at all four corners of the flat wooden bed, which was divided into three sections. After my wrists and ankles had been attached to the chains with manacles, my friend released the ends of the platform, which folded down. I was left attached to the chains with only my midsection still held up by the stand.

The music was perfect—Gregorian chants, as I recall. (I later found out that he was a defrocked minister, which helped to explain the love of ritual and the religious music.) The man was good at what he did. Nothing was violent; pain seemed to be only a punctuation point in the full body experience he gave me—hot wax mixing with sensual massage.

When we were done, he was disappointed when I declined a repeat performance the next day. He asked if I would at least be interested in working with him. It had been fun, but I assured him I wasn't slave material. If I was so adamant about my role that I wasn't willing to have a relationship as his bottom, maybe I wanted to be his sidekick. In return, he would show me the tricks of the trade; perhaps I would want to try all this myself. I decided to continue with the adventure.

The most important thing in being a leather hustler, he explained to me, was the costuming. On the first night that he had convinced one of his regular clients to hire both of us, I showed up in jeans and boots, chaps, and vest. My mentor was wearing all the same and a particularly vicious-looking motorcycle cap.

The client had been here before, so he knew where the entrance to the dungeon was. He knocked on the door at exactly the right time. My mentor let him in. There, standing in front of the client, was his fantasy: two leather tops, in full regalia, standing in the dungeon waiting for him to perform whatever duties they demanded. The customer was shivering with excitement and anticipation. He wasn't a bad-looking man. He was a bit pale, and he had an air about him of an office worker whose greatest thrill was creating a new filing system. But I admired him. After all, he had been willing to cross the line and enter into a world of sexual outlaws. That alone, I thought, indicated that he had something interesting in him.

In fact, I was turned on by his agitation. His eyes moved quickly over our costumed bodies and around the room with all its props. I could see how intrigued he was by the paddles and riding crops, how inspired he was becoming by the black leather hoods and restraints. The man had entered into his secret world, and it met his expectations. He was delirious to be here with us.

There was a carefully orchestrated dance that lead up to the client's being handcuffed and forced to his knees. I ended up fucking him while he sucked off the other top. When we were both done, and not before, we let him lie on the floor and lick our boots, one pair on either side of his face, while he jerked off. He was enraptured by the experience and paid our fee gladly.

For a while, I continued to work as an apprentice. I showed plenty of flair for what was possible and soon had clients asking to see me by myself. Within a month, I was set up in my own apartment, complete with leather and accouterments, a master for hire in San Francisco and later in New York.

When people discover that I, a mild-mannered WASP writer, used to hustle in California and Manhattan, their eyes light up and the lewd questions flow. I have come to realize that there are increasing numbers of men who aren't just asking for dirty stories they can enjoy vicariously: hustling has become something of a cottage industry in gay America, even in the age of AIDS—perhaps especially in an age of AIDS.

People are intrigued by the quick money, concerned about the dangers, seduced by the image. They want details. They want details because they are interested in the idea of hustling themselves.

Two other things happened to make me think more about my life as a hustler.

I was in Boston a number of years ago for a business meeting. I was dressed appropriately: suit, tie, polished shoes. I had some spare time, so I went to the Haymarket, a delightfully sleazy bar in the Combat Zone that, sadly, is no longer there. It was midafternoon, and I was looking for something to do for a while. I just wanted a relaxing drink, nothing more.

A very handsome young man came up to me. He was much younger than I, probably about twenty. He was friendly, outgoing, and clearly sexually interested. Now, there certainly are younger men who are mainly interested in older men, and I wasn't that much of an older man then. It could have been a regular pickup, or so my ego wanted to believe. But at a certain point my new friend made a coy announcement: he would certainly like to go home with me, but I had to understand that it would mean losing the income he would get from someone else, someone who would give him money. And he needed that income, he said apologetically.

Of course, it immediately became clear that I was the one from whom he wanted the cash. I was being hustled. I realized instantly that it only made sense. True, I was in my early thirties, hardly old enough to be unable to find my own tricks, but I was also dressed like a businessman and I was standing in a bar in downtown Boston which was not known for the high social caliber of its clientele. I was a mark. To this young man, I was an obvious trick. Why shouldn't he assume so?

I thought the whole thing was charming. I inquired into the fee that he would need—playing along with his game and phrasing it in more delicate terms. How much would he have earned if someone else were willing to pay him? He named a decent figure, and I accepted his proposal.

I discovered that I wanted the experience. I had been on the other side of this equation so often, I now had a chance to see what it would be like to change roles.

It actually was quite lovely. We went to the hotel room I already had. When we got there, he politely turned down my offers of room service. He was clearly a busy man and, while he was careful not to show too much desire to hurry, he wanted to be on his way.

I was faced with the immediate problem: what did I want? After all, here he was, a good-looking Irishman who was willing to give me just about anything I wanted, from the sound of it. I had negotiated untold numbers of sexual encounters with other men, but I found this situation awkward. The signals of regular tricking weren't here. In another—not monetary— situation, he and I would have already established a lot of what might happen with our banter during our cruising. But this was more straightforward. I was paying. I was going to call the shots.

I told him that I wanted to see him naked. He shrugged pleasantly and then undressed. I leaned back on the bed and watched, loving the luxury of having this show put on for me. When he was naked, he began brazenly to play with himself, complete with dirty talk that chronicled the adventures his dick had already had in the past couple of days, and the many other possibilities that it held out for me.

"No, don't bother," I said. I didn't want the whole performance. "Come to bed."

He also seemed awkward after I told him that I didn't want the verbal display. Having sex without the protection of verbal fantasies was obviously more difficult for him than playing a role would have been. He blushed, as though I had caught him in the middle of some naughty adolescent behavior, and then climbed on the mattress. We embraced, kissed, and I began to explore his bare skin. It was especially erotic to me to handle him that way—me totally dressed, him nude. It wasn't that he had a spectacular body; certainly there were men my own age who were better built, as they should have been, given the time they put into the gym. His youth carried him, though. I was just old enough to be able to appreciate the sweet touch of a younger man's body. There is a tautness to the skin that one can't really savor when it is part of one's own being. My own body was aging; not falling apart, simply maturing. Here was one that still had the spring of youth to it.

I was mesmerized by how hard his cock got and how long it stayed that way. It was a good-sized dick, one of those with a flared glans that make pornographers talk about mushroom heads. The skin on his shaft was almost shockingly white. His scrotum, though, was darker. It was a tight ball of wrinkled skin. He liked having his testicles played with, and I was happy to accommodate him by rolling them around in their soft purse.

I knew that he wasn't going to keep this muscle tone; he clearly wasn't doing anything to stay in shape. He was going to move toward fat, and in the near future, I thought. For that afternoon, though, I had paid my money, and I had access to his youth. I enjoyed it. I enjoyed it immensely.

Eventually I got undressed and we went about sex. It wasn't the most passionate I could imagine, and it wasn't the most professional that he might have delivered, but it was greatly enjoyable.

I was already concerned about safe sex and wasn't willing to fuck or be fucked. I was shocked when he made it obvious that he couldn't care less about safe sex. He was nervous about my health concerns.

I also wondered—I still think correctly—if I hadn't made him nervous by mentioning that I might write about our sex. Had I created too much performance anxiety?

After he left, I realized that hiring a hustler was a viable option for my future. I didn't feel waves crash on romantic rocks, nor did my earth move—but it had been exciting, interesting, and sexy to have employed another man for my pleasure. I became even more aware of the ads in the papers and magazines. Before, they had been reminders of my own past. Now they became options for my own future.

It was a bit later that I got a phone call from my friend Victoria McCarty, then the editor of *Penthouse Variations* and now also the editor of *Forum* magazine. She had a favor to ask. It seemed that a young man she knew had decided to try hustling. Victoria had been one of the people I had entertained with my accounts of my days as a prostitute. This young man didn't want the entertaining mythology, though, he wanted to know how to go about doing it; his interests were strictly nuts and bolts. Would I mind if she set up a conference call so he could ask his questions?

It sounded fine by me, and later that day I found myself talking to her friend, with Victoria, as always, enjoying her role as voyeur on the line. Since he had asked for advice, that's all I gave him. I went through every part of the sexual life that I could think of, explaining the ads, the tricks, the procedures. He asked some specific questions, and I answered them all as candidly as I could. The conversation took perhaps an hour, perhaps longer.

As soon as we were done and had hung up, the phone rang again. It was Victoria. "You must write this!" I wasn't even thinking clearly. Write what? "Everything you just told that boy. It has to be written!"

I laughed at first, but then thought she might just be right. I sat down at the typewriter and began to put down on paper all that I had told Victoria's friend. That original document became the central part of this book. There were many reasons why it didn't find its way to print—a conflict with a publisher, the appearance of AIDS on the scene, which made me wary of the subject for a while, and other priorities kept me from publishing it.

In the past few years, I have written so many self-revelatory autobiographical essays and books that I began asking myself why I didn't pursue this one book on prostitution more vigorously.

After all, I am now so exposed by my own writing that there is certainly no reason not to go into my experiences as a prostitute. I couldn't find a good reason not to return to this manuscript and resuscitate it with new data and new experiences. I know that other people's fascination with the topic hasn't decreased. I only have to look at the classified ads to know that there are many people out there who are working the phone and many more who are paying for it. A simple and clear-cut guide on how hustling works, what it's like, and how to do it seems to be appropriate now. If, after all, you are going to do something as important as sell your body, or buy someone else's for a period of time, then you should at least have access to expert advice on how to go about it.

A postscript: Victoria's friend did, in fact, go into the business. Later on, he sent me various notes and thank-you cards. I kept his address and a copy of his ad. I thought I should give him a final exam when I was in New York the next time. If one has sponsored apprentices, one does want to know how well they have learned their trade.

I called the number and made a date. Of course, he knew who I was. He actually offered me a free afternoon or evening, to thank me for my guidance. That wouldn't seem right, I decided. He was a professional, and I wanted to judge him on his own grounds. I insisted on paying the going rate.

I went to his house a few hours before I had to catch a plane home. I was exhausted after a long trip to the city with too many publishing lunches and too many late nights in the bars. I realized that while there had been suggestions of some very athletic sex, I really wasn't interested. I was horny, I did want to get off, but I just didn't want to do all that work.

After all, he was the hustler, I explained to him. What I wanted was him to be in his underwear and to give me the massage that he advertised in his ad. I wanted everything to be soft and slow and to take a long, long time.

He was more than willing. I stripped and sprawled on his bed. He got oil and began to rub me down. It was a finely wrought erotic experience. He was good at what he was doing; I was receptive to his skills.

I eventually turned over and exposed my hard cock. He slipped off his underpants then and knelt between my legs. He took both of our erections and rubbed them together with a healthy covering of lubricant. After all the foreplay of the languid massage, it didn't take long for both of us to come—especially not after he leaned over and began to suck on one of my nipples. When we were done, he cleaned me up. I dressed and paid him, and then went off to the airport, very relaxed and very happy. I had taught this one student well, I decided. It gave me a sense of great accomplishment.

MIND MASTER
Larry Townsend

During my final year of high school, a new awareness came upon me. I lived in a small midwestern suburb where sex in its varied modes was seldom discussed and never explained. The differences I experienced, therefore, were as strange to me as the Power I had once possessed. While my former playmates' attention and interest turned toward girls, I became more and more preoccupied with thoughts of the boys. I dated girls because it was the thing to do, and I behaved as my friends told me I was expected to behave. Yet it was the boys whom I desired.

Far more exciting to me than a petting session in the front seat of a car were the moments after gym when I showered with a group of classmates. I knew the size of every penis as well as I knew the faces of each and every boy in the class. I could have identified any of them by the one as easily as I could by the other. I knew the size, the shape, the length; whether a boy was circumcised or natural. And I knew if any boy displayed a greater "pride" on one day than he did on another. By all of this, I rediscovered a certain ascendancy, for my own precious gem was the most substantial of all. In fact, one fellow made a comment to the others which I overheard, and which started a most meaningful chain of events.

"Did you see that banana on Mickey?" he remarked from across the row of lockers. "Why, that stud's hung like a fuckin' horse!"

Though embarrassed, I laughed, because there were other boys around me. I was sure all of them had heard the exclamation. One boy in particular turned to grin at me, his gaze falling suddenly from my face and fastening in respectful awe on the evidence of my manhood. He looked away quickly, but between us was the beginning of a second realization.

This other fellow's name was Harold, and he was captain of the swimming team. He had a body like a heathen god, and his face should have graced a girl. But he was more than pretty; he was male! Second only to myself, he possessed a fullness of masculine potential unrivaled by any other classmate. Until this moment we had been casual friends, thought I suppose "mutually wary" might best have described our previous attitudes.

This particular day, however, we both became slow and awkward getting dressed, dawdling in the locker room until the other boys had gone. When we were finally alone, I was tying a shoelace for the third time and Harold was into the sixth or seventh minute of combing his long, golden hair before the mirror next to my locker.

"That guy was right," he mumbled without looking at me. "You do have a groovy piece of meat!"

Innocently, I looked up into the blue of his eyes from my posture of stooping to fasten the shoe. Whether at this moment a flicker of my former ability flashed between us or not, I have never been able to say for sure. Still, in that fleeting second when my gaze locked with his, I knew with total certainty what he desired. I think I blushed; I know Harold did, and within us both there swelled a warm rush of desire. It was a combination of youthful inexperience and equally juvenile inhibition that prevented either of us from expressing what he felt. The compulsion was strong enough, nevertheless, for us to leave the building together.

Because all varsity squads had gym during the final class period, we had completed our school day. (I was first-string left end on the football team that year.) Harold, I discovered, admired me as much for my robust physique and heavy-muscled body as I responded to his lithe, well-defined symmetry. Opposites attract, they say, and in Harold and me the old cliché had found its proof. Where he was blond and smooth of skin, I was dark with a heavy growth of hair beginning to sprout on my face and body. Harold's features were fine and delicate; mine were heavier, with a decidedly Latin cast. My eyes were dark, almost black, whereas his were a light blue, of Nordic type.

Together we walked through the deserted halls and grounds of the school, leaving campus by the rear gate, where students were permitted to park their cars. I had an old Dodge coupe, a relic of the thirties, and many years older than I. It was not quite ancient enough to be a classic, but I took as much pride in owning it as if it were, and I had expended on it the loving care of any teenager upon his most prized possession. Harold, who lived much closer to school than I, had no transportation of his own. With hardly a word exchanged between us, we got into my car and drove to my house.

My father, of course, was at work, and this was the afternoon when my mother played bridge. I hadn't been able to remember whether it was her turn to entertain "the girls" that week, and was deeply relieved to find our driveway empty. We entered the deserted house through the kitchen and went up the stairs to my room. Again, very little was said except for some polite remark by Harold regarding the well-tended appearance of my parents' home and my mother's obvious good taste in furnishing and antiques.

In my room, I sat on the edge of the double bed while Harold pretended an interest in my collection of memorabilia, carefully examining the various trophies and momentos I had collected over the years of my childhood. Watching him, I continued to be increasingly aware of the desire in my loins and equally conscious of the time. Precious moments were slipping by, and whatever was to happen between us must start soon, else my mother's return from her bridge game would prevent it altogether.

I knew—and again I suspect it was due to the creeping return of my Power—that Harold's wishes were the same as mine. He turned at last, looking at me with a bewildered yearning which I would have recognized even without my extra sense. He stood uncertainly in the middle of the room, his shoulders sagging slightly beneath the red letterman's jacket. His faded Levi's, worn low and beltless on his narrow hips, became like a coveted treasure chest to me. I watched the pulsing heartbeat beneath his T-shirt and seemed able to view the clearly-defined musculature of slender chest and belly through the opaque material.

With an unaccustomed though perfectly natural motion, I reached out for him. My fingers grasped the front of his waistband, and when I pulled gently at the cloth Harold stepped up to me, placing his legs on either side of mine. My chin grazed softly against his body as I turned my head to look up at his face. For several moments we remained motionless, our eyes engaged in a communication neither of us dared to voice. I felt his body tremble slightly as an answering tremor seized my own.

Slowly my hands slid onto Harold's hips, my fingertips resting against the hardness of his rounded buttocks. Without braking the bond of our mutual gaze, I was aware of the swelling in his crotch and a heated blush on the skin I couldn't see.

I leaned back on the bed, exerting a steady pull on my companion. He did not resist, and slowly, deliberately, his body descended on mine. My arms encircled his back and shoulders while Harold worked his hands beneath me. The caressing touch released the flood of our common desire. His face was only an inch or so from mine, and our eyes still stared deeply into each other's. Our lips came together and Harold's youthful sweetness flooded into me. His body pressed on mine and his erection ground fiercely against me through our clothes.

Our mouths parted for just a moment. I placed my hand against the back of his head, forcing his lips to mine again, and at the same moment encircled his thighs with one of my legs. Holding him strongly in my grasp, I rolled atop him. I turned my head a bit, allowing our open mouths to lock and our tongues to enter each other in a deep, penetrating kiss.

For both of us it was a new experience, though each of us would have at least claimed to have had sex with a girl. In fact, I had heard Harold boasting some days before, surrounded by a crowd of wide-eyed boys, about how he had seduced the prime beauty of his (co-ed) summer camp the previous year. How I recognized his virginity did not immediately occur to me, for the act of love was far too overwhelming. Only on later introspection did certain other factors seem important enough to merit my consideration.

Very quickly each of us shed his sweater, and our jeans were shoved off along with shoes, socks, and Jockey shorts. T-shirts went after that, pulled over our heads and tossed into a muddle on the floor. Devoid of all restricting fabrics, we pressed our eager young bodies firmly together. Each of us was rearing like a heated stallion, rubbing his cock against the other, reaching at the soap-scented flesh to hold the two shafts as one. I remember marveling at the massive girth they formed together, and how desperately we tried to impress each other with our total masculinity.

We rolled back and forth atop the bedspread, first one then the other taking the top position. The satin smoothness of Harold's skin inflamed me, while my own hairy body evoked a similar response in him. We kissed and fondled and explored, enthralled by the newness of touching the naked flesh of another boy. Wild though we were with the hunger of our craving, neither was sure exactly what to do. Both of us had heard what men did together, yet it had always been told in such a derogatory manner that we were each hesitant to make the first move.

It was the sheer wonder of the moment, I suppose, that finally overcame the rigid though poorly founded resistance. There was nothing nasty or evil in what we did; we both knew this. It was not at all like the filthy stories we had heard. Taking courage from this certainty, I finally pressed Harold's back against the bed. I sat astride his thighs, holding our bursting cocks together, while I stared down into the hypnotic blue depths of his eyes. His fingers stroked my heaving belly, tracing the ridges of flesh and sinew where ribs flattened out into hard abdominal muscle. He twisted bits of chest hair about his fingertips and squeezed my nipples gently.

Still holding our pricks fast with one hand, I began running the other across my companion's smooth, downy underbelly, up toward the hard little navel, following the deep channel that marked the central separation of his stomach ridges. I looked at his cock, where the loose foreskin had withdrawn and the wide pinkish head seemed to watch me with its single pulsing eye. I licked my lips, struggling for the courage to take that enticing flesh into my mouth, yet fearful of incurring his scorn.

Then, as if Harold had spoken to me, I knew he wanted me to do it. Through his mind raced an urgent appeal for me to absorb his shaft to the very base. Our eyes met again as I began easing myself downward across his legs. I held my own rigid mast in one hand and grasped Harold's with the other. When my balls hung between his knees, I lowered my body and bent forward to reach my prize. I held his cock straight upright from his body, forcing it against its will to receive me. The hardness of its upward thrust would have pulled it from my lips had I not descended fully on it, burying the softer flesh of the tip deep in my throat.

New at this, though fulfilling an oft-dreamed fantasy, I nearly gagged on the massive rod. But I wanted it so badly I refused to pause for more than a gulp of air before I descended with vigorous, renewed desire. I heard Harold nearly scream with ecstasy while his hips lurched up to meet my face and his shoulders pressed with all their force against the bed. I watched the glorious contours of his body writhe beneath me while I absorbed his length time and time again. His groans mounted in intensity until he finally grasped my head with both hands and forcefully pushed me away.

I could feel the craving within him now, and I knew exactly how close I had brought him to a climax. I also knew he wanted to reciprocate my act. Accordingly, I lay back against the bed, permitting my own erection to lay exposed for his attention. Looking across the hard expanse of my own body, I watched through the hedge of hair as Harold lifted my rigid penis, squeezing the base with his hands as he gingerly applied his lips to the tip. He licked at the fluid accumulated there and played his tongue inside the hole. I had no foreskin—oh, curse that barbaric rite!—but Harold ran his tongue about the cockhead and moistened the shaft halfway down before he drew back. His next thrust went deeper, until I could feel the spasms in his chest. Vainly, he tried to go down on my demanding cock as deeply as I had taken his.

Our youthful innocence was quickly fading before the rapid advance of our sensual awareness. I held onto Harold's head as he plunged and retreated along the column of my sex. He strained with gasping effort to reach the base, but he never fully succeeded. Tears streamed from his eyes and phlegm formed a heavy lubricating cover about my flesh. I could feel his hard rod slapping against my legs as he straddled one thigh, attempting to gain a purchase that continued to evade him.

In the end, I grabbed his shoulders and pulled him down on me. I rolled him onto his back and again assumed the seat of mastery astride his groin. Both our cocks were near the point of bursting, but as yet neither of us had achieved enough sophistication to receive a discharge of semen within our mouths. I worked our slippery masts together, one against the other, thrilling to the sensation of my balls sliding along Harold's cock. The tender undersides of both our shafts were already swollen with impending orgasm.

Within my loins I could feel the rapid buildup toward that final, sublime release. From Harold I received a similar impression of impatient yearning. I could have told this by his expression of mingled pleasure-pain and his tendency to hold his breath until his lungs demanded air, but I felt it more strongly than that, and I knew—even without the visual and auditory cues—he was racing along the path to ejaculation. I slid my hands more rapidly, causing the already-heated flesh to burn with fierce intensity. I looked at the dark redness of my own cock, in contrast with the pinkish tinge of Harold's shaft. Our hardness turned to rock, to steel, while I felt my balls draw up against my crotch, and a warmth of joy, so intense it hurt, began to flow between my legs.

A tremendous white eruption spewed forth across Harold's chest and belly. Watching as he released his flood of sperm, I gathered some of it in my hand and continued to jack us off with this new lubricating substance as my own seed boiled out on top of his. Huge, snowy globules spattered his golden flesh, and a puddle of our mixture lay in the hollow of his navel. Like the mingled blood that makes men brothers, our fluids joined on Harold's youthful body.

As I remained on top of him, milking the final drops from our still-rigid cocks, I received a flood of intense feeling from him. It was the type of impression I hadn't known since childhood, though before it had never contained such sensation. Dominating all the rest, I experienced a possessing love which in turn kindled a like response in me. My moving hand was evoking a gentle lust as our physical energies began to regain their strength. Then, as clearly as if he had spoken, I heard Harold ask me not to stop.

I dipped my fingers in the still-warm puddle, smearing the whiteness on our snuggling pricks. I felt myself grown softer for just a moment; then, I, too, began to swell toward a new thrill of discharge. Moments later the twin heads spouted forth again, adding girth to the pond that marked our joining.

In the moments following our second release, I began to realize what had happened to me. Miraculously, I was suddenly in total communication with Harold. What he thought, what he felt, his most intimate desires—all were as clear to me as if he had voiced them. I watched his face, wondering if my impressions were real or whether my imagination was the source of the turbulent wishes I perceived. I knew at once; it was more than this. The images were far too clear. Because the ability was not new to me, though something I had considered lost, I recognized it for what it was. My Power had returned.

Nor was it a mutual exchange. After I had watched Harold's face for several moments, wondering whether he could be receiving my impressions as well, he smiled. "What are you thinking?" he asked softly.

"You're a pretty neat guy," I replied.

"We made quite a mess, didn't we?" he laughed, looking down at his belly.

I glanced at him sharply again, for I knew this casual remark wasn't what he really wanted to say. He loved me, at least for that moment, but I knew he was afraid to speak. He was trying to hide a feeling he believed improper.

I stretched out on him, heedless of the sticky substance between us. I kissed him again, not only on the lips but on his throat and eyes as well. My singular knowledge caused a tender response within me, giving rise to emotions I couldn't ignore. I could feel Harold struggling inside himself, holding back words that wanted desperately to spring from his mouth. But society had worked its spell on him, and he was unable to express what he felt.

"I love you," I whispered in his ear.

The timeworn phrase was spoken before I realized I had said it. I think I surprised myself as much as him. I felt his body tense beneath me.

I pulled my head up a bit, so my face was suspended directly above him. "I love you," I repeated. "I think you're the greatest!"

At first he reacted with the tiniest indication of pain. His face wrinkled as some force within him continued to struggle against self-expression. Then his muscles relaxed as his brain released its restriction.

"I love you too," he muttered.

Tears began to flow again as his conditioned ideas of propriety continued their internal battle against his feelings. In the end he conquered them. He kissed me many times and clung so tightly to my body I found it difficult to breathe. The strength of his arms was amazing, and the intensity of his emotion—once he permitted the words to come—was overwhelming my senses until I could recognize only his tremendous waves of affection.

The sun had descended behind the houses across the street before we finally released each other. Quickly, we went into the bathroom and cleaned ourselves, each eager to wipe the other dry and to kiss whatever portion of his companion's body presented itself. Reluctantly, we returned to the bedroom and dressed. Our mouths were locked together for the final time when I heard the click of Mother's key in the front door.

She had won the prize at bridge that day; I knew it before she spoke. Later, my father's angry thoughts came to me before he had parked his car. It had been a difficult day for him at the office.

It rained the following morning. Torrents were gushing across the roof, thundering into drains and through them into the street when I left for school. The whole world seemed gray and drowned in the fury of cascading water.

I was glum as I started my old Dodge, for sometime during the night my Power had departed from me. The evening before, neither parent could deny my penetration, and their thoughts were etched as clearly before my eyes as if they composed a printed page. But that morning at breakfast, the bland faces of the two adults had presented the only clues to their thoughts. What they felt was hidden behind their eternal masks.

As I went out the door my mother called, "I want you home early this afternoon. It's Friday and I have a little surprise for you tonight!"

I could tell she was bursting with some silly secret, but not even a pattern of that intensity could penetrate my brain.

It must be something she's cooked up just now. I thought, *or I would have perceived it last evening.* Whatever it was, I would have to wait until after school to learn of it.

I went through my first two classes with the usual inattention. They were senior electives, and I had taken them because they were easy. They were also somewhat dull. My third class, however, was the only one I shared with Harold, other than last-period gym. In the hall outside the classroom I encountered several other friends and spoke desultorily with them.

Harold was already at his desk; I knew it, suddenly and without any doubt. He was waiting for me, anxiously watching the door, afraid I might not be in school that day. All of this I knew before I saw him. I was receiving his impressions!

Testing myself, I tried to penetrate the thoughts of the boys about me. I could not. Still, Harold's projections were as clear as they'd been the previous afternoon, and his mounting anxiety at my failure to appear was coming to me in waves of despair. I detached myself from the group of fellows and casually strode into the room. Immediately, I felt Harold's relief and pleasure. Smiling at him, I took my place—two rows over, behind him. Once seated, I tried to reconcile my own confusion.

Something was happening to me I couldn't understand, and the situation in which it was happening present a problem I couldn't take to anyone else for advice.

No one would understand it anyway, I told myself. *They'd think I'm some kind of nut! Whatever determines the fluctuation of my Power, it centers on Harold. Not only that; it must be based on...on emotion...on love?* My limited knowledge and understanding prevented a deeper interpretation. *Best to accept it*, I thought, *and not to worry about it*.

But I couldn't put it out of my mind. The teacher called the class to order and began the day's instruction. The course was solid geometry, another elective but one that counted toward college credit. It had always been a difficult subject for me, so I tried to concentrate on what was being taught. However, swelling surges of affection kept pummeling me, and mixed with them were visual depictions of Harold and myself, naked on my bed.

Through the eyes of my friend, I was seeing the projected image of my own cock, stiff and proud, descending toward his eagerly waiting lips. I saw myself astride a narrow waist, gripping two firm erections as they spurted their passion-fluid on a solid, rippling belly. Nor were all the perceptions a recapitulation of the past. I glanced at Harold, who was staring hard at the surface of his desk. I could see the grain in the wood and the partially sanded graffiti carved there by his unknown predecessors; but imposed on this, as if viewed through a gauzy film, I saw myself again.

This time we were in a forest glade with bright sunlight streaming against our naked skins. Some-where below us a stream bubbled pleasantly over moss-covered rocks. It was comfortably warm, without the searing, muggy heat our summers sometimes bring. The air was fresh and crisp, devoid of insects or other pests. Beneath our feet stretched a soft, close-cropped bed of grass. Harold must have pictured himself sitting on this, for I could see his lower abdomen, his legs and rigid cock—all as if I were viewing the scene from his eyes.

I stood before him, within the space surrounded by his legs. A film of moisture—sweat, perhaps— glinted on my flesh, tiny droplets gleaming like seed pearls among the hairs of my chest. I saw my upright cock from the underside, where its shadow formed a wide, dark band across my low-slung sac. I watched myself kneel between his knees, and I felt the pressure against the back of Harold's legs as I pushed them upward, turning his butt into range of my questing erection. I could feel the crush of coolness against his back as he pressed his body against the grassy ground. My cock descended toward him....

"Harold, either go to the board and solve that equation, or admit you don't know how!" snapped our teacher. She was a slender woman, fifty or so, with sharp features and an even sharper temper.

Her exasperated comment evoked a giggle from the class. Harold flushed with embarrassment, and his confusion tangled the threads of imagery I had been receiving. I felt his mind readjust to the problem Miss Lungley had written on the board, and the beginnings of its solution presented themselves. He slipped out of his desk and walked to the blackboard.

For the rest of the period we both concentrated on classwork, and though I continued to receive a series of thoughts and impressions, they were all to do with geometry. Only once, when he managed the courage to turn and look at me, did his previous pattern repeat itself. For that instant, Harold's thoughts were quite frankly sexual.

We each had one more class before lunch, so we went our separate ways with no more than a passing, "See you next period!"

Because it was still raining, we ate inside the auditorium. I saw Harold before I received any impressions from his mind, and it was not until he had seated himself beside me that I felt anything at all. Even then, it was weak compared with the blast of emotional projections I had experienced a couple of hours before. His feelings were the same, nonetheless, and while his immediate emotional state was diminished, his underlying desire was in no way decreased. I could not be certain of the cause; but here, too, my Power was fading.

We sat talking in generalities as we ate our sandwiches, afraid to say much else because of our close proximity to other students. I did feel the pressure of Harold's thigh against mine, however, and his guarded words assured me his craving had not lessened since Geometry.

We stood up reluctantly when the bell sounded, ending the lunch period. Being on different teams, we thought we might not see each other again until we showered after gym. I knew Harold wanted to repeat our experience of the previous day, and his wish was no greater than mine. We lingered in the hall to allow the others to go their ways.

"Will your folks be home after school?" I asked him.

He nodded. "Mom will be. How 'bout yours?"

"Same deal," I told him.

"There's always the car," he whispered, smiling.

I assented, and we parted like two conspirators. By then, I was receiving only vague impressions from his mind.

Later, in the car, it was a far different story. In fact, as soon as we had driven away from the school and were shielded from the view of passersby in a fresh downpour of rain, both arousal and mental images began concurrently. At that moment, of course, I was too preoccupied with sex to think about what was happening on my psychic plane.

Still, in retrospect, I think I achieved a glimmer of understanding. Obviously, in geometry class Harold had been physically excited by his thoughts. He told me he had sat there with a "raging hard-on" and had been afraid it would show when he had to stand up and go to the blackboard. In the auditorium at lunch he had been under better control. Thus, I reasoned, I received his thoughts most strongly when he was sexually stimulated. If this was true, the next logical deduction must be that, using sexual arousal as a channel for transmission, my Power would vary with both my state and my partner's state of desire. I already had concluded that I was in my most highly receptive condition during the height of sexual stimulation. How long afterward I would eventually be capable of sustaining my Power was something I could not yet judge. Experimentation in this area was to prove extremely rewarding—and most gratifying!

So at that time I did not know enough to predict the limits of my ability nor to establish rules for myself in using it. In the car with Harold, I did not care very much either way. I had discovered the new vibrancy of sex, and with this boy as my partner I was suddenly so happy nothing else made any difference to me.

That afternoon the rain provided well for us. I drove to the edge of town and parked overlooking the river. Few cars passed that way, and those that did were too intent on staying in their lane on the roadway to pay any attention to us.

The car windows were steamed from the cold mist outside and the heat of our bodies within. Fast-moving tracks of rain whipped down the glass, and we had to shout to be heard above the thundering clatter of water on the roof. At least, I had to shout; Harold's thoughts were coming to me so strongly I sometimes answered him before he uttered the words. My Power also allowed me to anticipate his physical desires. My goal that afternoon was to make him happy, and in this I was certainly successful!

Harold had taken my hand and slipped it inside his khakis while we were still driving. By the time we parked, he had stripped from the waist down and had unzipped my fly. His lips had possessed my penis and brought me to such a state of arousal it was difficult for me to drive the car. Once parked, both of us removed what clothing remained. Without heeding the possibility that we might be discovered, we began at once to enjoy one another's body.

I leaned back against the door, my feet reaching forward across the seat. Harold's golden body pressed between my thighs as his face traveled from my lips to my chest. With his tongue he pushed away the hair and with his teeth he nibbled gently on my nipples. Dominated by the impatience of youth, it was only a few heartbeats before his mouth ground down on my rigid cock.

As on the previous day, he struggled valiantly to absorb the entire shaft. He twisted his head and tried to force a greater penetration than his throat could take. There was determined frustration in the thoughts billowing from his mind, but the answer to his dilemma was there as well. Following the same fantasy I had perceived in geometry class, Harold was already considering another possible use for my unwieldy column.

I also wanted this ultimate expression of physical love, and the thought accelerated the surging of my own desire. Nothing else would satisfy the frantic craving—what I felt from Harold, what I felt myself. I complicated my partner's difficulties by such contemplation, for my penis responded by a further increase in mass. More from Harold's reaction than from my own, I knew my swollen member had burgeoned into a ponderous trunk, further constricting his windpipe.

I could feel Harold tiring; he wanted me to reciprocate his efforts. Immediately, I pulled his head from my groin, gently shoving his body back against the opposite side of the car. I swung my legs off the seat and leaned into the curve of his flesh. My forehead pressed against his trembling abdomen as my lips sought the flaring cockhead. Like an insect descending on a pollen-laden pistil, I fastened on his rigid protuberance and encompassed all of it with my mouth and throat. His accompanying groan of pleasure was echoed and emphasized by a warm flood of sensual delight. His thoughts of love and impending physical fulfillment engulfed me as his hands settled against the back of my head and neck.

Still raging within his pattern of desire was the wish I had detected earlier in the day. The space limitations of the car and the lack of proper lubricant made me doubtful, yet I couldn't ignore the urgent craving. I released his cock finally and strained to reach his balls. They lay heavily on the seat, two well-formed globes within their nearly hairless sac. I took them into my mouth, kissing them first, then fondling them with my lips. I sucked on the downy surface, drawing both testicles into my mouth and savoring the sweet essence of his sex.

Harold slid toward me, forcing his legs a bit further apart, inviting me by both gesture and will to descend lower on his body. From his crotch I could smell the scented soap he had used in the shower, mingled with the fragrant sexual odors of youthful manhood. I followed his demand and pressed my lips against his prostate, probing further with my tongue until I penetrated the pinkish tightness between his rounded cheeks. I moistened the opening until I felt it loosen, though I knew it would increase its grip the moment I withdrew my attentions.

I wanted the same thing as Harold, for the craving to press my cock deep into that hard, tight orifice was making me quake with expectation. Both of us were too eager to think of prolonging our pleasure; the sophistication to extend love's bliss comes only with greater experience than either of us possessed. I wanted to penetrate his anus...and I wanted to do it then!

I remembered suddenly that I had left a tube of hair cream in my glove compartment. That would solve the difficulty, I thought, and abruptly I drew away. My gaze met Harold's in an exchange of lust, mutual desire, and...love.

"Are you going to give it to me?" he whispered weakly.

I nodded. "Right now, baby."

I opened the glove compartment and found the tube. As I did this, I felt a surge of joy from Harold. He was uncertain, however, just what position would permit our act.

"Kneel on the seat," I told him, "facing it. Lean over the back, so I can get at it."

He obeyed immediately. "Going to do it dog-style," he mumbled.

"Man, you're going to think it's a full-grown stallion by the time I get through with you," I boasted.

He watched me over his shoulder as my trembling fingers unscrewed the cap. I gently rubbed the scented cream between his buttocks, pressing my thumb deep into his anus. I felt the muscles tighten and relax, fastening hard on the exploring digit. His cock was pressed against the worn upholstery and it throbbed in reaction to my ministrations. Without moving his body, he rested his jaw on the seat back, observing what I did, encouraging me in my preparations.

I took a final glob of cream into my palm and coated my bursting cock. Then I knelt behind him, my knees inside of his, my belly pressed against the back of his narrow waist. Because I was taller, the position suited us well, centering my cock in almost the exact location for its entry into the new world of sensation.

I placed the cockhead against his tender asshole, massaging both Harold and myself until the skin gleamed and both surfaces were so slippery they would offer no resistance. Gently, I placed my cock against him and thrust forward with steady, demanding pressure.

I felt the tip go in, while Harold groaned at the initial pain. His sphincter tightened in automatic protest. I made no effort to enter farther, simply allowing my cock to remain within the firmness of his grip. I laid my body against his back, encircling him with my arms and permitting the heated pressure of our flesh to reemphasize our mutual craving.

He trembled in successive spasms, but I felt his muscles relax. Gently then, a tiny bit forward and half that distance back, I pushed my cock firmly into his body. As I progressed, a tremendous swell of satisfaction flowed through me. When I knew Harold was prepared and willing, I completed my entry in a single, steady thrust. My shaft went in until I felt my pubic hairs pressing against his ass; his body rose slightly beneath me as if seeking a greater penetration.

"Stay still for a second," he gasped. "Oh! I wanted it, but I never knew how great..." He trailed off into a moan of total euphoria.

I gripped him firmly, my greasy hands rubbing the strongly scented cream against his chest while my fingers tightened about his pectorals. Feeling he was ready, I began to slide slowly in and out, creating a sensual completeness neither of us had ever known. We both were breathing hard, and our bodies shook with the delight of this new discovery.

Soon I was delivering a frantic, pounding rhythm. I shoved myself in to the very limit. The rushing, driving warmth of my loins merged with Harold's unrestricted delight. The glory of full possession seized us. There was no longer any hesitancy on our part as I rammed myself against him, thrilling to the impact of my testicles against his firm, rounded skin, the pressure of my belly on the rigid smoothness of his back.

I reached beneath him and grasped his trembling, swollen cock, working the loose skin back and forth across its tip, driving my companion to further heights of pleasure. Around our metal capsule rain still thundered in unrelenting fury, setting up a swift syncopation even more rapid than my own. Beneath us, the springs of my old car creaked and squealed in answer to my thrusts, while Harold panted and moaned with each delivered blow.

Our moment of orgasm was fast approaching, and both of us were eager to hasten its impending crescendo. My mind was full of my own and Harold's euphoria, so I had little interest in or awareness of what transpired beyond the steamed-up windows. But suddenly, another mind was there!

I halted my movements abruptly, and focused my concentration on the area behind the car. It was a sheriff's deputy in a black-and-white patrol car! He had pulled off the road behind us and was sitting in his vehicle, trying to decide whether he should step into the downpour to investigate or stay within the warmth of his dry cruiser, having convinced himself that the old car had been deserted.

Go away! I thought desperately. *Stay in that car and get the hell out of here!* So passionately did I want him to depart, I continued projecting this for several moments.

I could see what he saw then—his dashboard with its extra dials and gadgets. There was a white pad of paper in the center, with lists of stolen license plates. A microphone hung on a special hook, attached to a springy coil of rubber-covered wire. I could hear the heater turning and see the man's hands as they rested easily against the steering wheel. I saw his watch and his wedding band—all as clearly as he must have seen these things himself.

Get out of here, I begged in silent desperation. *The car's abandoned. Just forget about it!*

The sheriff's car remained another few seconds while the hands picked up the microphone and a voice called in to report no excessive rise in the river. The hands moved again, pulling the gear lever into first, and slowly the car purred itself back onto the highway where it disappeared in a cloud of steamy moisture.

"What's the matter?" Harold whispered.

"Nothing, baby," I assured him. I resumed my interrupted pounding, knowing that for the moment, at least, my Power was complete.

SINS OF THE CITIES
OF THE PLAIN
A n o n y m o u s

A few days ago George Brown, when a little under the influence of Bacchus, let me partially into another secret of his, which affords a partial clue to how so many unaccountable mysterious disappearances are always being mentioned in the papers.

"Do you know, Jack," he said, "what I do when things are a bit slack? I can always earn a pony (twenty-five pounds) if I take a boy of about eighteen to a certain house in Paris; in fact, they will give me an extra fiver for every year she is under that ago, so that a boy between seventeen and eighteen is worth forty pounds and all expenses paid, as they are in great demand for the rich visitors to Paris, especially for the Americans, who are nearly all sodomites. You heard of the case of General Ney, who shot himself the other day? Well, he was a regular customer to a certain Mme R. that I know, but they were too greedy, she and her ponce; always wanting money, and threatening the General to tell his wife and mother-in-law if he didn't shell out. So at last the poor fellow blew his brains out. If the boys turn out obstinate, they are outraged with brutal violence, and then disappear no one knows how, but I have nothing to do with that.

"A fortnight ago I went down Whitechapel way, and dropped on to such a nice, pretty boy. He was a shoeblack, and, although only about seventeen years of age, beautifully formed and well hung with fine light golden hair, blue eyes and cherry lips. I fell in love with him myself. Whilst he was blacking my boots I asked a lot of questions about what he earned and how he got along, and soon found that he lived in a refuge, where they kept nearly all he brought in every night to pay for his schooling and board, as he had no parents or relatives of any kind.

"Here was a chance for G.B., so I soon got him to promise to meet me near Moses' shop in Aldgate in the evening, and the result was I bought him a rig-out as a page. We had his ragged-school livery made up into a parcel and sent back to the refuge, and I took him off in triumph to my lodgings, a fresh place I engaged for that purpose that very afternoon. He was my page, and had a little bed made up in an anteroom next my own bedroom.

"I had four rooms *en suite* at three guineas a week in a nice street in Camden Town.

"Next day I bought him some more clothes, shirts, hose and underthings, and had him well bathed; in fact, he made a handsome little gentleman when dressed in mufti.

"He seemed delighted at the change in his prospects, and the jolly blow-out of good things at every meal; so in the evening, after supper, I asked him how he would like to go back to the Ragged School Refuge again, as I did not think I should keep him very long.

"You should have seen the tears come into his beautiful eyes, as he threw himself on his knees and begged I would keep him, that he would die for me, and do anything he could to please me.

"It was some time before I would appear at all moved by his

appeal; then I said: "Well, Tim, will you promise never, never, to let out any of my secrets or what games I may play with you? now swear it, sir, on the Bible!'

"So I made him take a fearful oath, which I felt sure had a great effect on him after his Sunday School teaching.

"'Bring me that small bottle of liqueur off the sideboard, Tim,' I said, as soon as he had taken the oath. I had a little of it in some water myself, and gave him some. You know, Jack, the stuff it is, and what an exciting effect it has upon everyone.

"'Now I want to examine your figure,' I said, 'because I won't keep a boy unless he is well formed everywhere; so just strip yourself, my lad.'

"I should not have thought he had so much sense of decency; but he blushed as scarlet as the most delicately bred youth could have done, and the sight perfectly delighted me, as it was a proof of his being a real virgin as yet.

"However, he did not hesitate, although the wavy blushes kept flushing across his pretty face as he threw aside his clothes, and presently stood quite naked before me, whilst the liqueur had such an effect that his fine little cock, quite six inches long, was as stiff as a ramrod, and evidently cause him considerable embarrassment.

"'Come to me, Tim. You look all right; but I must feel you all over, to see if you have any blemishes. How's this?' I exclaimed, touching his prick with my hand. 'Is it always sticking up like that? Put your hand into my trousers. You won't find me so. It's awfully rude, sir!'

"He was afraid of displeasing me, or I should never have got him to unbutton my trousers and put his hand on my prick; but he did, and pulled it out to view, as I ordered him to do. It was limp, but I knew his touch would have the magic effect very soon.

"'There, sir,' I said, 'why are you different to me? See if you can make me the same. Take the head in your mouth, and draw back the skin.'

"I could see he did not like it, but did it to please me. The touch of his warm lips and the soft pressure of his hand brought me up in a moment. It quite filled his small mouth; but I placed my hands on his head, and ordering him to suck it, and tickle it with his tongue, kept him to his task 'till the crisis came, and I almost choked the pretty fellow with my spending.

"'Ah, oh, delightful! It's heavenly, Tim. If you please me like that I'll never part with you, my dear boy!' I exclaimed, carried away by my feelings. 'Here; kiss me, my dear boy!' as I raised him on my lap, and glued my lips to his, sucking my own spendings out of his mouth. It was so awfully delicious, Jack!

"'Did that give you such pleasure, sir?' he asked in a kind of whisper.

"'Yes, Tim, my darling. I'll make you feel the same for yourself presently,' was my reply. 'You shall sleep with me, and we will now go to bed as soon as I am undressed. Take your clothes into your own room, and come back to me naked, just as you are.'

"We both got on to my bed in a state of beauty unadorned, and I sucked his little cock 'till I felt sure he must come soon, then, kneeling up on all fours, I ordered him to shove it into my bottom. He was too excited not to be ready to do anything I told him at once, and besides, there was no difficulty about his getting into me, as I could take a much bigger affair than his. Still, my fancy was awfully excited at the idea of having his virginity, and to think that his maiden spend with another man would be in my arse.

"The little fellow came quite naturally to the business, and fucked me so beautifully that I spent in his hands as they clasped 'round my body and held my prick as I had directed him to do. Then, presently, his shoves became more rapid and eager, and I felt his warm sperm shoot right up into me in a delicious jet of love juice, as he almost fainted on my back from the excess of emotion it caused him.

"'Oh! oh! what is it? How funny, how nice to fuel so!' he ejaculated, between laughing and sighing. 'Oh! I suppose that it's the same kind of pleasure that you felt when I sucked you.'

"'Now, Tim,' I replied, 'you know what it is like, you will let me do it to you. Isn't it beautiful?'

"He kissed me, and told me I might do anything I liked with him, he loved me so; only he feared my big affair could never be got into his small bottom, and I could see he was rather afraid of the attempt. But I soon reassured him, and got him to kneel up for me as I had done for him, then, anointing the delicious looking pink hole with some cold cream. I brought Mr. Pego to the charge. At first I could make no impression; but having got my finger in, and opened up the way a little, I succeeded in getting a slight lodgment, which made him scream with pain and apprehension, especially when I began to push on a little further.

"'Ah! oh! dear sir! Oh! oh! pray don't; you'll split me! Oh! oh!'

"Being afraid his cries would be heard, I reached a pocket handkerchief, and before he knew what I was about, had him effectually gagged.

"It was managed without losing my place, then with one hand putting a little more of the cold cream on the shaft of my prick, I gave a tremendous shove, and got a little further in. It must have been awfully painful, for he writhed and struggled to free himself from me, and went flat on the bed with a deep sigh, which would have been a scream but for the gag.

"The fact that I was inflicting awful pain only added to my lust, and regardless of consequences I pushed on 'till his virgin bottom had been completely ravished, and I could see little drops of blood ooze from him at every motion of my prick, which was also stained with blood and sperm.

"I had spent; but the idea was so exciting that I kept on 'till I had done it three times, and the tight aperture became quite easy, and I felt the gag might be removed with safety.

"From what I could see of his face he was both crying and laugh-

EVEN OUR FANTASIES

ing in an hysterical state, so I thought I had better stop for that night at least, and it was a long time before I could bring him 'round to perfect sensibility.

"I had him again the next night, but it was awfully painful to poor Tim; then I took him to Paris and sold him for a hundred pounds—he was so handsome I wouldn't take less."

THE MAD MAN
Samuel R. Delany

A bit after eight-thirty, the three of us got on the subway, rode down to Fourteenth Street, and walked down the empty cobbled streets toward the waterfront, by concrete porches under the meat warehouses' hook-hung awnings. At the Mineshaft's narrow doorway, we joined the GSA line—of about twenty-five, thirty guys—though it already went in and up the stairs to the second floor.

About five-to-nine, they let us start filing up.

The leather-capped cashier at the upstairs desk asked: "You're here for the GSA party?"

"Three of us," Pheldon said.

"All right." One after the other, as we shelled out, he stamped the back of my hand with a (waterproof?) marker. That made a slightly smeared, luminescent yellow-green star over the brown ligaments as my hand passed before a cold violet tube of black light, becoming invisible when I lifted it to look—a new wrinkle since last time. "So, if you want to go out for a little while, maybe visit another bar," the cashier explained to my frown, "you can come back in here and we know you've already paid. Right through there." He reached out to stamp the others.

Inside, men were lining up at the clothes check on the right side of the bar. One of the upstairs bartenders wore studded gauntlets and a metal-studded jockstrap like last time. The other was in lederhosen, with engineer boots and a black leather SS cap —though neither was the guy who'd given Tex and Horse the hard time, or who'd let me go down to look for my hosed-out shirt. Somehow ending up several guys ahead of us in line, Phel got rid of his coat and pants real fast and had already gone down. So behind Dave, I said, "You don't *have* to check your clothes. But I've been here once before, and I didn't. Take my advice and leave them up here. You'll be happier."

"I'm checkin' 'em! I'm checkin' 'em!" Dave hopped on one foot, corduroy pants around one ankle, plaid shirt already off one shoulder. Then he glanced up at me. "You're just gonna go down there completely *naked?*"

"Except my shoes," I said.

"Okay." Dave handed his clothes through the window. We put the elastic check tags around our wrists.

Besides his orange work boots and socks, though, Dave kept on a pair of brand-new-looking Fruit of the Loom briefs—which I'd gotten down once as far as his knees and twice as far as his ankles, back in The Cameo.

He turned to follow me into the narrow brick stairwell, a hand on either wall.

At the downstairs bar, though still generally subdued, there was more talk and laughter than last time. Once a big guy reached past me, leather vest swinging back from a pumped-up chest with a thick tit-ring through an outsized nipple. "Hey, there." I said, as he came back with a can of Schmidt's.

The big, bearded guy looked down, then grinned. "Oh, how you doin' there?"

"Back again," I said. "Seems I can't stay away."

"Know what you mean," Horse told me.

I introduced him to Dave (Pheldon was off somewhere in the back already)—and learned that Horse's *actual* name was Kelly. We talked some more—he was explaining something technical to me about sound patching, when suddenly he stopped and put his arm around my shoulder. With his other hand, he reached down and pressed low on his belly—tonight, besides his vest, he was wearing just a rented jockstrap and, like Phel, black engineer boots. "The pressure's kind of building up in there—in a minute, I'm gonna have to get off in the back and let some of this out." He took a breath. "You and me, last time we were here, we had a good time together, didn't we?"

"Yeah," I said. "We did—"

"The thing is," he looked down, then up, "the way I like to work it is not to do any serious messing around with the same guy—or guys—two Wet Nights in a row. You know what I mean? I like to spread it around, use different guys each time."

"Oh," I said, "yeah. Sure."

"It's just one of my rules. Tonight. For this place."

I nodded.

"Look," he said. "Three, maybe five months from now—we'll run into each other here. Then we'll get it on again. But that's just how I like to do it, you understand?"

"Sure," I repeated. "Yeah, I can dig that." I was a little surprised—and though I wasn't really thinking about any marathon piss-drinking session yet myself, I confess, I was a little disappointed.

He gave me another grin and a heavy pat on the shoulder. Then he took up his beer can and walked away from the bar. I turned back to Dave, who was on his second beer. "Come on," I said. "Let me take you back into the tub room and show you around."

"Okay." He picked up his beer and we moved away, through one of the brick arches, into a hall that led to the dim rooms in the back. A couple of times we started to make out again—doing pretty ordinary things to each other, while the sound of trickling water or —occasionally—a smack on someone's buttocks resonated around us. Once we found ourselves in a tight little circle with three other guys, playing with ourselves, now reaching out to feel each other up. Then one, another, and another—including Dave, cock out the leg of his drawers, and me—began to urinate. Warm, messy, fun — still, it was on the tame side. But Dave's briefs got soaked to near-transparency. And he kept grinning over at me as though the whole thing were pretty wiggy, so I guess it was a good introduction.

I left him at one of the tubs, watching some guy still in a business suit take it from the guys clustering around him, both clothed and naked: seven, eight, ten streams soaked his pin-striped lapels, his Gucci tie, poured into the open fly of his natty slacks.

"I'm going to move around a little," I whispered. "I'll see you in a bit."

Dave nodded in the half-dark. "Yeah. Okay...." and I drifted away.

Fifteen minutes later, I was back at the downstairs bar for a refill on beer. Thirty seconds later, with a (wet, rough) hand on my shoulder, Dave joined me. "Man, this is pretty fuckin' wild! He finished one can, put it down, leaned over, pulled one back from the four the bartender set out, and upended it for a long swallow. "I seen some stuff here tonight like I never seen before in my whole fuckin' life! There was one corner, where they had this leather...thing. Like a big swing. On chains. And one guy was in it, on his back, with his legs up in the air; and another guy had his whole goddamned *hand* up the guy's ass! I mean, to here...!" And, with one hand coming down halfway up his forearm, Dave demonstrated the depth. "That's fuckin' unbelievable! The guy with his fist up the other guy's ass was black, too. The guy takin' it was white." Dave shook his head. "That was fuckin' something. I don't know if I'm ready for that, yet." He took another drink of beer. "But it sure was somethin' to see!" He put the beer back on the aluminum counter. "I counted about nine colored guys here—not counting Puerto Ricans." Dave, wouldn't you know, had counted. "They ever have *more* black guys than this here?"

"I haven't been here that often." I shrugged. "So I couldn't tell you—but somehow I doubt it, though."

"You're all pretty nice-lookin'," Dave said. "It ain't sayin' nothin' bad about you, but I'd give almost any one of 'em I've seen here tonight a tumble—"

I ruffled his hair. "You'd tumble with any nigger who looked at you, wouldn't you, white boy?"

He grinned at me like a redheaded puppy.

At which point, having gotten rid of all his clothes, Pheldon stepped up and said, "So, how do you like being someplace where, any moment, someone may just walk up and"—letting go, he turned left, then right, to blitz the bellies, thighs, or buttocks of me, Dave—and everyone within four feet—"piss all over you!"

I laughed, as did the guys on either side of us. But Dave leaped back as though he'd stepped on a tack, bumping into one guy, making another spill half a can of beer, foaming down his hand to the puddled concrete. After saying "I'm sorry" a lot, "Oh, gee, fella, I'm sorry," Dave stepped back up, grinning and embarrassed. "Man, I don't know. I don't know..." he kept saying. "I don't know about this. I know I'm gonna come back here. Yeah, I know that. But I don't know...I mean, if I'm really ready for all this. But it's real interesting."

Cannonball-shouldered, mahogany-hipped Pheldon grabbed Dave by the back of the head and pulled him up close—beer splashed on them both. "Didn't I hear you say something about wanting a nigger to piss all *over* you, white boy?"

"Oh, Jesus...!" Dave grinned with idiot pleasure. "*Jesus*, man!"

Later, moving through the back rooms, in a blue-lit corner I came on Phel and Dave getting it on together. As I stopped to watch, Phel bent Dave's head back, deep-kissing him. Dave had his eyes closed, but Phel was blinking, eyes like ivory lozenges under the blue light.

And he saw me.

Now he began to push Dave down, as thought he wanted him to go down on his dick. "Shit," Phel said, breathing hard and hoarsely. "I think I'm gonna *piss* on this honky motherfucker! That'd really make me feel good." He turned back and beckoned to me. "Hey, bro'—come on over here, and piss in this white motherfucker's face with me."

I'd actually been carrying a pretty full bladder toward the tubs in the back, to see if anyone was in there who needed spritzing. But now I stepped up beside Phel, who put his arm around my shoulder.

Phel let go his stream.

Piss hit Dave on the cheek—he was sitting against the wall now. He shook his head once, but didn't try to get out of Phel's way. Dave reached for my cock—his rough carpenter's grip felt good and familiar. I let go—not as strongly as I might have, because just his hand had gotten me half-hard. But it arched out and struck his shoulder, to run down his chest. With his other hand, Dave began to rub the sheeting urine around.

"Go ahead, nigger," Phel repeated. "Piss on that white motherfucker! Look at him—that white boy *loves* nigger piss! Don't you, honky?"

Blinking up at us, Dave nodded. His mouth was open. Some of mine, then some of Phel's, got into it. When it did, Dave swallowed. But he wasn't into drinking it all, the way I'd been. He rubbed it over his chest, over his face, down his belly. One hand went under his briefs and he pulled out his cock. Balls slipping over the sopping rope his briefs had rolled into, he began jerking off.

Then a voice, real deep, said, "You pissin' in the sonofabitch's face, nigger? Just a second, here—lemme throw some juice at the white motherfucker, too!"

I looked up. It was the tall, 250-, 280-pound black with the glasses, whom I'd last seen, last month, urinating in the white guy's mouth when I'd first come into the Real Men's Room. His baseball cap was again on backward. He wedged up on the other side of Phel—he still had a beer can in one hand—and let go. In three waves of his cock, he wet Dave down from the bridge of his nose to his nuts.

Dave put his head back against the brick and beat his cock harder, looking up at one of us and, then the other.

Phel ran out first.

Still beating, Dave lurched forward on his knees and took Phel's dick in his mouth. His wet hand held my thigh. He came off Phel to go to the new man, who was still pissing—he gave the guy's thick, spurting dick three sucks, then he coughed or something. Urine erupted from Dave's mouth; it ran out his nose, too.

Again Dave fell back against the wall, wiping at his face with one hand, still beating his meat with the other.

In a voice deep as Darth Vader's and as country as Stepin Fetchit's, the new man intoned, "Suck that big black dick, white boy! You got three pieces of prime nigger meat here—don't you let it go to waste now!" And Dave lurched forward, now getting the new guy again for half a dozen sucks.

"Hey, there, little guy," I told said, "you're doin' real good there. Keep it up!"

Increasing his speed, now Dave moved on to Pheldon (the only one of us who, with his ten-and-a-half downcurved, uncut, graphite-blue inches, anyone could say had a *really* big black dick), to give him another dozen sucks.

Finally, he was back on my eight-inch, cut, mahogany prong. Inside his warm mouth, I felt my growing hard-on stop my stream.

The feeling it gave me was funny: suddenly I was overcome by a sense of just how happy the little white cocksucker was, with three black guys pissing all over him, with my black dick down his throat and two more prodding at his mouth.

I felt myself start to cum.

Because it's unusual for me to get off like that, though, and because I'd already cum with him once, I thought it was going to be one of those half-orgasms that starts but doesn't go all the way. I readied myself for it to peter out at the halfway point—like a sneeze that doesn't happen.

Pheldon was still holding me. Around beside Dave, the other man had wedged his leg against him and reached down to take Dave's pale shoulder in his dark, thick hand; his piss was still running, breaking over his own heavy fingers, dribbling down Dave's chest, getting all on my leg, too, where a wet Dave was hugging my thigh—warm and kind of electric.

Suddenly, instead of fading, my orgasm moved to new level—it *wasn't* going to stop! It kept on blooming! Then I kind of exploded inside Dave's throat. "Goddamn...!" I reached down and clutched his head.

He was still beating down there. His face was caught between my groin and Pheldon's. His free hand was groping for the other man's cock now.

Dave began to grunt.

Pheldon said, a little incredulous: "You *came*...?"

I nodded, taking a deep breath.

"God *damn*...!" Pheldon said, with both appreciation and envy.

Phel strengthened his grip around my waist. With his free hand, he hefted up his shift and began to pump. His fist was up against Dave's face, and he hit Dave's ear half a dozen times, so that I could see Dave's head jerk, and feel it through his mouth on my softening dick, till it slipped free.

Maybe it was just a theatrical gesture for Pheldon, but Dave raised his face; his tongue came out his mouth, blobbed with my cream; cum ran down the side of his chin onto his beard. With his eyes closed, Dave strained his tongue out and down to get the spilled jism back in.

"Look at that honky suck scum!" the big guy said. "Go on, Jim, make yourself feel good! Cum in his fuckin' honky face…!"

I reached over to hold Pheldon's balls; Dave's free hand was already there.

Leaning forward now, one hand on the brick, Pheldon shot. Some got in Dave's mouth; some splattered his cheek. Now Dave took about three-quarters of Pheldon's dick while Phel's dark fingers pumped the base, beating Dave's mouth.

Pheldon whispered, "Jesus H. *Christ…!*" and, using the wall, pushed himself upright again.

Dave collapsed away from all three of us.

His fist at his groin was pumping too fast to see. Leaning on brick, Dave's face strained up—with his bad teeth in the center of a grimace that was either pure pain or pure something else…. His grunts became a gasp.

Dave shot—up over his belly, spilling down his fist. Gasping, he moved his other hand from Phel's stomach to mine—then back to the third man's. He had finally finished urinating.

The big guy said, "Guess your white boy's all right down there, now." He gave Phel and me a grin, patted Dave's shoulder. "That was real nice there, honky." He stood up, and reached an open palm across to me.

Still breathing hard and kind of out of it, Pheldon just looked.

But I gave him (a very low) high five.

"Yeah…!" The big man said, and took another swallow of beer. "Ain't nothin' like peein' on a white boy, is there?" Nodding to us, he turned—"It just makes *everybody* feel good, don't it? Okay, fellas, so long—" and lumbered out of the light.

From the floor, Dave said, "Jesus!"

"Need a hand up there?" Phel reached down to lift Dave. "That's a cryin' shame, boy. I thought I was gonna get that load out of you. And there it is all over your belly."

"Yeah," Dave said.

I gave him a hand, too.

"What am I gonna do with this shit, now? I mean it's a shame to waste it."

"Isn't much you can do with it now," I said.

Still hanging on me, Dave said, "Usually I eat mine—when I beat off by myself. When I'm alone, I mean. I started that when I was a kid."

"Huh? Really?" Phel asked. "Well, knock yourself out. It won't be the strangest thing I've ever seen."

"You don't mind?" Dave asked.

I just laughed and, still supporting him, shook my head.

Hanging on me with one arm, Dave brought his other hand to his mouth and took a big lick across the back. Then he turned his hand over and ran the little finger, then his forefinger, into his mouth.

Letting my speech get a little blacker than it usually was, I said, "Cum and nigger piss—that should be a real treat for you, honky."

"Yeah." Dave grinned at me. "It is. Want some?"

"Why not?" I said. Dave held his hand up to my face, and I licked the mucus off his palm—surprised again at how hard carpentering had made it. "Good stuff."

"Oh, man," Pheldon said. He'd stepped away from Dave now. "Will you two fuckers cut it out? Let's go get a beer, huh?"

So we came out the arch and went back to the aluminum counter. (Pheldon never did arrive, though. Some guy in a leather harness got into that black dick of his while he was passing by; so he looked at us, smiled, shrugged, and we left him in the hallway.) At the bar, hopping now on one orange construction shoe, now on the other (both darkened with urine), Dave finally tugged off his briefs. "My socks are fuckin' scrungy, man!" He shook his head.

"So are everybody's, pretty much," I said.

Dave still had Pheldon's cum all over the left side of his face. But I didn't say anything. While he swigged at another beer, it made him look even cuter.

As usual, they closed the downstairs at midnight.

Upstairs, after he got back into his corduroys and shirt, and, when the bartender said something ("What's that on your cheek, guy?" "Oh, shit, man—this? Oh, Jesus—lemme get a napkin here. Oh, *shit*, you mean I been walkin' around with *cum* on my face all night? Oh, *man*...!"), wiped off his cheek and beard with a square bar napkin, Dave stayed through one more beer.

"But I got to go to work tomorrow," he told us. "And that's after I get back up to Port Authority and catch a late bus out to New Jersey!"

I gave Dave my number. Enthusiastically, he gave me his.

Pheldon, I noticed, abstained from this ritual.

"Now, my mom's name is Pat Collins," Dave explained. "In Elizabeth, New Jersey. So even if you lose it, you can still get me through Information." On his way out, he flung the wet wad of his briefs down into the green oil drum standing in the corner, with the ruffled collar of a plastic garbage bag flowering its rim. "I sure as hell ain't never gonna wear *those* things again!" Then, with a grin and a head shake, he went out the door for the stairs.

"Damn," Pheldon said. "If I was as much into black piss as that boy is, *I'd* have taken 'em back to Jersey with me as a souvenir."

"He probably would have if they were yours," I said. "Or mine."

"Well, yeah," Pheldon said. "There's that." And, still naked, Pheldon turned to move away, like a broad-shouldered black scarecrow, toward the bar's darker half.

Again, I stayed till closing.

Got into a couple of pretty wild scenes up there, too—this time, all within the rules. One—no kidding—involved the big black guy with the voice (I got his actual load) *and* Horse Bladder Kelly, who, by the night's end, was too drunk or too desperate to remember me, or his own rules, or something. Anyway, I had even more fun that time than I did the first. And, by the end of it, I was feeling just as good as before.

When the upstairs bartenders starting calling, "All in," I ferreted Pheldon out of the shadows, and (in all my clothes this time) rode uptown with him on the bus.

(The only problem, as Dave had said, was wet shoes and socks.)

We got off at Seventy-ninth Street and, as Thursday broke indigo and copper over the trees away toward Central Park, we went into a coffee shop just opening up and had ourselves an immense breakfast of pancakes, eggs, sausage, juice, and coffee.

On the other side of the booth's seafoam blue Formica table, back in his motorcycle jacket, Pheldon leaned toward me. "I think our friendship, John, has entered a new phase. And I would really be upset if this changed anything—I mean, because of it."

I frowned. "Oh, come on, Phel," I said. "I've seen your big black dick before tonight."

"But—before—*only* in photographs…of that orgy I had at my place last Christmas. To which you were *not* invited. And this is certainly the first time you've ever seen me dump my load all over some hungry dinge-queen's mug! I'd feel just awful, though, if the next time we went to brunch, there were these long and awkward silences because your mind was elsewhere and the ordinary demands of civility and gossip had suddenly become too great a strain."

I grinned. "Don't worry, Phel. That's not me."

"I hope it isn't," he said, sitting back and lifting a triangle of toast to take a very large bite. "Although most of my affections go toward the Daves of this world—as I have never made a secret of, at least from you—the fact is, John, I don't *have* a lot of black, gay men friends. You mean a lot to me."

"He was cute as a button," I said. "I kind of got off, sharing him with you. And *he* sure liked it."

"You did?" Pheldon asked, surprised. "You know, we really *are* friends, aren't we?"

"Even if we never get undressed in each other's presence again. Feel better now?"

Under his leather cap, Phel cocked his head. "You're a sweetheart!"

I laughed and held up my cup for the squat Greek waiter passing by to pour me more decaf.

Phel said he was going into the newspaper library early—

"Like *that*?"

"Nobody'll be there when I get in. Besides, after six years I've about got them trained—and I have a change of clothes at work, anyway."

—and he would stay till around noon, then come home early and take a nap.

I made halfhearted noises about going in today myself.

Good as I was feeling, though, when I got home I called in to work and told them I'd be out that day. With temp work, you can do that a little easier than at a regular job.

I'd been waiting for Dave to call. But now I decided, what the hell—I'd call him. (I'd always assumed that was the prerogative of the younger guy—and I was a couple of years down on him.) After work one evening, I phoned the number he'd given me—to find, after four or five tries, it wasn't even a New Jersey exchange.

I was a little surprised at that.

So then I called Information like he'd said.

There was no Pat Collins in Elizabeth, New Jersey.

Now people are always giving out phony numbers and phony names in sexual situations—a couple of times I've done it myself. But I hadn't been badgering him for his. I'd just given him mine and he'd volunteered his own back.

A couple more calls to the New Jersey operator, and I found out that there were only three Pat Collinses in the entire area code—none even close to Elizabeth.

One turned out to be an older guy.

One was a woman who'd never heard of Dave and didn't sound old enough to be mother of anyone older than three.

And the last one was no longer in service.

If I had to characterize Dave with only, say, three words, I would say good-hearted, affectionate, and naïve. But it was disappointing to find that the naïveté extended to his feeling that, just as a matter of course, he had to give out phony names and addresses to everyone he met.

"Well," said Pheldon, "I kind of had a feeling about the guy. That's why I didn't offer him mine—although I certainly had the urge."

"You mean you picked up on the kind of guy he was?"

"I had a feeling," Phel repeated.

Me? Talk about naïve.

But, as I figured when I thought about it later (and, when we got to talk about it later, Pheldon agreed), the guy was probably scared.

An alcoholic working-class white guy from New Jersey, who, at twenty-nine or so, realizes he's turning gay, that he likes to make it with black guys, and that he wants them to piss all over him, well—especially if he's also basically a nice, affectionate guy—in this country that guy has a lot to be scared of!

And I don't mean big, obliging niggers, either.

Sam, I've been writing this letter, as you might imagine, over a number of days now. Rereading it tonight, I've been wondering if there isn't, finally, something wrong with my portraits so far—of me, of the men I have sex with, of those I see having sex around me. It's not that any particular detail within them is untrue. (You have no idea how I've tried to discipline my account here and keep it strictly to the observed!) Rather, as the incidents from which such portraits are constructed pass in life, they occur in a context that, because I have, yes, omitted it, I feel falsifies them. The point is that, in these depressed sections of the city I've been describing, there is life. (And very much the life I recount.) But it functions under incomparable silences, in streets full of strangers, snarled in a net of degradation that, to specify with some rhetorical color (the old men in baggy suits with their adjustable aluminum canes still bearing the blue sticker, "Property of Bellevue Hospital," or the anorexic six-foot drag queen in shorts and bandanna, standing on the movie-house steps, giggling over a peach in her hand and hiccuping, "Oh, mah' Lord, this is a peach! Isn't this a peach? I could hit somebody with this peach and do damage!") is to distort it by the very gesture that takes the oppressively general and represents it as the humanized specific.

Just to take the few blocks on and off Eighth Avenue that cradle within them the Grotto, the Agape, the Hesperus, the Cameo, the Fiesta, and the Pit:

In those doorways, bars, porn-magazine and peep-show shops, the movie theaters where sight itself is so dimmed, in such theatrical darkness true vision is simply and largely absent. In one sense all the encounters that occur here take place on some vast and dreary Audenesque plain where a thousand people mill, where no one knows anyone else, and there is nowhere to sit down. Someone new coming here might never see some of the encounters I've described: there is such effort to hide them. Any exchange resembling real conversation takes place quietly and ceases when a stranger walks by.

The bourgeois visitor always goes home with reports of this area's violence, but that is to repress all mention and memory of what is truly terrifying here: the vast stasis, the immense periods of time—hours, days, weeks—when *nothing* happens, when psychic immobility reigns in the lives of those stalled here at an intensity people at jobs, people in families just cannot conceive of.

It's meaningful that, with the Strip below it, Hell's Kitchen a block to the west, the theater district just to the east, and midtown Manhattan right above it, this particular area has no name of its own—certainly no name that I, Pheldon, Mark, La Veuve, or any of the other people who, monetarily or emotionally, live in or off it all share and can use to speak about it in common. (Outsiders tend to call it by any of the names above—"Theater District," "Hell's Kitchen," "the Strip"—depending from which area they approach it, always feeling, as they pass into it and out of it, that something is nominally wrong—even as the city fathers from time to time write in the papers about tearing it down or destroying it.) When I made this point to him, Phel suggested, "What about calling it the Midtown Mausoleum and Take-out Service...?" But when it finally does develop some geographical sobriquet with which the tourists who stroll out of the Milford Plaza or straggle over from the theater to catch the uptown bus on Eighth Avenue can think about it fondly or fearfully in private, then it will no longer be the same place.

Talking about it with us one day at the Fiesta just before planting an upside down tumbler on the bar before us both (i.e., buying both Phel and me a drink on the house), La Veuve told us, "You know, you're right. Now I remember, about eight or nine years ago, a bunch of the regulars at the bars here started calling it the Minnesota Strip—because that summer four or five farm boys turned up hustling at the Pit who started out in—or at least came by way of—Minnesota. But that name only lasted a season. You're right—it doesn't really *have* a name. Or, at least, it doesn't seem to be able to keep one when it gets one."

Let me try, then, Sam, for a more generalized collection of—well, snapshots, instead of portraits. Let me move from the narrative totality I've been so far seeking to another, more abstract narrative level that might, finally, be more revealing.

Whether angry, fearful, or content (and there are those), the women who come here are insistently passive in a way that should be deeply studied by feminist analysts. (This immobility was, for example, the real object of a group such as "Women Against Pornography." And this area is precisely where they had their "shows" and organized their "tours," even as they were unable to grasp and grapple with the pornographic figure—because their true object was the ground that informed it—until they finally wandered away in muddled paranoia to persecute other feminists with better analytical tools than they.) When these knots are truly untied and teased apart for serious view, then real understanding of the psychosocial calamity in which we live may finally begin.

Outside the residence hotels (where the alcoholics and the drug addicts and the crippled and the mad and, yes, the merely poor and confused try to hide with dignity, sometimes succeeding heroically, sometimes failing at a degree of pathos unimaginable to someone who does not pass the momentarily open door of some twelfth-floor room, packed with newspapers and trash, floor to ceiling, in which a seventy-year-old woman lives), when we speak of women, we are seldom speaking about more than 10 percent of any visible group. That means, of course, that in *some* places, like the Times Square Motor Hotel, in its elevators, in its halls, in its high-ceilinged and gilt-molded lobby, in the hive of rooms above, when we speak of women we are speaking about 85 percent or more of the population!

In her forties and living at the Times Square for (I overheard her say) the last three years, Dodie looks more like sixty. Her pale face seems as if it has been smashed up and put back together hastily, a little makeup applied hurriedly to hide—ineffectually—the damages. Chain-smoking, in a small black hat, she sat all last night at the bar in Smith's, on the other side of the partition from the hot-plate counter, sipping gin and tonic, the only woman in a bar full of workmen, or men who would like to be through working, discussing her alcoholism with insight and intelligence, dispensing sympathy to every masculine problem presented her. One could wonder why I say such a woman seems "passive." She could as easily be called a gutsy, ballsy woman. She disagrees, she argues, she laughs loudly, she has strong opinions. Her sympathy? Isn't it simply the compassion of a middle-aged woman who's lived a hard life? But listen: she is sympathetic to every idea that is presented. All her considerable ire and hostility is reserved for whatever or whoever is absent. Were Governor Long sitting on one side of her and Reverend King on the other, she would be equally supportive of both (solely because both were male and there)—and equally and articulately against what each of them disapproved of (because it was not there).

It is not that her sympathy—or her antipathy—is false.

Or even hypocritical.

It is that neither, in their particular deployment of presence and absence, is finally sufficient. To deal with this world, certain things and ideas that are present must be said no to. Certain things that are absent must be hailed and hauled into play. And that is what it is almost impossible to imagine ballsy, gutsy Dodie ever doing.

In The Cameo, the hefty brown Puerto Rican woman arrives with her equally hefty brown boyfriend of five years. She's forty. He's thirty-three. They come to the theater so that he can get turned on so that later they can return to her furnished room on Forty-seventh Street, between Ninth and Tenth avenues and he can get it up; again, the same passivity. Yes, there are both white and black and young and middle-aged versions of this same couple, who, from time to time, come to the Cameo, the Grotto. Their relation may be more or less stable, their ages may be higher or lower; but all seek the same essential psychic commodity.

Black, white, Oriental, Hispanic, the high-school and college girls come with their necessarily protective boy or boys, simply to see what a dirty movie is. They, and even more so the boys with them, are, for the same reason as the girls, the ones before whom everyone else in the theaters grows silent. (We all feel that society—all that surrounds this strip of conflicting absences, this construct of desire at its darkest and lightest, all that finally secretes the discrete and shabby elements that, together, make up this space, so that somehow it is a part of, as much as it is apart from, the world—was built for them.) Sometimes the boys come here alone, for the same innocent reason as the girls it renders so much more, however momentarily, immobile: to see what's going on. Is it resentment we feel or just an endless and confusing separation? (Alienation?) Perhaps all the males (and indeed some of the females) on this side simply feel we should *be* them.

But the women conduct us to the truly less comfortable portraits.

I do not know this man's name, but he is as frequently at the movies as I am. Perhaps thirty-five, he usually wears a T-shirt and sneakers but never jeans: always a pair of old slacks, of which he has several. Over the two or three years I've seen him, his hair has thinned a little. More than half the time he has had a beard. (I fantasize that he is a good-looking bus driver, who probably works out of the Ninth Avenue garages up around Fifty-fourth Street—on an evening shift, possibly, which keeps his days free for the porn shows. But the chances are just as great that he is on some kind of welfare, or even that he does intermittent labor or "shape-up" work.) He stands near the back of the theater or just in the stairwell where he can still see the screen, his penis out of his pants and ill-concealed under a light jacket or, on colder days, a sweater folded over one arm, intermittently masturbating. Only if one of the homosexuals (like myself) pays him too concerted attention will he turn himself out of the line of sight or move to another location. When there is a couple present in the audience, he will contrive to sit two or three seats away from the woman and jerk himself with diminished motions, penis hidden only behind his free hand (which quivers while the other pulls and pulls), staring at her—until she glances at him, where-upon he looks away and hides himself again. Once I stood with him in the stairwell area of the Cameo with half a dozen other men. Most of us were masturbating, not really quite getting off on each other. For him, this was license to masturbate as well, though his interest was entirely in the actresses on-screen.

A couple who had been sitting in the balcony decided to leave. (He white with a short, muscular, well-knit body, she black, overweight, and in tight, electrically colored clothing somewhere between "punk" and prostitute.) Most of us hid our privates as, in the three-quarter dark (and certainly oblivious to the activity around), the white man led the black woman through those of us gathered there.

The man I've described hid himself too, instinctively, as one does in such situations, responding to what the rest of us were doing by the same mechanism by which a pigeon will fly when the group flies, and so an entire flock will take off, flapping—all at once it seems—at the flight of one, all, apparently, equally astonished. But realizing, with a look around him, why, an instant later he uncovered himself and, with the shoulders of his T-shirt back against the dirty blue wall (recently the management has repainted the same wall a fresh yellow), he rocked his hips forward so that his half-erect penis brushed the hip of the heavy young woman's satin toreador pants...closed his eyes, drew a quick breath, and settled his own hands before his genitals again, as, unknowing, unseeing, the woman hurried behind her boyfriend downstairs into the lobby's light.

Why is this portrait disturbing? Because I like this man. I don't mean just sexually—although once, perhaps a year ago, he let me play with that same semierect penis for some ten minutes, while we waited, silent in the dark, for the projectionist to fix the film (he is totally uninterested in blowjobs), whereupon he grew bored and walked away, terminating all physical contact between us ever since; and, as far as I've seen, all physical contact between him and any other male there. (He wants to be touched gently, almost ticklingly soft, not only on his genitals, but anywhere on his body. And only the men—or women—who, by trial and error have discovered that, will he put up with.) I like his reticence, his general carriage and personal demeanor, although—really rather rare for someone I've seen that many times—we have never exchanged an actual spoken word. And frankly I am uncomfortable liking him.

For on those areas of the social map where people, with the word "pervert," refer to a man basically heterosexual (not quite a homosexual, not quite an obscene phone caller, not quite a flasher, not quite a fetishist, not quite a rapist and certainly not an ax murderer), he is what they mean.

He has as many black and white and Hispanic relatives as does the Puerto Rican couple. One such—though he doesn't show up as frequently—is a white laborer of about twenty (possibly nineteen; certainly no older than I am), with tousled brown hair, who arrives at the movies after lunch in his soiled greens with two or three six-packs in a brown bag. Braver than the other, he will usually sit directly next to the woman in a couple to masturbate. (Rarely does anyone ever complain—so rarely, in fact, it's inconceivable some are not excited by the flashers around, so that even here some psychosexual exchange can occur.) Having already arrived drunk, over the next hours he will drink himself into insensibility, whereupon one or two shadowy figures will drift to his slumped, snoring form and, with razors, slit his pants open to pick out any loose bills, small change, or his wallet. When he wakes, he staggers from the theater, pants ruined and thready at both hips. The rip-offs—which plague perhaps one out of three men who fall asleep here— seem to be a part of the ritual for him. It's probably what keeps his visits so infrequent.

Once, bringing in three cans of Colt 45 with me from home, I drank one and, before I left, stopped at his seat and handed him the remaining two, still bound in plastic loops. He took them and, without looking at me, whispered, "Thank you!" then bent to stash them noisily in the brown bag with his other cans still under his theater chair.

Little Black Joe is perhaps the same age as this workman. But he is one of the most physically beautiful men I've ever seen. Certainly he had a year or two of weight lifting somewhere recent in the adolescence he has not quite left behind. He sells loose joints in the balcony and the restroom of the Cameo—and occasionally hustles. For as much of the year as he can, he wears sleeveless shirts or tank tops, stylish clean jeans, blue running shoes. He is nearly jockey short, and his totally unblemished face and arms are the color of bittersweet chocolate. There is nothing grubby about him —and, oddly, nothing effeminate. Indeed, his black masculinity is as saturated and as natural as his sales banter with the clients he sells his dope to. He also pimps for some of the younger black and Hispanic queens who hustle the older men in the theater.

Once, as I started down the Cameo's stairwell, I saw him at the turning, deeply kissing a young Spanish queen (a sixteen-year-old boy, most probably still in high school, who, with no classes after lunch, rushed there in a frenzy of seersucker and cologne). Joe stepped back. The other boy's thin arms dragged limply away from Joe's molded and muscled shoulders. Suddenly Joe's small hand whipped—*crack!*—across her face. (His cock, out of his fly, bobbed before the boy's belly, an accusing black finger, reversing all usual Freudian symbology): "You know you workin' for *me*, bitch!" he hissed, between full, smiling lips.

Rubbing her jaw, the queen (who, though small, is still half a head taller than Joe) whined, "You know, you don't have to *do* that!" then slipped from him to continue down the stairs.

As I came down, Joe pushed his still erect penis back into his pants and, indifferently, started up.

At the stairs' bottom, still rubbing her jaw, the queen joined two others, who had observed from below what I'd observed from above. "You know, I really think that guy is just kind of a little bit crazy!" she declared. "I really think he's a little crazy!"

Accepting her judgment, I've more or less avoided Joe since. Perhaps three times in two years, I've seen him the center of some altercation that has grown in one part of the Cameo balcony or the other, bringing members of the audience to their feet, staring in the dark. No blows have ever been exchanged in these, however, only loud words.

But the truth is, even though I avoid him, I like Joe too—though it is impossible for me to think of him as good, or trustworthy, or reliable. (Maybe I would if I were, as he is, into drugs.) But since I am here only for the sex, there is nothing he has that I particularly want.

Once, when I had just come into the theater and was standing at the back of the aisle, waiting for my eyes to adjust, someone brushed by me. I looked up into a gaunt black face with fire-engine red lips aglimmer with gloss: "Hi...!" came a light and throaty whisper. "Want a blowjob...?"

As I grinned and shook my head, I reached up to squeeze a bony shoulder under lace. "No thanks..." I whispered back. "I think we're both here looking for the same thing."

"Oh...!" The face nodded, still smiling.

Black lace rustled by me: light caught on the heel of a black pump as she moved off down the aisle.

She cannot be over nineteen and is probably a few years younger. Since then, I have seen her maybe ten times. Mostly she's been in her lace dress and makeup; perhaps three times, she has arrived as a very thin, gawky, and uncomfortable boy. All the time, however, she still says "hi" to me in that sweet, dazzled voice.

I say "hello" back.

And we part.

Sometimes I see him gazing wishfully at the older transsexuals who move about the aisles, most of them black, as we are, their surgical breasts displayed in net or lace shirts or simply bared in open blouses—male genitals bound tightly under Ace bandages between their legs before the women's underpants are slipped on: most of them can only afford the upper half of the operation.

Another man I like.

What makes these men disturbing? Why is it disturbing to feel camaraderie with them? I suppose because there is no economy that reconciles my actions around them with my emotional response to them, as well as my intellectual convictions about who they are as political/ethical beings. The greatest good for the greatest number? Most of them can be mildly annoying to someone at one time or another. But given any ten days in their lives, including their time here, you will not find them annoying *any*one. Yet the boys for whom society is made (as well as the city fathers a few of those boys will manage to become) would prefer that none of them existed—with a passion that dwarfs their merely sadistic delight in leering after the female prostitutes patrolling the avenue outside.

We are guilty that we are not them—are not those boys destined to run the systems and cities of the world: that puts a rift between us. They, on the other hand, are terrified, lest through some inexplicable accident, some magic happenstance of sympathy or contagion, they might become us. In most of them, we know, that terror can be repressed before adolescent curiosity. But we also know that that terror, given the license of adult exercise in the darkness of unquestioned moral right, can assume murderous proportions: our deviance, our abnormalities, our perversions are needed to define, to create, to constitute them and make them visible to each other and to themselves.

The descriptions I've just given you are not tales to displace or replace the stories of Tex and Mark and Pheldon and Dave. Rather, they are tales to be superimposed on those earlier stories. The first were tales of things I've done. The second recount what I've seen around me in the interstices of doing them. Neither set is complete without the other.

The polemicist in me, of course, would rather talk only about those encounters that are satisfying, that display true humanity, community, bonhomie (highlighted with the terminal nostalgia of impermanence)—and display it openly and unambiguously. But, equally true, to separate them as I have done here is to falsify them almost as much as to omit them. I wonder if I, having committed this exercise in context, can now move closer to some sort of integration.

As I walked down the aisle, a stocky businessman in his early thirties with glasses looked at me from his seat and, minutes later, when I walked back, was still looking. So I moved in before his knees and sat beside him. After a few minutes of fooling around (this guy, as I said to Phel the next day, was fucking hung!), he said: "Let's move someplace darker. It's too easy to see us here."

I explained to him the situation's optics: "You can easily see three rows around you—and ten rows away you can't. So ten rows away always looks darker, no matter where you are. And wherever you're sitting, it always looks too light."

"*Mmm*," he said. But he still wanted to move. After picking up his attaché case and moving us to two different locations in the balcony, he said, "You know, I think you're right."

"I know I am," I said. "Now I want you to look very carefully over there...." And I proceeded to point out six people in the process of giving/getting head.

He laughed out loud. "You know, I was up here for half an hour before, and I didn't see any of this."

I smiled.

And blew him.

(Turning a baseball player into a cocksucker...Sorry, Sam, but you probably won't get that.)

Afterwards he told me that it was his first time here. But not, I'm sure, his last. "The people are very nice here," he said as he was leaving. "They really act pretty nice to you, don't they?"

They do.

It is not, of course, a businessman's hangout, and the attaché cases are few and far between. In general, so are ties, leather shoes, and dress shirts. Because of this, about a week ago, when, with curly black hair and dressed in black slacks and a white dress shirt with the sleeves rolled up to his forearms, a tall young man came into the balcony, I noticed him. He sat down in the front row of the balcony's back section. As I passed, he kept looking at me. In my jeans and an old pair of running shoes, I sat next to him a little dubiously. I put my leg against his, my hand on his polyestered thigh. He smiled and put his hand on my crotch. No, this was not his first time here. He was very much into mutual sex, which can be a mixed blessing as far as real pleasure is concerned, but which nevertheless promotes a good feeling between people. Once, the uniformed security guard the theater's hired recently (to discourage the razor-blade rip-offs I told you about before) stopped in front of us. "Okay, guys. Take it somewhere else." We looked up and the guard walked on.

"What, does he just want us to get our feet out of the aisle?" my partner asked.

"I think so," I said.

So we moved back a row of seats. At one point, with my head in his lap, I took hold of his hand and was surprised to find it the hard hand of a laborer; I'd thought he was some kind of East Side office worker. Apparently not. In general, along with Dave and Mark, I count these among my most pleasant recent encounters.

Which reminds me of a third encounter, equally pleasant though more complex. Sometime last winter nearly a year ago, I saw a

Hispanic—about the same age as the last man I just described—sitting in the front row of The Cameo, in a brown leather jacket and knitted cap, masturbating. I sat a few seats away from him, finally moved a seat or two closer. He had very large hands and a kind of bemused expression as he stared up the screen. He also had a comparatively unique method of gripping his sizable, uncut meat—thumb buried down in his fist, so that his thumb knuckle kept brushing what would have been the upper part of his glans when his considerable skin was wedged back. Finally I leaned over and asked if he wanted to do anything. "Sure," he said. "But I'm hustling."

"Oh," I said, then got up and moved away, since I wasn't interested in paying. Later, I saw a heavyset white-haired man sitting with him. Apparently he'd found a customer. Over the next hour they both must have had a fairly good time, too. Between rounds, when the white head would disappear in the younger man's lap, both of them spent a lot of time laughing.

Over the next year I glimpsed him about three or four times, but I never approached him again.

Then, perhaps a week ago, as I was about to leave the Grotto, I saw him come in. On a whim, I lingered in the theater and finally walked down the aisle. He was sitting under one of the lights. He had taken his jacket off and was wearing sneakers, maroon pants, and a colorful shirt, though faded and frayed at collar, shoulder, and elbow. His pants were open. (His thumb was still tucked down in his fist.) I sat down directly beside him. This time there was no talk of hustling. But I learned very quickly what had provoked all the laughter of a year back. He was very into giving instructions. Once I started sucking his sizable uncut cock, he began to intone softly: "...very slow...yeah, real slow. Slower...okay, like that...no, stop for a second.... That's right, now a little faster...yeah, faster.... No, slower now...." Once I took hold of his big hand and, in the same way I'd been surprised by the hardness of the last guy's hand at the Cameo, I was surprised by the softness of those large brown fingers. "Lick it for a while. No, wait...I don't wanna do nothin' until we get to a good part in the movie.... Okay. Go on.... You can do it faster now.... Yeah, that feels real nice." Fortunately he had an ironic sense of the ludicrousness of his detailed urgings and pacings. So we both laughed. "Real funny, huh? Well, yeah...go on.... Hey, I'm gonna squirt now... I'm squirtin'—! Squirtin'—! Squirtin'! Ah, that was nice! Real nice!" He shot a fourth gout. "Good!" He followed with a fifth. "Yeah!" And a little sixth, final spill. "Wow!—that felt good!"

Sitting up, I said: "I liked it, too." I patted his thigh. "I hope we run into each other again."

"Me too!"

I—or at least the polemicist in me does—think of the above three encounters as among the nicest. Yet they are neither typical nor are they among, say, the half-dozen most sexually exciting ones I recall from the hundred-plus the last year has provided. Yet their general good feeling, the acceptability of the persons or their emotions, and the sense of exchange on more than just a physical level are parameters for something that I suppose is simply easier to speak of than certain other aspects of such a life.

Not only easier to speak of, but it also has its real importance—important enough so that when such encounters as the above three—as opposed to any of the others I've described—cease, one seeks out other cruising grounds. Several times since high school I've abandoned one area of the city for another, when forces I will never comprehend drive down the number of such accessible, satisfying exchanges, whose satisfaction is always, Sam, measured on a (or on several) scale(s) more complex than the sexual. Yet, in all cases, a dismal, gray, and unresponsive ground is the incomprehensible template against which they occur, not throwing them into relief so much as providing a necessary obscurity to their outlines, making them bearable, even possible (making them hard or impossible for we who indulge in them to speak of in any terms *save* the sexual, even as they are, in their actuality, wholly social), in a world that largely denies they exist.

But *could* this entire dithyramb of depression and recovering optimism be merely response to losing Dave?

THE LEATHERMAN'S HANDBOOK
LARRY TOWNSEND

A few years back, I used to be particularly hot for servicemen... Marines were by far my favorite choice. I was in the early stages of turning S in those days, and I found a lot of leathernecks whose basic masochism (I felt) had led them to enlist in the first place. It frequently took a little time, a little talk, and a little beer to bring out the best in them.

I lived in the San Fernando Valley at the time, in a small home I had bought on the G.I. Bill. I used to cruise the Hollywood area, trying to hit it just about the time the USO closed on a Friday or Saturday night. The Vietnam War was then at its height, and there were always a good number of guys in town from Camp Pendleton and El Toro. I picked up a guy one night who was hitchhiking with a couple of his buddies. They were trying to get back downtown to wherever it was they were staying. I have always been leery of taking on more than one serviceman at a time, but I was driving a two-seater Corvette, and this made it possible to offer a ride to just one of them. As I stopped beside the group—all three in uniform—I noted that any of them would have done nicely. But there was one I particularly liked. Fortunately, it was he who poked his head in the window.

"I can take one of you," I told him.

He smiled and nodded, though his expression was not definitive enough for me to be sure we were on the same wavelength. He turned to his friends and talked to them for a moment; then he opened the door and got in. He was eighteen, I discovered; small and rather slender, with light blue eyes and very close-cropped dark blond hair. He was obviously just out of boot camp, very spit-and-polish. I drove around with him for a while, trying to get him to commit himself before I made the long drive home. My usual procedure was to push the issue until the guy either indicated his willingness or rejected the whole scene. Sometimes, if he seemed to be just trade, I might do him as a warm-up and continue my search for a partner. I never wasted time driving home with a number I didn't feel had a fair potential for some two-sided action.

The Marine told me his name was Roger. When we shook hands his grip was firm, but his palm was very damp. I always took this as a good sign, because it meant he was a little nervous, and this implied his awareness of my intent. All these young kids were attracted to my Corvette, of course, and enjoyed riding in it. This gave me a little extra leeway to feel them out, simply by offering to "drive around for a while."

After fifteen or twenty minutes, I still had not been able to ascertain what Roger's bag might be. He was friendly and seemingly accepting, but I detected a certain element of lethargic unconcern—made me think of Lolita munching an apple while her older paramour attempted making serious love to her. Finally, I drove into a darker area and ventured putting my hand on his thigh—a sure way to resolve it, one way or the other. (If your quarry outweighs you by twenty pounds or more, I do not recommend this practice. With Roger, the size/weight advantage was mine.) When I touched him, Roger slipped down a bit in the bucket seat and hung his left arm over the back, turning slightly toward me as he did so. This was a sure indication that he wanted a blowjob, at least, and my usual S.O.P. was to get the guy's cock out and then see how much further he might be willing to go. Accordingly, I worked his zipper down the track, doing it with one hand and receiving no assistance when it hung up on a curl of cloth. I had reached a conveniently dark patch along a vacant curb before I actually got it out, so I pulled up, set the brake, put out the lights, and leaned across to use both hands. What I pulled out of his pants was an enormous semitumescent tube, warm and beautifully formed, slightly moist about the tip beneath an exquisite loose, wrinkled foreskin! This was obviously worth more than a quick session in the car, so I asked him if he'd like to go to my place for a beer.

"Sure, I guess so," he said casually.

All the way home, I continued to play with his fat, barely responding cock. It never got hard, and Roger never made any move to reciprocate. By the time I pulled into my garage, I was beginning to have serious doubts regarding his potential performance. But I'd extended the invitation and was committed for at least a beer and a blowjob. Anyway, it was still early, I thought. If I didn't get more than the bare bones, I could still go back for another try. Besides, Roger had a truly luscious hunk of meat! I took my Marine in the back way, noting that he never bothered to poke his iron back inside his fly. It flopped about in loose fleshy ponderance as he followed me with a rambling nonchalance that only heightened my previous apprehensions. As yet there had not been the slightest indication that he intended to reciprocate. We sat side by side on the living-room couch, and I opened a couple of cans of beer. Roger drank half of his in a single gulp, leaned back against the cushions with his thighs spread and his impressive manhood hanging down so the head was resting on the surface between his legs. I was about to resume my interrupted kneading of his cock when I realized my guest was glancing about the room, his eyes pausing every so often on the bottles I kept on a portable serving table.

"Would you like something stronger?" I asked him.

"Well, back where I come from," he replied in a bit of a drawl, "we like to use the beer as a chaser."

I brought a bottle of whiskey and a pair of shot glasses to the coffee table, pouring one for each of us. Roger bolted the double shot and washed it down with the rest of his beer. I got him a fresh one and we sat together drinking for about another half-hour. I was imbibing less than one for every two of his, and I was already feeling a glow seep through my guts, a flush of heat moving down both arms and legs. I had not touched Roger again since replenishing his can of beer. Suddenly he turned to me, his bird-of- prey eyes a trifle glassy. "Stand up," he muttered.

Not really sure of his intent, I stood. Roger scooted across the couch to sit directly in front of me, mumbled something about "eating crow" and buried his face in my groin. I could feel his lips moving against me through the cloth of my jeans. A few seconds later, he had slipped onto his knees between myself and the couch. He held up his hands, reached under my shirt and ran his warm, moist palms across my stomach and around the sides of my body. Eventually his fingers met at my fly, and he worked the buttons open awkwardly. He pawed down the left thigh and worried my rod free of its tight enclosure. By that time I'd sprung a full, raging hard-on. While his lips closed about the head, he unfastened the final button on my jeans and worked my balls free as well. He stroked and caressed them as he started sliding the entire extension deep into his throat. I was balancing myself by gripping the hard round of muscle above his shoulders, swaying back and forth from the violence of his motions and from my own reeling senses.

At length he sat back and looked up at me. His fingers began unfastening his shirt idly. He was wearing a light beige summer uniform, tailored to fit him closely. In a moment he'd bared his chest, and his narrow hips supported the sagging weight of web belt and the upper portion of his pants. His cock was finally erect, bouncing in fleshy majesty as—still seated—he reached down to untie his brogues. They were high lace-ups, and his trousers had been bloused inside them. It took him several moments to get them off, during which time he didn't say anything. I waited expectantly though, because I could tell he wanted to speak and supposed he was just a little bashful. I was still surprised, of course, at his abrupt change of manner, and almost paralyzed from the fantastic residual sensation of his hot eager lips about my joint.

"Can…can we go outside?" he asked in a choked whisper.

"Yeah…sure," I told him. My backyard was enclosed with heavy hedges on one side, the garage and laundry room on the other. There was a large unused grassy area in the very back…also surrounded by hedges, where the former owners had set a pair of T-shaped galvanized steel uprights to support a clothesline. Roger finished stripping off his uniform and stood up, moving with an imploring attitude toward the kitchen door.

I had slipped out of my shirt, but still wore my Levi's and boots. "Don't take 'em off…please," he begged in the same harsh whisper. He took my hand, still watching me with that intense almost-pleading expression. He must have expected me to refuse as he started once again for the door. Now, I would not say Roger was drunk, although he had belted down at least six or seven shots. But he certainly "had a glow on," and as a result he had broken through his former wall of reserve…just how far through I had yet to discover.

He paused a moment on the doorstep, getting the lay of the land before he made his way toward the back of my lot. Then he spun about abruptly. He faced me and knelt on the grass. He seized my cock and used it to draw me toward him until his lips could close about the crown again. He stayed there, naked, kneeling, moaning softly as he swung on me, twisting his head from side to side as he forced the mass of cock down his throat. He tried to hold it, choked and gagged, spewed up phlegm all along its length. After that, his lips slid fast and hard; he slammed his head against my groin, drew back, pausing when he held only the tip, savoring it with his tongue and looking up at me as I stood with my legs widespread, hands on my hips, swaying in response to his aggressive enthusiasm.

Without warning he released me and toppled backward. His body was balanced and suspended between his feet, which were doubled back beneath his ass; his arms supported the weight of his chest and shoulders. "Let me have it!" he rasped. "All over my cock and tits and belly!"

I was just green enough not to be certain, just experienced enough to guess correctly. He wanted me to piss on him, but the sight of his tight little body—flexed and hard in its present position, reflecting the night lights to further emphasize his physical beauty—all this contributed to such a hard arousal that I was doubtful I could comply. Finally I had to close my eyes and concentrate, willing my cock to soften enough for the other plumbing to connect. I tried to picture Niagara Falls, finally settled for the image of my bathtub faucet. The first drops came in a meager spurt, barely enough for me to feel it. Roger responded violently however, sighing and twisting as the spray struck his chest. Gradually the deluge gathered and built, seeped down my prick and struck him with a light steady trickle.

His moans seemed loud enough to wake the neighbors, but I didn't really care. I was spurting out across him, playing the stream up and down the center of his body, soaking him, feeling the splattered excess ricochet and strike my lower legs. On an impulse, I aimed the gushing flood against his throat and beneath his chin. At this point in my leather career, I had never had a trick who wanted it in his mouth, and I wondered. But Roger wasn't quite that far along. Instead he shoved himself upward, eyes and mouth clamped tightly closed, moving his face into the full warm rain of piss. I was almost running dry by then and tried to hold it back a little while he struggled onto his knees and knelt before me as he had before. Only now his head was bowed, so he took my final flow into his hair and down the back of his neck.

When I finally finished, Roger was kneeling in a wide puddle, splotches of mud and grass sticking to his legs and all across his backside. He reached out to seize my cock again, fondled my balls and the semisoftened shaft. He glanced around and spied the T-shaped posts for the clothesline. "Wow!" he whispered. "You ever use that?"

"Not for clothes," I told him. In truth I had never used it for anything.

"What do you use it for?" he asked softly.

"Get your ass over there and I'll show you," I said.

He stood before one of the uprights, facing it with his back to me. There were still a few strands of old clothesline dangling from the crossbeams, so I used these to tie his wrists to either end of the horizontal bar. I pulled the leather belt from my jeans before struggling free of them, then pulled my boots back on. I stood behind him, naked as he except for the heavy construction-worker footgear. "You want your butt warmed a little?" I asked.

"Yeah," he gasped.

"Yeah," I repeated. I slapped him gently across the ass with the folded belt. "Yeah? That how they teach you in the Corps?"

"Sir! No, sir!" he snapped.

"Would they punish you for saying 'Yeah'?" I demanded.

"Sir! Yes, sir!"

"Think I should punish you?"

"Sir! Yes, sir!"

I let him have it across the ass and back, hoping the sound would not produce a curious investigation from one of my neighbors, but aroused at the same time by the potential danger. My rod was again at full erection, and I was standing close enough for its jutting length to snap and slide across his cheeks, its contact interspersed with the crack of leather upon his taut, straining flesh. His tightly stretched body was gleaming with sweat, forming highlights along the upper sides of his shoulders and inside the wide V of his upraised arms. He had grasped the bar with both hands to ease the stress of his bonds, and this extra output of energy made his muscles stand out all the more.

After a while, I hung the belt over Roger's shoulder and eased myself against the heated glow of his ass, gingerly pressing my chest into the channel along his spine. I could feel the sticky moisture—his sweat, my own piss, the dried bits of grass and grime—transfer themselves to me. My palms grazed his chest as I drew harder against him, gripped down and closed about his nipples. I squeezed until I heard him suck in sharply. He reared back, driving my cock between his thighs so that it pressed desperately into the constricted hollow of warmth. Then he shifted his feet, and my prod surged upward, its spongy strength pressed upon the underside of Roger's crotch. He wriggled again, more deliberately this time as I lessened the pressure of my fingers. His hard, round cheeks were moving in a subtle shallow arc across my loins. He forced my cock to twist from side to side, enclosed by the firm-fleshed pincers of his legs.

"All you fuckin' Marines like to take it up the ass, don't you, punk?" I whispered harshly.

He didn't reply immediately, so I grasped his tits again, squeezing them hard and twisting the nipples until I made him bend his knees. This only drove his ass more deeply into the reciprocating arch of my body. "'Yes! Yes, sir!" he gasped.

By that time I had to piss again, so I quickly dropped my hands to his tiny hips, seized his buttocks and pried them open. I placed my cockhead to the crack of his ass, closed my eyes and waited for the flood to come. I never softened this time—at least not very much. As the stream of fluid rushed across him, I held my knees against the backs of his and rammed my cock deeper inside the recess. More by luck than design, I touched his puckered pink rosette and pressed against it while the warm flow continued between us. I entered him, sliding on the coating of my discharge, listening to his sighs and groans as my searing cascade found its terminus deep within his body.

I fucked him as he stood there, drawing back and hauling him against me, grasping his waist and forcing him upon my desperately pulsing shaft. I could feel the tides of heat rush through him, sensed the pool of moisture I'd deposited as it oozed out from his body, spilling against my thighs as I drove myself into him. My pounding thrusts made a series of slapping, rubbery sounds, the seepage keeping our contact slick and slippery—covering my balls as I forced him furiously against me. The metal frame was creaking from the hard use we were giving it, and several times I forced Roger backward until his toes were barely touching the ground.

The atmosphere about us was warm, but every time I drew back enough to allow the passage of air between us I was reminded of our being in the open, naked beneath the glow of sky, braving the danger of discovery. Neither of us was taking any further pains to keep our action quiet, and I shuddered later when I thought about it. At that moment nothing mattered but the urgency of our joining, the sensation of grasping flesh about my own aching, driving need. My lust boiled up in a surge of sensual fire. I slammed myself against him, sank my iron to its fullest. I reached around and grabbed his cock, remembering suddenly that its tremendous size had been the original incentive for bringing him home. I pumped it with my hand as I pounded against him, into him. I felt his bloated column fill and swell, responding to the battering of my own rod within his body. I felt him tremble, heard him gasp that I was going to make him cum. "Go ahead!" I whispered. "Shoot it, punk! Shoot your load!"

I came a moment after he did, while his viscous discharge trickled from him, and my hand began to rub its creamy essence across his belly. Thickly, it mixed with the half-dry residue of piss and the sweat that trickled down from the golden mat of hair upon his chest.

I released him, and we showered together before crawling into bed. He'd seen my camera, standing as it frequently did on a tripod in one corner of the bedroom. I was on the verge of sleep when Roger came back to life again. He urged me to take his picture, begged me until I ordered him to get his cock at full attention. This started us off anew, and our action lasted through most of the night. He stayed through until late Sunday afternoon, and I asked him to call the next time he got a weekend pass. Had he been a local boy, we might have had quite a thing going, because he returned three more times and later wrote me from his post in Vietnam. Then—damn that stupid war!—his letters ceased abruptly.

PETER THORNWELL

TORSTEN BARRING

Master Peter was late for his evening bath. Ivers was worried. It wasn't like the boy to forget his bath. He couldn't be occupied with his father, for Mr. Thornwell had left that morning for Liverpool, where he had some business to attend to and would be gone for a fortnight. The man often left his son in Ivers's care, knowing that the servant was devoted to the boy and enjoyed taking care of him. Ivers even bathed his Master Peter—as if he were a small child!—as if he were not almost fully grown!

Peter had been acting strangely, of late. He had always been uninhibited when it came to expressions of affection—lavishing hugs and kisses to an almost excessive degree. Now, with his dear mother gone and his indifferent father planning to send him away to become a ship's cabin boy, the beautiful youth seemed possessed of some kind of unnatural erotic frenzy.

When Ivers bathed him, he had always used a sponge. Lately, Peter had insisted that Ivers bathe him with his hands. Ivers would oblige, and the boy would make no effort to conceal his huge erection as he sighed with pleasure.

Ivers loved the excuse to touch the boy in his intimate places, but he felt it was wrong and suffered considerable feelings of guilt as a consequence. Guilty!—and yet utterly fascinated by Peter's huge cock. By the time Peter had reached the age of eighteen, his penis had begun to develop out of proportion to the rest of his slender, elegantly well-muscled body. In addition to making the handsome twenty-year-old footman bathe him, using his bare hands, Peter had recently cultivated a disturbingly bizarre habit at bath time. When Ivers had him covered with rich, foamy lather, Peter would hand him a stiffly bristled brush and insist that he scrub him as hard as he could—with particular attention to his nipples, his penis, and the crease of his arse. It was obvious that he wanted Ivers to hurt him!

Ivers had to admit that he took some kind of dark, mysterious pleasure in inflicting the required amount of pain and this was due to a long-denied and hidden quirk in his own nature that he had not the courage to examine. Why ever would he want to hurt the boy he loved more than himself? And—yet—if the boy wanted Ivers to hurt him, then how could he disappoint him?

Just the other night, when Ivers was preparing Peter for bed after his bath, the boy did a most amazing thing—something even stranger than wanting to have the most intimate places on his body scraped with an abrasive brush.

Peter always slept in the nude, even in the coldest weather. It was a chilly night, and Ivers was putting more wood in the fireplace so that his dear, lovely, naked boy wouldn't catch a chill.

Peter got out of bed, walked over to Ivers, and handed him a box of clothespins that for some unfathomable reason he had taken from the laundry and brought up to his bedroom.

Peter stretched out on his back before the fireplace and said, "Put the pins on my body, Ivers."

Ivers laughed nervously and said, "How absurd!"

Peter began to pull on his nipples which were exceptionally large with pointed, erect tits.

"Clamp the pins on my nipples, Ivers."

"What madness! I shall not."

"I've done it myself—lots of times—when I jack off."

"*No!*"

"Put them on my nipples, Ivers. I want you to hurt me. Pain enhances the pleasure when I jack off. I want pain on my nipples, Ivers. Put the pins on them. I insist!"

"Have you gone quite mad, Master Peter?"

"Yes. And I want you to torture me. Put the clothespins on my nipples! Torture my tits for me! Then put some on my cock. Right now! I want you to torture my tits and my cock!"

"Oh, Master Peter! I don't understand this sort of thing!"

"Yes you do! I saw your hard-on when I made you watch Dirk being whipped in the barn. You understand it—you're just afraid of it. Don't be. It's as old as mankind. I've read about it. In the library there are books that tell us things many people don't want us to know. But we know because we are men. We can never avoid suffering, whoever we are, however rich and powerful we are. Suffering is with us all the time. For life! My only liberation is the power to choose my own form of suffering. My choice now is that you should torture my tits and my cock with the clothespins. Can't you understand? I love you. The thrill of being actually tortured by a man I love would be the fulfillment of my best and wildest fantasy!

"Oh! If only you knew how much I love that kind of pain, you would oblige me willingly. Must I beg you? Torture me, my dear! Make me suffer exquisitely!"

Peter was stretched out on his back as if he were bound to a rack. His cock was absolutely stiff—lying far up on his belly, the huge mushroom head pointing above his navel and wagging in time to his heartbeats.

Ivers did what Peter so desperately wanted him to do. He did it expertly, as if from long practice, with the utmost sensitivity.

Peter directed Ivers to pull on the pins and vibrate them with his hands.

Under Peter's direction, Ivers became a skilled sadist! He inflicted exquisite agony on Peter's nipples and on his genitals.

Peter moaned and stiffened his entire body—arching up until his buttocks no longer touched the floor. How his muscles flexed!

The way he looked as he suffered! Never in all his life had Ivers seen anything as sexy! Sexy—and poetic, too!

Peter's disproportionate cock swelled to a size more suitable to a much larger man as Ivers fondled the pins that sent shivers of agony and ecstasy through the boy's entire body and soul!

Ivers's own cock was painfully hard. From this man two years younger than himself, he was learning things he had never dared to imagine. Things that had lain dormant within him all along. Things for which he hungered!

"I'm coming, Ivers!" Peter screamed. "Keep hurting me until I come!"

Ivers soon recovered his composure after Peter came. He had gone along with the mad game and enjoyed it. But when Peter attempted to make love to him, Ivers declined firmly. Peter had attempted to unfasten Ivers's trousers. He had been quite aggressive about it.

"Let me do you! I know how. I want to suck your cock, now, Ivers!"

"When and where did you get so wise, Master Peter?"

"At school, of course. There's nothing I haven't done. I know you want me to suck your cock. Why won't you let me?"

"Because I would never forgive myself! If I were found out, I'd be sent to prison and flogged!"

"Admit you want it! You've always wanted it! At least admit it!"

"Oh, very well, *yes!* Of course I want it. You're the most beautiful boy I've ever seen in all my life, and I love you. I've always loved you. But I cannot break the laws of society. I've already gone too far, and I know I'll be punished for it. Have mercy, Master Peter, and stop tempting me."

"Oh, Ivers, I'm sorry! Never would I want to make you unhappy. I only want to give you pleasure in return for the pleasure you gave me. I promise I'll never taunt you again. Oh, I'm wicked! Please, forgive me."

"You're not wicked, and there's nothing to forgive. You did nothing wrong by expressing the exact nature of your passion. I've heard of these things before.

"What you did was perfectly right, for you. It was also right for me to refuse!

"Come, now, my adorable, naughty boy. To bed with you. I'll tuck you in and kiss you good night. Then, resolutely, I will take my leave of you until the morning."

That episode had occurred only the night before, and Ivers wondered whether the boy was upset with him and was refusing to appear for the pleasant ritual of his bath which afforded the two of them an appropriate opportunity to enjoy a half hour's intimacy with each other.

Ivers looked throughout the vast house—in all seventy-five rooms.

Not finding Peter anywhere in the house, the servant went outdoors to search.

A sudden instinct carried his steps directly to the barn.

When he arrived at the door to the barn, he glanced through the tiny window and saw a pale, flickering light. No doubt it was cast by a lantern. Someone was within.

Suddenly Ivers knew what he had to do. He firmly suppressed the twinge of guilt that threatened to inhibit his resolve. He walked to the side of the barn where the bushes grew, sank to his knees, and peered through the hole—that peephole the existence of which he had learned from Master Peter the day the naughty boy had made him watch the naked Dirk receiving a whipping from his brutish father!

Two male figures were within. A hanging lantern bathed their completely nude bodies in a soft, shimmering erotic amber glow.

Both men's cocks were in a condition of full erection!

One was hanging suspended by his wrists from the barn's ceiling.

The other was lashing him with a whip.

The man being whipped was Dirk, the gardener's son.

The man whipping him was Peter Thornwell!

Ivers was so overwhelmingly aroused by the spectacle that he took his cock out of his trousers and, with an urgency beyond anything he had experienced previously, proceeded to masturbate.

Peter had seen Ivers peeking into the window. He ran outside, seized the footman, and dragged him inside the barn.

"Spying, were you?" he screamed. *"You are next for a whipping! I command you to strip naked at once!"*

"I knew you would look for me here," said Peter. "We were expecting you."

Ivers could not bring himself to take Peter seriously. Surely there was some reasonable explanation for this apparent madness. Perhaps he was dreaming—suffering, once more, one of those erotic nightmares that made his penis ejaculate in his sleep. He would wake up at any moment, have to change the bedclothes, and wash himself before he could get back to sleep.

Ivers was trembling before Master Peter and Dirk, both of whom were stark naked. Worse still, his erection was so huge that he could not get it back inside his trousers.

Master Peter was holding a whip in his hand and ordering his faithful servant to strip naked.

Seeing his condition, Peter took pity on Ivers and changed his manner. Calmer now, he loosened the ropes that held Dirk suspended by his hands and allowed the naked young man to stand on his feet.

"You're all right, Dirk?"

"Of course. My father has given me much worse than that."

Dirk rubbed his wrists to restore his circulation as Peter spoke calmly to Ivers.

"My dear friend, let me explain as well as I can what is happening here, and why. I am practicing— getting myself in condition for a life that is going to be quite brutal. I am going to suffer a great deal, and I shall be called upon to make other men suffer, too. That is why I whipped Dirk—whom I love almost as much as I love you, if possible. Dirk showed his love for me by allowing me to whip him.

"*Now I am going to whip you!* Oh, not for spying—I taught you to spy. I made you look through that hole and watch a spectacle that day that got us both aroused. I seized upon your spying on us as an excuse to whip you—part of my demonstration—because cruel men are also hypocrites who need excuses for inflicting their punishments on their victims. Dragging you in here with such mock-righteousness was part of my charade—a role I was playing in this theater of cruelty. A barn is an excellent setting for that kind of theater, don't you agree?

"I'm going to whip you because you want it as much as I do. But you have to be forced against your will. Paradoxically, forcing you relieves you of making a choice—for making that choice would burden you with guilt—and guilt, my dear friend, would spoil your pleasure.

"In addition to a good whipping, you would love for me to suck your cock. But allowing me to do it would, again, bring the guilt that would spoil your pleasure.

"Ah! I've an idea! A slight revision of my first plan. I'll make *Dirk* whip you while *I* suck your cock! And remember—you didn't agree to any of this. It was forced upon you by your cruel master, Peter Thornwell! Now relax and enjoy it.

"Dirk! Strip this man stark naked and tie him against that wall—over there, where the peephole is. Stretch him very tight—spread-eagled—*and make him stick his cock through the hole!*

"I'm going outside. I'll give you five minutes to get him naked and tied up as I've directed. Then—you will start whipping him on the buttocks while I suck his big, stiff, juicy, gorgeous cock!"

Hours later, the three young men were together in Peter's bed in the huge, quiet house.

They couldn't get enough of their kind of sex.

Ivers, so recently released from his inhibitions, surrendered himself completely to the twisted thrills Peter had initiated him into. One by one, he did all of the things he had longed to do. He played sadistic games with Peter's body—inflicting delicious cruelties while Dirk watched intently and stroked his erection.

He took hold of Peter's nipples with his long, strong fingers and abused them. He pulled the erect tits out from the marble-smooth chest. Pulled them, pinched them, twisted them.

One by one, he took those sexy boytits into his mouth. He sucked those swollen tits as hard as he could—enlarging them even more with strong suction.

"Bite them!" said Dirk, jacking his cock faster. "Bite down on those tits—hard!" he commanded, becoming increasingly excited by watching the erotic tit torture.

Ivers used his teeth on Peter's painfully enlarged tits as Dirk chanted at him.

"Keep torturing those tits until they never shrink back again. Make 'em stay hard and way out like that! *Torture the man's tits!*"

Peter pulled at Ivers's hair and ground his head hard against his chest—directing Ivers to torture his nipples with his suction and with his teeth until his capacity for nipple pain exceeded his usual threshold.

Peter asked Dirk to hold his arms down so he could not help

submitting as the agony on his nipples became unbearable and he began to cry.

But he wouldn't give in!

"No—don't stop! *Don't stop!* Torture my tits! Make the pain last so long I'll be unable to wear a shirt tomorrow. Make me feel more pain than I've ever felt in my life! Build up my pain! Make me learn to take more and more and more!"

Ivers pulled out one of Peter's bootlaces and tied it around the boy's cock and balls. He tied the lace so tight that the blood-engorged cock looked as if it might burst. Then, he licked the entire length of that giant cock—made it gleam with spit—blew on it, slapped it, whipped it with one of Peter's belts.

Peter's capacity for absorbing pain seemed limitless.

Ivers held a lighted candle over Peter's chest while Dirk held him down.

"Yes!" cried Dirk. "Torture his tits and his cock with hot wax! Let it drip right on those tits! *Burn 'em!*

"His *navel!* Let the wax dribble right into his *sexy navel!*—a drop at a time—that's it!—Now his *cock!*—All the way—up and down—dribble that scalding wax right on the head of his *cock!*—That's it!—Christ, that's so sexy!—I'm gonna *come* just looking at it!—Oh!—*Torture that cock—Christ, I'm coming!—Oh, God!—*"

All three men came at the same time.

Ivers and Dirk rubbed their combined come over Peter's chest and belly.

Then Peter and Ivers took turns spanking Dirk. They spanked his arse with their bare hands—then with a hairbrush—then with a belt—

They put clothespins on his nipples and on his testicles and spanked him again. They raped him, using the brush handle first—then their cocks.

They kept it up until Dirk came again—screaming!

On and on their games of sexual cruelty continued—giving

it and taking it—until all three men had come countless times.

Finally—completely exhausted—they slept.

Peter, in the middle, kept his hands clasped on the cocks of his two lovers.

He grasped their spent cocks with a desperate possessiveness, as if to let go for a moment would plunge him into an abyss.

THE SCARLET PANSY
ANONYMOUS

The voyage was over. Mason and Randall were congratulating each other on the number of delightful affairs they had consummated aboard ship. Bobby, was lamenting, "Oh, you two show so little discrimination that it's easy for you to have a good time wherever you go."

"We must be common," suggested Mason.

Bobby lifted her eyebrows and smiled, then voiced her own hope: "I'm waiting for Paris. There I shall be happy—many, many times. I'll stay there while you and Randy do your work in Vienna."

They debarked at Boulogne-sur-Mer, Mason and Bobby to hasten to Paris, and Randall to Berlin, which he planned to visit for a while before going on to the postgraduate schools in Vienna.

Randall's early Pennsylvania life now proved of use to him. There he had as a child picked up "Pennsylvania Dutch." At college he had learned German grammar and literature and his ear was "formed," so he had no difficulty in conversing with the Germans.

Once settled in the Adlon, he hastened to possess himself of a copy of *Freundschaft* (Friendship) and also bought a copy of *The Isle* to mail to Bobby. He had a few letters of introduction but also planned to make some informal acquaintances—"by intuition" as he called it.

The local slang amused him much—"*warmer Bruder, See Frucht, Tante*," etc.

Part of his first evening Randall spent in a small resort in Fuchtwangerstrasse. Later he went to a cabaret and still later, past midnight, to the corner of Unter den Linden and Friedrichstrasse to observe the type of night life there offered. Professor Jimmie Stay's description was correct. Here he saw Berlin's night wanderers in all their variety—men who looked like women; women who looked like men; and men and women who sold themselves to anybody and everybody.

He wrote Mason fully and added, "By comparison with what I see here in Berlin, Mason, you are worth 10,000 marks a night. Just for the camp of the thing, I have taken out a special license. At last I have a legal status befitting my station in life. One could quite well copy German methods in many things. Certainly Berlin is one of the most tolerant cities in the world. I like it better than Paris. Why can't so-called Christian American cities emulate her? Miss Savoy's conclusion gives the reason—'Americans do so love to manage everybody's business but their own. Religious people won't permit anybody to be happy if they can help it. To them anything that is enjoyable is a sin. Not content with being miserable themselves, they wish to make everybody else miserable, too.'"

Randall thought he had never seen such beautiful blond young men, but their youth made no physical appeal, for his fetish was for men of 28 to 35. He found that most Germans, once they had passed out of their teens, were likely to become fat, gross and physically repugnant. There were exceptions, of course, and one of these he met quite casually while visiting Potsdam. He was a man of title, tall, slender, blond, even more handsome than Mason Linberg. And he had never had a love affair!

"I am Count Karl von G.," he said simply.

"And I am Randall Etrange, an American visiting Europe for medical study."

The Count was very frank. "I did not know Americans could be so fascinating," he told Randall. "I do not know why I am following you, a person of whom I know absolutely nothing, but to whom I am drawn by some unknown power. We know nothing of each other, yet I trust you."

"For being fascinated, I kiss you," said Randall, "and for trusting me, I kiss you, more and more and more" (suiting action to word). He had to teach him everything about love, the most delightful of all instruction. But, what was more difficult, he had to make the Count believe that it was he who was teaching Randall.

Their friendship ripened rapidly. Together they visited theaters, museums, cabarets, and at the end of a week Randall became a guest at his castle. The Count's father was dead, but his mother, a very beautiful woman of middle age, still lived at the castle. Like so many Americans of mixed ancestry, Randall found himself much more at home with these Germans than he had ever been able to feel with the English or with any other Europeans except the Russians.

Many guests were present at the castle that weekend. One and all seemed to make an intensive study of Randall. His quite open love affair with the young Count caused no adverse comment, in fact, it was taken as a matter of course. A like situation in America would have led to much gossip, and condemnation, if not actual interference. What did surprise the Germans was that Randall appeared to be well educated. Randall was not much of a pianist these days, because medicine took so much of his time, but the castle had an excellent organ and the technique of playing that instrument still seemed natural to him. In more recent years he had made a practice of reading music daily. Thus he was able to help entertain these music-loving people. Then too, his horsemanship was good and he could hunt with them, though he cared neither for riding nor for hunting, unless Karl was with him. His ease in conversing with them also pleased, an accomplishment so unusual in English-speaking people. Too, he was able to discuss all of the newer psychology—a subject then beginning to be popularized.

True, Randall was unusual, but not more unusual than are many young Americans. His former life, that is the part that had to do with his personal advancement, seemed to these Europeans a story of fascinating adventure, rather than the account of hard work, which it really had been.

They pressed him with questions respecting his ambitions for the future. Knowing that these sincere and broad-minded people would not be shocked, he told them that he wished to do research work in venereal disease and, if possible, to find a cure for gonorrhea, that so-called "social disease," which has been fastened on mankind as a penalty for enjoying love. He told them of the work he had already done and of the theories he had formulated. This was fortunate, for the Count knew well a physician in Berlin who would be glad to put a corner of his laboratory at Randall's disposal.

Randall decided to defer his visit to Vienna when the Countess pressed him to remain another week.

Each morning, Randall and handsome Karl rode through the woodland paths of the estate. Sometimes they broke fast in the woods; other times they would go out on the great lake and fish all day. Everywhere they went, there was excuse for love-making. A typically wonderful scene would require that they stand arm in arm before the grandeur of the German countryside and view its beauties till they were so saturated with it that a new desire for love was aroused within them. Then they would embrace joyfully and kiss tenderly, the while murmuring sweet words of devotion, as they disrobed and exposed their warm flesh to the cool twilight breeze. How Karl adored to make love out of doors! His land afforded them privacy for miles, and when he put his throbbing, thick-helmed cock into Randall's hole, he would cry out as if he wished the world to reckon with his passion. He would milk Randall to come gloriously, and then he would feed upon the warm semen, cleaning its every drop from his lover's belly. They sought to draw nearer and nearer to each other, to become one time and again. So the lovely summer days passed.

Evenings, after dinner, there were the usual gatherings of all the guests in the huge reception hall. Acting was natural to Randall. The most finished actors are not those who appear on the stage, but those who must play perfectly several uncongenial roles in real life. Sometimes Randall would amuse them with impersonations, always with the help of Karl, fashioning fantastic drags from material usually reserved for other purposes: bedsheets, pillow cases and bath slippers turned him into a "white sister," regretful of having left "the world" before he knew what it was all about; lace curtains and a bouquet turned him into a bride who had experienced love before she had met her husband and was concocting schemes for further deceiving him. He was in turn a black woman nursing her half-white child; a New York society woman attempting an English accent, than which there is nothing funnier; and a Krankenschwester (nurse) who was in despair because the doctor she had loved too well was to marry an heiress, and the unborn child had not been disposed of. Most amusing to them of all, he was a Pennsylvania Dutch girl stamping through the mud to feed the chickens and pigs and, incidentally, to be loved by a yokel behind a haystack.

Near the end of the week a new guest arrived, the middle-aged and very distinguished Count von M., a man accustomed to having his way in most things, and especially in love.

Randall had been amusing the guests with his impersonations. When the Count von M. saw him, he experienced one of those sudden flare-ups of ardor for which he was noted. Randall had heard much of the man, who had an international reputation, and though he did not reciprocate his feeling in the least, he found it was pleasant to receive the attentions of such a renowned person; he encouraged him. For the time being he forgot Karl.

Dancing began. He danced thrice with the Count von M. As his partner was about to engage him for the fourth time, a servant stepped up announcing that Count Karl wished to see Randall at once in his apartments. He excused himself and hurried after the servant, whom he dismissed at the door of Count Karl's sitting room. Randall knocked, calling, "Karl, may I enter?"

"Yes," he answered in a strange harsh voice.

Karl was standing, gazing into the fire, his back to the door, but as he stepped within he wheeled about, a pistol in his hand. His face was flushed and wild-looking. He shouted, "How can you torture me so? You do not love me. I am going to kill myself here, now."

"Not love you? What can I do to prove to you that I love you, Karl?" asked Randall appealingly.

Karl let the pistol fall to the floor and stretched out his arms, "Oh, come to me, Liebchen, come to me and tell me you love me."

Randall went to his arms and smoothed his hair and patted his cheeks; tenderly he gave him his lips again and again. "That is my answer, naughty boy. Now, don't be jealous any more. The Count von M. is such a noted man that I thought it an honor to you as well as to me to dance with him. I do not love him. I do not even admire him."

"But he wins everyone," Count Karl continued. "He would ruin you."

"No, Karl, he could not ruin me. I am the only person who could do that. But I promise you here and now, Karl, that I shall be all yours, as long as you want me."

"And you will stay in Germany with me? You will give up America?" he asked.

Randall believed more in caresses than in words—the teaching of Miss Savoy. He remembered that whimsical person's advice: "Kiss their sensitive nerve endings," and kissed him a long, lingering, satisfying kiss. Then he explained gently, "Dear Karl, I have my work to do and you have duties of your own as well. My immediate course in life has been arranged. I must remain in Vienna for two years. But our separation shall be only temporary. I shall come to you and you shall come to me. So long as you want me, remember, I am entirely yours."

Then Randall kissed him again and again. Leading him to the bed, he tenderly laid him down and undid his jacket and his puttees. He would boldly show Karl tonight what the "ladies" back in New York would term in slang a "sixty-nine," quelling his lover's angst with a voluptuous new game. How far he had come since he had done this with dear old Teddy that first time! For today Randall was masterful, manipulating Karl's penis to a full and raging stand in seconds, even as his own thickened and rose to full mast.

Randall slipped his cock into Karl's pouting mouth, filling it like an overlarge pacifier, even as he took the Count's shaft into his own. Like an oiled machine, Randall undulated to and fro, pushing his cock down Karl's throat as he pulled Karl's member slowly and evenly from his jaws; then, tipping his lithe and agile body, pulling his cock back, still all the while gobbling Karl back down. This he kept up until at once they both began to pant and gasp as their cocks swelled to capacity. Only then did they simultaneously fire their weighty loads deep into one another's gullets.

"Ah, Karl dear," he murmured, "you satisfy me so completely. But the past has taught me that nothing so sweet can ever last. I warn you, dear, not to believe that Fate will make an exception of us. But

I shall never be to blame again for hurting you. Now, if you wish to die, let me die with you, happy!"

Karl laughed hysterically. "Die? Now? No, we shall live—for each other—just you and I, for each other," he repeated over and over, fondling him, kissing his lips, his cheeks, his eyelids.

They were very happy. Sometimes Randall thought of the cowboy and of others. All had something in common physically; all were tall, muscular, blond, vibrant with health. But Karl had the one thing the others lacked: the social and mental attributes of the educated and well bred. At last Randall had found what he had sought, unconsciously, so long.

The following Monday, Randall and Karl returned to Berlin, the former to plunge at once into some research work for which he found better opportunity there than elsewhere, the latter to prepare for the army maneuvers.

Karl's apartment was, of course, at his disposal, and so he left the Adlon. Evenings they dined at various of the famous restaurants and then sought out places where they could dance together.

Randall was doing exceptionally fine work. He found he could hire excellent technicians to assist him. This made progress more rapid, for he was thus able to devote all his time to direction and interpretation. His happy frame of mind made easy his many hours of work.

Count Karl had but recently purchased a new automobile, by that time beginning to be a practical success. They would roll luxuriously about the city in the evening or drive to suburban inns that were renowned for the splendor of their entertainment.

Often as Randall reclined in his arms he would speak softly and gently: "Beloved, this is heaven if there is such a thing as heaven."

And Randall would assure him, "Karl, my very dear Karl, our love is the sweetest thing in the world. Give me your lips again, dear."

They carried their devotion to the utmost limits. Even when dining they would sip their wine from one glass and share their food morsel by morsel.

"I had never dreamed there could be such happiness as ours," Karl often said. Then Randall would kiss him in answer.

Not a day passed but they would exchange gifts. Count Karl's were of course magnificent, for he was extremely wealthy. He gave Randall many beautiful pieces of jewelry, and Randall gave back lavishly.

Randall wrote to Mason, then in Vienna, telling of his happiness, and Mason, congratulating him, told of a wonderful new love affair of similar intensity which was taking his attention, and also of another one which the amorous and insatiable Bobby had begun in Paris.

So events went on week by week.

Near the end of July, Count Karl returned from Potsdam one evening in a highly excited frame of mind. His regiment was to go to Metz for the maneuvers. There was rumor of activity on the French border. It was even thought that war might ensue. The French were reported to be planning with their allies to attack Germany. To Karl, war-trained as he had been, this contingency seemed an occasion for rejoicing. To Randall, trained to think in terms of peace, the horrors of such an eventuality brought naught but dread. Of course, he had no thought of his own country being so unwise as to become embroiled in a squabble over European jealousies. Then too, he dreaded what Fate might have in store for Karl, and for himself too. But he did not refer to his formerly expressed fear that such perfect love could not last.

Karl insisted: "It will soon be over. If France retires from her arrogant position, I shall be with you—soon. If she does not recede, it will take less than a month to humble her. And I hope that she does not yield. Then we shall conquer her and occupy Paris in a month, and you and I will live there."

x   x   x

Together the Countess von G. and Randall went to see Karl depart. He kissed his mother dutifully. Randall he held a long time in his arms as he passionately kissed his cold lips. Randall was as one stricken with illness. Horror of the possibilities of the future had marked his face. He could not speak; only tears welled from his eyes, in answer to Karl's words.

When the train had departed there was a brief farewell to the Countess; then Randall hastened to his laboratories to try by hard work to submerge his dreads.

Less than a week passed, and the war broke out!

There were too-brief letters from Karl filled with words of love, telling of success and predicting further successes. Then nothing more from him. Anxiously Randall journeyed to the castle now occupied solely by the Countess von G. He found that noble lady grieving, but her sorrow assuaged by pride in a son who had given his life for the Fatherland. The report told briefly that Karl had been killed when a French mine exploded.

Randall condoled her as best he could, but already the Countess was beginning to feel the distrust which permeated all of Germany, the distrust of those who spoke English.

Randall returned sadly to Berlin.

During his absence his laboratories had been dismantled to make room for governmental activities, the preparation of immune sera and various vaccines. His copious notes, mostly in abbreviated shorthand, entirely meaningless to anyone else, had been confiscated. At that time what could not be understood was suspected. Randall volunteered to help them in their work. His motive was misinterpreted. After all, they knew nothing about him, and then, too, their own feeling of self-sufficiency precluded the acceptance of favors from outlanders.

Mason had written from Vienna that he too was persona non grata.

Randall acted quickly. He journeyed to neutral territory at once—Switzerland. But he was bored, without occupation. He had to shake off the frightful depression following the death of Karl. The newspapers gave little news. He was saved from the pseudo-patriotic piffle which cumbered the American periodicals during the war. The Swiss papers spoke of the work of the Red Cross. Randall decided to go to Paris and offer his services. Perhaps in helping to assuage the sufferings of others he would forget his own heartache.

SOLIDLY BUILT
Matt Townsend

The next day after working hours, in order to avoid meeting anyone, I went out to the house to see if Mark had been working, and it was hard to tell if he had been there or not. More wire had been strung, but not a whole lot. However, Bjorn and Tommy seemed to have finished the rough-in plumbing, and all of their extra pipe and equipment was gone. I was glad they were finished, and glad that I wouldn't have to face them very soon. God knows what was going through their minds.

I tried not to dwell on my problems with Mark. My primary concern now was whether he would finish the wiring. And as for the other—somehow I wasn't really angry. He had been a shit. No doubt about that. But those were his demons, not mine. I had thought that somehow I could help, but that was probably just presumptuous on my part. God knows it hadn't all been bad—far from it. But I hated to see it end that way. It just made me sad. Hell! I should know by now not to chase after trade. Oh, well. *C'est la vie.*

I went home, fixed a salad for dinner, and was just cleaning up when the phone rang.

"Hello."

"Hello, Mr. Tolbert?"

"Yes?"

"Are you the Mr. Tolbert who's building a house on Pine Mountain?"

"Yes."

"Oh, good. I wasn't sure I had the right one. This is Tommy, Tommy Baca. You know, Bjorn's helper."

"Oh, Tommy. Hi. How are you? What can I do for you?"

"Well," he stammered. "I just wanted to call. See we finished the plumbing today."

"Yes, I saw that."

"Well," and there was a pause. "I, uh, just wanted to…. Well, uh, you know, since I won't see you again, I just wanted to say thanks."

I wasn't sure what he meant, so I played it safe. "That's nice of you to call. Actually, it's me who should be thanking you. You did good work. It looks really good. But won't I see you when you do the finish work?"

"No, I go back to college in two weeks. I just work with Bjorn in the summers."

"Oh, I see."

And there was a long pause. "What I meant was thanks for, you know, the other."

"Oh, that," I blurted. "My pleasure. You were terrific. But I wasn't sure you liked it," I fished.

"Liked it? Hell, it blew my mind. Nothing like that has ever happened to me before. Wow!"

"Well, that's great," I laughed. "I liked it too. You were really hot."

"Yeah, man. It blew my mind," and there was an awkward pause. "Well, I just wanted to say thanks. I'll let you go now. Thanks, man."

"Hey, Tommy. Wait."

"Yes?"

"I was just thinking. Would you like to get together sometime before you go back to college?"

"You mean?..."

"Yes, Tommy, I mean just what you're thinking," I laughed.

"Oh, wow. Really?"

"Sure. I'd love to see you again. What's a good time for you?"

"Oh, anytime."

"Well, what's wrong with right now? Are you doing anything tonight?"

"No, not really."

"Well, then, let me give you my address."

"Actually, I know where you live. I'm quite near you, in fact. I was out riding my bike, and I rode by what I thought was your house. I saw the light. So I stopped at a pay phone and called."

"Good, come on over. I'll be waiting."

"Far out," and he hung up.

I barely had time to make the bed and pick up my dirty clothes before the doorbell rang. I ran a comb through my hair and headed for the door.

There he was, dressed like an Italian cyclist. Black cycling shorts, cycling shirt with Day-Glo writing all over it, a helmet, and cycling shoes. "Hi, Tommy. Come on in."

He looked very nervous, "Are you sure you don't mind. I didn't mean to barge in on you like this."

"No, no. It's fine. In fact, it's wonderful. Best thing that's happened all day. Come on in."

"I locked my bicycle out front. Will it be OK there?"

"Yes, I'm sure. This is a very safe neighborhood." And he came in and stood beside the door as though he were too embarrassed to know what to do. "Can I get you something? A beer, maybe? You must be thirsty."

"No, thanks, but I would like some water if that's OK."

"Sure, come on in the kitchen," and he followed me in silence.

As he gulped down two glasses of water, I marveled at his trim, youthful body, the way the shorts clung to every crevice of his hips and sculpted ass, and the prominent bulge in front. This was too good to be true. How lucky can you get?

"You want something to eat?"

"No, I'm fine."

After an awkward pause I let my eyes rove up and down his trim, muscled body and said, "Yes, fine. You look mighty fine in that racing gear. That cycling really keeps you in shape."

"Yeah, it works the legs, but I really need to work on my upper body," he stammered, shuffling in embarrassment.

"Looks good to me," I grinned.

"Thanks," and he stood there as though he thought I was just going to go down on him right there by the kitchen sink.

"Well, now. Why don't we go in the other room and get comfortable?"

"OK, whatever," and I led him into the bedroom. I knew he was too nervous to chat, so I figured I better give him the blowjob he wanted before he split out of embarrassment.

"Can I help you out of those clothes?"

"No, I can do it," and he set down his helmet, and slipped off his shoes and shirt. But when it came to his shorts, he turned around to pull them down. His shyness struck me as cute, but I didn't mention it.

"Would you like some music?"

"No, that's fine."

"Shall I turn off the lights?"

"No, that's fine."

"Do you mind if I get undressed?"

"Whatever, but you got to understand, Mr. Tolbert..."

"Whoa. Enough of this Mr. Tolbert stuff. Call me Jeff."

"OK, Jeff. But don't get any ideas. I like girls, you know. So I'm not about to..."

"Yes, yes. I know. I'd just like to be comfortable. Now why don't you lie down on the bed." While I undressed, I watched him sprawl spread-eagled on the bed and lie there staring up at the ceiling. He was youthful perfection. His tight, muscled body glistened in the light, and his already hard, surprisingly large cock arched rigidly up from a bush of dark blond hair—the only hair visible on his body.

Standing at the foot of the bed, I said, "You look good enough to eat."

"Good," he said slyly. "That's what I was hoping for. It's all yours. Help yourself," and he gave his hips a little thrust and grinned at me.

I knew he was expecting me to go down on him immediately, but I was in no hurry. So I knelt down and slipped his big toe into my mouth.

He gasped in surprise, "Careful, man, that tickles." But he let me suck on it, in and out, in and out. "Shit, man, I never. That's wild." Then I moved on to the other toes, one at a time, then two and three. Sucking and licking, while Tommy thrashed on the bed. "Weird, that's really weird, man, but wild. Do the big toe again. Yes, that's it. Fantastic." Then I did his other foot, while he thrashed and moaned encouragement.

Then I moved to the top of his foot and to his ankle. Licking slowly up his calf, my tongue encountered the stubble of his shaved leg. "You need a shave," I laughed.

"Sorry, it gets a little rough. Sorry about that." But I wasn't; it was exciting to feel the slippery smoothness, like muscled silk in one direction and slightly rough in the other. I inched my way up on the bed between his spread legs, licking over one thigh and then the other. And then down on the inner thigh. Around and around, and higher and higher. Then my tongue found the furry sack of his low-hanging balls. "Yeah, lick my balls, oh, yes. Suck 'em, suck 'em." I sucked in first one treasured little orb and then the other. Too big to get both in at once, but one was a nice mouthful. For a long time I nuzzled, and licked, and sucked. Then I lifted them up to find that sensitive spot just below them, between the balls and the ass. Tommy howled when I found it, lifting one leg up to give me access.

"Yeah, Jeff. That's great. Lick it. Now do my ass. I loved that. Do that again. Oh, God, yeeees!" and I lifted his leg higher and buried my tongue in the vulnerable spot. "Yes, I love that, do it, man. Do it. That feels so fucking wild."

"Here. Let me really get at it," and I shifted position and slipped an arm under each leg. He let me lift him up, so that his ass was spread wide before my face. There was almost no hair, so that the little, pink and puckering opening winked from between his milky white, muscled little cheeks. These were the Pearly Gates if ever I saw them. "Man, oh, man. What a beautiful little ass." I could have admired it for hours, but instead I began tonguing very lightly over the smooth surface of his cheeks and flicking my tongue over the tips of the sparse blond hair. Then I blew gently into the moist crevice, and I watched the orifice pucker in delight.

"Come on, man. Do it. You're driving me nuts. Do it."

So I slathered into the crevice, broad stroking the little canyon until it and my whole face were wet and slippery. I could have grooved on this for hours, but Tommy was writhing and demanding, "Eat it, man. Eat it. Get in there." So I zeroed in, kissing, sucking, licking and prodding with my strong tongue. "Oh, yes. That's it. Eat it. Stick your tongue in there. Oh, God, that's it. That's wild."

To my amazement, the puckered opening began to relax a bit, so that my tongue was actually able to penetrate somewhat, and that drove him even wilder. "Oh, God, yes. That's right. Way up there. Oh, my God, that's incredible."

As yet, I hadn't even touched his cock, but I knew he was close to cumming from the sheer eroticism. By now, Tommy was clutching his own legs to his chest and thrusting his hips up into my face. I licked a finger and began to toy with the opening. Round and round. Tongue and finger, and then only my finger, which probed into the relaxing orifice. Sliding gently round and round and dipping ever so slightly into the warm depth.

Now it was time. I quickly moved up to find his engorged cock throbbing and leaking precum over his abdomen, as he moved in the abandoned state of inflamed ecstasy. I sank down on his cock with a frenzy, swallowing the whole length into my throat.

"Yes, suck me, suck me, oh, yes," and his hands grabbed my head, his legs came down so he could pump with this hips, and he fucked my face. As I rode his bucking cock, I slid my finger deeper and deeper into his welcoming ass, and he seemed to be fucking my face as eagerly as my finger. He slammed his hips upward, and then ground backwards, impaling himself on my exploring finger. I thought he would cum any second, but he went on and on, thrusting his whole body in a mighty arch off the bed and grinding downward onto my finger, which was now moving easily in the relaxed tunnel. All the while, he was moaning and mumbling almost unintelligibly.

So I let a second finger slip into his ass, which constricted violently at first. "Oh, shit, what the fuck are you doing? That's too much," but I kept it there without moving it, as I continued to suck on his throbbing cock. Almost instantly, he fell back into his hip-thrusting movement, and his ass began to relax somewhat. Slowly, I began to wiggle my fingers, exploring until I found his prostate. When I found it, he howled, "Jesus Christ! Oh, fuck." Now my two fingers slid easily in and out, as he fucked himself on them while I sucked his cock. And he was just the perfect size—no gagging or gasping for breath, just a wonderful blowjob. I wanted it to go on forever, and he had amazing endurance for a teenager.

His wiry, muscled little body drove on and on. Oh, the joys of youth!

But then he began arching even higher, pumping up and up. "Oh, God! I'm there. I'm gonna cum. Fuck, yes. Fuck. Suck it, suck it. Fuck, yes, fuck it. Fuck me with your finger. Oh, shit. Take my cum in your mouth," and he clutched my face to his grinding hips, impaling me on his lust. And he came. God, did he cum. Blast after blast filled my throat. I let my fingers slide out of his ass and concentrated on savoring every salty drop he kept pumping into my mouth. "Oh, fuck, man that's fantastic. Jesus, yes, suck it. Take all of it. What a fuck, what a fucking fuck," and he fell limply unto the bed laughing.

"Wow, that was wild. What a fuck. You sure as hell know how to get a guy off. You're something else, man!"

"I'm glad you liked it," I grinned up at him.

"Liked it? Shit, man, I feel as though I just dropped five LSD tabs. That was fucking incredible."

It was nice to be appreciated, and I was thrilled that he didn't have any after-sex hang-ups. "You are the one who's incredible. You're about the hottest guy I've ever seen. What an orgasm! You were like a nuclear explosion!"

"Yeah, it felt like a nuclear explosion," he laughed. "But fuck, man. What were you doing to my ass? I thought you were going to rip me apart."

"I was under the impression that you kind of liked it," I laughed.

"Well, one finger felt kind of nice. But then you put your whole fist up there. At least it felt like it."

"No, just two fingers. And besides, once you stopped being scared, you got off on it."

"Well, I don't know about that, but you touched something in there that blew the top of my head off. What the hell did you do?"

"That was your prostate. I massaged your prostate. Blows your mind, doesn't it?"

"Well, it blew something all right. I didn't know what the fuck was happening," he laughed.

"Yeah, most guys don't realize what a turn-on their ass can be."

"No, I guess not," he laughed. "Well, thanks, that was a new one on me. But I guess I better be going soon. I didn't mean to take up your whole evening. This was really great."

"Take up my whole evening? Hell, I can't think of a better way to spend an evening. Don't rush off. Besides, I know you. In ten minutes you'll be horny again," I laughed.

"Hell, I doubt that. Look, it's limp as a noodle. After what you did, it won't get up again for a week," he laughed.

"How much you want to bet? I'll give it ten minutes, fifteen at the most."

"I seriously doubt it," he laughed.

"Why don't you just lie there and relax and see what happens?"

"You did wear me out, man. I'm totally drained."

"See? I wouldn't want you falling off that high-speed bike. Just relax for a bit. Want some more water?"

"Sure, what the hell," he grinned.

When I came back with the water, Tommy was propped up leaning against the headboard. He drained the cup and asked, "Aren't you tired? You ought to be, God knows. There's another pillow," and he indicated the place beside him. So I crawled in to lie next to him.

"Do you mind if I ask you something?" he said rather seriously.

"No, fine. Go ahead."

"Well, it's about yesterday. You know, at the construction site?"

"Yes, what do you want to know?"

"Well, don't get mad, but it's about the electrician, Mark. Why'd you let him do that? You're as big as he is. You didn't have to take that. He was such a shit, it made me really mad."

"It's a long story, Tommy. Let's just say that his need was greater than mine. You saw just the tip of the iceberg. It's a long story."

"So you knew him before? I thought so. But why'd you let him treat you like that?"

"He's been wrestling with some demons of his own for about a week now. There isn't anything I can do—he won't let me. But I really care about him. And in a strange way I thought it might help. And besides," I laughed, "without Mark I wouldn't have found you."

"Well, I felt bad about it. I didn't want you to think I was treating you like him. He was a real dickhead. Maybe you can excuse him, but I can't."

"No, but then you don't know the whole story. Now, can I ask you a question?"

"Sure."

"What did Bjorn say?"

Tommy laughed, "Oh, shit, he just kept muttering, '*Gott in himmel,*' and other Swedish nonsense all afternoon. "Now, Tommy, ve yust keep dis between us, right? Don't tell nobody, OK?" he mimicked. "I bet he went home and screwed his poor wife's brains out last night."

"So he's OK?"

"Oh, I think so. He'll get over it," he laughed. "He needs to be shaken up a little bit. Lord, I can still see him standing there, that monster prick jutting out, muttering, 'I yust don't know,' while you gave him a blowjob. But he flopped down on the floor fast enough when you told him to, didn't he," he chuckled.

"He sure did," I laughed. "And you—you're OK? At first, I was worried, but you seem fine."

"Oh, sure. I don't have any hang-ups. Sex is sex. You know, the liberated generation, and all that stuff. If it feels good, do it," he grinned. And then after a pause he added, "I'm not worried about you turning me away from girls, if that's what you think."

"No, that's not what I think, and not what I want either. In fact, I'm convinced that that isn't a choice anyway. You are what you are. But I'm glad you're cool about it."

"Oh, yes. It's cool. Don't worry."

Suddenly I had to hold him, touch him. I rolled over beside him, and began caressing his chest and stomach softly. "You're fantastic! Do you know that?"

"Thanks," he said quietly without any feigned protest. He let me cuddle up next to him and stroke his hard, muscled, bare torso. Not massive, but tight and alive and warm and youthful.

"You must have to fight off the girls," I said.

After a while, he chuckled, "I ought to hire you as my PR man. Maybe I can have you give me a testimonial or something, because I sure don't have to fight them off with a stick, let me tell you."

"You mean you don't have a girl?"

"No, not exactly. There are a few I go out with, but nothing serious. Well, there's sex now and then, don't get me wrong, but nothing serious. Nobody ever went totally bonkers, the way you did," he laughed.

"I'll be damned. You just haven't found the right girl then, 'cause when you do, she'll really flip. You're about the hottest thing in pants. With your good looks, a body like yours, and a big cock like this, they should be chasing you like crazy."

"Thanks," he grinned, "but I'm nothing special. Hell, yesterday I felt like a real piker next to Bjorn and Mark. And you, too. You're all bigger than I am. I haven't seen any other guys with a hard-on, except in some porn magazines. I'm beginning to worry a bit."

"Believe me, you have nothing to worry about in that department. You are way bigger than the average guy. And I'm kind of an expert in that area," I laughed. "Besides, you're still young. What are you, eighteen or nineteen?"

"Nineteen last month."

"Nineteen. Hell, Tommy, you're still growing. In the next two or three years you'll probably get even bigger. And you're a real hunk already."

"Thanks," and he beamed shyly. "Whether it's true or not, I guess I needed that."

"Believe me, it's true," and all the while I had been lightly caressing his chest and stomach, playing softly over the smooth, undulating surface of his cool skin.

"Ooooh, that feels nice," he said.

"Why don't you slide down in the bed?" I said. "Yes, that's better," and I was now able to kneel beside him and use both hands to stroke his torso. "God, Tommy, you're one beautiful guy. Your chest muscles are so hard and firm, and your skin is so smooth," and he lay there with his eyes closed and let me caress him and stroke him and worship at this altar of young manhood. And as I stroked my hands lightly over his body, I praised him. Praised the strength of his arms and shoulders, the narrow firmness of his waist and hips, the tight, hard muscles of his legs. And he seemed to enjoy my soft litany of praise.

Then I knelt down and kissed one little brown nipple. He gasped slightly as I began to lick it and suck it, and it grew, protruding sharply from his chest. Then I licked over to the other one and teased it into erection. Then, slowly and lightly, I tongued and licked and kissed all over his chest and stomach. Then up, up to his shoulders, down his biceps, and then to the curve of his neck. All the while, Tommy just lay there, his eyes closed, his face immobile, and every now and again he made little gasping sounds when I touched a particularly sensitive spot.

I licked and kissed the curve of his neck, and then took his earlobe between my lips, sucking it, knowing the sharp little tingles of pleasure it was producing. Then I stopped and looked down into his handsome face. Suddenly, his eyes opened and he whispered, "God, you sure know how to make a guy feel good."

"Shhhhh," and I touched a finger to his lips, and he closed his eyes again.

I traced a finger along each eyebrow, down the length of his nose, and over the curving shape of his lips, which were beautifully boyish. Not terribly full, but shapely and soft to my touch as I outlined them with my finger. Suddenly he nipped playfully at my finger with his teeth, but he quickly released me and let me go back to stroking his face with a light touch. When I played softly over the surface of his lips again, he said softly, "Go ahead, Jeff. It's OK," as if he were reading my mind. And I kissed him lightly on the mouth. Not long or deep, but a brief, tender kiss. He didn't respond, but he permitted it, and I was suddenly overcome with a desire to hold him.

I quickly stretched out beside him and drew him into my arms in a strong embrace. At first he just let me hold him, but soon his arms wrapped around me, and he shifted so that his body was pressed into mine. And I could feel his hard cock jabbing into my hip.

"That was nice. Real nice, man. But now you got me going again."

"Yes, I can feel it," but I just lay there, holding him.

After a minute or two, he said, "Come on, Jeff. You win. You got me all hot to trot again, just like you said," but I just continued to hold him.

"C'mon, Jeff. Quit screwing around. I'm ready. You wanted it hard, and you got it hard. So get down there now and suck on it, man. Come on."

"Well sure, I'd be happy to, but we did that already."

"I know, but now you got me hard again. C'mon, man. I really want it."

"Why don't we try something else?"

"Try something else? Like what? You mean...?" Tommy stammered.

"Yes, I want you to fuck me. I want to feel you inside me. Make you cum that way."

"But doesn't it hurt? I don't want to hurt you."

"No, no. You won't hurt me. I'd love it, really."

"Well, I don't know. I mean, hell, I don't know what to do. You'd have to show me."

"You don't have to do a thing. Just lie there and I'll do everything."

"Well, OK. I guess."

"Great, now let me get some lubricant." And I found the K-Y jelly in the nightstand. Tommy lay there on his back watching me, with a slightly bewildered look on his face, and his erection had softened slightly.

"What do you want me to do?"

"Nothing. Just lie there and enjoy."

And I bent over him taking his long, thick cock in my mouth. "Oh, yes. That feels so fucking good," he moaned, and instantly he was back to full, throbbing erection. I sucked on him gently, enjoying the taste of him, his size, the perfect fit, imagining what he would feel like inside me. When he was beginning to buck in earnest, I pulled off and just stroked his cock lightly with my hand. Then I blew on its wet surface, knowing the sudden cold sensation it gave him. "Oh, God. That's wild. But quit teasing me. Suck it, man. Suck it." But I just wanted to watch it, admire its size and perfect shape. The way it curved up and out of his hips in a mighty sweep of aching strength. Soon, very soon, I would feel it in me. "C'mon, Jeff, suck it." So I quit teasing him and went back to sucking him. "Yes, yes. That's so fucking good." He was hot and rock hard. So it was time.

"I'm going to put some lubricant on you now. It may be cold," and I slathered a little K-Y all over his raging hard-on. Quickly, I greased my ass and shifted on the bed to straddle him.

"I can't believe this doesn't hurt you."

"I'll go slow in the beginning, until I get used to it. Don't worry," and I aimed his cock at my ass. Moving the head up and down the crack, I had the urge to just sit on it in one mighty plunge. But I went slow, feeling the thick head pressing into my resisting orifice. Willing myself to relax, to accept, I pressed downward.

"It'll never fit, man. It's too tight."

And then it happened, and the broad tip of his cock slipped inside. The shocking wonder of first entrance hit me, not really painful, but tight.

"Oh, God. That's tight. You're so tight. Am I hurting you?"

"No, no. You feel wonderful, it feels great," and I began the slow descent, feeling more and more of his thick shaft slip into me, filling me, invading my depths until his hips were pressed into me and I knew I had taken his full length.

"Oh, Jeff. That's fantastic, it's so hot in there, so tight. I've never felt anything so tight. You got it all, man. Every bit of my cock is shoved up your ass. Oh, fuck, that feels so fucking good."

And I began to move on him, up and down, in slow, steady strokes, growing accustomed to his size and shape as the waves of pleasure began to wash over me. "Yes, yes, fuck me, Tommy, fuck me with that big cock." Tentatively, Tommy began to thrust upward to meet my movements.

"Am I hurting you? Tell me if I'm hurting you."

"Hurting me? God, no. You feel wonderful. Fuck my ass, fuck me with that big cock. Oh, you're so big." I fell into a steady rhythm, with long, full strokes. All the way in and all the way out to the very tip. Over and over, while Tommy kept thrusting and moaning about how tight and hot it was. Then I sat all the way down, grinding myself into his hips, making little circular movements trying to find the tiniest millimeter that was still not buried in me.

"Take it, yes, take it all. Feel my big cock all the way up there. So hot, so fucking hot. Fuck it, man, fuck it. I can't take much of this, I'm gonna cum soon. Oh, man, it feels so goooooooood."

"Easy there, Tommy. Let's make this last," and I stopped moving and pulled most of the way off.

"No, no. Don't stop. I don't know if I can, I'm so close," he moaned. Then I pulled off totally.

"Let's change positions," and I lay down beside him on my back. "Get up and kneel between my legs."

"OK. This is fantastic. I've never felt anything like that. You're so tight. Tighter than any pussy. God, what a fuck! And you like it too, don't you?"

"God, yes. I love it. Give it to me," and I lifted my legs up to my chest. He moved into position with his cock at the entrance to my ass.

"I just can't believe it. It looks so tiny and my cock looks so big."

"Give it to me. Shove it in."

"God, you really like it, don't you? Like the feel of this big old thing shoved way up there."

"Yes. Give it to me. I love it. It feels so fucking wonderful. Fuck me. Fuck me hard. Do it."

He slipped the tip into me and withdrew. "Wow. That's amazing. Those little pussylips just open right up and suck it in. Fantastic. You ought to see this." And he did it again and again.

"Come on, man. Give it to me. Put it all in and fuck me." I was aching with emptiness, aching to feel his tight, hard body on me, driving into me with all his strength and fucking me into delirium.

"You want it, Jeff? Tell me you want it."

"Oh, yes. Please fuck me. Do it, man," and I was wiggling my ass up toward him. He took my legs in his arms and pressed them up and over me, resting his hands on either side of my head, so that he was arched over my uplifted ass.

"Hang on, buddy, I'm going to fuck your brains out," and he drove into me with full force. Each thrust hit bottom and his speed was amazing. All I could do was accept—accept his driving strength, his frenzied climb to ecstasy, our frenzied climb. I'd had bigger men, stronger men, but I couldn't remember anyone who fucked with such total abandon.

We were both howling with pleasure, crying our passion, our words wild and mixed together: "Harder, yes, harder. Really give it to me." "So tight, so fucking hot, Jesus fucking Christ. This is so fucking good. Never felt anything like this." "So big, so fucking big. I can feel it in the back of my throat." "Oh, God, I'm there. Gonna cum." "Yes, yes, give it to me. Make me feel it." "Can't hold it, gotta shoot, gotta cum." "Yes, let me have it, I love it." "Take it, man, here it comes, take it. Aaahhhhhhhh. Yes, yes, yes, yes." And he filled me with his young, driving strength, his young abandoned lust for life and pleasure and sexual release.

He eased himself down onto me, resting his head on my chest, still gasping for air.

So it was over. God, I wanted it to last forever, but nineteen year olds are quick. So quick. But he felt wonderful. It had been a wonderful first fuck.

After a while, I said, "Are you OK?"

He lifted his head and looked at me, grinning broadly. "I'm fantastic. What about you?"

"I'm wonderful. That was totally mind-blowing."

"I know," he grinned. "You want me to move?"

"No, stay right there. I love the feel of your big cock up there. It feels so good, so big."

"I think you made it grow another inch just tonight," he joked.

"God, it feels like it," and amazingly, he did not seem to be getting soft. He was collapsed in my arms, but his cock still had life, and his hips began just the tiniest movement causing the slightest pressure deep inside me. Slowly, almost lazily, he fell into a small rhythm, so that his cock slid easily, but almost imperceptibly, in my fully relaxed ass, which was slippery with his cum.

It was wonderful. Slow and easy, with only the tiniest movement. He had cum so quickly that I was still longing for more, and I was grateful that he hadn't wanted to pull out as soon as he came. Now he was allowing me time to savor the feel of him, the sense of being possessed and of possessing him. It was wonderful. Amazing. And it went on and on.

Suddenly, he lifted his head from my chest and his dark eyes smiled at me, "You really like that, don't you?"

"God, yes. You feel so good, so big. And you're still hard. You just came and you're still hard, aren't you?"

"Yes," he grinned. "You ready for round two? Or are you sore?"

"Oh, no. Don't stop, it feels fantastic. I wish you could do it forever. Your cock feels so good."

"I love the way you beg for it," he laughed. "God, nobody has ever begged for it before, it just drives me wild."

"Yes, I love it, Tommy. I love your big cock inside me."

"And it really doesn't hurt you, does it?"

"God, no. You have no idea how great if feels to have your big cock fucking me."

"Well, it feels pretty good from this end too, let me tell you," and he fell into a slow, easy fuck.

This time there was no frenzy, just a long, slow fuck. Our bodies joined in a slow rhythm, and it was I who kept begging for more, for him to go faster and deeper. But he toyed with me, enjoyed the way I begged for it. His strokes were long and deep and deliberate.

Then he began withdrawing all the way out and waiting a moment before entering me again. It drove me wild to feel so suddenly empty, and I pleaded with him to slam it in. But he loved to tease me, loved to have me beg for his cock, and each time he would make me wait longer.

"C'mon, Tommy. Give it to me."

"You want it? You really want it?

"Oh, yes. Please. Please fuck me. Give me that big cock. Ram it in me!" It was a game, but it was real too, fulfilling some deep need in both of us.

"Beg for it, man. Tell me how much you want it."

"Oh, please, man. I want it so bad. Let me have it," and finally he would slam it in.

Finally, after many minutes, he said, "Enough of this fun and games. Let's really do it, man. I need to get off again." And he began to fuck me for real. In that position, I could wrap my arms around him and feel his driving body mounting to higher and higher planes of pleasure. My hands roamed over his strong back, down to the flexing cheeks of his ass. More than anything in the world, I wanted to bring him off again. I flexed the muscles in my ass to give him added pleasure, and he moaned in ecstasy.

I kissed his chest and neck, and without thinking, pulled his face down to me to kiss his cheeks and chin, all over his beautiful face. And then he was kissing me. Kissing me with all the passion in his driving body. In amazement, I returned his kisses. We were both too far gone to think about it. We just let it happen, accepted it with wonder.

But soon, he broke away howling, "I'm there! Oh, God, I'm gonna cum. I can't hold it back, man, I can't...," and I grabbed his driving ass and pulled him deeper in me with every powerful thrust.

"Give it to me, oh, yes, let me have it. So good! So fucking good. I want you so bad. Fuck me, fuck me!"

"Aaaaeeeeeeooooooo! I'm cumming. Oh God, I cumming!" and I could feel him shooting, convulsing in wrenching spasms of orgasm. "Take it, man, take it."

"Yes, oh, yes, yes, give it to me, let me have it." And he drove in deeper, and I held him there, giving, taking, possessing him totally. It was wonderful. I wanted him there forever. And I held him to me as he slowly relaxed and his breath became more steady.

He lay on me, totally drained and exhausted, and I held him, cherishing the beauty of this young man who had given me everything, let me lead him to new worlds and share in his wonder and joy. Given me his cock, his youth, his innocence, his wonder. He let me cuddle him, soothe him back from whatever realms he had visited.

This time, his cock quickly softened, and slowly it began slipping out. When it finally popped all the way out, he said, "Thanks, that was fantastic. Even better than the first time. Wow, what an incredible fuck. I thought I was never going to stop cumming," he laughed softly.

"Yes, it was really great. You are something else. Wow. I can't believe you can cum twice in a row like that."

"Me either. It's never happened before. Wow. And you—you were really going there. Does it make you cum too? It sounded as though you were cumming."

"No, I didn't cum. It was just as good though. Totally different, but just as good."

"Good, I'm glad. But I've got to get off now; you drained everything out of me, man," and he rolled off me onto the bed. "Wow, I'm really wiped out now, man. How are you?"

"I'm fine, just fine. Let me get a washcloth and clean you up."

"Yes, I must be a mess," and he looked down at his soft cock. "Well, I'll be. I thought it would be all dirty. You know, covered with...," and he stretched it out to inspect it. "But it isn't. It's just slippery with cum. Wow, that's wild."

"Things aren't always what you expect, are they?" I laughed.

"No, I guess not," and he lay back on the bed. "Wow," he grinned. "You can say that again. What a night! Goddamn!"

THE MISSION OF ALEX KANE:
GOLDEN YEARS

JOHN PRESTON

Alex Kane didn't have a hard time making sense of Cactus City. It was like any other small county seat in the Southwest. One big main street, a few shops, a courthouse, a couple of middling motels. It was the center of life for the surrounding area, but not one that was made for a hot time.

Alex had flown into Yuma Airport that morning and rented a car. He'd driven the three hours to Cactus City, admiring the stunning vistas that lined the highway at the same time that he was astonished by the lack of inhabitants. This was one of the most sparsely settled parts of the United States. There had been dozens and dozens of miles that Alex could travel before he saw so much as a shack at the side of the road. All of Arizona's population seemed to be clustered on the banks of a few rivers, none of which came close to this town.

He had spent some time reading local newspapers and wandering through the small stores on the street. He hadn't found a clue about anything to do with his goal in coming here. Normally Alex was able to get information quickly and easily. He'd just go to a gay bar, allow himself to be picked up, and he'd have a source—almost always a good and trustworthy one. Alex remembered Erin Frost, the gay leader in Boston who had helped him out on one of his last cases. Now, that had been a mixture of business and pleasure, double servings of both! But Cactus City wasn't going to have a gay bar. Not by a long shot. Alex doubted there would be an Erin Frost, either.

When Alex had wandered into the one decent-looking restaurant in town, he wasn't expecting anything but a beer and a meal. It was immediately obvious that the other people in the dining room's bar had greater expectations.

It was Friday night, and the working people of Cactus City were celebrating loud and heavy. Alex smiled at some of their antics and made his way to the bar. He ordered his usual Budweiser and overtipped the bartender. He turned to face the crowd and study it some more, resting his elbows on the mahogany surface behind him.

As he scanned the diners, Alex noticed a single male standing in the corner across the way. Alex Kane had no time to waste on seducing straight men; he couldn't be bothered with all the games that came with them. But he did decide that this man certainly looked interesting.

For the most part, the people here were dressed in the expected Western clothes. Some, probably lawyers, bankers, and salesmen, were wearing an embarrassment of pastel polyester—they must have thought that was the "in" thing this year. The women looked as though they shopped out of a Sears catalog, and they probably did. All in all, the group was happy, singing along easily when a favorite country-and-western tune came over the loudspeaker, laughing loudly at their jokes and just pleased that the weekend had arrived.

It was easy enough for Alex to become moody. It was always so appealing to look at what appeared to be simple lives and to want to have that kind of existence for himself. If he were just another guy living in Cactus City, then most of his problems would be solved. But that was an impossible speculation. He wasn't just another guy, and he never would be again—if he ever had been before.

Alex drove those little touches of self-pity from his mind and scanned the room again. That same man was still standing in his corner, still slouched against the wall. Alex looked at him for perhaps a beat too long. Then he took his eyes away. If this had been a gay bar, Alex would have sworn the man was cruising him.

Could he be?

Alex looked back. Now that he had caught Alex's attention, the stranger had a bigger smile on his face. He nodded his head in a slight but overtly friendly manner. Alex certainly would have been interested if this had been a gay bar. The guy was at least Alex's own six feet. He had a shock of curly blond hair and a thick blond moustache. His teeth gleamed when he smiled. His eyes were a light blue, noticeably light even from this distance.

The jeans and cowboy shirt the man wore showed a lot of wear. But they were also made for his body. The denim pants hugged his solid thighs and bulged at his crotch. His shirt was buttoned only halfway up. The hair on his chest—so unexpected on a blond—was thick and just as curly as that on his head. The skin was darkly tanned.

The man winked.

What the hell! Alex thought, more surprised than he was used to being. The guy must have sensed that. His smile broke out even more. He stood straight and walked over to where Alex was standing. His hand was outstretched. "Luke McDavid," he introduced himself.

Alex took that handshake and made his own introduction.

"I know you're not from here," Luke said. "I know everyone in this town."

"California," Alex explained. He always used Farmdale's address when he had to have one. The reality was that Kane lived most of his life in a succession of hotel rooms. That was too difficult to explain to most people.

"Here on business?"

"Yeah. I'm looking into some property near here for someone."

"Ranching?"

"Maybe."

"Well, I have a great idea. If you want to talk ranch land, you *have* to talk to Luke McDavid. I just happen to know everything there is to know about such things in this whole county. And I will insist on sharing all that knowledge with you...over dinner."

The smile and the invitation were both authentic and added up to an honest-to-God come-on. Alex smiled, "I'd be happy to have dinner with you. But if you're giving the information, I guess I better pick up the tab."

"Don't be silly. No one picks up the tab in Cactus City when he's with Luke McDavid. You just come on over to the dining room of this establishment and we'll get down to some serious talking ... about business."

Alex followed the big man to the other side of the partition, where the tables were set for the evening meal. Luke didn't wait for a hostess, he just picked out a table that suited him.

They sat down, and Luke began to ask Alex some more questions about what type of real estate he was looking for. Kane thought he had done his homework for the assignment; he had learned all the right terms and key words about a transaction like this from Farmdale, but Luke seemed to come up with various questions that made Alex feel as though he were missing something.

A waitress came up and handed each of them a menu. "Rebecca, how's my sweetheart?"

"Oh, Luke McDavid, don't you go playing those games with me. You've broken more than enough hearts in this town, leading poor girls on to think they could get ahold of what they can never have. Bad enough it's you; you don't have to go importing more good-looking men we can't hope for." The waitress looked right at Alex Kane and sighed. "Why are all your *friends* so damn good-looking?" Rebecca shook her head and walked away, leaving the menus in their hands.

"What the hell's your story?" Alex Kane asked, not angrily, with a touch of humor in his voice. "I just don't understand how you can act this way in a small town. You came on to me as though we were in a bar on Folsom Street or on Christopher, not in Cactus City. Then the waitress in the local steakhouse treats it like it's just matter-of-fact that we're gay. You haven't even said anything to me yet. How could you have been so sure?"

Luke obviously enjoyed all this. His eyes sparkled more brightly. "Oh, well, so far as you're concerned, I was sure only because you were looking back. Now, all that sixth sense we're supposed to have about one another is foolishness. But there is a certain way that men look at one another and let each other know that something's going on. You had it. You looked back. I didn't do all that by myself, you know.

"Besides, there are things you notice. You aren't a cowboy, I would've known if you were. But you got the right kind of jeans on, and boots and all. And you aren't wearing a gold chain—that's a straight man's dead giveaway; they all wear gold chains around here. You're also too good-looking. You can always tell a gay guy when he's good looking and has a tight body, certainly one who's our age. Straight men have bellies by the time they're your age—about thirty or a little more?"

Alex nodded. "Thirty-two."

"See, and you got a body like a high school athlete. Put all that together and it spells gay.

"Rebecca? Well, after a while, in a small place like this, the word gets around. Small towns aren't as bad as most people think, not really. Now, you can't go and seduce their children, and they might have trouble if you wanted to have a gay-liberation parade down the center of town or something. And I know you would have trouble if you were a newcomer. But I was born and raised in Cactus City, and they all know me and they've known me forever. I just let them joke and I joke back, and we all keep it at a friendly enough level.

"They're used to my having a *friend* come and visit every once in a while, though it's been a long while this time around, I must admit. So they just take a few liberties."

"How do you manage—just with friends visiting?"

"Oh, the old animal urges get to me, and I make some mad dashes to Los Angeles or Las Vegas when that happens. I have a little plane of mine out in the county airport for just those events. I used to have some visitors—you know, married men in the dead of night, the kind that are scared to shit that someone will see their car in my driveway, so they'd walk two miles instead. But that got to be more trouble than it was worth, so I cut it out.

"Thing is, I'm happiest here. I've tried to live other places, but I just can't hack the city and its ways. So I don't get laid as often as I'd like, but I get things I care about more. Not that I don't like it when I do get my chance to climb in the sack." Luke lifted up his bottle of beer and toasted Alex playfully.

"Pretty presumptuous, aren't you?"

"Hell, Mr. Kane, it isn't presumption to say I'm the best fuck in Cactus City. I'm probably the only one you could get your hands on!" Luke took a deep drink of his beer and slammed it down on the table. "What you see in front of you is all you're going to get here. And something tells me you've done a hell of a lot worse in your time."

Alex really did like Luke's puckish manner. And if he really was a native, he fit the usual category of Kane's sexual partners: men who had information they'd give in exchange for a night with him.

Looking at the way the man's shirt had spread open when he had leaned across the table just now, revealing a larger look at that hairy chest with those well-developed nipples. Alex was perfectly willing to concede that this was going to be a pleasure—especially once he got a look at Luke's nipples. They were large, well developed in a way that nature had nothing to do with. They stuck far out from the planes of his pectorals; bits of flesh that had been teased and tortured and played into greater size, size so great that Alex felt his mouth water from the idea of getting them between his teeth.

Suddenly Rebecca was back beside them and broke the spell that Luke's chest had been weaving over Alex's mind. "Now, what are you going to have?" she asked. "Least, what are you going to have that's on the menu and that's legal?"

Luke smiled at Alex. "If you follow my lead and have a sirloin steak, rare, a salad with house dressing, a baked potato, and we split a side of onion rings, you'll have a damned good meal. You choose anything else, I am not responsible for your doctor bills."

"You win. That sounds fine."

"Two Luke specials," Rebecca said as she gathered up the menus. "You wouldn't have done too bad with the fried chicken. It's not bad tonight."

"All that means is that it's not deadly poison tonight," Luke insisted.

"McDavid, you are a pain in the butt. Or at least I wish you would be. Just once, I surely do wish you would be." With an exaggerated sigh, she left.

Luke and Alex talked easily for a while longer. Then Rebecca was back. She put a bottle of French wine on the table. Alex was impressed. He recognized it as a particularly good St. Emilion, one that Farmdale enjoyed. Luke had taken a corkscrew that Rebecca had placed beside the bottle and was opening it. He saw the question on Alex's face.

"Well, you see, when it was time for me to go off to college, my daddy and me finally compromised. I'd study animal husbandry, the way he wanted, if he'd let me go to Cornell, the way I wanted. I picked up a few things out East. Let's just say that a taste for good wine was one of the less exotic."

Rebecca returned with two glasses for them. Luke poured each of them full. "I had them buy a couple of cases of this for me. Private stock, you could say. I eat here a lot. Gets a bit lonely eating by myself all the time. Even if all I get is some background noise from these fools, it helps a lot. I got some business in town often enough anyway; bankers, insurance brokers, and the like. So I try to do it here.

"Back home I get a little more fancy in the kitchen than just steak and potatoes, anyhow. Another of the exotic things I picked up at Cornell."

"A gourmet cowboy?"

"Well, hell, those gay genes got to come out some way besides my cock and asshole!" Luke loved that joke and nearly spilled his wine as he laughed.

The dinner was as good as Luke had promised. The steak wasn't the chemically tenderized stuff of a big-city restaurant. It had the firm texture and full taste of lean range beef that burst in Alex's mouth. The wine went with it impeccably. The potato was baked to perfection—not microwaved, he knew that. The salad dressing had been made with buttermilk and some tart spices. By the time they were done Alex thought he had gained at least another ten pounds. He was sitting back in his chair, contented and happy with the food and the company.

"I do hope you're expecting this little evening to continue," Luke said. His voice wasn't as challenging or joking now. It had a touch of seduction to it, soft and alluring in a way, though nothing that came from the big man's mouth could ever be less than masculine.

"Oh, yes," Alex replied. "I most definitely am."

"Good. The coffee here's for shit. Why don't we just get along? Don't worry about the check; I insist on paying it. You're a guest in our fair city. I have a tab here, and Rebecca will just take care of it all for us."

"You're on," Alex said.

They drove over the backroads after leaving the state highway. Luke's place was at least twenty miles from Cactus City, but that kind of distance didn't mean much in this part of the country. Alex Kane knew that.

The ride wasn't all that comfortable. Luke drove a monster of a four-wheel-drive truck. It bounced and jerked with every bump. It didn't buffer its occupants from the realities of the highway like Kane's rental car did with its super-suspension and power steering and power brakes and God knows what else.

They stopped at one point. Luke had been giving Alex a guided tour through this part of Arizona, and now he pointed out a large and imposing Victorian mansion. It was out of place in the middle of the near-desert. "That's where I grew up." There was a wistful tone to Luke's voice.

"Do your parents still live there?"

"Nah, they're long dead. It's been at least ten years since." He put the vehicle back in drive and started them on their way again. "My father built it for my mother when they got married. He was trying to make it easier for her to move here. Didn't do much good, the woman always wanted to be back East—she was from Baltimore. She hid it as well as she could, but we always knew.

"She'd keep on trying to civilize everyone around here. She'd have poetry readings and musical evenings and all that. Dad was the biggest rancher around, so all the other ranchers' wives would feel obligated to come. But they didn't really have any passion to match her interest in art. She tried to get it going in me, but I was drawn out to the range with my father.

"She was a good woman. Like I say, she tried to hide things, but there used to be this look on her face when Dad and I would go out in the morning, most often on horseback in those days. We'd try to contain ourselves in the house and be proper gentlemen for her, but our hearts were always outside. If she hadn't loved the two of us so very much, I guess she would've left this place long ago. But she stayed till her last days.

"I loved them both. And I loved that house. But it was a woman's house. Dad and I always let it be that. When they'd gone, I just couldn't see a bachelor living there with all the flowery wallpaper and the fine antiques she'd collected. It's off to a corner of the property, so it was easy enough to divide that acre it sits on and let it go on the market. I built myself my own kind of house farther in. More my own style."

Alex soon got to see what Luke's "own style" was. The house was a single-story building, sleekly lined and showing the sharpest attention to architectural design. It was constructed of obviously local materials: rough stone and hand-hewn woods combined in a way that allowed the structure to almost melt into the natural surroundings. It was understated, at least in the sense that Alex wasn't really aware of how large or luxurious it was at first glance.

After Luke had parked he led the way into the house. At first it appeared to be one gigantic room. A state-of-the-art kitchen was separated only by a waist-high divider. Food processors, pasta machines, microwave ovens—all the latest gadgets were evident. The floors of the room were stone, but not cool to Alex's feet when he had followed Luke's example and left his own boots by the door. Obviously there were heating elements in the material.

The inside walls were of the same stone and wood as the exterior. There was an enormous fireplace at the opposite end of the room from the kitchen. Only a few large pieces of furniture formed an arc facing the hearth. Between them and the cooking area was a huge and obviously handmade dining ensemble. It was baronial in size and appearance.

Farmdale would have been comfortable in a place like this, Alex realized. Whatever else, Luke was rich.

The cowboy had sauntered down the other end of the room and was striking a large wooden match to light the already-assembled wood in the fireplace. When the flames had begun to flicker, he turned to Alex. "It'll take a while for this to really get going. Want to warm up in the hot tub first?"

"Hot tub?"

Luke gestured to the side wall of the room. Alex hadn't noticed the large sliding-glass doors. Outside was a wooden platform, the centerpiece of which was a wooden tub. Alex smiled, "This is the life of a cowboy?"

"Yep—1990s version," Luke answered. He began to unbutton his shirt as he went to the doors. "Come on, let me show you how the latest model works—hot tub, that is."

"I don't need to know how a hot tub works," Alex said as he watched Luke pull his shirt off. The two cultivated nipples were standing at attention, just asking for someone to do something with them. Alex knew he was going to be the one to handle their situation.

"Well, then, I guess you'll just have to be satisfied with the basic cowboy model's way of doing things," Alex answered.

Stripped to the waist Luke walked over to where Alex stood and wrapped his arms around the dark-haired man. They kissed. Luke stood back suddenly. "Jesus!" He said the word in two long syllables. "What the hell was that all about?"

Alex Kane smiled. People often reacted to him that way. He had trained his body to be the most efficient tool possible. The countless hours of work, exercise, and physical awareness had heightened his sensuality. Those same things that had made him a fearsome fighter had created a depth of sexual ability that always seemed to take people by surprise. A simple kiss, a light embrace, a tender caress; any of them became greatly magnified when Alex performed them.

"It's just something you learn." Alex gave Luke his stock answer.

"Well, teacher, I want some more lessons. Right now." He grabbed Alex's arms and pulled him to the patio.

In a matter of minutes, Luke was naked. He lowered his body gingerly into the steaming, swirling water of the hot tub. The slow entry gave Alex a chance to appreciate just how well built Luke was. That blond hair seemed to cover all his body like a thick pelt, but not one so dense that Luke's muscles weren't obvious. The body hair certainly couldn't cover the length of Luke's expanding penis. The cowboy had a beefy cock, just a hefty serving of meat that Alex knew was going to taste as good as tonight's steak dinner.

Finally Luke's torso was submerged. "What's the matter, you shy or something?"

Alex just smiled. He finished unbuttoning his own shirt and pulled it off. He peeled off his socks, then unbuckled his belt and let his jeans fall to the ground. His undershirt came next. Its removal was enough to evoke a low whistle from Luke. "Just like a fucking statue."

Alex Kane's body didn't have the bulk that Luke's did, but those torturous exercises had produced a definition and a sharpness of each individual muscle that left him looking as though he had been the model for most of the great artwork of ancient Greece. But when he slipped down his cotton briefs and stood totally naked in front of Luke, the cowboy had other thoughts in mind. "Hell, no wonder they put a fig leaf over that! They'd have half the men and half the women fainting dead away. It's like seeing one of those Greek columns turned into flesh."

Alex smiled again and walked over to the tub. When he put a foot into the water, he understood why Luke had taken so long to immerse himself. It was hot! The cowboy reached over and took one of Alex's calves in his hand. "Smooth like silk," he seemed to say to himself. Then he raised his voice, "Just slide in slow and easy. You'll get used to it."

Alex followed the advice and soon had almost all his body in the water. The unseen jets made the tub into a mechanical massage device. The pounding flow of water relaxed his muscles, and the warmth was seductive all by itself—and in addition, Luke was giving it plenty of help. He had taken Alex's cock and balls gently in his palms and seemed to hold them tenderly and almost lovingly. That sensation was accompanied by the wonderfully erotic surge of water that came out of the jets and seemed to fuck Alex with its pressure. He felt as if he was having sex with two beings; one human, the other mechanical, both of them awfully good at what they did.

"Not often I get to have this, a hot man in my hot tub, my hands on his crotch. Feels good." Luke's voice was lost and sensual. He moved around in the water so his back was to Alex. There wasn't much doubt what he wanted. Alex moved a bit and let the jets of compressed water rush against Luke's buttocks. "That's not enough, man," Luke insisted. "I need the real thing."

The real thing was getting itself ready for the invitation. Alex's hard cock moved into place, positioning its hard knob against the walls of Luke's sphincter. There wasn't any need to push hard; Luke was willing, ready, and able to take the whole length inside him in one long, sensual motion.

"Ride me, Alex, ride me!" Luke commanded. He began to buck against the invasion of Alex's dick, forcing Alex to hold tightly to the cowboy's shoulders while he fucked the hard round ass with all the bravado of a frontiersman.

"Spear it! Man, fuck that ass!" Luke was in his own world now, lost in his sexual drive. Alex forced his hips against the firm butt and felt the juices gush inside himself. In only seconds, he was flooding his fluids in the cowboy's ass.

Alex could feel Luke's muscles clenching his cock tightly. He knew Luke was coming himself, and soon he could see the stringy white come floating to the surface of the hot tub. Luke reached out and waved the ooze onto his body, using it as though it were a bath oil. "Isn't a damn thing better for the skin," he laughed. "Organic and everything!"

They laughed at the joke while they disengaged, Alex's softening cock finally slipping out of the tight confines of Luke's ass. They both sighed and then leaned back against the side of the tub.

"It's a big place for a single guy, Luke," Alex said finally.

"Yeah," Luke was still fondling Alex intimately. "I always hoped maybe I'd find someone to move in with me. That's why I wanted a man's house, not something like my mother's, but I guess I always hoped I'd have another man to share it."

Luke probably felt Alex stiffen. "Oh, don't worry," he reassured him. "I know the signals well enough. You're not one to want to move out to Arizona and live in the desert for the rest of your life. I'm not going to make any moves like that on you."

"Sorry, Luke."

"Sorry? Hell, I knew who you were, and I had an idea what you were as soon as I saw you. You don't have the hunter's look about you. That kind of hunter I mean anyway. You're an honest, open guy, okay by me. You're a big boy and so am I. This is for tonight, maybe one or two other times while you're in town. That doesn't bother me. But you asked me a question, and I gave you an answer."

Luke moved slightly away from Alex. His mind was drifting. "You know, I thought I had that once, that guy. When you asked me back at the restaurant if I did much and I said not recently, it was because of him. Liked him a lot, really did. He was from L.A.—that's where I met him. Lust at first sight, so we thought everything would be perfect. I had the house, he could just get some kind of job in the town to make himself feel independent—it's hard when you got a place like I do and the money to go with it; people are always worried about taking too much from you.

"But it was like my mother all over again. He was a fish out of water. He wanted theater and movies and God only knows what else." Luke was far, far away now. "It was hard to watch it happen. He did all those things that my mother didn't. He started to blame me, find unnecessary fault in me.

"You could just see it, like it was a movie script. At first he was willing to try anything so long as it meant we could do things together. I taught him to ride, and we'd go all over hell on horseback. I was even teaching him how to fly that plane of mine, thinking he could go over to Phoenix or up to Las Vegas when he wanted to get his culture-fix.

"But then it soured. You could watch his reactions as they changed. Everything was wrong. There was nothing good about the place, the desert, the state, the truck, the plane—nothing had a single redeeming value. Then, one day, he understood that what he was saying was something different. He was saying that *I* didn't have any redeeming value. And that was that. Two years and goodbye!"

They sat in the water silently for a spell. "Do you want me to leave, Luke?" Alex felt he had to ask the question; the cowboy had left him so far behind.

"Oh, hell, no!" It was as though Luke had been awakened from a trance. "Hell, no! After all this time I got a number like you in my paws, you think I'm going to let him go? You're crazy." He pulled Alex to him. Kane let the big hairy man drag him over and embrace him. Luke's hands found Alex's cock again. "I'm perfectly happy with a perfectly honest night with a good man. I'm downright appreciative!

"I shouldn't go on about things in the past. I learned my lesson. I won't try to take any more fish out of water. But that sure as hell doesn't mean I can't try to find myself an amphibian!"

They got out of the tub soon after that. Naked, dripping with water that Luke told Alex to ignore, they went inside. The fire was roaring, its bright flames sending wild and energetic shadows over all the walls. There was a large bearskin spread in front of the fireplace. Luke collapsed on top of it, face up, looking right at Alex.

"Like what you see as much as I like what I see?" Luke asked. He had spread his legs. His cock was slowly but surely filling with lust—it had begun to arc up, away from the nest of blond pubic hair. His balls were pulled so tightly beneath it that they were nearly invisible. But Alex had seen how very large they were.

Kane dropped to his knees beside Luke. His own cock was becoming erect. He reached over and laid a palm on Luke's warm belly, where the beads of water from the tub had plastered the body hair to his skin. Alex ran his hand up and down, each movement taking his palm closer first to Luke's nipples, then to Luke's now fully hard cock. Alex kept up the motion, coaxing Luke on and on to a higher peak of passion.

Eventually his hands found those hardened pieces of flesh on Luke's chest. After a bit of pressure, Luke moaned as the nipples were manipulated. Alex kept up the seductive actions until Luke surrendered to his peaking passion and lifted his hips off the floor.

"Please, Alex, oh, man ... please."

Alex bent down and took the blond-haired shaft in his mouth. Luke grabbed hold of Alex's hair and held on to it as he directed the motion of Alex's mouth. He wanted it soft and slow at first, making sure that he dragged Alex's lips right to the tip of his cock. But he couldn't keep that pace for long. Soon he was directing Alex with an ever-greater frenzy of desire. Alex could feel the cock expanding in his mouth. He knew the cowboy was going to come soon.

Alex struggled to get his head out of Luke's grip, then he moved to cover the cowboy's body with his own. Their two stiff cocks rubbed against one another and against one another's belly. The pressure of their bodies built as they kissed each other's lips. Soon they couldn't hold back any longer. They began to breathe more heavily into each other's mouth, and finally the warm flow of come shot from their dicks and made their bodies slip and slide against one another.

SKIPPER
Paris Kincaid

He stopped the boat just inside the international waterline. He dropped anchor and came down from the pilot's seat.

I watched him as he worked, putting the deep-sea fishing poles into the brackets and setting out the deck chairs. His longish blond hair stirred in the breeze, and his muscular ass swayed beneath his white cotton shorts. Suddenly I was not at all interested in fishing.

He smiled at me every time he caught my eye, his teeth white in his sun-bronzed face. He would wink and nod his head a little. When he finished setting the pole, he waved me into a chair and helped me bait the line. I sat there for a good two hours or so without a nibble. Finally there was a prodigious tug on my line, and I nearly flew out of my chair. Skipper leaped down from the pilothouse and wrapped his arms around my waist and put his hands on mine as we tried to reel in the largest marlin I'd ever seen.

He was a fighter, but we weren't about to let him go. And once we had him on deck, I let out a yell of victory and went downstairs to the galley for a hard-earned beer. After stowing the fish, Skipper followed me down.

"Congratulations!" he said. "That's one big fish."

I beamed at him. "Thank you. I'd never have landed him myself." I went over and shook his hand. Suddenly he was in my arms. My mouth ran across his, and his lips parted beneath mine, our tongues fencing, tasting each other.

He sighed as I broke the kiss, and he moved in closer, seemingly reluctant to have me leave him. I shook my head and put my hand on the bulge at his crotch. His cock leaped up into my hand. Grinning, he turned and stripped.

After a few moments, he stood naked before me and opened his arms wide. He was beautiful—wide muscular shoulders, narrow waist, a nice eight-inch cock nestled in a thatch of blond pubic hair. His legs were long and toned from walking on pitching decks. They swayed up and down from the movement of the deck beneath our feet.

He walked over to me and tugged the shirt over my head. He brushed his fingers down my chest until he reached the waistband of my shorts. He pulled them down, his fingers brushing lightly against the bulge of my cock as he passed. I stepped out of the shorts and kicked them across the room. Skipper sank to his knees.

I felt the wetness of his tongue glide from my toes up to my knee, where he stopped and reached around to tickle the tender underside. Working his way upward, he circled my groin with his tongue, never once touching it to my cock. It didn't matter—I was already hard.

When he finally wrapped his lips around the base, I thought I was going to break. He dragged his lips up the shaft, following them with little swirls of his tongue. When he reached the head, he swirled his tongue around the ridge of flesh there, and along the slit.

Dropping to my knees, I threw him back and entered him, plunging my cock into his tight hole until I was buried within him. As he lunged in and out hard and fast, each thrust met with a low cry from Skipper and the battering of his balls against my sweaty body.

I felt it start as an almost-painful contraction low in my balls which shot what seemed like gallons of cum up the shaft of my cock to bathe Skipper's bowels in liquid fire. As I spent deep within him, he cried out and shot his own wad, spurting jet after jet of creamy, hot cum, coating my torso and his with the sticky mess.

Pulling out in a backwash of cum, I collapsed to the deck and put my hand on his stomach, feeling the stickiness there. Skipper smiled. "Caught yourself another fish, huh?"

I laughed. "Yeah. Stuffed and mounted, too."

ROADIE
Michael Chelsea

I wander onstage to look for Teddy. I have never seen the place so empty before; but then, I am usually busy before a show. I warm up, bending at the knees and waist, jumping up high and landing in a split, then popping back up again into a spontaneous pirouette.

Teddy leaps onto the stage and begins to climb the rigging, motioning me to follow.

On the catwalk, Teddy looks hungrily at me and unbuttons my shirt. Pushing the shirt over my shoulders, he exposes my chest. He takes a nipple into his mouth and sucks on it gently.

Teddy's hands are at my hips, feeling for the double row of buttons there. My own hands find the buttons of his jeans, undoing them, and I'm anxious for my first sight of him.

He is huge; a thick nine-inch cock planted in a patch of brown pubic hair. His balls are full and round. Teddy undulates out of his clothing.

Fully erect now, he falls to his knees to worship my prick with touch and tongue, licking it as if it were candy, long wet strokes up and down the shaft.

Teddy draws me down onto the catwalk with him.

His mouth at my balls, he sucks at them and licks at the line that divides the sacs. Suddenly he growls and turns, offering me his own cock.

I take it greedily. Teddy's rod is thick, and I almost choke on it; but I open the back of my throat wide enough to take him. He slides his cock in and out of my mouth as I provide counterpressure with my lips and tongue. I can taste the precum that forms at the tip. I hear Teddy groaning as my cock jumps in his mouth.

He turns again, raises my knees and buries his face in the crack of my arse. He licks at the hole and takes the precum from the tip of my cock onto his finger to lubricate the opening. He takes his prick in his hand and guides the head toward my tight hole, slowly pushing it in. I throw my head back in a mixture of agony and rapture as the head of Teddy's prick is followed by the rest.

He moves in tight circles within me. He dances out of the tight opening and dances in again before changing tempo as the heat rises, marking four-quarter, then five-eighths time.

I feel as if I am going to explode; the driving rhythm of Teddy's cock in my arse and my own cock's being caressed by his writhing torso, cause flights of ecstasy unknown until now.

The music starts and I am engulfed by the white-hot explosion of his cum, jets of milky white jism flowing into my bowels, making me all warm inside.

The release is immense. As I cum, Teddy falls to my chest, the fluid bathing his abdomen. I touch him there, where it lies, thick and white upon his belly. I feel my cum between my fingers and am surprised as Teddy takes my hand and puts my fingers in his mouth. He takes his other hand, finds some cum of his own, and serves it to me. He tastes strong, bitter; it is a masculine, musky taste that tingles at the back of my throat.

Rising, Teddy fetches our clothes; as he dresses silently, as I do the same. We have been up here too long.

Teddy climbs down the rigging at stage left. I climb down at stage right a few moments later.

TOUR GUIDE
Thom Spencer

"**C**ome on, Martha, I'm getting our money back!"

Just like that, I was the only one left.

I walked over to the tour guide, stood next to him, and braced my arms against the rails of the display case. I read his name off the badge on the lapel of his coat.

"You've got to admit it, Steve, it *is* pretty lame." I said, not unkindly.

He looked at me, his eyes moist, as if he were about to cry or something. "Don't worry," I assured him. "I won't abandon you." He looked at me gratefully.

I sort of liked him. He was a young guy—well, younger'n me, anyway, with dirty-blond hair. He had a conventionally handsome face and who-knew-what under his clothes. He wasn't a bad tour guide, just saddled with stupid exhibits.

We continued walking through the halls and I ended walking not behind him, but next to him. Every once in a while, my hand strayed across to rest on his ass. He didn't seem to mind. Beneath the suit, it felt like a particularly nice ass. An ass I wouldn't mind touring.

Sensing my mood, he veered off and opened a door between displays. Pulling me in, he shut the door behind us and braced a chair under the knob.

He removed his jacket and draped it over the chair at the door. I looked at Steve, a brow raised. He shrugged. "I'm tired of telling you about things you don't give a shit about." He paused. "Don't take this the wrong way, but I noticed that you were, uh…"

"Interested?" He nodded and licked his upper lip with the tip of his tongue. My breath came faster and I approached closer. He fell to his knees and opened the fly of my pants. My cock, already semihard, popped out and he took it greedily in his mouth.

He wrapped his lips around the base of the shaft and pulled upward, following the suction with warm swipes of his tongue. He lapped his way around the ridge of flesh at the head and darted the sharp tip of his tongue past the slit at the top. Running his tongue back down the shaft to the base, he continued licking his way around the heavy mass of my balls, tracing every fold and seam with the tip of his tongue.

He wetted me down thoroughly, his chin damp from spit and precum. Grabbing his shoulders, I turned us both and eased him down to the floor until he was lying beneath me. I opened his trousers and bared his cock, which was already hard from blowing me. I left it alone and raised his hips a bit. Feeling my way with a finger, I probed his hole and sighed as I felt how tight it was. Raising him up a bit more, I guided the head of my cock until it was just inside the sphincter.

Steve gasped and shuddered. Penetrating slowly, I filled him completely and began to thrust in and out slowly, taking my time, and making it seem as if it took forever to embed myself in his tight hole.

Seating myself to the hilt, I moved my hips and felt my cock touch the sides of his passage. He raised his hips to grind against mine, his cock brushing against my belly, our balls slapping together. I began to thrust faster, slamming in, pulling out, then ramming in home again. He rose to meet each thrust as I reamed out his tight hole.

Stuffing my throbbing cock deep into his ass, I shuddered and came, spewing oceans of hot, steaming jism up into the depths of his bowels.

As he felt me spend, he cried out, clutched his cock in his hand, and milked it of its load, squirting jet after jet of creamy cum against the ridges of muscle at my torso.

Withdrawing from him, feeling the stickiness of my own cum on my cock, I propped myself on my elbow and leaned over his cock, which lay quiescent against his belly. I ran my tongue over it, tasting its salty muskiness, and watched it twitch beneath me. Chuckling quietly, I kissed it before tucking it away. "Ah, Steve, cheer up. You're not that bad a tour guide."

THE CONSTRUCTION WORKER
LARRY TOWNSEND

F or his first several days in the hidden valley, Dick existed in a peculiar quandary. Well accepted by the other men, he did not lack for companionship or advice in getting used to the customs and routine. The work was not very difficult—certainly not very different from what he had done all his life. Mike presented a bit of a problem at first, as he was obviously infatuated with Dick and displayed a possessiveness that was unjustified on the basis of what had passed between them. Dick was able to handle the situation gracefully enough to create no ill feelings, however, and the little welder soon accepted his new roommate as a friend, instead of the lover he had first envisioned.

With domestic discord averted, Dick began experiencing sex with a number of other men. A casual observer would have said he was getting all the sex he could want, and for a week or so Dick deluded himself into thinking he was. Except he was not. Working every day under Jimmy Alvarez's guidance, the newcomer found himself more and more attracted by his boss's confident, self-possessed manner. Because of a continued indifference to Dick's increasingly obvious interest, the foreman became the dominant object in the big construction worker's thoughts.

Alvarez was certainly attractive, and while it was probably his position and his attitude that heightened his appeal, there was more than sufficient physical basis for Dick's unflagging desire. The foreman was extremely well built, just over six feet tall. While the other men seemed to know little about him—Alvarez having been at the project longer than any of his subordinates—he had presumably been hired for his language capabilities, as well as his unquestioned knowledge of construction work. Fluent in both English and Spanish, he was able to make himself understood whenever there was contact with the natives. He also did some occasional interpreting when it was necessary to contact the local authorities over the radio-telephone. This was not very often, Dick learned, as the present regime that ruled the country was either indifferent or well paid to leave the Institute project alone.

Thus Alvarez stood in a unique position. He was intermediary between the administration and research staff on the one hand, and the three dozen construction men on the other. After his single conference with Laslo, Dick had no further contact with the project head or his staff. He took his orders from the foreman, and other than an occasional, passing word from Warner Denier, the chief engineer, Dick's sole contact with the powers-that-be was through Jimmy.

To make the situation more profound, and certainly not to dissuade his burning lust, Dick would frequently look up from his work to see Alvarez standing a few feet away, watching him. There would be an expression of poorly concealed interest on the foreman's face, and the ever-present bulge along his left thigh would generally indicate a more-than-casual response to the bare-chested body of the bearded workman. But he never spoke except in regard to work, leaving Dick to wonder—and to dwell upon—his persistent, accelerating desires.

In keeping with his Spanish name, Alvarez had a dark-visaged attractiveness that seemed to be especially suited to his position of authority. His facial features were sharp and angular, like some classic Western cowboy. His swarthy complexion was further darkened by the sun until it seemed to blend with his deep auburn hair. This was cut fairly short, although Dick suspected it only looked so severely trimmed because it was always carefully combed, frequently concealed beneath a wide-brimmed Stetson. Even his hat reflected a certain willful personality, with the sides turned up until they formed two nearly parallel lines.

From what Dick could learn from the other men, Alvarez kept largely to himself. He had a room at the end of the barracks building, this being the only one with its own outside entrance. The extra door permitted the foreman to come and go without entering the main portion of hallway, and he seldom went into a room occupied by any of the others. When he did, however, it was not to have relations with any of them. If there had been secret assignations, these remained subjects no one was willing to discuss. The foreman's bag seemed to be to watch.

Still, Alvarez had been on the project for a long time, as had most of the construction workers. Only a few of the personnel had been there less than a year. So, despite the infrequency of his visits to the main portion of the barracks building, there was hardly one among the men who had not experienced the surprise of looking up from his preoccupation with a sex partner to find the foreman standing quietly in the doorway, observing them. In fact, his nickname among the crew was "Miss Eyes."

The one time when Dick's conversation with Alvarez concerned more than work assignments came the second day he was at the project. The current on the fence had been turned off, as it always was during the day. Dick was told to take a machete and to knock down any vegetation that seemed in danger of growing into the mesh. Thus, he had to walk the entire periphery of the camp, along the outside of the twenty-foot barrier. Most of the other men were at work on the tower, also outside the fence, and only a short distance from the gate.

By noon, Dick had worked his way to the end of the fence, reaching its terminus on the north side. At this point it abutted a sheer, granite cliff that formed the eastern barrier of the site. Dick was returning toward the gate, intending to work the southern half after lunch, when he was suddenly confronted by two, nearly naked men. Each man wore a headband, breechcloth, moccasins, and nothing else. Dick had come upon them so suddenly that all three stood in momentary confusion. Both men were red-haired, and while each was darkly tanned, Dick could see their skin would normally have been quite fair. Jarred by this unexpected contact with the supposedly hostile natives, the big construction worker did not know exactly what to do. The half-constructed tower was a good hundred yards away, so he was completely on his own—or so he thought.

After a few seconds, one of the natives jabbered at the other in a peculiar patois that sounded less like Spanish than some clicking Arabian tongue. Another moment of hesitation and both seemed about to flee into the underbrush. At this point, their motion was arrested by a sharp command in their own language, and Alvarez appeared around the corner of a building, just inside the fence. He spoke briefly to the men, who executed a sort of bow, first to him and then to Dick. After this they left, walking easily and unhurriedly into the jungle.

"Just a pair of lovers," said the foreman. "You scared them."

"I scared *them?*" laughed Dick. "I expected an arrow through my gut at any minute. Didn't know how many more might be hiding in the bushes."

Alvarez chuckled. "They're curious, that's all," he explained.

"Wanted to see what was going on. They'd heard about the bearded giant and wanted to see if there really was such a thing."

Dick grinned self-consciously. "But I thought they were hostile," he protested.

"Well, they are and they aren't," continued the foreman. They had turned toward the gate, walking together with the high fence between them. "I wouldn't want to run into a pack of them at night," he said, "but when they come around like that during the day they're usually just curious or looking to trade some handicrafts for food and trinkets. They know we've got rifles, you see, and they aren't about to attack us in force. They'd never make it in daylight, and at night they can't get across the fence."

"You seemed to speak their language pretty well," Dick remarked.

"It's basically Spanish," Alvarez told him, "except for a few odd words in English or Dutch...a little Aztec here and there. It's sort of like speaking Yiddish to a German. You stumble on an occasional Polish or Russian word, but mostly you can understand each other."

"You'll have to teach me enough to do some trading with them," Dick said smiling.

Alvarez returned a knowing grin. "You might prove a good student, at that," he said.

They had reached the gate by then, and were joined by other men on the way to lunch. The foreman excused himself and went to check the work site before following the crowd of men toward the mess hall. *He sure is strange*, Dick thought, *strange and sexy!*

Several days later, Dick's frustrated attraction for the seemingly indifferent foreman had reached a stage where he could think of little else. He tried to imagine what Alvarez must look like beneath the tightness of his Levi coat and pants. The sex that swelled along the left thigh left little doubt of its substance; yet the true form and shape...and size.... Dick found himself aroused just thinking about it. In consequence, and in a largely unrealized attempt to overcome his frustrations, Dick embarked on one of the wildest sex sprees of his life. In less than a week, it seemed he had tried out half the camp, and was always ready for more.

The cooks and maintenance people—all apparently gay—were lodged in a second barracks building, located on the far side of camp. As Dick visited there more than once, his fame was spreading through all the worker types until there was not a man on the grounds who did not know him and greet him when they came face-to-face. Those he had not yet possessed were willing, and those who had experienced his talents were anxious for more. It was just as it had always been for him...except for Jimmy Alvarez. Frustrating! And frustration became obsession.

Added to the discomfort his passion for the foreman was creating, Dick was experiencing another peculiar bent. Big and powerful, both physically and verbally, he had always dominated those with whom he had relations. It had never been any other way, nor had Dick ever desired that it should be. Despite the many tight little rears he had penetrated, his was still a virgin ass. He had never felt the slightest inclination to submit himself for another to fuck.

Now, he found a gnawing curiosity, sometimes even a desire to allow someone else to take the stronger role. He wanted it, and yet he didn't want it. It was as if some heretofore repressed craving were being unleashed within him, rising to do battle with his well-established mode of behavior. Dick could not understand it, and it troubled him. It troubled him to a degree where he began to feel a need to think it out, to be alone—and in his present living situation that was nearly impossible.

The answer came on a Friday night, about two weeks after his arrival. Following the long established American custom, the work crews took a two-day weekend. Except for some light gardening and housekeeping activities about the camp on Saturday morning, there was no work assignments between Friday afternoon and

Monday morning. Movies were shown in the mess hall Friday and Saturday evenings, and sometimes a group of guys put on a short play or sketch. Naturally, there were some who attended these performances and some who did not. Thus, a man could disappear during this time without causing anyone to wonder. And if he failed to come to bed later on…well, his roommate would know there were many other beds where the missing man might be.

A couple of days before, Dick had heard the foreman talking with Warner Denier, complaining about thefts of materials from the building site outside the gate. It was nothing large, just occasional pieces of lumber and small tools if anyone neglected to pick up all his equipment at quitting time. It had to be some of the natives, of course, but whether it was just a few marauding kids, or whether the place was overrun with savages after dark, no one could tell. Denier had told Jimmy not to worry about it, as long as the pilferage amounted to so little. And there the subject was dropped.

The gate was normally closed after the work crew returned to camp, and the current was turned on before dark. On this particular Friday, however, there was about an hour's worth of finish work still to be done on one of the lower floors. A couple of men had volunteered to work after dinner to complete it. Thus, the gate was left open later than usual, and Dick decided to take this opportunity to slip outside.

He crept past the room where the two men were working and climbed through the maze of beams and girders onto the upper level. It was fully dark by then, and no one had seen him. He settled down to wait, sitting in a dark corner of the uppermost floor. He had been there less than an hour when he heard the workmen packing up their tools eighteen floors below and preparing to depart. Dick looked up at the clear, star-sprinkled sky, puzzling over the many unanswered questions he had about himself…and about the Institute.

The purpose of this very building, he thought—that had never been explained to him. Nor did the other workmen seem to know. Judging by the amount of plumbing, it was designed as an apartment complex. Either that or offices where people could remain at night. But twenty stories of apartments? Here, in a valley surrounded by tropical jungle, accessible only by air? He shook his head. The whole thing was so strange...the whole set-up a peculiar enigma.

Everyone seemed to be gay, although there was never any interaction between the administrative staff and the men. Still, Dick had seen the beautiful young man who served Laslo as secretary-receptionist. *If he's not fuckin' that pretty little ass, I miss my bet*, thought Dick. And the other officers, too. Each of them had a staff of assistants, and every one of them was a living doll! *Always keep their distance...wonder if they know what goes on in the barracks...must! How could they not know? It couldn't be just coincidence that all these guys...*

There was a noise on the lower floor, and Dick leaned to his side, peering through the shadows. A long shaft stretched into the darkness beside him, used during the day as an elevator for tools and equipment. Dick had made sure the lift was all the way down, so he had an unobstructed view. Except it was so dark, he couldn't see a thing!

He waited, holding his breath until he heard a muffled bump, followed by a scraping noise. After this was a momentary silence, until Dick heard the distinct clicking of footsteps coming up the stairwell. This was really puzzling, because whoever approached him was wearing shoes—boots most likely. And the natives went barefoot. He pushed back more completely into the shadows, waiting to see what was about to happen.

Heavy breathing echoed in the stairwell as the climber paused to rest. Electric current had been turned off in the building when the workmen left, diverted to the high-tension lines on the fence. The mysterious intruder was thus deprived of the elevators. A few moments later the footsteps began again, louder as the man neared the upper floor. Finally, a shadowy form emerged from the open doorway and moved to the side of the room facing out, across the valley floor.

Had it not been for the wide-brimmed Stetson, Dick might not have immediately recognized the visitor. However, only Jimmy Alvarez wore such a hat, with the sides pulled almost against the crown by a leather strap. As Dick watched from his place of concealment, the foreman sat down on the littered floor, gazing out upon the moon-silvered landscape. Obviously he did not suspect Dick's presence, as he was mumbling, talking to himself. He pulled a cigarette from his shirt pocket and struck a wooden match against the rough surface of unfinished flooring. After this, he sat quietly, smoking until the glowing coal had reached the filter. Then he snuffed it out and stood in the open frame of window.

Although there was not yet a roof over the structure, the crisscross of beams and rafters cut off most of the light from directly above. This caused Jimmy's body to stand in almost total darkness, outlined only by the silver-white reflected off the surrounding forest. For Dick, the display was all the more exciting. The hard, trim body, sheathed in close-fitting, blue work clothes became a silver-haloed silhouette of masculinity.

For a long while, Jimmy Alvarez stood gazing across the plains and forests, his hands braced on either side of the gaping window frame. He seemed almost in a trance, motionless, mesmerized by the vast beauty of this unspoiled, mountainous valley. Then, still moving slowly and without any apparent motivation, he began to remove his jacket. The night was warm, of course, as all nights seemed to be in the valley. Maybe sweating from the climb, thought Dick. The blue Levi jacket fell to the floor, and much to Dick's surprise it was followed a moment later by the light gray work shirt!

Now Alvarez paused again, posing in the opening, bare torso

glittering in the increasingly brilliant moonlight. From Dick's position, the hard, muscular symmetry seemed etched against the star-studded vault, dark flesh against the darker velvet sky. Jim stood motionless for a much longer time, legs spread, hands against his waist. Dick could hear his heavy breathing, wondered why he should be out of breath...until the big construction worker detected a repetition of syllables. The foreman was whispering some kind of prayer or tuneless chant...reciting a verse, perhaps, but not in English.

Finally, the rasping intonement ended. Alvarez stooped to take his jacket and Dick expected he was about to put it on. Instead, the foreman pulled a tightly wrapped skein of rope from his pocket—rope about the weight of a clothesline. He dropped the jacket once again and began fumbling in the darkness above his head. Eventually he succeeded in looping the rope across a beam, and drew both ends down so they hung almost in contact with the floor.

Without further hesitation he stripped completely, again pausing to gaze across the landscape. Completely nude, he flexed his muscles and ran his palms over his upper arms and shoulders, testing the strength that rippled beneath the tight-pulled skin, riffling the heavy growth of hair upon his chest. Then he replaced his boots, slipping his bare feet into the high, leather coverings. He pulled the wide, black belt from his discarded Levi's and buckled this around his waist. That he was in the process of some peculiar, secret ritual was now obvious to Dick. Watching the uninhibited display, he felt a twinge of embarrassment that he should be here, observing this normally taciturn individual bare not just his body, but very likely the innermost, personal cravings of his soul. If he could have slunk away unobserved, Dick would have done so, though he would surely have wondered ever after—never knowing what followed this strange beginning.

For a moment, the naked performer turned sideways to his

observer, allowing Dick a profile view of the splendid body. Even more beautifully defined than Dick had expected, the foreman displayed a physique that might have rivaled Dick's. Except for being a few inches shorter and slightly less bulky, Alvarez was the equal of his own perfection. Hanging free and heavy, the foreman's cock completed the picture of total virility. It made as close a match to Dick's as the latter had ever seen. Even soft, it possessed an aura of forceful power. Jimmy had paused again, momentarily frozen in a pose that seemed to satisfy whatever drive was motivating his secret rite. His body arched, hands pressed tightly against narrow hips. His legs bent slightly at the knees, and the corded muscles of his abdomen became the interior of a crescent formed by the curve of his upper body.

Without his touching it, Jimmy's ponderous column began to grow, swelling steadily as the flesh expanded and the bursting flower of crown slid free of the loosely surrounding foreskin. The foreman's body began to tremble as he watched his fast-erecting sex, and Dick wondered if he might somehow ejaculate as a result of just this self-induced excitement. But no, once the great shaft was completely hard, pointing upward toward the arc of the foreman's tense and hard-flexed torso, Jim stood upright. He braced his feet once more before the unglazed window, facing toward the distant Aztec buildings.

When he finally moved again, it was with a slow, deliberate twist. His feet remained planted, while his upper body turned sideways, forcing him to bend his knees, every ounce of flesh and sinew strained to stand in deep relief against the skin. Gradually, his arms moved up and he took hold of the dangling rope. While Dick watched in steadily increased excitement, Alvarez tied one end about his neck. Carefully, he pulled it taut with a hard, downward force that brought him to a rigid, vertical stance. Holding the untied end, he pulled so the noose tightened harder about his throat while he brought the other length behind his back. Passing the loose end between the cheeks of his ass, he brought it up in front and secured it about his cock and balls.

He left the excess rope to dangle from the knot he formed about his genitals, so a trail some three or four feet in length remained. Then he dropped his weight slowly upon the rope, bracing his feet together on the window ledge and leaning backward through the opening. He was thus suspended above the multi-story drop by the bindings about his neck and sex. Gradually, he spread his booted feet more widely apart, thus forcing an increased tension upon the ropes as his toes inched along the edge of window, eventually touching the frame to either side.

Watching this, Dick's cock had lengthened and swelled until it was a painful force within its confines. His balls were squeezed back against his thigh by the pressure of his arousal, and touching the head of his thrusting cock, he felt a spot of moisture seeping through his jeans. Fascinated, he dared not move lest he make some sound to betray his presence. As it was, his heart beat so loudly he felt in imminent danger of being overheard.

Once the suspended figure had achieved its full spread-legged posture, the fingers began pulling up the dangling end of rope below the balls. The foreman passed this up, pulling the free end over the top of his belt buckle and down between the leather and his lower belly. Thus, the rope hung from between the belt itself and Jim's flaring, hard-risen sex. He now proceeded to loop the rope about first one wrist, then the other, tying his hands in place above the heavy patch of pubic hair. It took a little time to do this, and required some careful manipulations on the part of the performer. *Wonder how many times he's done it*, Dick thought, *...wildest thing I've ever seen! Tying himself up, hanging his ass out like that! Held up just a rope around his balls...another around his throat...wow!*

Slowly now, straining to reach their goal, Jimmy's fingers moved to grasp his sex. The motion must have caused an increase in tension on the binding about his prostate. The resulting sensation made him moan in heated ecstasy as his hands began massaging the length of his cock. He never hurried but moved with a firm determination that promised a not-too-distant release.

Dick could see the outline of movement, though the foreman's entire lower regions were in a shadow. Still, the widened crown stood far enough removed above the rest of his body that moonlight glinted off the tip, providing the observer with a constant awareness of the furious passion displayed before him. Dick's entire body was bathed in sweat by now, and his own desire had reached a point where it made no difference whether Alvarez would welcome his intrusion or not. He had to join the other man. Having dreamed of possessing him for days, he could not pass up the opportunity. Seeing the totality of his object's form—despite the peculiarities of the circumstances—Dick's craving became an impulse he could not refuse.

Unfolding from the shadows with a lithe, animal grace, Dick's tremendous form suddenly took shape before the foreman's startled eyes. At first it seemed as if some nebulous, ghostly specter were manifesting itself from the gloom. Jim's first impulse was terror, as this unknown thing rose seemingly from nothing to confront him. Then fear became embarrassed shock as he realized who it was.

Naturally, Jim's bindings were such that he could free himself. However, it required a process of several minutes' duration. For the moment, he was helpless, his body bound and stretched into the opening. Besides, shocked dismay held him frozen until Dick had approached to stand directly before him, the giant's booted feet upon the very line of window sill that separated Jim's.

"Beautiful!" whispered Dick, and for a second Jim suspected a note of sarcasm in the tone. His eyes sought the towering workman's gaze in the darkness, and only then did the sincere admiration of the other's expression convince him. Undismayed at finding him in this condition, Dick was fully aroused and preparing to join in the ritual.

Quickly, the bearded young man stripped the clothes from his massive body. Never moving from his position between the other's widespread legs, Dick discarded every vestige of civilized accoutrement. A pale, silver glow from the sky reflected off his powerful chest and shoulders, fading to a deeper gray where the foreman's shadow fell across the lower portions of his body. Dick felt the rough, unfinished floor beneath his feet, but would not have bothered to cover them had Jim not broken the silence by whispering, pleadingly, "Your boots." He gasped hoarsely, "Please, put on your boots...your belt...unless..."

Dick stood at his full height before the other, his fingers tracing the curve of leather. The heavy belt was doubled in his hands as he gazed into the shadow that obscured the other's expression. "Unless?" he whispered. "Unless...what?" He knew, of course, though the certainty had come more slowly. He knew what his foreman wanted, and he knew as well that forcing the man to ask would only increase the essence of his supplication. It would heighten the fantasy of their interaction and further emphasize the reversal of their customary relationship.

"Unless?... Unless you're man enough to use it," gasped the foreman. His voice was harsher, more hoarse and strangled each time he spoke. But the very act of hanging there, half choking on the rope that bound him, was driving his lust to a higher, more feverish peak.

Dick reached out, seizing the smaller man behind the head, pulling him foreword so he swung inward, hanging sideways as the rope about his genitals forced the body to turn. The wide, rigid back was directly in front of Dick now, and the small, firmly rounded buttocks gleamed whitely in the darkness. Grasping the rope between the prisoner's neck and the supporting beam above, Dick steadied his erstwhile boss in submissive bondage. Drawing back his right arm, he brought the heavy loop of leather down across the foreman's ass with a resounding crack.

Jim's whole body tensed, and a moan of satisfaction escaped his tightly drawn lips. "That's it!" he whispered. "I know you've wanted me," he gasped, "and I've been teasing you for days. Doesn't that piss you off, man? Doesn't that make you mad enough to...to..."

"To whip your fuckin' ass?" growled Dick. "You better believe it does!" he assured the prisoner. With that, he administered another blow, this one more than hard enough to raise a welt. He half expected the foreman to object, but regulating the severity of Alvarez's punishment seemed to be solely in the hands of the man who administered. Dick released his hold on the rope and stepped back to give himself a better range of the back and ass.

Each time the belt fell across the foreman's body, Dick heard him gasp and moan in satisfied response. Though the effects of the whipping were evident even in the depths of shadowy darkness, the captive seemed more than willing for his humiliation to continue. And while Dick might otherwise have assumed the role of master without compunction, and delivered whatever treatment his partner seemed to require, he found himself recalling the newer impulses he had experienced since coming to the hidden valley. Each time he struck the other man he seemed to feel the blow himself; it was this response, rather than his active role of master, that aroused him. His craving was to submit, and this was a desire he had never known before.

Still, his years of habit and conditioning forbade his asking the other to change places with him. He might have wished it, but he found himself unable to express such a formerly untenable thought. Instead, he did another penance for his brutality. While a lesser expression of supplication, it was almost as out of character for the Dick MacPherson of Appletree and Plumb. Without warning, he stepped around in front of his prisoner. Looping the belt around the narrow buttocks it had just been used to warm, Dick dropped onto his knees before the other's crotch. His hands held the leather that passed behind the other's ass, and using this as a lever to command the motion, he began forcing Jim's groin to swing against his face. His lips grasped the wide, softly rigid crown, and with a gagging, choking determination, he forced the full, tremendous shaft through the constricted passage of his throat.

The restricted hands of the foreman strained against their bindings as he grasped the other's head between his palms. Undulating his hips, he drove himself against the other's lips, forcing the fullness of his swollen pride deeper into the stretched and straining orifice. He felt Dick's strangled acceptance of his bulk and held him desperately against his crotch for several moments. His boiling seed rose swiftly, charging furiously through the passages from his taut, bound balls. As his flood of sperm burst into Dick's waiting mouth and throat, Jim released the gagging supplicant, and allowed him to take the full, hot load across his tongue.

After this, neither moved until the spasms of release subsided and the trussed-up captive relaxed against his bonds. His cock, still fully hard and quivering in unabated sensuality, remained fixed between the tightly gripping lips. Dick gazed up at Jim, across the glistening, sweat-covered ridges of his belly. The foreman's chin was tipped slightly backward, his eyes closed while his mind derived full measure of satisfaction from their act. Without looking down, he seemed to know the other was watching him and through emotion-tightened lips he began encouraging Dick to find his own fulfillment.

"Any way you want it, baby," rasped the foreman. "Anything you want...don't ask, man; just take it...do it...anything...no matter what. I'm all tied up like a fuckin' hog for market, man...nothin' I can do about it...nothin' I wanna do about it. Come on, baby, anything you want...anything...."

Slowly, Dick stood up. His own rigid manhood extended powerfully before him, colliding with the foreman's as he came to stand against him. Again, the smaller man had curled his body, leaning backward so the rope would tense about his neck. His entire form was arched in a display of rigid, hard-flexed muscle. Dick seized him about the waist, held the moist, heated flesh against himself. Roughly, he kissed the prisoner, standing between the other's doubled knees, and leaning down to possess the gasping mouth. Dick's tongue plunged between the other's lips, forcing Jim to savor his own essence where it clung to the mouth and tongue of the bigger man. The foreman's hands, bound still against his crotch, were pressed upon the bearded giant's groin. The fingers traced a heavy weight within the sac, felt the underside of an eager, waiting shaft.

And abruptly, while this first total, full-length contact between their bodies was yet unbroken, a strange, unfamiliar emotion crept unbidden into Dick's awareness. It was not what he desired that mattered! Whereas his passions had reached a stage where he would normally have followed blindly into whatever direction his lust might lead him, this was not what he wanted now. He felt compelled to do what Jimmy wanted. He knew the most important aspect of their joining was for him to please this other man. Dick crushed the smaller form against him, kissing the foreman deeply as before, but with a semblance of tenderness his former possession had lacked. He had beaten Jim because that was what the guy had asked for...what he had demanded. He had sucked Jim's cock—done him for trade, almost, and that was not his usual way. Now, when the time for his own fulfillment was at hand, Dick found he wanted to make his partner happy, regardless of whether it satisfied himself.

Intermeshed and inseparable from his lust, Dick felt a protective tenderness for this man. While the sensation was foreign to him, something he had never known, realization was slowly dawning. Love? It *was* love! He really, truly, had fallen in love with another person! How permanent this would be, or why it came about...these questions made no difference. The simple status of being in love, of feeling the object of that love pressed hard and naked against him...for the moment that was enough. Nothing else mattered.

He wanted to say something of this newly discovered feeling. But he knew, somehow, he should not. For now it made no difference, anyway. Jim Alvarez was his, and there was no one else...no other person or thing to come between them, to distract the interest of either. "I'll do what you want," Dick whispered. "If you want me to whip your ass some more, I'll do it. If you want me to suck your cock again, anything...what I want is to please you," Dick admitted. "Tell me..."

Jimmy pressed his face into the hollow of the other's neck. His breath was hot and almost fluid upon the moistly heated skin. "Fuck me," he gasped. "This may be the last chance you get, so fuck me, man...fuck me so I feel it to my navel! Do it to me tied like this...standing up, facing out across the valley. Ram that big cock up my ass, and shove all that muscle against my back. Push me so tight on this rope it makes me choke...and then don't stop...keep it in me..." The foreman's fingers seized both their pulsing cocks, pressing them together so their widths combined to form a ponderous mass. Both shafts were hot and trembling, ready...waiting the command to enter, to penetrate, to drive the flaring crown to where it might deliver its heated load...

Ignoring the peculiar justification in the other's request, and in fact unmindful of the warning implicit in his words, Dick did as Jimmy asked. He repositioned the rope against the other's ass, and following the smaller man's instructions, he hunted in the discarded jacket to find a tube of lubricant. "I use it sometimes...by myself," the foreman explained. "Only now...now its going to be used like it should be...like it should but seldom is..."

He stood firmly in the window once again. His feet were spread wide apart, his back rigidly straight except for its slightly forward curve as Jimmy arched outward, hanging again with his weight against the collar of rope. His tiny ass trembled slightly in anticipation as Dick's heavy fingers began working gel between the cheeks, probing the anal opening as he deposited a sizable glob within the canal. Then he rubbed another goodly amount upon his prick, and stepped into position behind the waiting prisoner.

Placing his hands against the other's groin, Dick centered his cockhead and slowly drove himself between the foreman's cheeks. The smaller man wriggled slightly to more precisely align them. As Dick felt himself in place, he grasped Jim's loins and eased the solid, trembling body against himself. He moaned in pleasure as he felt his cock slip inside and the tightness of the sphincter closed about him. Slowly, then he drove deeper. Jim's hands, still bound above his crotch, came to rest on top of Dick's. Their fingers intermeshed, and they held together with hard, unabated strength. The further Dick's manhood sunk within the foreman's body, the firmer his grip became upon the giant's hands.

With this additional contact, each was speaking without words, telling the other something he dared not say was true. On Dick's part, at least, it was a conscious gesture, something symbolic of the feelings that swelled within him. Yet, despite the depths of these feelings, Dick was reluctant to express in words what his mind and body told him. What Jim felt, he could only guess, and the lack of communication this night was but the start of a long, protracted period of uncertainty.

For the moment, pure, glorious, physical sensation carried Dick into the furthest reaches of total, blissful pleasure. What he must say tomorrow or the next day was a problem for the future. Right then, it was enough to drive his sex deeply, knowing his possession was an act of love. What the other felt must remain a matter to be discovered at the proper time...was something which would surely express itself. A relationship this great could not be so short-lived that a few days made any difference.

So Dick thought...so he convinced himself. But what forces were at work to restrict this reciprocal expression, the big construction worker had no way to even guess.

GUY TRAYNOR
TORSTEN BARRING

Where was I? Ah, yes. The play he wrote for Daryl Eliot and Brendan Chinn:

I played Skye, a leather-clad young hoodlum. A pot- and rock-addicted high school dropout who corrupts his best buddy, Chad, (played by Brendan) by talking him into dropping out of school and riding off with him on his motorbike to an infamous brothel in Mexico.

I could say it was close to home—that play—or close enough to my most private boyhood fantasies, at least.

He came up with a really kinky idea for the relationship between the two teenagers: Chad, the "sensitive" one, makes the crucial mistake of confessing to Skye, the "tough-butch" one, his more-than-platonic feelings for him.

Skye is revolted to learn that his best buddy is "queer for him" and rejects him brutally. Chad withdraws into himself, lonely and miserable, while Skye gets high, listens to recordings of The Sex Pistols, and swaggers around making every effort to look like his idol, Sid Vicious.

But Skye's conscience bothers him. He misses the handsome kid who so obviously worships him. He decides to "help" Chad with his "sexual problems."

Skye bursts in on his old buddy late one night. Chad is in bed. He always sleeps "in the raw," of course. Skye is in full leather—a fantasy vision in the night.

Skye announces to Chad that the two of them are riding across the border to Pilar's Cantina where Chad will, by God, get laid! It's what Chad needs, Skye insists. No best buddy of a superhip, superstraight stud like Skye could possibly be queer. Skye has it all figured: Chad is still a tender virgin. Of course he hero-worships the handsome, pot-smoking leatherboy—which is only *natural*—*all* the boys in the little California border town dig Skye and think he's the coolest. It's only because Chad hasn't made it with a woman yet that he thinks he might be "homo," and his good buddy is going to fix him up with one of Pilar's girls: maybe Conchita. Or even Concepcion. Maybe both of them together! By the time Conchita and Concepcion get through with Chad he'll know he's just as straight as his old buddy, Skye.

"Believe me you'll rise to the occasion," Skye declares.

The play's title is *Rising to the Occasion*; and it has less regard for logic than any play he ever wrote. And "Mexico"—a country he had never visited or even read much about—becomes another all-male NEVERNEVERLAND.

Chad yields to Skye and the scene ends with a preposterous turned-on motorcycle duo fantasy right out of the pages of *Drummer:* Chad is still naked. He doesn't take time to put on a single stitch of clothes. He simply jumps on the back of Skye's motorbike and rides all the way to Mexico—*stark naked*—with his arms around his Leatherboy Hero!

The scenic effect was one of his technical triumphs: The motorbike was mounted in front of a wide, high screen, which was like a movie's "back projection." The bike's wheels spun freely while the bike remained in place. The motor loudly boomed and sputtered while "on the road" background music accompanied the projected images of wide-open country flying by at eighty miles per hour!

All the while, Chad's beautiful naked body molds itself to the leather-clad back and buttocks of the handsome homophobic biker he adores!

The next scene finds the boys at Pilar's Cantina—but the setting is designed to keep the female characters offstage. A balcony overlooks a courtyard. Doors open from the brothel's second-floor rooms onto the balcony. On the ground floor is the Cantina. Music is heard: A man's voice, accompanied by guitar, singing a Mexican love song. One of the doors opens and Chad appears on the balcony. He is still naked. He is nervously smoking a cigarette. He leans against the balcony railing. His manner suggests that he is quite distressed.

Another door opens and Skye appears, also naked. He sees his friend, goes to him, and stands beside him. He puts his arm around him and presses his naked thigh against Chad's naked thigh. "How was it?" he asks.

The song from the Cantina abruptly stops. Silence— except for crickets singing. "Look! A falling star!" cries Chad, eager to change the subject (and, at the same time, an opportunity for the playwright to enhance the al fresco mood of the scene: crickets, falling stars, two beautiful young men naked together on a balcony in the moonlight).

But Skye presses his question: "How did it go?"
"It *didn't!*" Chad cries, as he flings his cigarette into the night.
"What do you mean?" Skye demands.
"I mean—I didn't rise to the occasion."
Suddenly a gunshot is heard. A Young Man bursts through the

back door of the Cantina and runs across the courtyard. A moment later a mob of men run out of the Cantina in pursuit of the Young Man.

"There he is! Get him!"

"Is he hit?"

"No. I missed."

"Shoot him!"

"Kill the gringo!"

"No you don't! I want him alive."

There is a barbed wire fence far downstage—stretched across the footlights. The Young Man attempts to climb over the fence, as if he intends to seek sanctuary by leaping off the stage onto the auditorium's front row seats.

The Young Man cries out in pain as he becomes entangled in barbed wire. The angry mob rushes to the Young Man. They grab him and pull him off the fence.

One of the men is tall, dark, sinister looking, and uniformed. He is El Perfecto—Commandante of Police—and a regular customer of Pilar's.

High up on the balcony, Skye and Chad are joined by many more naked men, all of whom have deserted their female partners and rushed out onto the balcony to see what is taking place in the courtyard.

El Perfecto shouts up to the balcony, crowded with stark naked men: "No women! Keep them all inside! Tell Pilar I said keep her girls back, this is men's business down here. You men up there, stay and watch what happens to gringos who cheat at cards in my town. *Stand there naked and watch and remember!*"

The offstage Singer is heard again. His gently strumming guitar and tender love song rendition provide ironic counterpoint to El Perfecto's demonstration of what happens to gringos who cheat at cards in his town.

"You there, José and Juan, make the gringo more comfortable.

Take his clothes off and tie him up against the barbed wire."

While José and Juan are taking all of the Young Man's clothes off, El Perfecto strips to the waist.

"Pedro, my friend, I seem to have left my whip inside. Get it for me, por favor."

When the Young Man is completely naked, the other men join José and Juan in the task of roping the Young Man's arms high above his head and pushing the front of his body against the multiple strings of barbed wire. The Young Man screams as the barbs penetrate his naked flesh. His thick, *extremely long PENIS* is especially vulnerable as it is pressed sharp and hard directly against one of the tightly stretched wires.

Smiling and stripped to the waist, El Perfecto takes the whip Pedro has fetched for him, and, with great and ever-mounting passion, proceeds to lash the Young Man.

At this point I should like to note that Guy Traynor, at my request, cast Damien Draco in the role of the Young Man who is stripped naked, bound against barbed wire, and lashed by El Perfecto.

I must admit that Damien was very good at screaming. It was his specialty. He could scream for long periods of time without getting hoarse. Perhaps that was why Guy had Damien tortured on stage more often than any other actor in his company.

I should like also to mention that El Perfecto was played by Mario Di Palermo, the heterosexual Italian who was flogged the evening I first met Mr. Yakamoto and his son.

El Perfecto continues to whip the naked Young Man until he faints. El Perfecto is not satisfied. The Young Man has not suffered enough. The Commandante of Police decides to subject the Young Man he has stripped and whipped to more punishment.

"Revive him," El Perfecto commands, "then fuck him! All you men. Every one of you. *Rape the gringo!* I've warmed his ass for you with my whip. You first, Pedro; then Juan; then José. Get naked, all of you, and rape the gringo. I want to watch."

High up on the balcony a young male voice shouts "*NO!*"

It is Chad's voice.

Skye attempts to calm his outraged friend but Chad angrily shouts, "*You got me into this!*" and punches Skye in the nose. Skye falls back into the arms of one of the naked men on the balcony.

Chad leans far out over the balcony railing and denounces the Commandante of Police, calling him, among other things, a "Sadistic Spic."

"Seize that man!" shouts El Perfecto. "He is under arrest!"

Chad attempts to escape but he is seized and held by several of the naked men.

Skye again attempts to intervene but the man holding him warns, "Don't get mixed up in this. You cannot help your friend now."

Skye's "protector" drags the dazed teenager into one of the rooms.

El Perfecto points to Chad with his whip. He shakes the whip as he says, "I have special treats for a boy just like you—*in my jail!* A special little room with very special instruments for your pretty young body. You think this whip is harsh? When you feel my other little toys on your naked body you'll BEG for my whip!

"There are many pretty young lads like you in my jail. They have been there a long time. They call my jail '*EL DIABLO*.' Some of them have even learned to like it there. Perhaps you will be one of my lads who learns to enjoy PAIN!

"*BRING HIM TO ME!*"

The naked men on the balcony tie a rope around Chad's wrists and lower him down from the balcony into the arms of El Perfecto's men. Holding Chad aloft like a sacrificial offering, they carry him to El Perfecto.

El Perfecto strokes his hands over the teenager's buttocks. He pinches the boy's nipples. He gropes the boy's huge fully erect cock.

"Yes. Yes. Nice. So nice. You will make GOOD TORTURE!—*TAKE HIM TO EL DIABLO!*"

The next scene takes place in El Diablo Prison. The stage is divided in order to represent two connecting rooms in the prison. A partition—center stage—separates El Perfecto's private office from his TORTURE CHAMBER! In the office area, Skye, wearing only his leather codpiece, is pleading with El Perfecto to spare his good buddy. On the other side of the partition, Chad, still completely naked, is bound to a vertical RACK, being electrotortured by three of El Perfecto's interrogators.

Electrodes are attached to Chad's nipples and penis. One of the torturers is seated at a table operating a "telephone" crank that sends excruciating charges of electricity into Chad's sexual organs. Each time the man at the table turns the crank, Chad emits a piercing scream and his nude body tenses into a mass of corded muscles.

Skye becomes increasingly upset as he listens to his friend's pitiful screams in the next room.

El Perfecto informs Skye that Chad has committed a serious offense. He can release Chad only if Skye can pay a fine of ten thousand dollars. Of course Skye can't pay—and El Perfecto knows it! He is leading the handsome American Leatherboy to exactly where he wants him.

"Oh, come now, my handsome American friend—you must make an effort. Surely if you try hard enough you can find a way to—*rise to the occasion.*"

Skye insists that he hasn't that kind of money but he will do anything El Perfecto demands—anything that Skye can do—if only the Commandante will free Skye's best buddy.

The inevitable—if not to say "predictable"—has now arrived—the moment the audience has been waiting and hoping for: The homophobic Skye—stark naked and handcuffed—on his knees—performing fellatio on *El Perfecto!*

The graphic sexual torture of Chad continues implacably as Skye performs his "painful duty."

When at last the act is done, Skye begs, "Let my buddy go now—you promised!" But El Perfecto insists that the "fine" has been only partially paid. *More payments are due!*

The remainder of the play is devoted to Skye's "rising to the occasion"—*in the Torture Chamber!*

El Perfecto gets naked and directs the proceedings: He has Skye put on the Rack beside Chad and both boys are electrotortured together!

It goes on and on:

Skye is made to suck Chad's cock!

Skye is put over a whipping-horse and made to take a whipping from Chad.

Then Chad is made to fuck Skye.

Then Skye is made to suck the cocks of the three Interrogators.

Then Skye and Chad are made to assume a sixty-nine position and suck each other's cocks while El Perfecto lashes the copulating boys with his whip—on and on—

The Finale of the play finds Skye and Chad back on Skye's motorbike, riding back to California.

Both boys are stark naked and their bodies are covered with marks left by El Perfecto's whip.

"Sorry I didn't rise to the occasion" says Chad, his arms around his lover's waist, his head resting on his lover's shoulder.

"That's cool, ol' buddy," says Skye, smiling. "I did."

They both laugh as the curtain falls.

Rising to the Occasion went over big with the audience.

The next one was even kinkier. If possible.

He admitted that I was strongly influencing his writing. More and more, his plays were exploring and exploiting the retarded adolescent appeals of the Male Adventure genre: those timeless, ever-popular, escapist "Buddy Stories"—but with their covertly implied homosexuality thrown once and for all into arch relief!

He liked me. He trusted me. He wasn't bullshitting when he told me he wanted to make me into a star. But even as I steadily rose to the front ranks of his theater company I was nurturing an attitude that would lead to my downfall. For no single actor was The Star over the name of *Guy Traynor*. I was still just one of the guys he trained—and when I got, as my Dad used to put it, "too big for my britches," those tight britches—to be sure—got pulled down for some serious BARE-BUTT DISCIPLINE.

Then I would betray him. And by betraying him I would also betray Rex Cormack, whom I never wanted to hurt. And those betrayals would lead to disastrous consequences for us all. Consequences I would spend the next eighteen years trying to flee from.

Even now I don't understand what he thought he was trying to prove with his theories that took a little Jesuit Drama from the seventeenth century and mixed it with some nineteen thirties French Theater of Cruelty and a pinch of Actor's Studio navel probing, and *voilà*:

The Traynor Style!

Theories. It was all talk. What he thought, wrote, and taught in his classes. What did any of it have to do with what the audience saw on the stage?

They put the Marquis de Sade in a lunatic asylum. He, also, raved on and on in an effort to prove some kind of cockamamie philosophical justification for whatever gave him a hard-on. Much of what de Sade wrote seems to me to be long-winded attempts to validate his perversion. (Unless, of course, it loses something in the English translations I've read.)

The Marquis de Sade and Guy Traynor. I wonder if they were both Puritans at heart. Or reverse Puritans, if there's such a thing.

It was his pose of "complete honesty" that pissed me off! If he wanted to be really honest why didn't he say—simply—that some men get their rocks off by inflicting pain—and/or receiving it? What kind of philosophical validation does that require?

Rex Cormack was a man who was truly honest with himself. And yet he worshiped Guy Traynor and saw no fault in him. Was I missing something?

I suppose the fallen rebel artist feels like Lucifer: Cast out. And it makes him so crazy he can't keep his mouth shut.

The failed Artist-Actor-Poet-Playwright—rejected by the Establishment—whatever gives him a hard-on isn't good enough as a fall-back position. He has to fashion his own insanity into a work of art and fling it at the world that has committed the irremediable atrocity of underestimating him.

That may not altogether explain Guy Traynor. But I have to identify. I've no choice but to identify. Because I'm so much like him—?

Ah—so *that's* why I'm writing this book.

It's about me—isn't it?—this book?

Last night—when Chip dropped by—I called him "Rex"—and quickly corrected myself. (Too late—he noticed.)

And in the course of our conversation I started to ask Chip something about Titman Burns and, in so doing, I referred to Titman as "Daryl." (And got another of Chip's little worried glances.)

The story of Guy Traynor will not—cannot—be over as long as I'm alive (and my very knowledge of that fact will probably be the death of me).

Guy Traynor teaches Drama History to a bunch of tight-panted narcississies in a boy's prep school in—

Quick! *THE WHIP!*

Back! Back! What was the next play? The one that was even kinkier than *Rising to the Occasion?*—if possible—Oh Christ—

The whip! AGAIN!

x x x

There—there now—see?—It doesn't matter how crazy I am as long as *I KEEP WRITING!*

By the time rehearsals for the new play had begun, it was apparent that he was grooming Daryl Eliot and Brendan Chinn as replacements for Arthur Banton and Travis Hedrick, who were approaching the twenty-five-year-old retirement age.

In some plays, Brendan and I acted together as a team. In others, we were assigned parts opposite Arthur or Travis—sometimes both.

I played opposite Travis in *Floggingson's Sacrifice*.

Take the two main characters from *The Lives of a Bengal Lancer*, mix them with the "Masochism equals Heroism" theme out of *Four Feathers*, and throw in the cult of loinclothed pain worshippers ruled by a raving madman from *Gunga Din*, and you have *Floggingson's Sacrifice*, by Guy Traynor.

Along the way you might even detect traces of *Lawrence of Arabia*; *The Charge of the Light Brigade*; *The Corsican Brothers*; *Beau Geste*; *Ben Hur*; *Damon and Pythias*; and every history-bending, homoerotic BUDDY SAGA that ever was!

Was the action taking place in Africa?—India?— Other?—Did anybody care? Of course not. What mattered was handsome young men in uniform—and out of uniform—cartoon soldiers acting out every cliché in his fetishistic Catalogue Raisonné.

He had sent questionnaires to all his subscribers, asking them to reveal and give detailed descriptions of their fetishes and return the completed questionnaires to him. They did, and the most requested fetishes appeared in *Floggingson's Sacrifice*.

It could be said that the plot of the play was merely a hook on which to hang the fetishes. It was his biggest success.

For my role as *Prosper Floggingson*, the much-too-eager-to-please son of the "strictly by the book," *General Floggingson*, I had to let my hair grow long—after which it was dyed blonde and curled.

I also was required to cultivate the polished manners of a young

English aristocrat. It was the kind of part Travis would have played when he was eighteen or nineteen. In fact, he assigned Travis the task of coaching me in diction and body movement. The dashing and almost-too-glamorous Englishman was extremely gracious toward me and I enjoyed the hours I spent with him. He seemed almost eager to pass his assets along to me. He even told me he was looking forward to retiring and becoming *Trainer in Charge of Fencing*, a post for which he was exceptionally well qualified, having displayed his dazzling swordsmanship in many of his stage roles, most notably in *Escape from Torture Island*, in which he played a wrongly convicted prisoner of a penal colony on an uncharted island in the South Pacific in the seventeenth century who was released from the torture rack by a corrupt Governor only to be mad e to fight a duel to the death—*in the nude*—with all five of the Governor's insane, opium addicted sons!

He didn't want Daryl Eliot to be typecast after playing a Leather Punk in *Rising to the Occasion*.

I was glad because Prosper Floggingson represented the kind of Sexy/Sensitive Boy Wonder who knows No Fear and Looks Great With His Clothes Off that I had always wanted to play.

Travis was given the part of Prosper's unwilling and resentful (at first) roommate and mentor with the interesting name of Grant Payne!

General Floggingson (played by Mario Di Palermo) is distressed to learn that his only son—handsome, eighteen-year-old Prosper— has been assigned to his Regiment.

"How stupid of the High Command!" he complains, "There is no room for family feelings in the military. Especially in wartime. They should know better than to send a general's own son to serve under him. It's unfair to the boy. Unfair to me. Unfair to the other men. They'll accuse me of favoritism unless I'm ten times harder on my own boy than on all the others. And they'll bitterly resent the lad and take it out on him."

But the High Command had spoken and General Floggingson, like any soldier, must obey orders from his superiors.

Personally, privately, in his secret heart of hearts (which he must conceal beneath his stern demeanor, of course) the General adores his son. Never has a son worked harder to please his father and more than live up to his expectations.

Likewise, Prosper thinks the sun rises and sets on his old man. He has, in fact, *requested* to be assigned to his father's command—a request that should have been denied for the reason the General has explained. How-ever, against all reasonable judgment, Prosper's request is granted and the "still-wet-behind-the-ears pup"—newly out of *Officer's Training Academy*—arrives with the altogether too eager determination to be the *BRAVEST AND BEST SOLDIER THAT EVER WAS!*

Enter Grant Payne, the meanest, toughest, most feared officer in the Regiment.

The men under General Floggingson have good reason to hate and fear Grant Payne: Flogging is the punishment for all infractions of rules; and Grant Payne is the man who cracks the cat-of-nine tails!

The General sends for Payne and informs him that young Prosper will be his roommate!

Payne can barely contain his revulsion and outrage in his General's presence. Payne has never had a roommate. He is the only man in the Regiment who bunks alone—for the simple reason that every single soldier in the Command would rather face the firing squad than room with the notoriously sadistic Grant Payne!

The General has decided to take Payne into his confidence and personally explain the reasons behind his decision to put the two highly incompatible young men together:

"Put yourself in my place, Payne. Comprehend my dilemma: I cannot even acknowledge the lad as my son. I am compelled by duty and rank to treat him as I would any man newly assigned to me whom I've never laid eyes on in my life. Even so, the men will assume a natural favoritism on my part unless I'm hard on him to the extreme. They will kill the boy with a thousand and one displays of their predetermined prejudice against him. He won't stand a chance.

"But—if you come down on him—*HARD*—and make of his life a constant Hell, they'll be on his side—don't you see?! And you, by your own repeated declarations, don't give a damn what the men think of you.

"So—you'll be doing my boy—and me—a great service by systematically brutalizing him. The men will all be for him! They'll love the lad with the same fervor that they loathe you—and *me*. You and I will be the villains and young Lieutenant Prosper Floggingson will be the darling mascot of the whole Regiment!—and I fancy it will make him a happy boy as well as a good soldier.

"I know I can count on you, Payne. Dismissed."

I must briefly interrupt this synopsis of Floggingson's Sacrifice to mention that Mario Di Palermo was extremely touching as the *General*. In praising Mario's performance, Guy reminded us that Mario never wanted to be on the stage—and that his complete lack of ego was the clue to his simplicity and conviction. He seemed to be saying that if Mario had wanted to act he wouldn't have been half as good.

I'm still trying to fathom that enigma because— Damn it!—I can't altogether dismiss it.

Meanwhile—back to the play: Having established its deliciously perverse premise, the rest of the piece concentrates on the sado-masochistic relationship of Grant and Prosper. It's all there, in their scenes together:

Prosper—made to kneel, naked, with his hands tied behind him, and polish Grant's boots with his tongue, while Grant lashes him with his cat-of-nine tails.

Grant—constantly lecturing Prosper about what a "real man"

is and what a "real man" does: "A real man always sleeps in the raw—a real man ought to be able to take a little pain, and like it," etc.

Prosper—made to kneel by his bed, naked, and say his prayers, before getting a bedtime spanking over Grant's lap. Then made to sleep naked so Grant can spank him again, first thing upon awakening.

Grant—training Prosper in the manly art of not breaking under torture ("In case you're captured by the enemy") by tying him to his bed, naked, and stubbing cigarettes out on the most sensitive parts of his body.

Night after night, the men of the Regiment hear Prosper's screams—and they see him limping painfully through the day, bravely enduring it, and never complaining. It is obvious that Payne constantly tortures his young charge and the men marvel at the manly way the kid takes it!

Both young men thrive on their relationship! Prosper approaches perfection as a soldier. The General is delighted that everything is going so well.

Prosper outdoes himself when he saves his father's life in battle. However—Irony of Ironies!—in order to save the General's life, Prosper has to disobey a direct command, an offense punishable by death!

The General orders his men to retreat. A moment later he takes a bullet in the shoulder and falls off his horse. Prosper, seeing his father's grave peril, breaks ranks, returns, and rescues the General in the nick of time. A second later, and the General would have been run through by an enemy bayonet.

Prosper kills the enemy soldier, swoops the General onto his horse, and rides him to safety.

BUT—*THE LAD HAS DISOBEYED THE GENERAL'S COMMAND AND MUST BE PUNISHED!*

All the men are greatly relieved when they learn that the brave and beautiful lad they have come to love will not be stood before the firing squad. After much soul searching, General Floggingson has decided that young Lieutenant Prosper Floggingson "shall be stripped of all his rank, ribbons, honors, medals, insignia, and uniform (including regulation underwear)—and shall be bound to the whipping post in the compound at High Noon before the entire Regiment—thereupon to receive 100 LASHES ON HIS COMPLETELY NUDE BODY."

It was Payne who convinced the General that the shame of a soldier's being stripped totally naked and flogged on all parts of his body—including his genitals—would serve as an example to the men quite as effectively as the Firing Squad.

The public stripping and heavy flogging of the General's son is carried out with great pomp and ceremony. The lad's roomie, Grant Payne, administers the naked whipping, during the course of which some of the assembled men are heard to mutter curses and imprecations of darkest loathing for the man who wields the whip—and for the ungrateful General who has a book of rules where his heart should be!

Prosper takes his whipping like a man. But after— alone with Payne—he weeps. He feels utterly disgraced. Nor can he comprehend Grant's heartfelt justifications on the General's behalf (spoken with unaccustomed tenderness by Grant as he rubs soothing lotion on Prosper's whip welts).

The heartbroken boy cannot accept Grant's declaration that the General is, in fact, more proud of his son than ever. Prosper finds it hard to believe that his father loves him and is proud of him after having his own son stripped stark naked and flogged before all the men in the Regiment! "It was not the whipping that hurt so much as Dad's harsh judgment!" cries the inconsolable youth.

Determined to redeem himself, Prosper, on his own, embarks upon what is a most dangerous, if not foolhardy mission: He stains his face and body a deep shade of brown, dons loincloth and turban, and sets off in the dead of night to infiltrate the murderous Cult of the Dragonoids.

The youth's daring plan is to impersonate a Dragonoid Slave, participate in the cult's bizarre ceremonies, and learn the details of their leader's plot for World Conquest. He feels that he might sufficiently redeem himself in his father's eyes and be a really good soldier if, single-handedly, he can save the entire White Race from being conquered and enslaved by *PYTHA-KOKULA—SUPREME RULER OF THE DRAGONOIDS*.

The role of PYTHA-KOKULA was played by Arthur Banton. It was Arthur's first character part and he played it with great relish. He made an incredibly sexy-looking villain, wearing nothing but a snakeskin thong, and with his entire body stained to the shade of chocolate.

Guy's racism was as ambiguous as everything else about him. He did not want to use black actors in the company. But he thought handsome white actors made up to look black were incredibly sexy! For the big Final Act, in the Temple of the Dragonoids, half of the company was on-stage wearing only snakeskin thongs, their mesomorphic bodies made up with Max Factor's "Egyptian—#4" which was one shade lighter than "Minstrel."

Pytha-Kokula has proclaimed himself a God. When he addresses his people he refers to Himself in the third person:

"Pytha-Kokula is angry. Pytha-Kokula must be appeased." Etc.

Pain—*inflicted on the nude bodies of handsome, virile, young white men*—is the only thing that can appease Pytha-Kokula's anger—of course.

His people have arranged for two exceptionally suitable men to be tortured that day. Pytha-Kokula is delighted.

Conspicuously inconspicuous in his disguise among the throng of PAIN WORSHIPPERS is Prosper, who nervously glances left and right, the better to simulate the correct responses and genuflections of Pytha-Kokula's followers.

The first white man to be tortured is brought out. He is the young son of a missionary couple whom the Dragonoids slaughtered in a recent raid. When they saw how beautiful the boy was, the Dragonoid's warriors spared him and brought him to their leader. The chaste and innocent but sexually well-endowed youth would make "good torture" for the anger-appeasement of Pytha-Kokula!

The pain worshippers gasp at their first sight of the Missionaries' Son. He appears to be extremely young. He is wearing short pants (very tight!) and nothing else.

Guy cast Marcel Heurtebise in the part of the Missionaries' Son because the Frenchman looked so outrageously young—sixteen, at most—despite the fact that he had recently turned twenty.

"STRIP HIM!" commands Pytha-Kokula.

I shall always remember how the audience gasped—louder than before—when Marcel's shorts were ripped off and his incredibly thick, swinging, long penis was revealed.

This was Marcel's specialty: To appear so very young, thin, and rather fragile—then be forcibly stripped naked for the big shock effect that his enormous cock invariably produced! Even audience members who had seen it before gasped with amazement when those short, tight pants were ripped off!

"Put the naked beauty into the cage and lower him into the Pit of Vipers!" shouts the insanely fanatical leader of the Dragonoids.

It was rather strange that no member of the audience, to my knowledge, ever voiced an objection over being cast in the role of a Viper. Yes—the audience becomes the "Pit of Vipers" when the Missionaries' Son is put into a cage and the cage is lifted up, swung out over the audience, and slowly lowered.

Lower and lower the cage descends, only to rise again, quickly, whenever a member of the audience attempts to insert his hands into the cage to grope the naked boy!

Here was a clear example of how he "forced" the audience to

participate in the action, although I seriously doubt if that was the sort of thing Artaud had in mind when he wrote his *Manifesto on Acting*.

When the audience has been teased long enough, the cage is returned to the stage. The naked boy is dragged out, hung up by his incredible penis, and whipped until he loses consciousness.

"*NEXT!*" shouts Pytha-Kokula. Prosper gasps when—to his amazement—Grant Payne is brought out!

It seems that Payne guessed what Prosper was "up to" and where he was going—although no clearly credible explanation is offered as to how Payne gets himself captured.

Prosper and Grant exchange nervous glances, observed by Pytha-Kokula. Pytha-Kokula now begins to suspect that Prosper might possibly be an English Spy in disguise. He orders all the Dragonoid Slaves to drop their loincloths. He observes that Prosper's body has a thin strip of pale, white flesh about his loins, in the manner of a man who has sunbathed wearing only a bikini. Prosper has to think fast: "Yes, I am white!" he declares, "but I am devoted to the Great Pytha-Kokula and desire to serve and follow him, always!"

"Very well, then prove your words by torturing the handsome English Officer!" screams the demented Pytha-Kokula.

Poor Prosper. He has no choice He must publicly torture his own roommate! Pointing to Grant Payne, Pytha-Kokula shouts "*STRIP HIM!*"

The fiendish Dragonoids seize Grant and tear all of his clothes off!

When Prosper falters, Grant, in a whisper aside, says "Do it, Lad! You must TORTURE ME! I can take it!"

The two Englishmen are rescued—eventually. It is explained that Grant left word that he was going after Prosper. "And if we're not back by dawn, come after us." (My God! How many times has that line been used!)

EVEN OUR FANTASIES

The rescue party arrives to slaughter Pytha-Kokula and all the Dragonoids. But not too soon. Not before the audience gets to enjoy the kinky thrill of watching Prosper pay Grant back for all the Sexy Abuse the kid took in the previous scenes: With only a little coaching from Pytha-Kokula, Prosper hangs Grant by his balls and whips him. That done, the General's son brands his roomie's buns with a heated iron and sodomizes him!

And—incidentally—the White Race is saved—and the General expresses his complete satisfaction with his customary dignity and reserve.

Final Curtain.

End of the Play.

But not the end of my story. Not the end of me.

LEATHER AD: S
LARRY TOWNSEND

Master,

I saw your ad in the *Underground* and thought I'd write. Enclosed is my photo. I'm 27, 5 feet 9 inches, 150 pounds. I would like to know more about your instruction in leathercraft.

If you're the sort of man who enjoys enforcing his domination over others, I'd like to hear from you. As my master you'd naturally have the right to humiliate and punish me and force me into acts of degradation.

Your obedient slave, Layne [phone, etc.]

The picture was of a young man in white jeans, wearing work boots and a leather jacket. A single chain was looped through the right shoulder strap, and a small medallion hung in the center of his chest, against a loose-fitting white T-shirt. His hair appeared to be a medium brown—like Johnny's—and in general, he had the fresh, all-American-boy appearance I found especially attractive. I called him, and we arranged to meet for dinner Wednesday night.

Layne's a sharp one! I've seen his picture, but he's never seen me. He's not taking any chances…going to look me over before he gets himself involved at my place or his…easier to say no if you're in a restaurant or bar. He looks good, and he knows it… Well, I've had no complaints so far.…

We had arranged to meet in Hollywood, across from a newspaper stand just off the Boulevard. Layne was temporarily without transportation, he explained, and would appreciate my picking him up. He said he would be dressed as he had been in the picture, so I should be able to recognize him easily. I had gone home after work, showered, and changed into Levi's, boots, and leather jacket. We'd go to a gay place for dinner, I thought, and afterward…

I pulled up across the street from the newsstand and sat in my car listening to the final bars of a new record being played by my favorite disc jockey. I didn't see Layne at our meeting place and simply remained in the car, watching the movement of the evening crowds at the corner. I had noticed several men standing about the news rack, but hadn't paid any particular attention to them. From the edge of my line of sight, I was vaguely aware of a fellow approaching my car, but I assumed he was going to get into the vehicle parked either in front or in back of me. He limped as he moved, and he was forty-five or so, with coarse, salt-and-pepper hair. All of these details registered only later, however; at the moment I was concerned with watching for Layne's arrival.

Suddenly, the limping man was beside my open window, shouting something at me. I turned my head to see what was going on, when the guy yanked open my car door and started striking me on the shoulder. He grabbed my shirt and would have ripped it off me, had I not shoved him back with my arm. He continued mouthing some gibberish I couldn't understand, and made a move to seize my door handle again. I quickly depressed the lock and rolled up the window, starting the engines as I did so. He was still standing in the street shouting something about having my license number as I drove away.

Now what do I do? Some idiot screaming at me in the street, and Layne's due any minute. Shit! That's Hollywood for you! I drove around the block, parking on another side street for fifteen or twenty minutes. It was ample time, I hoped, for the nut to have gone away and for Layne to have arrived. I drove back and spotted my date waiting for me on the corner. I called to him, and he quickly got into the car, his expression indicating his satisfaction at my appearance. The screaming kook was nowhere in sight.

We ate at a gay place on Santa Monica Boulevard, and I told Layne of my peculiar experience. After a couple of drinks, we both laughed about it, and I forgot the incident for the remainder of the night. Layne was certainly everything he had appeared to be in his photograph, and both his physical being as well as general demeanor were excitingly masculine. Since it would avoid the necessity of my having to run him home, Layne suggested we go to his place instead of mine.

He directed me through a maze of streets that wound and twisted into the hills above the main area of Hollywood. "How did you get down to where you met me?" I asked.

"A neighbor dropped me off," he explained.

"This is a bad place to live without a car," I replied.

He laughed. "I don't need a car," he said. "I've got a Harley, but it's down right now."

We pulled into the curving drive of an old Spanish-style house, and Layne took me into the garage to show off his handiwork. He did, indeed, have a cycle, except he had the engine in pieces, laid out carefully on a cloth. "I'll have it back together tomorrow," he told me. The rest of his gleaming machine stood intact, however, in a wooden rack to hold it upright.

"You know, I've often wondered what you guys do when it rains," I remarked. "A bike's great, but it must be hell in winter."

Layne chuckled again. "Well, I've got a roommate," he said. "He won't be home tonight," he added quickly, "but he's around most of the time, and he's got a car."

He unlocked a door in the side wall of the garage, leading me through a service porch and kitchen into the main part of the house. The living room, like the exterior, was Spanish adobe, with a high, beamed ceiling. The furnishings were in keeping with the design of the house, but the decor items were definitely not from any book on interior decorating. Just as chains had been the strongest stimulant to Jason, I saw that Layne's thing must be rawhide. Several wide lengths of it were tied to the beams, hanging in loops against the wall. The lamp shades and a few of the bases were decorated with strips of the material, and one entire wall had been covered with an interlaced design of rawhide of various lengths and thicknesses.

Layne offered me a drink and began picking up several odds and ends of magazines and items of clothing that made the room appear untidy. Watching him move about the large chamber, my mind drifted inexplicably to Jason and that mysterious chain he had worn about his waist...*his nuts. Never did explain it, but I know he doesn't have a lover. Must have put it on himself! Must go around all the time with that thing on him, binding across his groin and pulling on his sex every time he bends or stretches. Goes to a gym, though...must not wear it there! That'd create a stir! Imagine, some stud coming into a shower room with his nuts chained to his waist! They'd lock him up...*

When Layne came back with our drinks, he had removed his leather jacket, and I was surprised to note the collection of tattooed scrolls on both of his arms. He followed my glances and grinned sheepishly. "Had it done when I was a kid," he said. "I've got a few more...here and there," he added with a restrained laugh.

"They're sexy," I commented.

Layne shrugged. "Hope so," he said. "I'm stuck with 'em, now."

"Let me see the rest," I suggested, smiling.

Again he shrugged, and, kneeling on the floor near my feet, he lifted the T-shirt over his head. Two flying birds were engraved on his chest, one above each nipple, and a full-rigged sailing ship was emblazoned across his belly. He allowed me time to examine them, then hopped around on his knees, so I could see his back. There he had a large, snarling lion's face that covered most of the area between his shoulders.

"You really went all the way, didn't you?" I said. I was surprised now, because Layne's outward appearance—at least with clothes on—did not bespeak this type of bodily decoration.

He laughed softly, standing up with his back still to me. He unbuckled the belt and dropped his jeans from his waist. His firm buttocks gleamed at me, a lighter color than the rest of him, and for a moment I failed to see the final bits of his artistic display. Then I noticed blue marks on the underside of his cheeks. He bent forward slightly to display them. Along the lower curve of his left butt it read: KEEP IT GAY; and below the right it said: FUCK ME, BABY!

"You must have been a pretty wild kid!" I said.

He looked at me over his shoulder. "I still am," he replied. With that, he turned, allowing my first look at his equipment. *Jesus, another one!* Layne's cock was long and slender, hanging softly from his almost hairless groin. He wasn't circumcised, and through two small holes in his foreskin, he had a miniature padlock. "My friend put it there," he said, "but I've got a key," he added with a smile.

"Maybe I should make you leave it on," I suggested.

"Well…" said my companion, "…you could, but it's better without…."

I nodded. "Probably is," I laughed.

He started to pull his jeans back up, and I held out a restraining hand. "I like it this way," I told him. I kept my voice low, but the tone was a definite command.

"Okay," he replied meekly. "Whatever you want."

He bent down and removed his boots, slipping the Levi's off and replacing his feet in their leather coverings. He sat down on the thick Persian rug, his elbows about his knees, looking up at me with a suggestive smile. His balls lay on the intricate design of floor-coverings, his cock with its artificial terminus on top of them.

"You must be into rawhide," I said after several moments of silence.

He nodded. "The most!" he replied. "Rawhide and bikes...that's my bag!"

"And little locks on the pee-pee," I added.

"Have you seen this?" asked Layne abruptly. He picked up a magazine from under a table beside my chair. He flipped it open to an article on brutality in a Marine Corps prison barracks. There were several pages of drawings, showing the prisoners bound and suspended in a number of uncomfortable positions. Layne read a few sentences from the victims' descriptions of their treatment. "Really turns me on," he whispered. "All those guys getting their asses whipped by guards...probably big studs in uniforms...wow!"

I saw his cock move on its own as he spoke, saw the flesh expand and press against the restraining lock. "You'd better take it easy," I said. "Pandora's Box is about to explode."

He stood up laughing and slipped a key out of a pocket in his discarded jeans. Quickly, he removed the lock, allowing his swollen cockhead to poke free of its enclosure. He looked down at himself, then glanced slyly at me. "Ever seen a bull led around by a ring in its nose?" he asked.

I thought a second before answering, though his message seemed pretty obvious. I got up and pulled down a couple strips of rawhide from about the beams. Taking the thicker one, I walked in back of him and bound him so his forearms overlapped, his hands tied into the curve of the opposite elbow. I had never secured anyone exactly this way before, but it seemed a newer, better use, something possible with the rawhide, though difficult with chains. I then took the remaining rawhide, a strip about the size and length of a bootlace, and slipped it through one of the holes in Layne's foreskin. I knotted it and led him several paces about the room.

He had an ecstatic look on his face during the first few moments, but gradually he assumed the pose of a beaten, dejected captive.

"Your ad said photo," he whispered. "There's a Polaroid in the hall chest if you want it."

"Show me," I commanded, pulling once again on the leather lead.

He followed me docilely, inclining his head toward the proper drawer. I opened it and took out the camera. I took a couple of shots and was about to lead him back into the living room, thinking to suspend him from one of the beams, when he made the suggestion that must have been on the tip of his tongue from the beginning.

"You might get some better pictures in the garage," he muttered. "It's kinda groovy...."

I had removed my clothes by this time, replacing just the boots. Thus, both of us were almost totally naked. "How 'bout the neighbors?" I asked.

"There's an automatic door," he explained. "Just push the button on the service porch and it'll close."

Garage? Bike's out there...what else? Didn't notice...the bike! Wild!

Without waiting for further suggestions, I did what I thought he wanted. As soon as we were in the garage, I led him by his cock-halter to the Harley. It was firmly held by the wooden supports, and I had him mount the saddle. I then pulled him forward, so he was lying prone, with his belly against the seat. Using the rawhide strips that hung about the walls of the garage, I tied his neck to the center of the handlebars and his feet to either side of the rear wheel. Reaching under him, I wrapped the strip of rawhide on his cock about the underside of the seat, and pulled his balls backward, so they protruded between his legs. I tied them near the top of the scrotum, and ran the two loops down, securing them around the back of the seat. He was now tied securely atop his bike, his neck and genitals bound so firmly he dared not move a muscle.

I went back into the house for the camera, photo-graphing his predicament from several angles before using my belt to administer the blows I knew he awaited. Layne squirmed and gasped as I struck him, his muscular movement causing the tattoos upon his back to move. At times, it almost seemed that his lion was preparing to roar. The cheeks of his ass were glowing a bright red before I finished with him, and I heard him begging me to let the leather strike his balls as well as the solid curve of his ass.

I was hot enough to do whatever he wished, though judging from the cries that broke from his lips, I must have caused him fantastic pain. Because of the position in which I had tied him, I couldn't help seeing the dark pink of his anus, almost breathing as I whipped him, and the tattooed command upon his cheek...*FUCK ME, BABY. KEEP IT GAY. Fuck me...Fuck!*

I'll fuck him! I lubricated my cock with saliva and rubbed more moisture into his asshole. Then, balancing myself against the wooden supports, I positioned my cock and drove it in. I could feel the sphincter contract desperately to bar my entrance, and Layne bellowed in impotent protest. As I ground my hips against him, I knew I was increasing the strain on his bindings, but I never slowed. The groans and muttered exclamations of agony only drove me on as I rammed my hardened cock up his ass, driving myself into him until I fired a heated load...and still I didn't stop. My cock had never softened, and my lust subsided for only seconds. I rested briefly and started once again, my excitement only heightened by his softly whispered gasps and pleas for mercy.

The heavy motion of my violent thrusts against him caused the bike to bounce and vibrate within its stand, giving a feeling almost as if we were in motion, driving over a roughly surfaced road. The squeaks of the springs and metal frame, and the protesting groans from the wooden uprights added to the illusion. I wrapped my arms about my victim's chest and rode him furiously, finally bringing my legs together and bracing myself so my toes were supported by the rear of the wooden framework. I raised my entire body, holding it stiffly straight as I dropped my weight time and again upon his bound and helpless form. It took me a long while to culminate my second release, but when I came, it was with a rushing roar of sensation through my brain and a frantic trembling of my total being. I pounded and wrenched, driving myself into him until I felt my balls contract with the violence of their discharge, and I fired my second bolt of sperm deep inside the trussed captive.

Layne shot when I did. I had felt him trembling toward his climax, and I knew by the frantic, gasping moans when he actually spewed his sperm across the leather seat. Even after I had come, after my balls were drained and I knew I couldn't conjure up another load, my iron remained hot and hard, and I held it in him, impaling him as the weight of my body pinioned him upon his beloved bike.

When I finally pulled free and got up from him, I left Layne bound upon the cycle. A stream of creamy fluid oozed from his ass and another collection of semen was dripping from the seat beneath his belly. *Man! Shot from just my fucking him! Never touched his cock, never did more than shove my big iron up his ass and let him have it!*

I took a couple more pictures of him, allowing the secretions to dry upon my gradually stiffening prick before I straddled the front wheel and shoved my groin against his face. I made him clean me thoroughly before I stepped away.

Like to leave him there! Body's stretched across that bike, tied down so he can't move...both his things—rawhide and bikes...nothing else...just him and his things. Naked boy on a bike! Layne's eyes followed me as I circled his helpless form, still finding excitement in what I saw, despite having twice shot my load into him.

"Beautiful!" I whispered. "Really nice!"

Layne asked me to stay overnight, and I agreed. *I'll have to rush in the morning...get home and change for work...hellofa lot better than sleeping in an empty bed, though...much better!*

ISLANDS OF DESIRE
Peter Heister

The peninsula of Peloponnesos extended southward into the Mediterranean Sea. Near the center of its southeastern half, a region known to the local people as Lakonia, the city of Sparta had grown slowly and built up its military force until it dominated all of the surrounding land. Anacraeon and his companions journeyed south from Camarina, following the coast until they had entered Cynuria. They traveled westward from there, through huge tracts of land that had been divided among the Spartans. Armies of slaves worked the land constantly. These were the Helots, Timon explained, who occupied a sort of a middle ground between slaves and nonslaves. They could not leave their work freely and were forced to wait on the Spartan citizens, cooking and cleaning and serving them meals when they were not working in the fields. But the Helots had no master, no one Spartan they could call their owner. They were entrusted to the stewardship of a Spartan for a time, but passed into other households regularly and moved from farm to farm. Because all of Sparta was responsible for the entire body of Helots, few frictions developed between the Helots in the field and the Spartans commanded to watch over them. Indeed, the Spartans themselves, though nominally free, lived lives of such subjection to the authority of the State that they were nearly slaves themselves.

"How many free Spartans are there?" Anacraeon asked as they passed through the fields and watched the guarded expressions of the Spartans and the Helots.

"Five thousand," Timon answered. "Some say more, perhaps as many as fifteen thousand. The number of Helots is incredible in comparison, perhaps one hundred thousand."

"One hundred thousand!" Anacraeon cried out. "How do they keep them under control?"

Timon shrugged and shook his head. "Every Spartan spends his life in military training. When they are children, they are taken from their mothers and put into a herd of boys and girls. Then they are trained in fighting and wrestling and the peculiar skills of citizenship. All the males enter the army; they have been trained as soldiers from their infancy. When they are thirty, they become full citizens. They watch the Helots carefully, and every aspect of their lives is designed to maintain control of the Helot population, as well as to increase the hold of the city over the neighboring lands."

"It does not sound like a fitting life for a man," Anacraeon said.

"It is not," Timon agreed. "Their upbringing breaks their individual will, and they live by their leaders' commands. On the other hand," he conceded, "they elect their leaders. Much of their condition is the result of Fate, of being born Spartans. Who can change the reality? If the Helots were to find a charismatic leader, they would sweep away the Spartan State immediately. I was told in Athens that the Spartans once offered freedom to one thousand of the Helots. Any Helot who asked for his freedom, until one thousand, would be counted. Then, when they had accumulated the

Helots to be freed, the Spartans had them killed. They reasoned that the ones who asked for freedom would be the ones most likely to lead a revolt; the most dangerous and intelligent of the Helots. The spirit and will of the Helots have been broken ever since."

Anacraeon shook his head but did not speak. Like most Greeks, he was conservative in theory and in practice—slavery was a fact to which none but the squeamish objected—but the execution seemed even to him unnecessarily cruel and capricious.

Timon went on, "Despite their constant training, they have suffered great losses recently which even the Athenians have heard of. It suggests that their military prowess is not what it should be."

"How do they find time for business?" Anacraeon asked.

"They find no time for business," Timon answered. "Their affairs are entirely decided from birth. They leave nothing to the last minute, nothing for chance to determine. The infants are evaluated at birth, and any defective babies are flung from a sacred cliff near the city."

Anacraeon shook his head and wondered. What were they getting themselves into? Soon they had passed through the fields and the scattered outposts, and the road before them assumed a military straightness. The city of Sparta appeared before them, and they entered through the city gates. The Spartans were plain to look at, dressed in simple garments undecorated by gold or jewels. They moved about with stern and serious expressions, and at first Anacraeon feared that they would be arrested for entering the city. Who could say what strangers would meet with in this savage place? But though many of the citizens looked on the strangers with suspicion, no one bothered them as they walked into the simple city. Almost every city in Greece had high walls surrounding it, but the Spartans had little to fear. Their city spread outward, over the plains and the hills, wherever their influence could reach. Some saw that the travelers were not

Spartans, but most people walked past them with little interest.

The city had many surprises in store. At first, more than anything else, the presence of women on the street astonished them. In Athens, women were kept under lock and key. They were sheltered as girls, forbidden to leave the house without one of their parents or a slave to accompany them. As they grew into young women, they were guarded even more closely. An unmarried young woman was never seen, and even after marriage, it was rare to see a beautiful woman in public. But here, among the Spartans, handsome women walked as freely as the men. At first Anacraeon had to guard himself from staring at them, but soon he accepted their presence. On Psara, relationships between the sexes were much more casual than in the regulated life of Athenian society, but Timon took quite some time to accustom himself to the free movement of the women.

"You are not from around here." a tall, handsome Spartan said to them at last. They had paused in the central square, where a row of temples and city buildings rose majestically to the heavens.

"We are not." Timon disguised his Athenian accent a little.

"We have come from the islands." Anacraeon gestured to the east. "It is said that your city is in need of soldiers, and we are looking for work."

"Sparta has many soldiers," the Spartan said. "I do not know if you are needed here." He considered for a moment. "I will discover what I can, though I doubt it will be of much of help. Meet me here as the sun sets this evening, and I will take you to my mess hall."

Before they could accept or decline—for it mattered little to him what they said—the Spartan had left them.

It was already late in the day, and Anacraeon and his friends wandered through the streets. What a busy people! Anacraeon thought. They were always in a hurry, but at the same time they seemed dissatisfied with their lives. Their grim expressions never varied, and he began to suspect that they would be jailed for smiling or for laughing publicly. Were they different in private? In a large open field near the edge of the city, Spartan men and women underwent military training all day, practicing with their javelins and swords beneath the hot sun. They struck and parried, sword clattering against shield, spear being thrown across the field, while wrestlers grappled in the afternoon sun. It seemed even stranger that the women wrestled as well, and the sight was more then Timon could bear. He looked away in horror, while Anacraeon and Pentheus laughed at his exaggerated modesty.

Nearby, to set the tempo of the military training, a poet recited the famous Spartan lyrics: "Stand close to your enemy and strike; attack with the long spear and the heavy sword; set your foot to his foot, your shield to his shield, face to face; battle bravely." It was certainly not the most beautiful poetry Anacraeon had ever heard, but it well expressed the humorless mood of this strange city to him. The three travelers looked about and listened, but they were afraid to wander too much. There was no agora in the center of the town, no common meeting place where they could safely watch the Spartans in their daily life. Even watching the military training had its dangers, but they remained. Before they knew it, the sun touched the horizon. They returned to meet the Spartan in the city square.

"Who are you?" Anacraeon asked as the man came toward them.

"I am Chilon." Anacraeon was struck with how similar it was to their meeting with Timon, though then it had been a species of attraction that had drawn them to the Athenian. Recalling that day, Anacraeon looked at Timon and saw again the strange beauty of the young man's face. But Timon was listening closely to Chilon, who was telling them he had spent his day on the practice field.

"We saw the field," Anacraeon said.

"It occupies most of our time when we are home in the city. We spend our days with our companions, and our nights with our mess unit. Other Greeks are content with the units that nature has given to the animal kingdom, but we prefer a more rational arrangement."

"Not all animals live with their mates and their offspring," Anacraeon disagreed.

"Nor do all human creatures," Chilon said. They had reached a small building built around a central courtyard. Chilon led them into the dining hall, where a half dozen young men sat about, talking and drinking diluted wine and waiting for the dinner to be brought in. Helots stood in attendance, and the wine was poured and watered and mixed by a plain-faced girl.

"How did your people come to be like this?" Pentheus asked, once they had been seated and given wine.

"Lykurgus," Timon answered.

Chilon turned to him and nodded. "Yes, it was Lykurgus who established the agoge, the body of laws that governs us. While he walked among us, we thought that he was a man; but after his death it was revealed by the oracle that he had been and was a god."

"Though of course that is open to dispute," another of the Spartans said.

"Leon," Chilon said, "it is unwise to say such things before strangers. These men could easily be agents of the krypteia—the secret police," he added for Anacraeon's benefit when he saw the look of confusion on the islander's face. "Lykurgus established the common ownership of the slave class. He took the countryside surrounding Sparta and divided it among the three thousand citizens of the time. Before Lykurgus, we were an undisciplined people, poor, at the hands of Fate; but afterward we grew to dominate everything in our world."

"Have you changed your society since then?" Timon asked. "Surely everything cannot remain as your lawgiver made it."

"What changes there have been are unknown," Chilon said. "We do not, as in Athens, study the past and memorize its information, and we cannot know for certain what the agoge originally was. Our lives consist solely in training for war and threatening our neighbors with war, and occasionally warring."

"Now you forget the krypteia," Leon said. "It is time for dinner." Leon motioned to the Helot by the door, who nodded and stepped outside, returning soon afterward with a tray containing many containers. Bread, diluted wine and a strange stew of chopped meat and vegetables formed the entirety of the meal. But after experiencing the grim life of the Spartans and their colorless public life, Anacraeon and Pentheus were not surprised by the lack of flavor in their food.

"Much of what we believe about Lykurgus may be mythic," Chilon said as the dinner came to a close. Pentheus and Anacraeon had discussed their home on Psara, and Timon had been persuaded to say a few things about Athens. "But our myths cannot be far from the truth. Sparta has risen to its present state of power by the ruthless system we follow. Yet even among us are some who see the drawbacks of living the way we live."

"War is the natural state of affairs between the cities," Timon observed. "This is simply the truth, and I admire a people who are able to embrace the truth."

"But is there a way to escape this truth, to change the reality?" Chilon asked. "Why can't two neighbors agree to continue without fighting? Why can't there be peace without victory?"

But these questions interested Chilon's fellow Spartans not at all. Leon, who had spoken up before, shook his head and dismissed Chilon's speculations. He turned to Anacraeon and posed several questions about Psara. How had it existed for so many years without fighting, without an army, without a fleet of warships? At first he could not believe it. He managed to interest Areus, one of Chilon's mess mates, in the strange stories that Anacraeon related.

Chilon and Timon, who discovered a certain affinity for each other, got up and went for a walk in the courtyard, where they discussed Chilon's theory of peace through diplomacy. To Areus and Eurycrates and Leon, Anacraeon described the simple life of the fishing village, the unrestricted life of the young people. Even the Psarans had the habit of keeping the young women at home unless shepherded by brothers or parents. But one of the Spartans lost interest in Anacraeon's story and approached Pentheus with a gleam of interest in his eye.

"You look strong." The Spartan poked Pentheus's muscled arms with his fingertip. "I wonder if I could take you down."

Pentheus looked at him and smiled confidently.

Eurycrates was a handsome dark-haired young man with eyes that seemed almost black. His dark curls fell down upon wide muscular shoulders, though his waist was narrow. His jaw was square and his lips were deep red. He stared boldly at Pentheus, his bushy eyebrows furrowing inquisitively. His arm, as it extended toward Pentheus in a friendly competitive gesture, rippled with muscles. Before Pentheus could answer, the other two men in the room explained to Anacraeon.

"Eurycrates is a wrestler," Leon said to him. "He is always challenging strangers to a match."

"Pentheus has had little training," Anacraeon said, forgetting that Pentheus had spent hours every week with Locrus and Iapetus, practicing holds and rolling about in the open meadows.

"I will go easy," Eurycrates said, standing up and looking down at Pentheus. The low tables were taken away quickly, and the couches were pushed against the wall. The dining hall was larger than it had appeared, and there was ample room in the center. Eurycrates stripped down, and Pentheus watched him a moment before taking off his own garments. Though Pentheus was huge and stout, with a barrel chest and wide hips, Anacraeon was not sure he would be able to take down the muscular Spartan, whose muscles were round and bulging. Eurycrates's calves were huge and thick, and his thighs were made up of long strips of muscle and tendon, running up to his slender waist. Above the strata of hard muscle on his flat stomach, his chest rose up into two huge pectoral muscles, and his wide shoulders supported his huge neck and enormous arms. Leon and Areus had oiled the wrestler, and Anacraeon oiled his friend.

"The winner must take two out of three," Leon pronounced, going to the center of the room and beckoning the wrestlers forward. Then, when Eurycrates faced Pentheus, standing a yard apart, Leon stepped back and clapped his hands.

Eurycrates sprang forward like a panther, but as his hands seized Pentheus's neck, he was stopped by the Psaran's greater mass. Eurycrates struggled, tried to push against Pentheus, but failed. Pentheus, though larger, could scarcely move himself, and he waited patiently for the Spartan to make the first move. Their heads together, their arms encircling their opponent's shoulders, the two young men pushed and circled, grunting as they struggled and exerted themselves with all their might. At last Eurycrates moved like lightning across the night sky, his legs darting swiftly toward Pentheus and toppling the islander quickly. Pentheus fell to the floor, and Eurycrates raised his arms in victory.

"Another time," Pentheus said, getting up from the stone floor and brushing himself off. Dirt had clung to the oil and sweat on his back, and Leon had moved forward to begin the next match. He counted out, then stepped back and clapped his hands. This time, when Eurycrates sprang at him, Pentheus seized the wrestler's hands deftly and pulled him off balance. Grasping Eurycrates by his narrow waist, he quickly threw the Spartan to the floor, then helped him back to his feet for the third and final match.

Leon stepped forward, and the other men in the room held their breath with anticipation.

Eurycrates and Pentheus moved together warily when Leon clapped his hands. As before, they seized each other and circled, each vying against the strength of the other, each waiting for an opportunity. Pentheus was surprised by how his body remembered the strategies he had learned on Psara, but at the same time he knew the wiry Spartan possessed a hundred tricks he had never experienced. Pentheus shook free of the wrestler's hands; but before he could throw him, Eurycrates had again grabbed his shoulders. And then—suddenly—with none of the spectators even seeing from where the movement had come, Eurycrates had tried to kick out Pentheus's feet. The Psaran countered, throwing the Spartan to the floor easily, and Anacraeon and the others cheered Pentheus's victory.

"You are stronger and quicker than I thought," the vanquished wrestler said as Pentheus helped him to his feet. They walked together to the couch and sat down, as the other men set the tables and couches back where they had been. Eurycrates, though beaten, remained at Pentheus's side, and when the others had brought a goblet of wine to celebrate the win, Eurycrates and Pentheus took large sips from the goblet. A splash of the red wine fell onto the Spartan's chest, running quickly down the oiled flesh and across his rippling stomach, where it pooled near his pubic hair. Pentheus, who watched the liquid flow, reached out and brushed the liquid from Eurycrates, and when the two men made contact again, an electric spark passed between them. Eurycrates looked up at Pentheus, whose face had reddened with a sudden flush of blood.

Watching the sudden arrival of Eros, Leon and Areus turned their attention to Anacraeon. "What a handsome face!" Leon touched Anacraeon's chin, which had not been shaved for several days. "Your face is so long, and your lips so beautiful, that I think that you must be from Persia or Egypt."

"I don't know where my family comes from," Anacraeon's face grew warm with the Spartan's touch. "Perhaps you are right."

"It is a shame that your face will be damaged in battle," Areus said. "Unless, of course, the gods see fit to spare you the scarring that comes to most soldiers."

Anacraeon looked over to Pentheus, beside the beautiful glowing body of Eurycrates. In the lamplight, with his body oiled and his skin flushed with exercise, Eurycrates was truly beautiful. Pentheus and Eurycrates gazed into each other's eyes, moving together almost imperceptibly. It was like a vision, a dream, an erotic fantasy, and Anacraeon found himself aroused by it. Leon and Areus touched Anacraeon's body through his tunic, until Areus loosened the clasp and let the garment fall to the ground.

Eurycrates slid from the bench and knelt at Pentheus's feet. Then he began to kiss the Psaran's feet, his curly black hair falling against Pentheus's legs as Eurycrates moved his attention higher.

Pentheus began to grow aroused. His thick member had begun to stir to life in the forest of black pubic hair. Eurycrates kissed his way up the seated man's thighs, his tongue passing over the swelling cock, his lips kissing his stomach and hips. Pentheus's cock grew hard rapidly, rubbing against the firm muscles of the Spartan's chest. Eurycrates's nipples rubbed against the swelling organ, and the Spartan growled with hunger. His body had awakened completely to pleasure, and when Pentheus reached down to stroke his own sex, Eurycrates pushed his hand away roughly and took the tip of the organ between his lips. Pentheus had swollen completely, the huge cock jutting upward from his groin, the round, wide tip disappearing into the Spartan's warm mouth. Eurycrates sucked on the head, laving it passionately, before kissing up and down the length of the organ. He held it in his hands, amazed at its width— he had never held a heavier organ or tasted a saltier cockhead. Then Eurycrates returned to the tip and devoured it hungrily, slowly, inch by inch.

Anacraeon watched the scene unfold before him as Leon and Areus stripped. The two naked men rubbed his body, seized his throbbing cock and stroking it, rubbing their own hardness against his hips and thighs and buttocks. They moved to their knees and began to suck on Anacraeon's long cock, which they shared between them like a toy. Leon sucked on the long shaft, which he took easily down his throat. Then he pulled back and aimed the cock at Areus, who had more trouble swallowing Anacraeon's long organ. As Areus sucked on the head, his hand holding the base of the hard cock, Leon took Anacraeon's balls in his mouth one by one, sucking and tonguing them. Then Leon sucked on Anacraeon again, while Areus stroked his legs and moaned encouraging words. Anacraeon was on the verge of orgasm, but he did not want to spill his juices yet. He took Leon's head in his hands and held it still, to hold off the impending orgasm. Leon held the cock in his throat without moving. He had done this before, and he knew how to prolong the experience. Then, when Anacraeon's hands loosened their grip on his head, Leon pulled back slowly, feeling the foreskin moving on the surface of Anacraeon's hard cock, and he offered the cockhead to Areus to taste.

Behind the two Spartans, as they knelt and sucked on Anacraeon's shaft, Eurycrates took Pentheus's cock from his mouth. He bent over, offering his flaring muscular buttocks to the Psaran. Pentheus crawled between his legs and slowly slid his shaft into the awaiting hole. Anacraeon's cock grew even larger as he watched, and Leon and Areus turned about to see what was going on. Eurycrates had closed his eyes and began to growl with excitement, as Pentheus's wide member stretched his ass open. Inch after inch was inserted, until at last all of Pentheus was inside the kneeling wrestler, who felt the islander's hips against his upturned buttocks.

Eurycrates had been taken beyond thought and reason by the excitement of Pentheus's cock driving into him. He muttered and moaned and growled as Pentheus began to fuck him with the huge hard prong. Leon moved closer, until his hard cock was pressed against Eurycrates's face, and the wrestler parted his lips and sucked down Leon's cock. Leon lay on his back, his cock rising upward into Eurycrates's mouth, as the force of Pentheus's fucking impaled the wrestler on Leon's cock. Areus straddled Leon's face and pushed his cock into Leon's mouth, then reached up and began to suck on Anacraeon with renewed vigor. Though he could plunge only half of his length down Areus's throat, Anacraeon pulled back and pushed his hips forward, watching the tableau moving in front of him. Eurycrates, moaning as Pentheus fucked him from behind, bobbed his head up and down on Leon's cock. Areus, on his knees, sucked on Anacraeon as his own sex sank completely into Leon's mouth. Anacraeon remembered how good it had felt to have the entire length of his cock luxuriating in the warmth of the Spartan's throat.

Suddenly—and soon—Anacraeon came. He had been lost for several minutes in a haze of pleasure, and the head of his cock began to spurt into Areus's mouth. Areus pushed himself forward, swallowing the entire spasming shaft once, then pulling back to catch the load on his tongue and gulping down the thick fluid. He moaned, his own cock blasting into Leon's sucking throat, triggering Leon's cock to burst into Eurycrates's throat.

As the taste of Leon's spicy come flooded his mouth, Eurycrates moaned, his ass spasming around Pentheus's huge cock, which began to pump its own fluids into the wrestler's ass. As Leon's come flowed into his mouth in billowing jets and Pentheus's cock pumped its own warm juices deep within him, Eurycrates began to come violently, his cock ejaculating huge blasts of sperm into the floor beneath him. With every thrust of Pentheus's cock, as the Psaran pumped the last of his sperm into his tight ass, Eurycrates shot out a thick measure of heavy white sperm, until at last the final spasms of his orgasm brought forth only a small dribble of sperm, which dripped in long white ropes from the end of his bright red cock. The five men collapsed together. Several minutes later, when Chilon and Timon returned from their conversation and their walk, they entered a room thick with the smell of fucking and sucking, sweat and sperm.

Timon looked at Chilon and raised his eyebrows. "Just what are the customs of your people?" he asked philosophically, looking at the entwined mass of arms and legs and torsos and heads.

MILES DIAMOND AND THE DEMON OF DEATH

Derek Adams

I kept having the wildest dreams. I was wrapped in cotton batting—all pale and fuzzy and cold with damp—and the handsome man in the gray suit was there, hovering over me. It was really strange because he was floating above the ground, moving his lips without saying anything. Then he was prodding me. Then we were both sailing through the air. Suddenly the fog rolled in from the Sound, wrapping everything in its clammy tendrils.

Then, somehow, there was a purring sound, and it got nice and warm. I stretched out my hand. My fingers curved around a solid lump that kept growing till it was too big to fit against my palm anymore. Oh, man, it had felt so good pulsing against my skin, so warm and firm and comforting. I ran my fingers down its entire length, my belly fluttering with butterflies, as I realized how big it was. I remembered looking around for it, but being unable to see it. Then everything had gone blank again.

My body jerked and my eyes flew open, but it was still dark. I was aware of a pain in my side and back and of the weight of a sheet against my body. I squinted into the darkness, but there was no sign of the man in the gray suit. Then I reached out, pushing my hand beyond the slight stiffness of the crisp sheets, hoping to find that big, warm, comforting lump again. My fingers brushed something, then curled tight around a man's big, firm balls. I squeezed, groping farther for the stalk of his cock. I found that just about where you'd expect such a thing to be in relation to the balls and began tugging rhythmically. My dream felt so real, and I wanted to keep it near, to keep the sensation alive. I bent my arm, coaxing the fat lumps of his manhood back over toward me, maybe even close enough to bury my face in it and get a whiff of my mysterious man's musky funk. Maybe, if I was really lucky, bringing him close enough to feel his power against my cheek.

"Miles." He knew my name, was calling it from across a great distance, coaxing me on.

"Yes," I moaned sexily, my fingers tightening a little more. I could feel the powerful shaft rubbing against my wrist, stirred by the pleasurable little bolts of pain I was causing him.

"Miles! Jesus Christ!" The tone was more urgent now, and I could feel the man's powerful hand on my wrist, his grip tightening, even as mine did. I raised my head, mouth open, tongue flickering out like a serpent's, still drawing him closer, pulling relentlessly on his nuts. His cock snout brushed my cheek and I lunged forward, engulfing the big hot knob, lapping hungrily at the thick, veiny shaft.

"Stop that this minute, dammit!" My eyes flew open when a huge hand grabbed my own privates and began squeezing in a decidedly unfriendly way. The room was no longer completely dark—there was a flickering pinpoint of light above my head that was illuminating a massive forearm, thick in russet fur that gleamed like copper wires. My gaze traveled over the curve of a big biceps, across a broad chest, dense in more russet fur, and up a thick neck to a very handsome, very familiar face.

"Rudy?"

"Let go of my fucking balls, Miles. If you don't, I'll pop yours like a couple of grapes."

"Rudy!" I eased my grip, but hesitated to let go. Rudy had such big, pretty balls, tucked into a big, floppy sack covered with more of that copper silk. I know a man shouldn't feel that way about a business partner, but I couldn't help myself.

"Let go, Miles!" Rudy's grip became absolutely painful. I let his tempting orbs slip through my fingers. I glanced down and was secretly gratified to notice that his dick was standing straight out from his body, making me flatter myself that maybe he'd been just a little bit interested in his old buddy.

"You really are a disgusting pervert, Diamond," he grumbled, setting the flickering light—a candle stub, as it turned out—down near my head. "I sit up half the night with you, worried that you might be dying, and you reward me by trying to suck my cock. What would Jackson think if he saw that?"

"Jackson's not the jealous type, Rudy. You know that. Besides, we've done it before."

"That was strictly under duress, Miles. And I didn't enjoy it even one little bit."

"You are such a liar, Rudy." I winked at him and sat upright. My sheet, which turned out to be an old newspaper, fluttered to the ground, leaving me naked in the middle of my old office. "How'd I get back here?" I indicated the cramped cubicle where we'd camped out the night before. "I was doing some research out at Grizzard's place. Then I'm not sure what happened."

"I can't help much, I'm afraid," Rudy sighed, perching his bare ass on the floor beside me. "Jackson and I left Lena's when she shut down for the night. When we got back here, you were spread out on the doorstep, half-naked and out cold. There wasn't a soul in the vicinity who could have brought you there, and nobody asleep in the doorway with you was in any condition to recall much of anything about your arrival. Jackson and I checked you out and decided to bring you on up here. Jackson said you had no broken bones and your pupils responded to light, so I figured you didn't have a serious concussion. Besides, we didn't have a quarter to call an ambulance." Rudy sighed plaintively.

"I feel like hell," I muttered, wincing as I took a deep breath. It felt as if someone had been at my ribs with a hammer.

"You don't look so hot, either," Rudy announced, sounding entirely too pleased to make me happy. "Don't worry, though. You were just a little bruised." He turned toward me, and I could feel his gaze burning into the side of my head. I chose not to look his way. "What happened to the clothes, Miles?"

"Uh...I don't know, Rudy. Maybe I was robbed after I got knocked out." I had a vague memory of coming up short in the clothing department after my encounter with Grizzard's sexy son, but I didn't think it was the ideal topic to broach with Rudy—at least, not when we were alone.

"Forget it, Miles. I know what you were up to."

"Why, Rudy, whatever do you mean?" I was shooting for a tone of injured innocence. I didn't even come close to the target.

"Miles," Rudy growled, latching onto a tuft of my belly fur and pulling hard enough to bring tears to my eyes. "I examined you when we found you, remember? You were covered in dried jism, Miles. Barring a masturbatory interlude—which seems highly unlikely, knowing you as well as I do—I suspect you were with someone. Typically, Diamond, every time you fuck, you lose your clothes. I know that may sound mean, but it's true. I'd just like to know where I might look if I were going out to search for the only clothes we owned collectively."

"Well, I imagine they're in the custody of Mr. Nicholas Grizzard."

"You screwed Grizzard?" Rudy sounded shocked.

"Not exactly. I screwed a Grizzard family member." Rudy's eyebrows shot up. "His son, to be exact."

"You screwed an innocent child?" Rudy really sounded shocked now.

"Hardly. He was fully grown, and he was far from innocent. Actually, he seduced me." Rudy looked at me doubtfully. "In any case, my investigations were cut short when Grizzard Senior came on the scene unexpectedly. Sorry, Rudy, but I just couldn't help myself."

"No doubt, Miles." Rudy stood up and stretched mightily. He raised his clasped hands high over his head, exposing the damp tendrils of hair in his armpits. I was tempted to lick him, but contented myself with sniffing at the acrid musk that rose off of him. "Look, I'm going to hit the museum first thing when it opens. Then I'll go to the library if I feel a need to do more research." He folded his big arms across his bare chest and looked at me quizzically. "I don't know why, but I have to admit you've got me intrigued by whatever it is you think you overheard when doing God-knows-what at that museum yesterday."

"Hey, Rudy, people have been trying to kill me ever since I left that place." I nodded my head sagely.

"There are any of a number of possible motives for that, Diamond," he shot back at me. "As a matter of fact, I have my own private list of favorites."

"Very funny," I groused.

Rudy draped a heavy arm across my shoulders and gripped my bicep till it ached. "Besides, if things don't improve suddenly, we'll all be dead of starvation within the week."

"Thanks, Rudy," I muttered, slipping away from him. "You know how bad I feel about all that's happened lately. I just sort of let things get out of hand."

"Yeah. Sort of. Don't talk about it, Miles. It just makes my fingers want to curl up around your neck and squeeze—real slow and hard."

"Oh, I see." I let that conversation die. It didn't seem to be leading anywhere that I wanted to go. "Where's Jackson?" I hadn't seen a sign of him since I'd come to with my hand in Rudy's crotch.

"I'm over here, Miles," he muttered sleepily, his voice coming from someplace to the left of me. "Come on back to bed," he called to Rudy. Rudy slipped off the desk and snuggled in beside his friend. I heard them settling down to sleep and lay back on the hard floor.

"I'm cold," I muttered a few minutes later, after my efforts to cover myself with a section of newspaper had been less than successful.

"Come on, buddy," Jackson murmured. I sat up and crawled over to them. I snuggled against Jackson's hard torso and was asleep almost as soon as my cheek nestled against the full curve of his thick arm.

They say things always look more cheerful in the light of day, but I think that they—whoever the hell "they" might be—exaggerate. When we woke up, it was to the prospect of a gloomy gray sky spitting rain against the grimy windows. I tried to ignore it by closing my eyes and going back to sleep, but Rudy and Jackson got up, and there was very little to be said for a solitary stint on the dirty tile floor.

I struggled to my feet, every joint aching, my ribs screaming at me with every breath I took. I eyed the greenish purple streaks that adorned my left side from armpit to hip. The previous night came back to me in garish detail. "Car," I announced.

"Pardon?" Rudy looked at me inquisitively.

"I was hit by a car last night," I clarified. "I was crossing the street so I could talk to the man in the gray suit, when a car roared out of nowhere—with no lights, I might add—and tried to kill me."

"What about a man in a gray suit?" Jackson asked. "Was he the one who tried to run over you?"

"No, Jackson. To tell the truth, I'm convinced that he's the man who's been saving me ever since I caught wind of something going on at the museum." I mentioned the occasions when I had seen the man.

"So you think he's following you?"

"I don't think so, Jackson. I'm beginning to get the feeling that he's following the same leads I'm following."

"But at a safer distance," Rudy quipped.

"Much safer," I admitted ruefully. "Still, whoever he is, I'm glad he's on my side."

"You assume that," Rudy shot back, ever the skeptic.

"I assume he's trying to keep me alive. That seems safe enough, based on his performance to date."

"Maybe you should try to get closer to him."

"Jackson, every time I try to get close to the man, I'm nearly killed."

"Maybe that's the message you should be taking to heart," Rudy remarked grimly. "Maybe we all should."

"Come on, Rudy," I protested. "I know we're on to something. I can feel it right here." I inadvertently clapped a hand on my bruised ribs and groaned out loud.

"No doubt, Miles. I'm sure you can also feel it here." Rudy grabbed at his crotch. He caught one big ball, but the other spilled out between his fingers and drooped fetchingly against his muscular thigh.

"Come on, guys!" Jackson shook his head. "I don't know about you two, but I'm hungry. As a matter of fact, I'm addicted to food. It'll be a tough habit to break, and I'd just as soon not go cold turkey on it. Keeping that in mind, let's get dressed and try to see our way clear to rounding up some cash." We divvied up our meager supply of clothes and managed—barely—to make ourselves decent. Rudy headed for the museum, Jackson went off in search of some of his former associates who might be able to offer temporary employment, and I wandered off into the misty morning without a clue.

I didn't flatter myself that I would be welcome for a repeat performance with the curator of the museum, regardless of the prowess I had displayed in that quarter the day before. If Corliss and Grizzard were in cahoots, as I suspected, they had probably been in contact about my recent unauthorized visit to Grizzard's estate. Even without that bit of information, Corliss didn't strike me as the type whose disposition would improve with repeated fucking. Besides, I suspected that even if he hadn't orchestrated it, he wouldn't have been too distraught if I had ended up under that bus that had so nearly been the cause of my untimely demise after our last session. Going to the library to assist Rudy with research seemed pointless, given the fact that I sometimes have trouble looking up names in the telephone directory. Job hunting seemed pointless as well. I was back to the short trousers that seated six and a torn T-shirt. It was not an ensemble likely to inspire prospective employers. Still, I had to do something.

Imagine my surprise and delight when I encountered the following sign taped up in a Pioneer Square window after I had walked only a few blocks: male volunteers needed for full-body massage. fop wages paid. inquire within. Well, this seemed almost too good to be true. I looked at the storefront—there were a few framed pictures of handsome young men and a discreetly lettered sign that announced the talbot agency to the world at large.

The young man at the reception desk eyed my costume somewhat askance, but seemed more interested in my biceps and the stretches of abdomen that showed through the rips in my shirt than he was in my unorthodox daywear. In any case, he pushed a buzzer and the door directly behind his desk swung inward. I stepped through the portals and within twenty minutes, I had showered, shaved and shampooed, and was sprawled naked on a massage table in a delightfully warm cubicle that smelled pleasantly of eucalyptus oil.

I was on the verge of drifting off to dreamland when the door opened and two people entered. I opened my eyes sleepily, but the vision that confronted me snapped me wide awake. The man in the lead was approximately my age—mid-thirties—and he had obviously spent a good part of his time during those years working to hone his body to its current peak condition. He wasn't too bulked, but he had the definition of an anatomy chart: squared pecs, lats that flared like wings, abs you could cut your fingers on, and legs in which every individual muscle was clearly carved into sharp relief. He wasn't a particularly handsome fellow, but his arrogant air of self-assurance—not to mention the obscenely large bulge in the front of his spandex shorts—took your mind off that little defect almost at once.

His companion had the face of an angel—and the body of a big man. He probably wasn't a day over eighteen, but he was well over six feet tall and had to weigh in at around two hundred thirty pounds, minimum. The guy was obviously into the weights; his muscles looked like they were ready to pop right out of his skin. He had grown a beard, probably to make himself look older, and had a dense coating of downy, brown hair on his chest and forearms, but his pink cheeks and timid expression made him look like a cherub who'd had a bicycle pump jammed up his ass and been inflated to the bursting point. His skimpy shorts barely covered a bubble butt that made my tongue twitch just looking at it, and his powerful legs were almost, but not quite obscured by gleaming ringlets of chestnut fur. He saw me checking him out and blushed scarlet. I liked him immediately.

"Today we learn the art of massage," the older man announced, kicking the door shut and taking up a position on my right side. "We'll concentrate on the following areas. First, the chest." He clapped a hand on my left pec and began tweaking the meaty knot of my tit. "This leads down to the belly." The man's hand slipped down the center of my torso and he began twirling the lock of hair that grows right below my navel. This particular lock of body hair is very sensitive; its roots grow down and twine around my nuts. I groaned and he tugged it a second time. "Then we'll work on the thighs." He put a hand on my knee and began working his way up the inside of my thigh. I shivered slightly and spread my legs a little wider. "Finally, Nate, we'll concentrate on the genital area." He twitched the towel from around my hips and tossed it aside.

"Plenty to work on here, right, Mr. Jamison?" The young man definitely sounded as if he was warming up to today's lesson.

"I promise you that you'll have all you can handle, Nate," the instructor assured him. I turned my head and had another look at his overstuffed crotch. I had a feeling that Nate was in for a day of it.

"Uh, just what am I supposed to do?" I asked, raising my head and looking from man to man. I knew exactly what I wanted to do—at least to the delectable, overblown Nate—but wasn't sure quite how I was supposed to be earning my money.

"I'd say you're already well on your way to doing it," Jamison chuckled, reaching out and collaring my cock. He squeezed his fingers tight, and my prick grew a good inch. Jamison then proceeded to smack me in the belly with my own meat a few times. The little grin on his face broadened as my knob approached my navel, covered it, then surged right on by as it reached for my sternum.

"Ooh!" Nate moaned, his eyes glittering hungrily.

"We subscribe to the old adage that the customer is always right—provided he's got the cash to pay for what he wants," Jamison continued. "I'd say Nate is at a point where he should be able to handle just about anything. I'll leave it to you to test my theory."

"Ooh!" Nate moaned again, a little louder this time. It was a simple but heartfelt little noise that came from deep inside of him. I wondered casually just how many times I could get him to repeat that or a similar noise during the next half-hour or so and decided it would be worth my while to find out.

"Begin!" Jamison barked, suddenly sounding like a drill instructor. I glanced over at him—his face was grim. I feared that poor

Nate was going to be judged by a harsh taskmaster. The young masseur moved around to the head of the massage table and pressed his hot hands down tight against my pecs. His fingers were stubby but strong, kneading the mounds of firm muscle vigorously.

I looked up along his thick arms, watching his own impressive pectoral muscles twitch and jiggle as he worked me over. He stared down at me intently, his mouth set in a firm line, his nostrils slightly flared. I hated to do anything that might break his concentration, but I longed to see his serious expression change.

I raised my arms over my head, careful not to disturb his own firm grip on my pecs. My fingertips brushed the fabric of his shorts. Then I made first contact. I ran my fingers against the tender skin of his inner thighs and up inside the leg holes of his pants. The higher I reached, the wider his eyes got, till they practically bugged out of the poor boy's head. Then I bumped against his luxuriantly furry balls, and his belly ridged like a washboard as he sucked it damn near back to his spine.

His stubby little prick was already peeping over the waistband of his shorts, gleaming a ruddy pink, so I went the other way, tracing the ridge of his cock that ran from balls to asshole. His crack was clenched up tight, so I contented myself for a few minutes with an exploration of his muscle-knotted ass. Surprisingly, it was totally innocent of hair, with just enough silky fuzz to make it clear that it hadn't been touched by a razor.

It didn't take long to get annoyed by the constraints of his damned shorts, so I took what seemed to me to be the only logical course of action—I gripped them firmly by the waistband and ripped them off of him. Nate sucked lots of air, but held his ground, never letting go his grip on my pecs. As a matter of fact, this steady pressure was in danger of separating muscle from the connecting tissue. I didn't want to hurt his feelings, but the pleasure was diminishing. Fortunately, at about the same time that Nate's shorts went south, his instructor stepped in to help him focus his efforts.

"Tits!" he snarled, stepping up to Nate and leaning toward him menacingly.

"Huh?" Nate gaped, inexplicably confused by his instructor's simple command.

"I said 'tits,' you fool!" Jamison rasped, his hand shooting out and latching onto the prominent pink point capping the unfortunate Nate's left pec. Jamison pinched hard and yanked viciously, stretching the little nubbin of flesh a good half an inch from its perch.

"Oooh!" Nate sobbed, his big eyes watering. "I'm sorry. I just...I just—"

"You just what?" Jamison growled, still torturing the young man's big nipple.

"Nothing!" Nate whimpered, his thumb and forefinger closing on the meaty points on my own chest. A bolt of pleasure raced from tits to balls and my cock flopped against my gut. I groaned noisily to alert the two men that Nate's temporary oversight had been corrected. Jamison released Nate's nipple, stepped back a pace, and leaned against the wall. The simple act of pinching the young man's tit had added at least two inches to the length of the instructor's cock. It looked more than ever like a club. If it got any harder, it was in danger of causing his expensive spandex shorts to explode.

Nate's relief was so great that his whole body relaxed, including his gorgeous, tight buns. Ever the opportunist in matters of the heart—or crotch—I moved quickly and wedged as many fingers into his hot, furry crack as I could manage. His buns clenched again almost instantly, but it was too late. I had achieved my goal and wasn't about to back off—even if he managed to break all my digits.

Fortunately for me, the pressure he applied was more pleasurable than painful. I wriggled my fingers around till the ball of my thumb made contact with the springy ring of muscle guarding his rear entry. I probed gently, but the little pucker remained firmly closed. I poked again, still without result. My interest piqued, I probed and poked and prodded, all to no avail. Nate was airtight at this end, and I got the distinct impression that—up until this instant, at least—his asshole had always been strictly a one-way street. I shifted my hands slightly, assessing alternate plans of attack in order to achieve my goal. The very thought that I might actually be dealing with an unpicked cherry made my prick so hard that it rose up off my belly, throbbed mightily, drooled a big dollop of hot lube, and then continued to levitate, unsupported, a good two inches above the level of my abs.

I cupped his ass, took a deep breath, tensed my muscles, and began to lift Nate. He sucked air again, but didn't protest even when his feet left the floor. It was a struggle, but I managed to raise him till he was hovering directly over my face. His hands were planted on my chest for balance, and he had to spread his legs to avoid getting his knees cracked on the edge of the bench. This all worked perfectly to my advantage, offering an eye-popping, mouth-watering view of the dark, glossy curls clustered around his pinky brown, desperately puckering manhole as I stared up at him.

Nate was getting heavy, so I let him down, seating him directly on my face. My nose was wedged in his crack, his balls were bouncing off my chin and my field of vision was obscured by his succulent cakes, but his asshole was planting hot little kisses on my lips and I was now well on my way toward becoming a very happy man indeed.

It soon became apparent that I'd just been trying to open the oyster with the wrong knife. What had been so totally resistant to my thumb gradually gave way to the gentler promptings of my long, wet, slippery tongue. I contented myself with swabbing his muskily delicious pucker at first, teasing him till he began to relax, finally letting me into his previously untapped pleasure cave.

"Ooooh!" Nate sighed. If I could have spoken, I would have

seconded his opinion. As it was, my prick just got harder, feeling like it was going to split the skin. Nate's defenses gave way and my tongue plunged up into a moist little tunnel that was smooth as silk and fiery hot. I wiggled my tongue and Nate, in turn, wiggled his firm ass. He was obviously a very good student.

I slipped my hands up along Nate's muscle-slabbed sides, made a little detour at his rib cage, and stopped to get acquainted with his nipples. He tensed up, but instead of gripping them with the ferocity of his instructor, I took a gentler approach, merely pinching the little tabs of flesh gently as I coaxed him to lean forward. Once again he caught on quickly. Within seconds, his other pair of lips smacked against my bulging juicetube.

Nate lapped at the goo oozing out of me, then began exploring my prick, inch by inch, vein by vein, moving slowly and thoroughly from my comehole down to my balls, then right back up to the top. As he rolled forward, his cock rubbed in the valley between my pecs, and his weight shifted so that I could raise my head. I looked over at Jamison—he had his dick out of his tight pants, stroking the long, veiny shaft as he looked enviously at me. He had a mean-looking piece of meat, thick as a bottle of beer, long enough to probe the innermost depths. I winked at him—then got back down to business with the succulent Nate.

I licked the hairs away from Nate's hole, then plunged my tongue deep into his tight channel and wiggled it around. After a couple of minutes, I popped my tongue out, watching the gaping little hole as it struggled to clamp down tight again. The poor boy's heart just didn't seem to be in it, however. All I had to do was blow on his tailpipe. He opened wide, flashing me glimpses of his hot pink interior.

While I lay there, nibbling his tender lips, Nate was putting on a pretty impressive display of cocksucking. I didn't know who had been his lucky guinea pig, but I almost envied the bastard who had had the opportunity to offer his prick for this sort of practice. After kissing my knob passionately enough to convince me he was serious about it, Nate had swallowed me in one gulp, not stopping on the downstroke till after he had bumped his nose against my balls. My head flew up off the table and my tongue plunged in him to the root. He backed off me slowly, keeping his lips tight all the way, jarring me with rushes of intense pleasure that had all the fur on my body standing on end.

I knew I wasn't going to last long, especially when he began rubbing my big balls against my inner thigh, stretching the cords out till I felt an ache in my gut. I definitely had other plans for Nate's hot ass besides having it serve as a tasty snack while getting my dick sucked, so I blew air up in him to open him up and smacked him hard on the curve of his delectable, silken asscheeks.

"Time for a change of pace," I announced.

"Huh?" Nate came up off me with a big, wet slurp.

"I want you to turn around and squat over my hips," I explained, tugging one of the sodden curls in his crack. "Come on, buddy. I'm way beyond ready."

Nate did as I asked him, hunkering down on the table above me, looking nervous. I reached between his legs and pushed my prick back till my sticky knob made contact with his slimy little hole.

"Uh...no!" he squeaked, his muscles tensing. "No...oooooh!" I thrust my hips up and breached him. His backdoor was defenseless, totally undermined by my high-powered rim job. By the time his muscles could respond, they were gripping about halfway along my rigid shaft, doing nothing but intensifying my good feelings.

"I—I can't," Nate protested, his hands balling into fists, his thighs tensing, ready to spring up from the table. His instructor saw trouble coming and jumped into the breach. He clambered up onto the table with us and clamped his hands on Nate's broad shoulders, pushing him down. "Oooooooh!" Nate howled, his mouth wide as my cock stabbed into him up to the hairy hilt.

Jamison kept up the pressure, throwing his weight in against Nate

EVEN OUR FANTASIES

to make sure the young man didn't make another attempt to get away. Not content just to hold him there, he began bouncing him up and down, hands under his arms to lift him, then back on top of his shoulders to thrust him down onto my rigid spike again and again.

Gradually Nate's look of anguish faded. His howls subsided as the last of his cherry was battered away. My knob started bouncing off the fat lump of his prostate, and pleasure won the age-old buttfucking battle over pain. Nate started doing his squat thrusts unassisted and Jamison was able to move aside, taking up his post beside the table again, pumping his prick in rhythm with Nate's bouncing body.

I was teetering on the edge when Nate tipped the scales for me. His asshole spasmed, gripping like a vise, and his mouth gaped in a little circle of purest pleasure. "Aaaaaaah!" he sighed, varying his vocabulary somewhat as the jism began pumping out of his stubby pink spout, splattering my sweat-slicked torso with creamy white beads of pungent balljuice.

About the third time his fuckchannel clenched down on my spike, I let fly, searing his bowels with my hot load. Nate looked down at me and his hands clutched his belly. "Man, I'm burning up inside!" he cried, starting to come all over again. I was so taken by his enthusiasm that I sat bolt upright, pushed him back onto his shoulders, and pounded him till I churned out a second load myself. I shot off in his ass, and Nate's eyes rolled back in his head as he felt my hot sperm laving his battered manhole.

About the time that my balls were starting to climb down off the top of my cock, Jamison stepped over to the table, inserted the bloated head of his prick between Nate's pouty lips, and braced his hands against Nate's massive chest. The young man began sucking noisily, moaning ecstatically as his instructor began to feed him a natural testosterone-laced snack. Nate swallowed greedily, but still the scum overflowed, bubbling out around the plug of Jamison's cock, trickling down Nate's rosy cheeks.

I would have gone for a third round if Jamison hadn't taken matters in hand and pried us apart. "Thank you, sir," he said sternly, "but there are other lessons for Nate to master before we can send him out on his own. You can shower up and collect your money at the front desk."

"It's been a pleasure, sir," Nate gasped, his big chest still heaving. He got to his feet and hobbled out of the room, looking distinctly bowlegged. I winked at him as the door swung shut behind him. I had no doubt that he was well on the road to a stellar career as a personal escort.

I was in the tiled shower room afterward, standing under a pulsing jet of hot water, beginning to feel just a tiny bit guilty about having such a good time while Rudy and Jackson were out scrambling to get us all back on our feet. On the other hand, I had earned thirty dollars for my efforts, which made a significant contribution to our kitty. Truth be told, I couldn't wait to tell Rudy all about it. He would be livid.

I was contemplating the gratification potential of that encounter when two men walked into the changing room and began to disrobe. I glanced over my shoulder at them when they stepped into the tiled shower. They were both young, hot, and very well groomed, making me assume that they were a part of the stable of young studs who worked for the agency that Nate was apprenticed to.

"Bitch of a day," said the first one into the showers, a tall brunet with a trim body, a classically handsome face, and an enormous prick.

"Your day couldn't begin to hold a candle to mine," retorted the redhead who came in right behind him. "I'm just finishing up one of the worst nights of my working life." The redhead looked familiar, but I couldn't place him right away. I had the feeling I had met him just recently.

"So?" The brunet put a hand on his friend's shoulder and pulled him under the water jet.

"So I was out doing the deluxe number on this rich dude in this big barn of a place on Lake Washington. We had us some dinner—candles, wine, soft music, the whole works—then he suggests that maybe we'd like to sit in the sauna for a while. So I said, 'Sure.' So we go downstairs, and there's this hot dude humping the fucking shit out of this blond kid. Kid's good-looking, acts like he's having the time of his life, taking it right up the old money hole."

"So, what's the problem?" The brunet wasn't getting it. On the other hand, I had a feeling I knew exactly what the redhead was talking about.

"Hey, there wasn't no problem with the fuck. The blond kid was doing a good ten-to-twelve on this big pork stick—we're talking world-class cock here, Jim. Nice piece of meat. No, the problem was with this dude I was supposed to be with. Turned out the blond kid was his son, and old Dad wasn't taking it near as well as junior was, if you get what I'm saying."

"That's disgusting," the brunet growled, wrinkling his nose.

"What?"

"Fucking some dude's son."

"Uh...you're some dude's son, Jim."

"Oh...yeah. I guess so." Jim shrugged. Lucky for him he had a pretty smile and a big dick. He wasn't likely to make it as a rocket scientist.

"Anyway, Mr. Moral Majority, the kid's legal—and humpy enough to give a corpse a hard-on. I personally think Dad was just jealous that this other cat got onto him first." Jim wrinkled his nose again but kept quiet. "So, anyways, my night was fucked. This dude—the one who was putting it to the kid—he jets, and they can't find him. Do you believe it? Twenty grand invested in security gear, enough guards to make up a private army, and this fucker gets clean away. I had to laugh. That was before I had to go back and listen to Daddy bitching and pissing all friggin' night long."

"Why didn't you bug out?"

"Couldn't. I was making big bucks. Then, once we got into it, I got sort of tied up, y'know?" The redhead chuckled and showed a faint rope burn on his wrist. "Anyway, the dude fucks the hell out of me—three friggin' times, and me on an all-night basis instead of hourly. Then, to make it worse, he talks in his sleep, and I gotta lay there all night listening to him piss and moan in his sleep about what a bitch his life is. He kept going off about how people were trying to get what was his and how the fuckin' curator who was tryin' to fuck him wasn't going to take him for a fuckin' ride."

"What fucker was trying to fuck him?" I couldn't blame Jim for asking. The redhead wasn't a world-class raconteur.

"Hell if I know," the redhead shrugged.

"Uh...what's a curator?"

"What am I, a dictionary?"

"Excuse me for asking," Jim snapped, sounding just a little miffed.

"All I know is that he was worried about some stupid collection of crap he kept on talking about."

"So?"

"So I nabbed one on my way out this morning. Shouldn't have, but there it was on a table in the man's office. What can I say?"

"You're an asshole, Gary." Jim laughed. "Think it's worth anything?"

"Just looks like some damned pottery trinket to me, but the guy sure seemed to be all hot about it. He was bragging how he was a big-shot expert on stuff like that. When I made some comment about it looking like junk, he told me it was worth more than I'd ever be. Said it was something Colombian."

"Something Colombian? Like maybe drugs?"

"Nah. It's not hashish. I checked it out already."

"Well, like maybe the drugs are inside it, guy."

"So, maybe we'll break it open. Maybe. Later." The redhead grabbed his buddy's huge honker. "Now, why don't you let me suck on your big old prick? I didn't get any breakfast this morning on top of all this other shit."

As the redhead hunkered down to service his buddy, I rinsed off quickly and made my way out to the drying area. Hell, there couldn't be that many men who had caught their sons getting nailed the previous night—especially not men who had collections of pottery things and didn't trust curator fuckers.

I dried off quickly. Then I did a couple of rotten things. First, I stole both guys' clothes: shirts, pants, shoes, socks, the works. I had the feeling that they were both in a much better position to replace them than I was to acquire them legitimately in the first place. I refrained from taking any cash or identification—that would have been too dishonest. My heart soared when I pushed aside a jockstrap in the redhead's gym bag and unearthed a little stone carving about seven inches high. He had a fierce expression, a potbelly, an elaborate headdress that resembled bird feathers, and a tiny little hard-on. He wasn't likely to win any beauty contests, but I kind of liked the little bugger. Besides, if he was kin to the figure they had been discussing at the museum, he might be worth enough money to take your mind off his appearance. Money could do that for people—and statues as well, I guess. I grabbed it and stuffed it back into the gym bag, along with my other loot. I was tempted to stick my head in and thank the redhead for all those nice things he had said about me and my mighty mantool, but figured it might be counterproductive. As I left the room, I apologized silently to the two horny men in the shower.

KISS OF LEATHER
LARRY TOWNSEND

The Eagle's Nest was a large, almost empty shell when Vic first arrived. The bar entrance was off a long, narrow courtyard, sheltered from the street by an eight-foot wooden fence with a small opening in the center. Parking places for cycles were marked off along the cement surface, and at ten o'clock, Vic's Triumph was one of only three bikes occupying the area. He had dressed in faded blue Levi's and denim shirt, with black boots and a wide, leather belt. The evening was so warm he had not bothered with a jacket. He left his crash helmet hanging from the handlebars, though he quickly discovered the custom of the leather group was for bike riders to bring their headgear inside, where the bartender hung them ostentatiously from special pegs above the bar.

A dozen early arrivals lounged in groups of twos or threes in various parts of the room, while a high volume blast from the jukebox made the place sound full and active. Dimly lighted, mostly from concealed, amber sources, the room looked more inviting and intimate than Vic had expected. Leaning his elbows on the bar, he sipped at his beer and watched the other customers with interest. His conversation with Shaperstein earlier in the afternoon had not alleviated the uncomfortable feeling the man had originally created. Obviously, the fellow was suspicious of Vic's personal activities, and had hinted at this when they spoke. The lieutenant had brought a sheaf of papers to Vic's apartment, and their discourse over these had also been unsettling. They had sat at the dinette table and carefully gone over reports of suicide and accident investigations covering the last six to eight months. This alone had not left Vic with any too comfortable a feeling.

Not all the deaths they discussed had been within departmental jurisdiction, of course, and on these Shaperstein could not give him any first-hand information. What pattern there might be was unclear, and there was no obvious reason to expect foul play. But there had been too many cyclists—obviously gay cyclists—dying off.

"I don't really expect you're going to find out much," Shaperstein had told him. "But the captain's got this wild hair up his ass, and all we can do is go along with him."

After the lieutenant left, Vic had called Allen, telling him the whole story, and asking for whatever advice his friend might be able to offer. "My God, what a blast!" Allen had shouted, almost shattering Vic's eardrum. "Christ, I'd give my left nut for an assignment like that! I've wanted to go into that place for months, but I don't dare because some vice prick might recognize me, and then it's so long Charlie!"

"I only hope I'm not going to get my own ass in a sling," Vic had replied. "There's a lieutenant in charge of the case. Name's Morry Shaperstein, and he—"

"I know him," Allen interrupted. "He thinks all the world is queer except him. But he's never been married, either. Probably a closet queen," he laughed.

"I don't know what he is, but he makes me feel more like a suspect than an investigating officer," Vic shuddered.

"Well, listen," Allen had told him. "Just play it cool, and don't give him a chance to prove anything. He can suspect all he wants; after all, you're supposed to be playing a role."

"And that's something I wanted you to help me with," Vic replied. "Is there anything I should do, especially?"

Allen had chuckled and, hearing his amusement over the wires, Vic had been able to visualize the handsome features contorted into their habitual grin. Allen was probably sitting in his living room, or maybe lying in bed—most likely naked, or wearing only a pair of Jockey shorts. Vic could not suppress his own excitement at the thought and he wondered if it showed in his voice as he continued speaking.

Allen had told him what to wear—the costume Vic had assumed. "And no shorts," the smaller man had emphasized. "Let all that gorgeous meat show itself. You might have to fight them off, but at least you won't lack for conversation. Then there's the matter of chains," he went on.

"Chains?" Vic had responded laughingly.

"No, it's very much a part of the scene," Allen assured him. "Not everyone wears them, of course, but lots of leather guys do. You use like a choke chain—you know, the kind they put on dogs. You loop it through the shoulder strap of your jacket, or around one of your boots. Left side for 'S'—or top man; right for 'M'. Or you can hang your keys on whichever side you want to be."

"My God," Vic had said, "that's pretty open, isn't it?"

"It can save a lot of disappointments later on," Allen assured him.

"And if you're not really sure, or like to go either way," he concluded, "hang your keys in back, down the crack of that nice, fully-packed ass."

"I'm a little too nervous to make a proper answer to that!" Vic replied lightly.

"Just stage fright," Allen replied in the same vein. "All actresses get it on the eve of their debut."

Now Vic stood at the bar of a well-known gathering place for gay leather boys. Nothing he had been told made him any more at ease. So far, no one had spoken to him, and Vic began to wonder if he was going to attract the kind of attention the department hoped he would. It was the bartender who finally broke the ice.

Vic had finished his first draft and shoved the glass back for a refill. A second man had come in to help behind the bar, and the original fellow took Vic's order. Returning with the foamy drink, he paused to look at his new customer.

"First time in the Eagle's Nest?" he asked softly.

Vic nodded. "First time for a lot of things," he replied. He hoped his grin had the knowing quality for which he was striving. He took out a cigarette, which the bartender quickly lighted for him. The man was attractive, though beneath the leather chaps and frilly, long-sleeved shirt he was probably as skinny as Captain Mallet. "I'm Lewis Thorpe," he said, extending his hand.

Vic shook hands with him, surprised at the coldness of the fingers, until he remembered the fellow had been handling frosty bottles and glasses of beer. "Have you worked here long?" Vic asked.

Lewis smiled warmly. "Right from the first," he assured the other. "Got a small interest," he added in a whisper. "See, I'm secretary of the Lancers, and it keeps the fellows coming in. They're a nice bunch; I'll have to introduce you around."

"I'd like that," said Vic. "Must be a good club, huh?"

The bartender grinned broadly. "The best, man, the best!" He turned to tend some other customers as the bar started to fill. "Don't go 'way," he called to Vic.

Within minutes, it seemed, the place was packed with men. Some were dressed like Vic, but a good twenty-five or thirty wore leather pants and jackets, despite the heat. With the number of bodies all crowded together, the room seemed to shrink while the temperature and heavy haze of cigarette smoke continued to increase. Among the group of customers Vic noticed several guys in cowboy hats, western shirts and boots. Some of them were appealing and he wondered what their scene might be. He made a mental note to ask Allen next time they spoke.

Vic was on his third beer when there was some commotion near the door, but by then the crowd was so thick it was impossible to see what was going on. There were a couple of loud guffaws, and a few moments later a big, leather-clad figure pushed his way through the milling mob of customers. He was an older fellow, probably in his late forties, maybe a little more. He had heavy features and close-cropped, grey hair. He wore a double loop of heavy chains on his left shoulder, and the Lancer insignia on his back. Everyone seemed to know him, and many customers spoke to him as he made his way to the bar. Handing his white helmet to Lewis he ordered a bottle of beer and turned to face the room, leaning his back against the wooden edge. The men around him kept up an animated conversation, until Lewis stretched across, whispering something into the bigger man's ear.

The newcomer and several of his cronies turned their gaze on Vic while the bartender whispered. The looks from the several men were frankly appraising, and Vic was uncomfortable under their stares. He wondered if they might suspect he was a cop. Then the big man stood up straight and walked to him. Extending a huge ham of hand, he introduced himself. "I'm Dick Moreno," he boomed. "Skinny Minnie, here," he said, pointing to the bartender, "tells me you're new in town."

"That's right," Vic replied. "Just in from the corn belt."

"Big Dick is president of the club," Lewis added from behind the bar. "Don't let those chains scare you; underneath he's just a big loving doll."

Moreno shot him a menacing glance and returned to smile at Vic. "Just ignore our lady here," he said. "She's pissed off because I don't hold her on my knee for dictation."

Dick Moreno introduced several of the other fellows who had followed him. There were a couple Vic found attractive, but his immediate attention was riveted on an especially handsome young man whom the others called Bobo. Like all the Lancers, Bob "Bobo" Conway wore a white silk vest over his leather jacket. On the back, the club emblem of a mounted knight was imprinted beneath the words: Lancers M.C.

After several minutes of questioning by Moreno, Vic's worries began to fade. His cover was good, and his story had been well rehearsed. The department had obtained Iowa plates for his Triumph, so when the others trooped outside to examine the machine there was no apparent doubting of his explanations.

Probably because of his status within the Lancers—and Vic soon discovered that this was the most prestigious of all the local clubs—Moreno was well known and constantly being called to join one group or another within the bar. His obvious interest in Vic was not enough to overcome his normal, gregarious nature. Finally, he absented himself to have a beer with several other men.

"Stick around, now," he said off-handedly to Vic. "Maybe we can show you a thing or two later on."

"I'd like to show you a thing or two myself," mumbled Bobo, who was standing just outside the door with Vic and a couple of others.

Vic looked at him and smiled. "Maybe that could be arranged," he replied.

Bobo reminded Vic of Allen in that he was dark and carried himself with an unaffected masculinity. Casually handsome, without seeming to be overly aware of it, he appeared a friendly, open personality. He was just over twenty-one, and had been initiated into the club only a few weeks before. All of this he explained to Vic when they went back inside and stood together in a corner of the crowded, noisy room.

All around them, masses of dark-clad bodies pressed together, sliding past one another like fish in an overstocked aquarium. At one end of the room the management had turned on a concealed, ultraviolet light. This projected over about a third of the area, making white shirts and items such as plastic buttons glow brightly in the otherwise dim interior. Several guys made effective use of this, Vic noted, as a number of well-muscled bodies seemed arrayed for inspection along the wall. Well defined, carefully worked physiques were most effectively displayed in white, form-fit T-shirts.

"I'll bet you could put them all to shame," Bobo remarked. "You've got a great body."

"You look pretty good yourself," Vic replied self-consciously. Bobo's frankness and seeming innocence was refreshing, but there was an almost childlike quality about him that was also a little disconcerting. Bobo's obvious attraction was flattering, however, and several times Vic felt a warm stirring in his loins as they spoke.

"How come an attractive guy like you isn't married to somebody?" asked Bobo at length.

Vic shrugged. "Well, I am, sort of," he lied uncomfortably, thinking of Allen. "My friend is still back east, and we...well, have an arrangement. You know."

Bobo nodded. "That's the best way," he said sagely. "Safer, too. I mean, having two guys living together, even if they aren't strictly lovers. You never know what you're going to pick up on the streets these days."

"Oh?" asked Vic, raising his eyebrows in surprise. "What do you mean?"

"Well, you're pretty safe in a bar like this...unless you run into the Vice," Bobo explained. "But if a guy doesn't make out and cruises the streets later on...well, there's no telling what he might get into. A lot of guys I know go for hustlers, I guess because they seem so butch. Anyway, you can end up with a knife in your back while the guy's kissing you."

"The Kiss of Death," Vic said solemnly.

Bobo sighed. "Yeah, one of the hazards of being gay, I guess." He looked Vic in the eyes and smiled. "I hope you're not going to kill me," he said lightly.

"I didn't know you were going to give me the chance," Vic replied.

"Any time, man," said Bobo. "I think I'd let you do about anything you want."

Moreno joined them a few minutes later, still laughing, and now obviously feeling the beers he had been pouring down with his many friends and acquaintances. "Bobo been keeping you warm for me?" he asked.

"More like for himself," commented another fellow who had been standing nearby.

"More likely," echoed Dick, much to Vic's relief. The older man sighed resignedly. "One of the problems of growing old," he added with a good-natured laugh. It may have been a bit forced, but Bobo returned the grin gratefully.

"We gotta keep our kids happy," said Moreno, patting the younger man on the shoulder. "Maybe we can have a workout some other time," he added to Vic. He winked. "See you," he said, and turned to join another group by the bar.

"He's a nice guy," said Bobo. "Supposed to be a great top man, too."

"Certainly seems popular," Vic observed.

Bobo's apartment was surprisingly large and well appointed. It was furnished with expensive-appearing velvet chairs and couches mostly Spanish or Mediterranean in design. The place was extremely neat and clean. Vic complimented the boy on his housekeeping.

"A girl has to keep up appearances," he laughed. "My ex left me most of this stuff. Said I'd earned it for putting up with him as long as I did."

"Oh, I didn't realize..." Vic began.

Bobo waved a hand "Oh, it's all over with," he said. "I moved in with Frank when I was eighteen. Just came out here from New York, and green as hell. Anyway, I met him the first week I was here, and I guess I fell in love with him. Or at least I thought I did. So I moved in. He's a decorator and gets all this stuff practically for free. He was nice to me, and we got along all right; but he was older, and after a while it wasn't very exciting."

"Must be tough to break up something like that," mused Vic.

Bobo shrugged. "Oh, not really," he replied. "Things just kept getting worse and worse...not fights, really. We just weren't the same kind of people. I bought a cycle, and I started running around with other guys who rode—guys my own age or not much older. I did things with them, and I liked it. Frank couldn't understand it. He's pretty square in a lot of ways. Anyway, he found himself another boy a few months back, so it made everything a lot easier. I moved in here, and Frank insisted I take all this stuff. I still see him once in a while—we're good friends, and all." He leaned his hard body against Vic, kissing him lightly on the lips. "See, it isn't all so bad, and I don't have any hang-ups."

"Not even afraid I might stick a knife in you?" Vic asked lightly.

For a moment, Bobo's face blanched white. "I'm always afraid," he replied. "Even with you, I guess I'm not going to be quite sure until you...well, until you demonstrate that you're..."

Vic held Bobo's blue eyes in his own gaze, while his fingers played about the other's crotch, fumbling the zipper open and working his hand inside. The boy's cock lay soft and damp with sweat inside the leather covering. Gingerly, Vic pulled it out, caressing the tip with his thumb, massaging the pliant flesh as he attempted to make it respond. He looked questioningly at the other young man.

Bobo seemed uncertain. "I'm always nervous," he explained.

Vic kissed him again, very deeply this time, seeking the full sweetness of his mouth. Bobo's tongue flicked between Vic's teeth, and their arms went around one another, as Vic pressed the boy backward upon the couch. He could feel the straining muscles beneath the coarse fabric of Bobo's shirt, the hardness of his midsection, the expanded growth between his thighs, as the cock finally reacted to their mutual passion and desire. As he lay his full weight upon Bobo's chest, Vic forgot everything except the frantic craving of the moment. All thoughts of his job, of Shaperstein—even Allen—all were momentarily suffused into another time, another world.

Bobo had turned the stereo on, bringing in one of the twenty-four-hour FM stations. They lay clasped tightly together while the swelling waves of the Liebestod seemed to engulf them. Vic was lost to everything external to himself and to the warm, demanding lips, the firm, entwining body...he started violently when the soft voice of the announcer broke in.

"Let's go in the other room," Bobo whispered.

Together, still clinging to each other's hands like adolescent lovers, they walked slowly into the bedroom. Like the rest of the apartment, it was large and provided with heavily carved pieces of costly furniture. On either side of Bobo's ornate, king-size bed were large commodes surmounted by tall, rather rococo lamps. The only light was a dull reddish glow from one of these. From hidden extension speakers the music began again, this time a medley of light, symphonic arrangements.

Bobo stood beside the bed, looking into Vic's face seeming to study him, waiting. Vic started to enfold the boy in his arms, but Bobo slowly slipped from his grasp, descending in a graceful, almost floating motion to his knees. He unfastened the buckle on Vic's wide leather belt, then one by one the buttons on his Levi's. Gently, he pulled the material over Vic's narrow hips. The lengthening penis flipped forward, leaning obliquely outward from its dense tangle of blondish hairs. Dim red light reflected in highlights along the heavy flesh and upon the contours of Bobo's face as he looked up questioningly at Vic.

"Can I?" he asked softly. His tongue traced the edges of his lips and he kissed the very tip of the hardened shaft.

Instinctively aware of the other's desires, empathizing his own responses to Allen's skillful mastery, Vic paused a moment before giving his consent. A heartbeat later, Bobo's lips surrounded the flaring head. Gradually, he drew the fullness of Vic's cock into his mouth and the pleasurable intensity of this contact coursed in throbbing, swelling rhythm through the larger man. When his entire length had penetrated the kneeling body, Vic placed his hands behind Bobo's head, forcing the lips hard against his groin, experiencing both the pure physical rapture of their joining and the accompanying emotional satisfaction of his dominance.

As Bobo ground his face into the mass of silky pubic hair, feeling the subtle moisture of the scrotum stretched across his chin, his hands began unfastening the buttons on his shirt, shoving the material away from his upper body. Gradually, Vic relaxed his grip upon Bobo's head, allowing him to work his mouth slowly, eagerly, back and forth along the rigid, questing expanse of flesh.

Vic spread his legs a bit further apart, thus preventing his Levi's from slipping down. He placed his hands upon the shallow hollows at his hips, silently watching. The boy kneeling before him was now totally nude from his hard, well-defined shoulders to beyond the gentle curve of his ass. The leather pants still clung to his thighs and lower legs, but the darkness of the material was lost in the depths of shadow. A rosy glow emphasized the two powerful arcs of muscle along Bobo's back, and the pattern of his dark hair was sprinkled with tiny flecks of crimson.

Vic removed his shirt with quick, deft movements, despite the trembling excitement now gripping his body. He tossed the cloth aside and looked down again at the boy. Bobo had placed his hands behind him holding them together against the small of his back.

Drawing away at last, he allowed the full, glistening length of Vic's bursting erection to reveal itself. He held just the tip within the grip of his lips, wriggling his tongue into the tiny opening, kneading gently at the flesh with his teeth.

Reluctantly, then, he released it completely, allowing the springy hardness to stand upward, thrusting its trembling extension toward the ceiling. Bobo slowly licked along the underside until he reached the thick folds of wrinkled skin. He ran his tongue against the sac, feeling the heavy balls move gently to either side as he savored the area between them. Taking first the right, and then the left, he absorbed the entire mass of flesh, creating such a sudden rush of voluptuous swelling within Vic's body it was necessary for him to grasp the boy about the back of his head and neck, holding to him for support lest the furious flood of his own craving make him lose his balance.

Finally, Bobo stopped the maddening ministrations. He sat back on his legs, gazing upward at Vic for several moments. He mumbled something the taller man could not hear, and pressed his forehead to the floor between Vic's feet. His hands still remained behind his back; each gripped firmly to the opposite wrist, as if pinioned in their positions.

Grasping Bobo gently about the shoulders, Vic pulled the boy upward until he stood facing him. He crushed the hard youthful body against his chest, cradling the head within the hollow of his throat. He could feel Bobo's lips caressing the skin of his neck and the tongue probing at the hairs in the cleft between his pectorals. The hands, however, had remained in place, mutely expressing the other's desire.

With his cock pressed tightly between the hard walls of their bodies while Bobo's erection had slipped into a warmth between his thighs, Vic sighed as passion obliterated whatever restraints or inhibitions he might normally have felt. Still, he hesitated, not knowing exactly what he should do, and not wanting to exceed the limits of his companion's desire. However, Bobo responded as if the thoughts had been spoken. He whispered simply, "Second drawer, beside the bed."

Still holding the boy against himself, Vic reached over and pulled the drawer out of the commode. A number of items were arranged neatly within; on top of the others was a short, black leather strap. Gingerly, Vic picked it up. Still uncertain, he held it momentarily.

"That's it," Bobo whispered.

Looping the leather around Bobo's wrist, Vic pulled it tight, allowing the buckle to fasten in the innermost hole. "Now you're the boss," mumbled the boy. "You can do anything you want, and there's nothing I can do about it."

Vic fastened the strap to the other wrist while the boy still faced him. Thus Bobo stood before him in the posture of a prisoner, his hands firmly secured behind his back, and his head bent slightly forward as if in helpless, abject submission. Vic knew this posture, and from his own experience he was aware of the other's wishes. He pulled the cover and the blankets down from the bed, exposing the lower sheet. Hastily he removed the rest of his clothes, as the Levi's had fallen about his ankles, restricting his movements. Bobo did not move from where Vic had left him, and as he returned his attention to the prisoner, he was aroused again by the magnificent symmetry of the body, the exquisite detail of youthful musculature, outlined and subtly emphasized by the dim, reddish light.

Bobo's back and buttocks were illuminated most brightly, and the hard, curving surfaces seemed to glow from within. The front of his body was largely in shadow, although the light glinted upon his shoulders, along his side, and down the length of his thighs. The light also filtered softly between his legs, causing the dark hairs about his pubic area to stand out in the darkness, while the thrusting head of his cock welled outward from his groin, also catching the reflected gleam along its underside.

Waves of music continued to engulf them from speakers beneath the bed, as Vic seized his captive. Lifting him bodily, he dropped the boy roughly upon the bed. He pulled the boots and the leather pants from about his ankles before throwing himself full length atop the prone, helpless figure.

Bobo gasped as Vic's full weight crushed him, momentarily knocking the wind from his lungs. But as his breathing returned to normal, he gasped in pleasure when the larger, more powerful man kissed his face and throat, gently taking the skin between his teeth, and teasing the flesh to a tingling sensation. Vic's mouth sought after Bobo's nipples. He explored the chest until he found the nub, hard and pointed at the apex of the well-formed pec.

His lips surrounded it, grinding down forcefully upon it, pulling the skin within himself, as again his teeth pressed upon the pliant flesh. His possession became more intense, his pressure more decisive, until he was sure he must be hurting his captive. But Bobo made no sound to indicate this, and his moaning pleasure drove Vic onward, until Bobo's writhing spasm assured him he had brought the boy to the ultimate pinnacle of passion. Vic moved to the other side, working at it the same way, while he held the first nipple in his hand, playing his fingers about the hardness of the tip.

He glanced at Bobo's face, the perfect configuration outlined and glowing softly within the brightest circle of illumination. The eyes were closed and the expression was one of impassioned satisfaction, pleasurable contentment. Vic pressed his face against the solid abdomen, ran his tongue along the faint trail of down until he reached the cock, fully expanded against the ridges of Bobo's belly. He took the crown within his lips, playing his tongue about the tip, pulling the foreskin downward over the head, shoving it back again. Gradually, in unhurried stages, he moistened the shaft with his tongue, and slowly absorbed the length. Bobo's penis was classic in its form and unaltered perfection, but it was not immense, certainly not a challenge to the swelling pride that Vic now pressed against the sheet, as he lay his face upon the other's loins. Forcing the boy's manhood deeply within himself, Vic found he could pull in the balls, as well. This he did, and when the entire mass was enclosed he could feel the other respond in languid arousal. The legs extended to either side of him twitched against the muscles of his shoulders and the entire form of the captured body writhed in ecstatic pleasure.

At length, Vic released his hold upon Bobo's genitals and resumed his position atop the other. He shoved his mouth down upon the boy's, thrusting his tongue deeply inside, while his shaft probed between the other's legs. Bobo brought his thighs together, fastening upon the powerful rod, thus joining their bodies in a dual, momentary fusion.

He reacted fully and eagerly to Vic's persistent kisses straining to lift his head and press himself as tightly as possible against the possession of the other. Vic could feel the continued movement of the solid form beneath him, the questing hardness of the erection against his belly. When his lips finally parted from Bobo's, the boy lay still and silent, except for his labored, gasping intake of breath. His eyes were closed and his entire body relaxed, as if gathering strength for its further efforts.

Vic traced his lips across the boy's cheek, kissing his eyes and forehead, too tenderly, perhaps, because Bobo whispered, "Please, let my hands loose…let me loose, man."

Vic rolled slowly off the smaller form, pulling the boy on top of himself. Reaching behind Bobo's back, he released the strap, and the youngster's arms came free. Gently, they joined behind Vic's neck, as Bobo kissed him once again. Vic's eyes were closed, now, and though he felt him move, he did not realize what the boy was doing until he heard the muted clink of metal. He opened his eyes just as Bobo sat up, straddling his thighs. The other smiled at him, rocking forward a bit so their two cocks lay parallel, then joined them by the pressure of his fingers.

Bobo massaged the uneven lengths, and with his other hand he brought a pair of handcuffs down upon Vic's groin. They were not the regular equipment the officer was used to seeing, but a cheaper, less efficient mechanism. "I want us joined," Bobo whispered, working one side of the cuffs around Vic's cock, and underneath his balls. Vic heard the sliding click of ratchets, as the metal band closed about him, exciting him as it brought a gentle pressure to bear upon his prostate. Bobo locked the other cuff about himself, thus chaining them together.

Reaching into the drawer, Bobo extracted a jar of cream, which he now applied to both cocks. The unimaginable sensation of his motions brought Vic very close to a climax, and only with a tremendous effort of will did he withhold his ultimate release. The boy worked his lubricant thoroughly onto both of them, finally smearing a good amount onto their bellies and chests. Then he lay himself on Vic, circling the massive chest and shoulders with his arms, and wrapping his legs about the bigger man's thighs. He kissed Vic with a heated, forceful depth, exceeding even the passion of his previous demanding contacts.

While they were so fully joined, Bobo applied his full weight to one side, toward the center of the bed, so as to pull Vic over. When he realized what the boy was after, Vic pushed himself on top, again crushing the slender form beneath the weight of his body. When they had remained together for a while, rubbing their bodies, one upon the other, Bobo reached between them. His arm slid easily over the well-lubricated surfaces, until his fingers closed about Vic's massive cock. Easing himself gradually upward on the bed, he was able to shove Vic's cock between his thighs. The great shaft pressed firmly upon the underside of his body, its greatest weight thrusting against the crotch and prostate. Bobo forced his thighs and buttocks forward, surrounding Vic's flattened hips, locking his legs behind Vic's hard-muscled ass. The bigger man's cock now rested, almost perfectly positioned, above the tender opening. Vic was nearly bursting with heated desire. The metal ring pressed harder against his flesh, because the chain had stretched taut.

Vic stared into the half-opened eyes beneath him, knowing what his companion desired, yet afraid to move lest he release his pent-up energies too soon. The boy seemed to realize how close Vic was, and for several moments they both lay still, twined in their mutual embrace. Both were completely comfortable, and for a moment they were satisfied to simply savor the exquisite floods of overwhelming, physical sensation.

At length, Vic reached down and centered the short length of chain that joined them, positioning his shaft at the entrance of Bobo's canal. His fingers probed gently inside the opening, where a tiny pulse beat rapidly against the flesh; the anal lips seemed to beg for their impending fulfillment. Carefully, then, Vic inserted his wide crown, pressing firmly into the yielding flesh, until he felt himself inside, sliding easily down the lubricated passage. Bobo's legs increased their pressure against his ass, and the boy's cock, compressed between them, welled hard against his belly.

When at last his long descent was completed, Vic held himself pressed against the opening. He shoved downward with all his strength, at the same time gathering Bobo's slender form against his chest. With his powerful arms encircling the boy's body, Vic could feel a slight motion from the other. Bobo gently undulated his hips, causing his cock and his midsection to slide in a subdued, restricted rhythm against the heavy weight of rigid bone and muscle possessing him.

Vic gradually withdrew his cock; then, coming slowly up from the tightness of the gripping sphincter, he extracted nearly all his probing flesh. When he felt the cockhead seized by the anal muscles, he drove the thrust and slowly increased the speed of his powerful strokes. Bobo groaned in constantly mounting volume, until the pounding of Vic's massive manhood brought the boy's thirsting desire forward, upward, toward the final peak of eruption.

The increasing violence of this great stud's hammering, thudding beat soon caused the metal bands to tighten about both their cocks, until the excitement of their swollen flesh was too great for restraint. Almost without warning, the final moment was upon them. One second Vic felt an unequaled ecstasy of possession, and the next he exploded into the furious outpouring of release. He felt his seed rocketing furiously, deeply into the other, as he continued to plough his shaft far beneath the skin, deep inside the warmth of Bobo's being.

Nor was the final sensation of his coming denied the recipient. At the same moment, between their slippery midsections, the boy shot forth a searing stream of fluid, further lubricating their bodies as they moved in unrestricted opposition. With the feeling intensified by the pressure about their privates, each sustained a prolonged, completely draining ejaculation. To Vic, it seemed he must have released a quantity of sperm that exceeded the capacity of his body, and yet the flow continued, driving him into a state of near delirium.

When the flow finally subsided, they lay in exhausted euphoria, still joined as they had been before, their bodies still pressed together as if they were permanently cast into a single entity. When Vic finally sat up, his cock was yet half hard and still expanded to a size that filled the channel where it remained encased.

"Oh, man," Bobo gasped. "You're really something!" He reached awkwardly into the drawer and handed Vic a small ring of keys. "Boy, are we a mess!" he laughed.

Vic unlocked the cuffs, and Bobo wriggled out from under him. He padded into the adjoining bathroom while Vic remained kneeling on the bed, watching the round, firm buttocks as they disappeared into the darkness beyond the doorway. Bobo returned a moment later with a warm, wet towel, which he used to sponge them both. He took a cigarette from the nightstand, lighted it, and lay back upon the sheet. He took a drag, and passed it to Vic, who took it, and stretched himself out beside the boy. He allowed his body to touch Bobo's, still deriving full pleasure from their closeness.

They smoked in silence until the cigarette was almost gone.

"I guess I better get going," Vic murmured. "I've got a friend coming by for breakfast in the morning."

"I wish you could stay," Bobo replied.

It was tempting, but Vic knew Shaperstein would be around looking for him. The lieutenant seemed to rise at the crack of dawn, and it would not do for him to suspect Vic had spent the night with another man. "Wish I could, too," he said truthfully.

"Well, look, there's a run tomorrow," Bobo told him. "It's a special thing, sponsored by the Zealots— they're another club, you know. They were going to call it off when Jack got killed, but now it'll be to raise money for his funeral, because he didn't have any family. Will you come with me? You'll have a good time, and meet a lot of groovy guys."

Vic accepted the invitation and told Bobo he would be back around one o'clock. Forcing his un-willing muscles to respond, Vic stood up. He dressed beside the bed, fascinated all the while by the beauty of this slender, sleepy boy. Bobo opened his eyes, smiled as Vic bent to kiss him, and fell asleep before Vic let himself out the door.

Vic mounted his cycle, trying to start it without making a roar that would wake the entire neighborhood. Once on the street, the harsh, crisp air blowing across his face, he began to recover his strength. He was not really sleepy, he realized, for many thoughts were suddenly coursing through his mind. Instead of going home he headed his bike out the main boulevard, streaking westward along the deserted streets. Briefly, the turbulent city was at peace. Vic encountered no one, passing only darkened buildings and parked, silent cars. His was a solitude the city dweller can experience only in the final, pre-dawn hours. But Vic hardly noticed his surroundings. His mind struggled to assemble his thoughts, and to order his emotions into their usual, well-controlled pattern. Right now, nothing seemed to fit.

He had greatly enjoyed his few moments with Bobo, and he knew he had probably just finished one of the most completely fulfilling sex experiences of his life. Yet there had been a missing element, and this became increasingly clear as he lengthened the distance between himself and that comfortable king-size bed. He rode on, through the suburbs and on to the main highway, beyond the area where lights illuminated the roadside. There was only an occasional light standard now, and before him the final darkness of night hung like an impenetrable wall above the ocean.

He had been drawn in this direction, as if an invisible magnet had fastened its field upon his bike. He cut off the highway and rode across uneven turf to a crest above the cliffs. He realized, only when he stopped, that he must be very near the spot where Jack, the young Lancer, had fallen to his death.

What might lie beneath all the fear and suspicion, Vic could not yet understand. The momentary dread he had noted in Bobo's eyes when he had jokingly suggested he might be a killer, came back to him with heavy impact. Yet this might have been no more than the uncertainty of a single person, a fear that had its roots in some childhood trauma, or in the groundless rumors then current among the leather group.

Vic shrugged to himself. If some terrible evil was hiding in wait, biding its time to strike again, he had not found any tangible evidence of it. But tomorrow he would rejoin a part of the cycle group, and he would learn more about their feelings, maybe something of their secret fears. Tonight, the seething turmoil of his mind was centered more concretely upon the problems of his own existence.

Forcing his thoughts away from his assignment, he tried to unravel the tangle that complicated the usual simple sequence of his daily routine. Irritatingly enough, he could not. To accept his own homosexuality was disturbing enough. He had known this for years, but only in the last few days had his orientation been so clearly defined. He could live with this. Many others did, and not all of them seemed unhappy. He was attracted by the leather crowd, and he liked what even most gay people considered "way-out sex." Well, that need not present a problem either. He lived in an area where there seemed an ample outlet for whatever kind of sex he wanted.

Vic had been sitting astride his bike, legs angled to either side, both feet touching the ground to support his balance. He dropped the kickstand into place and walked to the edge of the rocky precipice, staring down into the seething waters. The tide was coming in, and huge waves smashed against jagged, stone outcroppings. He could see only the foaming, phosphorescent whitecaps and the upper edges of rock. The water, the sand, all the rest was blended into a single mass of darkness. Like himself, he thought—his "ego," the police psychiatrist had called it. (At the academy, all recruits had an interview with the headshrinker.) Was his job the basis of his present discontent?

He was a cop, but he liked being a cop. Was that it? No, he decided. There were other gay policemen, probably a good many more than anyone ever suspected. He could go on for years, and no one would necessarily point a finger at him. Even remaining single would not give the game away; there were many officers who never married.

No, in the final analysis he had to admit it was Allen. What he felt for the little guy was something he could not define, or maybe he was simply not ready to define it. "What the hell?" he told himself. He swung his leg over the seat, remounted his cycle. In the same motion he struck the starter and swung the machine around, back toward the city.

"You're still young," he said aloud. "Plenty of time to figure that one out." He smiled to himself at last. Yes, plenty of time. Allen would be around for a while, and that thought, at least, made him happy.

He twisted the speed control on his handlebars, and the Triumph leaped ahead, its roar drowning out the pounding surf, as he left the ocean far behind. Maybe some of his confusion would remain back there as well. He wondered. Only time would tell.

The first brilliant fingers of morning yellow were beginning to streak the sky when he reached his apartment and wearily climbed the stairs to bed.

REUNION IN FLORENCE
Sonny Ford

The next day was calm, as before, and we were made to resume our rowing. At midday, the Turk manning the observation post on the mast suddenly began shouting excitedly to his fellows, who were lazing about on the deck. Since the Turks themselves were freed from the task of rowing, which would have been their duty had they not had us to row for them, they had become indolent. Wine was drunk at all times of the day, though drunkenness was rare. From time to time, particularly toward evening, we witnessed them smoking those exhilarating herbs whose effects I was later to come to know well. In such a manner were they lazing about at the time the observer warned of danger ahead. "Mamluk! Mamluk!" I heard the Turks shouting excitedly. They began organizing for battle, a contingent of them casting us back into the hold. I do not know exactly how the battle was prosecuted, save that the ship picked up speed considerably as the Turks began rowing. Though the Turks had one cannon aboard, it was not used in the assault, as the captain feared that this weapon—then a new invention—might explode from its rear and wreak more destruction on his crew than on the Mamluks. Apparently, our ship was able to maneuver its bow into a broadside slash against the Mamluks' ship, for the force of this collision thrust the bow of the ship suddenly upwards, rolling all of us in a mass toward the stern. Such a slash no doubt disabled the Mamluks' vessel, but this act must merely have goaded them into a degree of ferocity which the Turks could not match, given the days of idleness they had enjoyed. After the shock of the collision, we heard a din of screaming and clanging and the stomp of many feet above us. This was followed by the sounds of hand-to-hand battle, screams and clanging, the slash of steel, the groan of death, and, finally, silence, which was followed by the jubilant sounds of victory.

Suddenly the hatch was thrown open. We were ordered up to the deck to be inspected. As I emerged from the hold, I grew sick from the horror which lay about me. About thirty bodies lay strewn about the deck, even as the Mamluks, seemingly unconcerned whether the bodies were their own or the enemy, were throwing corpses overboard. The deck, the masts, and the sides of the vessel were all strewn with blood. We were ordered to line up in three rows for inspection, many of us slipping and sliding in the blood as we did so. A bearded Mamluk with a scimitar in his hand walked up to the French knight who had translated the note and squeezed his private parts, saying, "Christian, eh?"

Looking to my left, I saw a contingent of Mamluks standing guard over twenty or so captured Turks, who apparently constituted those of the Turks who had not been slaughtered in the battle. Among them stood the lad who gave me the note who, though looking frightened, surveyed the scene with sensibility. The Mamluks forced us Christians to clean up the gore of the battle, as they meanwhile retrieved their valuables from their own ship, which was sinking. We were again placed on the rowing benches, still naked, this time in the company of some of the captured Turks, who were allowed to retain their clothes. The Turks were permitted to row nearest the sides of the ship, where rowing was easiest. Four Mamluk brutes filed up and down the company of rowers with whips and scimitars in their hands, lashing us Christians with the whip or jabbing us with the point of their scimitars when the spirit moved them. At dusk, we Christians were thrown below, while the Turks who rowed with us were allowed to sleep elsewhere on the ship.

Would that our service as rowers had been the extent of our suffering! The very first night of our captivity by the Mamluks, the hatch was removed, and ten Mamluks fell through among us, two of them carrying torches. We were made all to line up in the hold along either wall of the ship, where a selection process took place. Two of the men who wielded the whips and scimitars were among them, heavily armed. In fact, it was one of these that selected. Only two of us were chosen at a time, and it was my great misfortune to be one of the first two who were selected, the obnoxious Pierre being the other.

Pierre and I were pulled from the lines by the hair of our heads, thrown down upon the floor of the hold, and made to sit up on our knees. As Pierre and I sat thus, side by side, two Mamluks, one of whom wielded a whip, threw off their clothes from the waist down, and quickly stimulated themselves into a state of excitability. It was Pierre who got the wielder of the whip thrust into him, but the brute whom I was forced to accept had much the larger organ. These brutes, like the Turks, had naked heads upon their shafts. The thought of swallowing such an engine sickened me. As the brute neared me, a Mamluk approached me from the rear, tying my arms together, then grabbing my hair so as to force my head to jut upwards, meanwhile, with his other hand, forcing my jaw open. The brute committing the assault then thrust his member into my mouth, causing me to gag and cough as entry began. The Mamluk behind me screamed at me, after which he removed his hand from the region of my mouth and, with his free arm, boxed my neck in the crook of his elbow, thereby increasing my gagging. As the Mamluk before me forced entry, the one behind slackened his hold around my neck, so that I was able to catch my breath. Slowly, at first, he jammed his member in and out of my mouth, his stern countenance seeming to soften in the midst of his enjoyment. His eyes narrowed into a squint and his lips pursed upwards into a tight smile of pleasure, giving him the look of a Chinaman. The Mamluk behind me released his grip around my neck (while continuing to hold my hair) and dropped his hand to my own private parts, where he began handling my member with quick, jerky motions.

The thrusts into my throat became deeper and quicker, and, notwithstanding my own discomfort and pain, my member reached its own expansive proportions. On seeing this, a Mamluk holding a torch passed the flame to one of his comrades and fell down upon the floor by me. Suddenly he encapsulated his mouth over my organ, thereby increasing the tension in those regions. This made the fellow jabbing into my throat all the more excited, his thrusts becoming more and more violent. Finally he slowed, preparing for the final thrusts which would unload that shower which I was loath to swallow. Rather than withdrawing his member a bit so that I might catch my breath, he jabbed all the more deeply in slow, deliberate thrusts, each thrust unloading a shower of viscous material directly into my throat. As this was done to me, my own member retracted slightly, only to be forced into stricter attention by the ministrations of the Mamluk below.

As soon as the brute towering over me had left off, the Mamluk behind me pulled me down so that his fellow still attending me below could have the larger measure of my organ. For a moment, he left off his stimulations to my organ, so that he might lick and swallow my balls, soaking these poor, innocent fellows with his spittle. At that moment, the Mamluk who had pulled me to the floor, who was then holding my chest down, threw off his own trousers and mounted me upon my chest. His face appeared reddish in the light created by the torches.

Though his skin tone was dark in the way one sees among the Moorish peoples, his physiognomy was like that of Christians, for he had fine, regular features and blond hair. Nonetheless, his mien and behavior were those of a renegade, for there was no grace about him. Though I had hardly swallowed the load that had so recently been thrust into me, this Mamluk quickly fell upon me, bracing his hulking frame upon my neck and chest and thrusting his hot, distended member into my throat. As he entered me and began his thrusts, his hips rubbed against my nipples, producing unwanted excitement below. The Mamluk upon my lower parts, who meanwhile kept my member incorporated into his mouth, sensed my excitement and gave hand to me alternatively with his mouth. I closed my eyes, fighting the movement of my own bodily liquids to a point of discharge. A nearby Mamluk, seeing that I had closed my eyes, kicked me rudely in the right side. This new fiend, whom I could see from the corner of my eye standing over the Mamluk who was thrust into my mouth, was totally naked, with an erect engine distended outwards from his body, the underside of which I could see looming ominously over me. He knelt down and picked up my right hand, which he placed over his member and began forcing me to stimulate his flesh. This I did, for I could hardly protest, both of the other Mamluks meanwhile continuing their labors. I could not well control my hand, and apparently produced far more stimulation than I intended, for this fellow, suddenly plucking my hand from his organ and abruptly dropping his frame upon my face, jammed his horrid appendage into my throat alongside that of the first fellow. The two of them thus positioned on my chest with their bodies facing one another, commenced kissing and hugging each other as they forced double entry into me. I could not see anything that was going on about me, as two bodies obstructed my vision. The newcomer on my face achieved fruition first, discharging a cascade of liquid into me, whereupon the other achieved his goal, leaving my mouth and throat deluged.

This unpleasantness had only a brief debilitating effect on my own member, which continued to respond to the efforts of the fellow below. The two on my face removed themselves at length, leaving their comrade still operating upon me. The two who left off grabbed two Christians and thrust them down upon the floor on either side of me, so that they lay parallel to me, there now being three of us that were operated upon. On seeing my comrades on either side of me, I looked at them plaintively and was met with looks of fear. They, like me, were unable to control the excitability of their members. Seeing this, I again became stimulated and looked down at the Mamluk working on me. Another Mamluk, seeing my head start up slightly to witness my own suffering, walked over to me quickly and jabbed a club across my throat so as to force me down again. Realizing finally that the quicker I might discharge my load, the quicker I might find surcease of suffering, I let my thoughts fly to Tristan, whereupon, almost in an instant, the liquids of my own excitability coursed to the terminus of their goal. The Mamluk sucking me felt the liquids reaching the head and thrust my member deeply into his throat, whereupon he parried the member in and out of his head in jerky, strong movements, so that the liquids were drawn from their deepest reservoirs. On each parry, he constricted his mouth about my shaft, so as to force maximum discharge. On his leaving off, I was deeply pained within my groin, as though my loins had been ruptured and their vessels torn out.

Amidst the travails of that night, for reasons I little understand today, it was I who suffered most. Every other Christian I can remember was operated on, but it was I who was most often and most cruelly victimized. And scarcely at all could I control my own member which, though once, twice, thrice discharged, continued its outpourings. At last, perhaps after midnight, the Mamluks left off and went up on the deck, themselves exhausted from their extensive labors.

Rowing proved unnecessary the next day, as the wind came up and we were able to set sail. Although this boded well for the sores upon our bodies, particularly since we no longer had a surgeon to minister to us, it boded poorly for our comfort, for we were made to stay below through the heat of the day, the hold becoming stifling with the heat and with the stench of our bodies. Since we were not allowed to go above to relieve ourselves, some took to relieving themselves in a corner of the hold. This created a noxious stench and a congregating of flies, causing the Mamluks to alter the place of their barbarous assaults upon us. Periodically, the hatch cover would be removed, and three or four Mamluks would drop below among us. Holding their noses, they would select several of us to be the objects of their pleasure. The poor fellows selected would be sent up above, where they were taken to separate quarters for the Mamluks' enjoyment, and then returned to us. Strangely, I was not first selected. Finally, about midday, two Mamluks, one of whom was the blond fellow who assaulted me the previous evening, came below and grabbed me. I was surprised that I—and only I—was then selected, none of my fellow Christians being chosen to accompany me. These two had really been assigned to take me up for reasons having nothing to do with their pleasure. But they could not resist having sport with me.

After taking me up to the deck, they threw me into a small boat, which was suspended from one side of the ship, and entered the boat after me. After lowering the boat halfway towards the water, they forced me to lie face down on the bottom of the boat with my chest propped upon a seat which bisected the boat. With my chest thus raised and my rear thus flat upon the bottom of the boat, they began operating upon me. Quickly, they pulled their stiffened members from underneath their clothes, one entering my mouth and the blond one entering my rear. The discomfort I felt at being propped up on the hard wooden seat and having my mouth unceremoniously entered in such a position was exceeded only by the pain I felt in my rear. I had sustained the injury of forced anal invasion but twice in my life, and then only by knights of proportions not so gross as those now visited upon me.

At first, the pain in my rear was excruciating. But gradually, as the blond man neared his goal, the anguish became less harsh, and it felt as though a lubricant were easing the pain occasioned by his operation. Of course, I was unable to look back to examine the status of my battered rear, as my attention was more than filled by the other fellow operating upon my face. Finally—almost simultaneously—the loads of the two burst upon me, and they left off.

Still lying upon my back, I looked back at my rear and saw the source of the lubrication I had welcomed. Emanating from my rear was a course of blood which had begun to run over the bottom of the boat. Quickly, pain set in, and I began to moan. The two Mamluks drew the boat up to the side of the vessel and pushed me off onto the deck. Mamluks lolled about, their attention drawn to me. I must have been a sight. The members of the crew gave out various shouts and calls to their comrades, apparently in derision of my state. I was the only person on board wearing no clothes, and bruises and cuts covered my lower parts. From my rear exuded blood, which mingled with clots that I could even now feel forming upon my rear and legs. I had bruises and raw red places upon my chest and midsection, and similar ugly marks no doubt covered my face. The two brutes pushed me towards a compartment near the bow of the ship, opened a door, and shoved me in.

Inside the compartment stood a tall, dark Mamluk brute who wielded a small knife with a long, sharp blade. The two who had just assaulted me grabbed me by the arms and shoulders and thrust me down upon a table on which lay some old cloths. Staring up at the knife-wielding brute, I could not guess what was to follow. On hearing an order from the seated man, my two assailants left the compartment for a few moments, returning with some powerful straps and ropes in their hands. As the three of them exchanged comments in a brisk fashion, peppering their speech with hearty laughter, the two with the straps bound my feet tightly together, then tied the straps as tightly as possible to some fixture within the compartment that I could not see. They also strapped my wrists together, then anchored the straps binding my wrists to another fixture, so that my arms were stretched out as far as possible above my head. Further to immobilize me, they bound my chest, waist, and thighs to the table on which I was spread. While this operation took place, the bantering and laughter continued, the one with the knife ever leering at me.

By the time this binding process was complete, I was so stricken with dread that I could not focus my eyes upon one or the other of my persecutors. The knife wielder turned away from me and reached for a strap, on which he slowly and deliberately sharpened his knife. As I realized what was to happen, I began struggling violently; but try as I might, I could scarcely move at all. Clasping my member with one hand and wielding his knife with the other, as though he were skinning a cucumber, the brute began cutting a slit into the skin which covered the head of that most private and sensitive of bodily appendages. I screamed at the top of my lungs. With violent pain, the knife cut a large slot into the skin and then, slowly, it wielded its way around the head which had ever stayed hidden when not brought to attention. Sweat poured off my face and body, and my screams degenerated into sobs and cries. When I thought I would surely die from the pain inflicted on me, the world was lost to me entirely.

The next I remember, water was being thrown on my face, startling me into consciousness. Pain of the deepest sort, emanating from that extremity on which these louts had done their foul business, enveloped me. Peering down at my lower parts from my still-bound position on the table, I could see naught but a raw, red, viscous mass of flesh, the cloths on the table on which I lay being saturated with blood. The Mamluks were as merry as drunken lords, and gleefully thrust into my face the bloody skin which had so recently been my part. As they removed the straps from me, I nearly fell off the table. Although I could not stand—much less walk—the brutes forced me to perambulate upon the deck. At one point, I fell face forward, pressing my raw, red lower parts against the knotted planks, whereupon I screamed in violent pain. They paraded me before the crew, who laughed and jeered at the grisly deed that had been done to me, after which they pushed me into a compartment near the one from which I had just exited.

As I was shoved in, I fell to the floor, again experiencing an agony of pain, and lay there crying for long moments. Noticing figures in the compartment gathered about me, I expected to sustain further abuse and, perhaps, finally to die. But this did not occur. My companions were not Mamluks, but Turks—the Turks who were themselves captives of the Mamluks and who had so recently been my captors. One of them turned me over, so I now looked up at them. Absent among the faces was the lad who gave me the note, whose shining countenance instantly would have calmed me and reduced my pain. The Turks had some liniment and ointment with them, which were quickly administered to me. They also possessed a sheet, which was swaddled about me, whereupon I was placed on a cushion. Water was given me to drink, and I quickly feel to sleep.

When I awoke, it was mid-afternoon. The Turks were of all different ages and walks of life. A man approaching middle age who had a full head of deep brown hair and sported a moustache and beard in the Spanish style, came over to me and spoke to me in my native tongue, which he uttered somewhat haltingly, and with an accent.

"I am he who wrote the note for young Omar, whom you have met more than once. In my old country, in Navarre, I was briefly the Sultan's emissary to your country, and thereby was able to learn your language. I have become an exile from my native country and now perform diplomatic and other service for the Turks."

"Pray, good sir," I blurted out, "what shall become of us? Will these brutes kill us one by one while they commit their pleasures upon us?"

"Nay, lad, be not afraid for yourself. You are with us now, thanks to Omar's intercession. We are sorry that it took us so long to rescue you from your tormenters. I hope that your suffering has not been unbearable. For your fellows below, I can offer little hope. The Mamluks have many, many slaves, and probably are not in need of more, save for ransom. They know that the more valuable Christians are aboard other Turkish ships, so they view your comrades as worthless other than to become Mamluks. The leader aboard this ship is not entirely stupid, and he may yet think of what hearty Mamluks your companions would make. You, on the other hand, are under our protection, thanks to Omar's intercession, and will be ransomed with us. Be sure you do not let the Mamluks know of the unique nature of the complement of Turks they have captured. Perhaps you know not of this until this moment. You surely would have known sooner or later, for you would have guessed why young Omar wished you saved and not the others. If the Mamluks knew of our predilection, they would treat us as they do your brothers, since they know that we would fear to complain to our Sultan."

"And what of this Omar? Is he safe?"

"Alas, though the Prince is safe from danger, he is not safe from affliction. The first mate of this ship, who has a liking for young lads, has taken a fancy to him, and Omar is locked in his quarters. This mate will suffer at the hands of his emir when he returns to Syria for so treating a Muslim prince being held for ransom, but he cares not about the punishment which will be his. Do not worry that young Omar's fate will be as harsh as that which has been yours."

This man, whose name was Faisano, further explained that the Mamluks and the Turks, though constantly warring with one another, respected each other, and had developed an organized method of capture and ransom which, unfortunately, did not normally apply to Christians. Though many of the Mamluks were lovers of men and quite public about their predilection, this was not true of the Turks, who generally eschewed those of my proclivity. Abdullah, the Crown Prince, was an exception to this. Being a lover of men, he had secretly assembled an entire company of men like himself. Those of the captured Christians known by him and his agents to be similarly oriented were to be added to his company.

For me, at least, the remainder of the voyage was uneventful. At every opportunity, those of the Mamluks who wanted Christians vented their desires as they felt. Several Christians experienced deep afflictions from the miseries visited upon them. This, in combination with the cramped, ugly condition in which they were kept, resulted in the spreading of disease among them, and several died. When some of the illnesses which they had contracted were seen to spread to the crew, the captain put a stop to these practices, isolating the Christians from the crew and tending more mercifully to their needs. Indeed, the hold of the ship was washed each day. These measures quickly reversed the deterioration, and most made it safely to the Mamluks' port, which lay in Syria.

For my part, I was accepted wholeheartedly among the Turks. Faisano began immediately to teach me Turkish, which I studied so assiduously that, by the end of the voyage, I could speak the language fairly well. This brought me ever closer to Faisano, who became as a father to me. It was at this time also that I began learning to read and write. To this day, I write better Turkish than I do any other language.

THE INITIATION OF PB 500
KYLE STONE

Somewhere at the edge of Micah's fogged consciousness was the sound of running water. Gradually, he became aware of someone gently touching his face. He opened his eyes. There were three of them. Three tall men with dark luminous eyes and heavy eyebrows. Although distinctly alien to him in some subtle way, the impression he received was one of caring, of kindness.

"You are Healers," he said, and they smiled, as if they understood. But then they looked at each other, and once more he heard that strange liquid language slide back and forth between them. He sensed that it was this sound that had formed a background for his dreams for some time now. He wondered where he was and how long he had been here. Slowly he absorbed the details around him.

This was not Base Gamma 1, that much was obvious. He was naked, supported on jets of warm air above some sort of bed. His long blond hair was unbraided and cascading over the pillow as if it had been arranged that way. A white light glowed above him from some unknown source. Alien symbols covered one wall. He felt the first ripple of fear.

"Where am I?" Micah looked from one dark face to another. He felt for his I.D. tags but they were not around his neck.

The Healers seemed pleased when he spoke, but they obviously had no idea what he was saying. One of them began to stroke Micah's forehead, moistening his dry lips with a soft sponge.

Flashes of memory came to Micah, fragmented pictures of violence and pain. The uprising! Flight! Could Royal be dead? He felt his eyes fill with tears at the thought of his lover, and he turned away from the alien faces. I am alone, he thought. Does anyone know I am here? His eyelids fluttered and he was lost in darkness again.

Micah awoke to the realization that he had been moved. Now he was in a small room with walls of some sort of padded material. Muted sunlight filtered through the thick greenish glass of the ceiling. In the wall at the foot of the bed was a panel of shadowed glass he suspected might be a two-way mirror. He was still naked, but now he was lying on a narrow bed, his wrists attached with soft restraints above his head. His ankles were tied to the foot of the bed, his legs spread apart. He knew that he had been quite delirious at times. He pulled experimentally, trying to bring his legs together, but it was impossible. Though the material that bound him was soft, it was very strong.

Two young men came into the room, wearing some kind of one-piece white coveralls as the other three men, tight at the wrists and ankles. They were talking softly together, the liquid syllables of their strange language slipping swiftly between them. Micah flushed, painfully aware of his nakedness. As the men talked, one of them laid his hand over Micah's left nipple. Micah tensed as the hand traveled down his stomach and touched the hollow of his groin. To his horror, he felt himself respond to the casual touch.

He turned his head aside, feeling the flush of embarrassment spread over his chest. The man took Micah's chin firmly between his fingers, turned his head back, and smiled down at him. Then both men laughed. They undid the restraints that fastened his feet and began to move his knees, bending his legs back and forth, knowing hands feeling the stretch and pull of every muscle. They repeated the procedure with his arms. Apparently satisfied, they helped him to his feet.

"At last!" Micah exclaimed, and they nodded, almost as if they could understand. He felt a little shaky, but well enough. "Where are my clothes?" The men looked at each other, puzzled. Micah gestured to their coveralls, then to his own nakedness. They nodded, smiled, and turned away.

"Perhaps they are taking me for a bath or a shower," Micah thought as he followed them out the door.

To his relief, there was no one in the narrow hall. It was very quiet, almost hushed. Then they came to a set of double doors, and the Healers ushered him through to a different world.

Here it was warm and bright and noisy. Startled by the contrast, Micah looked around. Two burly dark men, wearing bright red tunics with an emblem on the shoulder and black pants, stepped forward at once, as if they had been waiting for the Healers. One of the men wore a black earring. He laid his large hands possessively on Micah's shoulder, feeling the muscles of his arms and thighs roughly. Incensed at this treatment, Micah broke free. The next thing he knew, his hands were caught in a grip of steel, twisted behind his back, and snapped into handcuffs. It was a harsh reminder that he was a prisoner here, after all, not a patient. When Micah looked around, the Healers were gone.

The man with the black earring slapped his bare ass and gave him a push down the corridor toward the glass doors leading outside. Horrified, Micah realized they were taking him outdoors, naked, just as he was.

"You can't do this!" he cried, turning around.

The man peeled off his belt and hit Micah with it. The leather uncurled against his flesh, shocking him into anger and tears. But the man was not finished. With a fierce growl, he hit him again, and then again. Unable to shield himself with his hands fastened behind him, Micah turned away and stumbled down the corridor, the leather stinging his back and thighs and ass. These barbarians, whoever they were, probably had no treaties with his people. There was no higher authority to complain to. He would have to endure. The door opened before him and he stumbled through into the sunshine and a crowd of people.

To his surprise, no one seemed to notice the sudden appearance of a naked, bound man in their midst. His guards slipped the belt into the handcuffs and used it as a leash to pull him along through the busy crowds. Micah couldn't take in anything but the hum of activity and the fact that now and then hands touched him, prodded him. Curious hands. Rough. Male.

At last the crowds diminished and they came to a narrow gateway leading into a field. When one of the men pushed him roughly through the opening, Micah snapped, turning and pushing back. It was a mistake. At once the belt whistled through the air and tore into the flesh of his shoulders, chest, and thighs. This time the man continued to beat him without mercy until Micah screamed and dropped to the ground in agony. The other man threw a pail of cold water over him, pulled him to his feet, and shoved him into the field. Then they took off his cuffs.

The taller of the two men clapped his hands and made a circular motion, indicating he was to jog around the field. Shaking, Micah threw back his long hair. He was used to having it in a braid, and he found it distracting down. The man with the black earring was taking a whip from a table near the gate.

"Shit!" muttered Micah. He would not be whipped like an animal! The belt was bad enough. He quivered for a moment, hesitating between his pride and common sense, then turned and began to jog.

His muscles were cramped from the long convalescence and he ran much more slowly then usual, but as long as he kept going, the whip was not used. At last he heard the clap of hands that signaled he could stop. With relief he came back and dropped to the ground in exhaustion. Sweat poured from his body, dampening the fine gold hair on his chest and dripping from his armpits. As he panted on his knees, his hands were again cuffed behind him. The brown-haired man wiped his face and produced a silver bottle with a rubber teat, which he thrust into Micah's mouth. Incensed, Micah spat it out, pulling away. The man grabbed Micah's long hair and pulled his head down till his forehead was on the ground. He held it there while the other man began to hit him, his open hand making the muscles of Micah's unprotected ass dance. Micah tried to pull away from the intimate and painful contact, but it was impossible. It went on and on, the sound of the naked hand against his bare flesh loud in the air. The stinging sensation grew and grew, the heat spreading and deepening, making him more conscious of his buttocks than he had ever been before. And in spite of the torment, he knew that the hand belonged to a strong man who had him at his complete mercy, a man who thoroughly enjoyed what he was doing. Although Micah twisted against the blows until he cried out, he was dimly aware, too, of a glimmer of pleasure, sensed through the haze of his pain.

At last, to his shame and utter mortification, he came onto the grass. His hope that his tormentors would not know was shattered at once. The slapping stopped and he was jerked upright. The man who held him reached down and pulled his slack cock, wet with his own come. Both men threw back their heads and laughed. Then the brown-haired man produced the bottle again and forced it into Micah's mouth. Quivering with pain and humiliation, Micah sucked at the bottle. From the vaguely familiar taste, he guessed it was a kind of liquid protein, similar to what was used at the Base. As he sucked, the big man wiped his tears away. Then he felt the man's hand slide between his legs and along the crease of his ass and push its way inside him. He stiffened, but the face of the one who fed him was warning enough: He was to allow this invasion or suffer the consequences. He could hear the rustle of clothing behind him and knew what would happen next. Panic swept through him. He was about to be raped and there was nothing he could do about it. These men had total power over him. The bottle was finished and the brown-haired man forced his head down into his lap, holding Micah's ass in place for his friend. Micah felt the tip of the man's fat cock, then a sudden lunge. He screamed.

"No!"

He almost passed out from the pain. His body was drenched with sudden sweat. It seemed like forever, a lifetime of agony. Then it was over. The man who held him pulled his head up. The man who had fucked him presented himself to be sucked. Broken and crying, Micah sucked the man clean.

How long had it been since he walked out into the sunlight of his torment? One hour? Two? It seemed like a lifetime. They led him back to the building by a different route and he followed docilely. They went into an outhouse with a stone floor. It was open on one side. The big man who had raped him pointed to the shower and turned on the water. He held the shower head aimed at Micah's head, shoulders, genitals. Micah was ordered to bend over, but he didn't care anymore. He was exhausted and the hot water stung his bruised and scratched body. The man's hand directed the water up his anus, cleaning away the blood.

When it was over, he stood under the radiant heat while his long hair was brushed and dried. Finally they led him back to the main building.

This time they took him to a small room with a narrow cot equipped with the same restraints as before. He lay down on the bed and was manacled on his back, his legs spread apart. Even so, he fell asleep almost before they had left.

He woke up to the rough hands of the brown-haired man, who was taking off his restraints. Micah's jailer handcuffed him and led him to another room overlooking the valley. Here he was made to kneel on the floor and a large dish of stew was set in front of him. The man left. Micah was very hungry. He looked at the bowl, bent down and sniffed it. He was drooling for its wonderful rich goodness. But there was no way to get it except by putting his face in the plate. He pushed his knees further apart and bent over, trying to lick up the gravy and keep his balance at the same time. It was slow going. His long hair kept getting in the way, but finally he figured out how to shake it back to one side. At last he lost all dignity and pushed his face into the dish, smearing his nose and cheeks and chin in his eagerness to get a mouthful of the food. He finished off by licking the dish clean.

His jailer arrived almost at once and laughed when he saw Micah's greasy face. To Micah's shock, he leaned over and licked the gravy off his chin and nose. There was something erotic about the silken touch of this stranger's tongue against his skin. His jailer ended by kissing him, forcing his lips apart, exploring the greasy mouth inside. And Micah let him do it, wanted him to do it. He dropped his eyes when the man released him. What is happening to me? he wondered.

After that, he was taken to a large hall fitted like a gym. He was provided with an odd sort of jockstrap, then put through his paces. Apart from the fact that he was almost naked, it was much like his usual workout at home, except abbreviated because of his convalescence. He would, he supposed, have to work his way back up to par.

This routine went on for weeks. Mornings, he went running in the field, made to go faster and faster, the whip used less and less sparingly. Then he would be forced to service one or the other of his trainers, sometimes both. Then he would be fed his bottle of protein. After that, the shower and a nap. Lunch was always the same, stew on a plate on the floor, which he was forced to eat like an animal while his jailers watched, sometimes eating their own meal at a table on the terrace. At times, they fed him pieces of unfamiliar fruit as a treat, but for this he would have to cross the room on his knees. He learned never to touch his genitals or anus, never to pee without someone else placing his cock in one of the clear plastic bottles, always to kneel with his knees spread wide apart, so that he was constantly on display for their pleasure. He found that his blond hair was endlessly fascinating to these large, dark men and they played with it constantly. They found his fair skin and pale pubic hair equally alluring, and constantly touched him, running their hands over his smooth ass and the soft whiteness of his inner thighs. And although his mind rebelled, his body responded. He was often hard after their touch, and the sting of a slap would bring him quickly and humiliatingly erect. It wasn't long before they played him like an instrument. Most mornings ended with Micah hard and hurting with the desire to be fucked or masturbated by their rough hands. They rarely disappointed him.

After weeks of exercise, Micah's physical condition was better than ever. His body was tanned a honey gold all over and his muscles were firm. Although the punishment never faltered, he sensed that his trainers were pleased with him and, in spite of himself, this made him proud. But he reminded himself every morning that he was Micah Starion, a Nebula Warrior, and his first duty was to escape from this place of humiliation. He rarely had the chance to see much of the area they kept him in, since every day was spent going to the field, or in the gym, but he got the impression they were in some sort of fortress high on a hill. But where? It did not look like any part of Zeedon, the place he and Royal had been headed when the instruments failed. He lay awake at night, trying to remember the star charts so that he might get some idea of where he could have crashed.

And then he would remember Royal and his heart swelled with the pain of his loss. They had had so little time together. He could still feel the sting of Royal's mark being burned into his ass as a sign of their union, only two nights before the disaster. It seemed disloyal now to regret that he had never had the chance to put any sort of mark on Royal. It had been understood between them that this was a one-way thing. It was never discussed. And now his strong, powerful lover was dead, and he was left a prisoner, alone in this foul place!

Yet in an odd way, he found his life falling into a certain comforting rhythm. And this was why he sensed a change at once when they began to treat him differently. It was not that they were any more gentle or any less demanding. They still slapped him with their calloused hands and pulled his hair and thrust their fingers inside him, twisting him with pain. But they no longer used the long curling whip or beat him with the belt. They began to rub oil into his skin every afternoon. Then one day, he noticed three new men watching his performance in the field. One of them especially caught his eye, a tall, rugged man with slate gray eyes. Unconsciously Micah put on a burst of speed, raising his head proudly and throwing out his chest. He would show them what a Nebula Warrior was capable of! A few days later, the gray-eyed man was in the gym, and the next day, he was with a group watching in the afternoon.

Then one day the routine changed. After his lunch, he was taken to a different room. It was similar to the shower place, but there was a sort of high table in the middle and a cupboard at one side. Apprehensive at this break in routine, Micah looked around, trying to figure out the use for such a place. There was a shower here, too, he noticed, and a large tub on a raised platform.

The big man with the black earring, whom he had named Simon, after Simon Legree, threw him into the shower stall and turned on the water full force. Micah fought to keep his balance on the stone floor, bracing himself with both hands against the glass of the walls. Then his long hair was soaped and washed. At last he was allowed under the radiant heat unit.

After that, another man appeared whom Micah had not seen before. He was friendly with Simon, the two men talking with the ease of old acquaintance. As they talked, for the first time, Micah thought he detected a name—something that sounded like Kee. This man, too, wore the red tunic and baggy pants that seemed to be some sort of uniform, but he was shorter than Simon, with an unfriendly, suspicious expression in his small black eyes every time he looked at Micah.

Kee clapped his hands and pointed to the table in the middle of the room. When Micah hesitated, Simon made a threatening move toward him, and Micah decided it would be less humiliating to climb up himself. They pulled him onto his back, attaching his ankles and wrists to the now-familiar restraints, his legs apart as usual.

It was then that Micah saw the long open razor. He broke out in a cold sweat. He began to struggle, even though he knew from bitter experience that it was useless to try to break the restraints. Kee paid no attention, but began to assemble what he needed for the job at hand. When he was ready, he slapped Micah's face to get his attention, then began to spread lather on his chest. As the open blade descended, Micah froze. He did not consider himself a hairy man, but he had some hair on his chest that narrowed to a thin line, fanning out again just above the pale bush of his pubic hair. He lay motionless as the thin steel blade swept over his body, and he held his breath in terror. Kee was obviously experienced at this job, but Micah followed the flashing blade with his eyes until his face was pushed to one side and his cheek and jaw covered with lather.

As soon as this was finished, the whole table was tilted abruptly backwards, and the section between his ankles dropped away. Kee moved between his legs and grasped his balls.

"No!" cried Micah, not able to stop himself from struggling in his panic. Did they intend to make him a eunuch? "No!" he shouted again. "Oh God, please! No!" But if that was their intention there was nothing he could do. To his surprise, Simon laid a hand on his chest. It was a gesture of reassurance, and Micah looked up at the big man gratefully as Kee began to trim the hair around his cock.

When Kee was finished, Micah turned over. This time the procedure was less frightening, but Micah was relieved when it was over and he was lying under Simon's hands, having soothing oil rubbed into his raw skin. Simon was doing a quick, professional job this time, no lingering, exploring fingers, no pinches or sudden exploratory probes. Then leather bracelets were slapped on his ankles. They were wide, studded with silver, with a metal loop on one side. Although they were not heavy, the unaccustomed weight made Micah very aware of his legs when he moved.

Kee clapped his hands and pointed to the stool beside the table. Micah climbed down. He felt even more naked, now, with no body hair except an abbreviated bush of pubic fuzz surrounding his cock. He sat on the stool, feeling the rough wood against his ass, while his hands were cuffed behind him. Kee began to brush his long hair back from his face. Then he took the razor and began to scrape away at Micah's hairline. Now what, Micah wondered, feeling his forehead getting higher. Long golden locks began to fall to the floor around him. Would he soon be bald? But Kee stopped, satisfied with whatever effect he had been after, and then he began to rub something into Micah's newly exposed forehead. It was a sort of cobalt blue dye, Micah noticed, close to the color of his eyes. It came to him that these people must consider this a cosmetic thing, a sort of beauty ritual, maybe. Kee added designs using a white paste and then forced the locks around his ears into a series of glass beads, which were pulled and twisted into a painful coronet around his head.

"I must look like a nightmare," Micah thought, wincing as Kee gave a final twist to his painful coiffure and pushed him off the stool so suddenly that he staggered. He would have fallen, thrown off balance by the weight of the anklets, had not Simon caught him.

Then Simon took his place on the stool and pulled Micah down across his knees. Micah could feel the push of a plastic bulb against his anus and tried to unclench his muscles, knowing from bitter experience that Simon would only use force if he didn't comply. By now, he knew enough to hold the liquid inside, and release it when Simon tapped his buttocks. What was happening? Micah worried, as he tried to concentrate on not angering the man who was handling him so casually, easily, as if he were a child.

Simon pulled him upright and the two men inspected their handiwork, walking around him as if he were an object on display. They seemed satisfied with what they saw, but they were both very serious, with none of the almost playful cruelty Micah had become used to.

By now, dinnertime had come and gone and still Micah was no nearer to knowing what was going to happen to him. He sensed a growing tension in his two keepers that put him even more on edge. Micah's stomach gurgled loudly. Abruptly, Kee pushed him to his knees and produced the familiar hated silver bottle. There was something so demeaning about being fed that way, having to stretch out his neck and raise his face submissively toward his handler, who often held the bottle just out of reach. But Micah was starving and he opened his mouth, sucking greedily on the rubber teat. It was unusual to be fed liquids at this time of day, and the drink had a bittersweet aftertaste that was also not what he was used to. Micah was so hungry he ignored the slight unpleasantness, trying to get all the liquid as quickly as possible.

A gong sounded from somewhere deep inside the huge complex. At once Kee pulled the teat from his lips. Simon straightened up and adjusted his red tunic. He picked up a blue leather collar studded with glass beads like the ones in Micah's hair and fastened it around his prisoner's neck, then attached a light chain to the collar. Kee opened the door, said something to Simon and stood aside. Simon pulled at the chain and led Micah down the hall to a large carved wooden door he had never been through before. Simon beat a rapid tattoo on the brass panel in the middle of the door and, after a moment, it opened.

Before them three steps led down to a wall of mirrors. Micah stopped, almost falling when he caught sight of himself in the glass. Could that be him, that tanned naked barbarian with the startling blue eyes that matched the painted ribbon of blue high on his forehead? The same color was repeated in the beads that formed a headband restraining the long blond hair that fell over his shoulders. Micah's mouth fell open, but he had little time to get used to his new image before Simon pulled on his chain. A hallway stretched in two directions on either side of the mirror. Micah was led to the right. Men in brown uniforms hurried by, carrying trays full of succulent meats and gravies and platters heaped high with colorful roots and other vegetables. Micah's stomach growled again. Now he could hear noise coming from the door at the end of the hall where all the servants were coming and going. Simon led him to the door, opened it, and pulled him inside.

They were in a large courtyard, open to the skies. Automatically Micah looked up, trying to see the position of the stars, but he had no time. Simon kept pulling his chain and he was forced to look where he was going or risk the humiliation of falling. He might be a prisoner, but he was still a Nebula Warrior and he was determined to preserve as much dignity as possible.

The space was full of the sound of deep voices and laughter, the clatter of plates and cutlery, the clink of glasses. Where were the women? Micah wondered. So far, he hadn't seen any. Bright lights shone on a platform in the middle of the courtyard, and it was here that Simon led him. He clapped and pointed, indicating that Micah should mount the three steps. When Micah stood in the middle of the bright circle of light, he felt Simon slide a clip onto first one anklet, then the other, forcing him to stand with his legs far apart. Then he felt Simon withdraw behind him.

Micah squared his shoulders, feeling his muscles swell as he did so. He looked down on the dark, upturned faces and felt a sudden thrill of superiority. He remembered Royal's voice: "You cannot be humiliated unless you agree to it." He, Micah Starion, did not give them that right.

It was when he felt the first casual touch on his thigh that he realized there had been some sort of tranquilizer in the drink. Just as we do with animals led to the slaughter, he thought. A tall man wearing a white tunic reached up to finger Micah's left nipple. When it grew hard under his touch, the man gave it a savage twist and Micah jerked away, almost losing his balance.

"No," he told himself. "You must let them do what they want. You must not react. You must not give them that satisfaction."

But his body betrayed him. It was impossible to control the physical evidence of the pleasure their hard hands gave him, or stop the tears when they scratched and twisted and squeezed. They weighed his shaved balls in their calloused palms. They were fascinated with his hair and pulled at it unmercifully, twisting it in their fingers and lifting it to their lips as if to kiss it. And then Micah saw him, the man with the slate-gray eyes who had watched him earlier. He was bare-chested, and Micah found himself wondering what he looked like under the soft suede leggings that hugged his long legs so tightly. His cold stare moved over Micah's body appraisingly. Micah could almost feel it against his sweating skin. Although the man didn't touch the prisoner, his eyes seemed to cut through to what was most private and vulnerable inside Micah's soul. Sweat trickled down his smooth well-defined chest. He wanted that man. He made himself look away.

The prisoner shivered. He was glad of the numbing effects of the drug he had been given. It was getting hard to keep his concentration, but he was aware of a change in the atmosphere of the place. Many of the men were shouting as Simon read out what sounded like a list. The clamor went on for some time, then died away.

The complete silence was alarming. Micah blinked, trying to concentrate. And suddenly, he knew. He was not a prisoner! He was a slave! Micah's head jerked back as Simon pulled him down from the platform and led him to the man with slate-gray eyes. Everyone was shouting now. One word. A name?

Attlad! Attlad!

His master!

Attlad stood beside the open fire, holding a long rod. Simon pushed Micah down on his knees as Attlad raised the rod. For a moment, their eyes met.

I am a Nebula Warrior, Micah thought. It is my duty to fight the enemy. But he didn't know who the enemy was anymore. All he knew now was that he wanted Attlad, this strange, alien male, and the man wanted him. Their desire was so strong it was almost palpable, vibrating in the air between them.

Then his vision cleared.

"No!" Micah lunged forward, taking Simon by surprise and pushing him off balance. Micah kicked out fiercely but the anklets threw off his aim. He fought viciously for his pride and his freedom, tearing at arms and legs with his teeth, kicking and pushing with his powerful shoulders, but the drug slowed him down, and he was not used to fighting with his hands cuffed behind him. At last he lay on the floor, held down on his side by four of the men. Screaming his rage and terror, he watched in horror as Attlad lifted the branding iron and pressed it to his right bicep.

Pain shot to the center of his being. He smelled burning flesh. His brain felt as though it was in flames. Micah passed out.

BEWARE THE GOD WHO SMILES

LARRY TOWNSEND

Tape File No. 686: MASTEN, Gregory K. (Con't)

I was so stunned by what had happened...or what appeared to have happened, I just hung there, both hands pressed against the stones, chest raised, my cock still in Ken's ass, but growing softer by the second. It was like nothing I had ever seen, or even dreamed of. We were in a long hall, obviously below ground, with a row of stone gods along the wall in front of us, and a facing row along the opposite side. To our left, gazing down the double ranks of idols was the largest of them all, a great huge statue of Osiris, carved out of dark, green granite.

Moving as if in a dream, or a trance, I slipped free of Ken and stood up. We were both stark naked, of course, which made it seem all the more as if I must have been dreaming.

"Do you often have dreams where you are nude?"

No, not often. But I have had a couple like that, and I certainly wouldn't be running around without clothes unless it was a dream!

"Well," I said, "I don't know where we are, but at least our old friend Anubis came with us."

"It's not Anubis," said Ken flatly. "It's Seth."

I looked at him in surprise, because I couldn't imagine his knowing this, at least not knowing it and sounding so certain about it. "I don't get it," I said. "I thought..."

"They told me," he said.

"They? Who are they?"

And that's when Ken explained how it had happened to him before. He almost cried, because he said he hadn't meant to get me into it. But after a couple of days he'd convinced himself it must all have been his imagination. "We really are here, though, aren't we?" he asked.

"I guess we are," I said.

"But how...?"

I shrugged. "You got me, baby," I told him. I started off, down the row of idols, looking at each one and trying to figure out just what kind of place we were in. I thought at first it might be the basement of the museum...that we'd fallen through a trap door of some kind. But Ken assured me that wasn't it.

So, I examined each idol in turn. Next to Anubis— or Seth—was Troth, the god with the baboon head, who was supposed to be the keeper of wisdom. Next to him was Sobek, the crocodile god of water, worshipped much further north, and generally thought of as belonging to Heliopolis. Between him and Osiris was Isis...the sister-goddess of the Nile. I trotted on, further down the row, my bare feet making a whispering sound against the stones, and even this subtle noise echoed along the empty vault.

I cannot tell you how strange and helpless I felt, a single, naked mortal surrounded by the huge stone effigies of the mighty Egyptian gods. The air was dry and warm against my skin, and other than a slight mustiness there was an almost total absence of any sensory stimuli. I could see the gods, of course, but they were silent, placid in their unmoving grandeur. There was no sound whatever, and even the temperature was benign, neither warm nor cold, and the air about me was as still as the ranks of silent deities.

Near the end, the hall became so dark I could not make out the features on the farthest idols. Had I climbed up on them, and peered into their faces I might have discerned their identities. But to touch them would have required more courage than I possessed. Instead, I started back toward Ken. He stood watching me, rooted to the spot where I had left him, as if afraid we might somehow become separated if he moved.

My thought was to take one of the torches that guttered on the wall behind Osiris, and use it to light my way into the dark end of the hall. Until that moment, I had not considered the possibility of another person being anywhere near us. It was as if the stillness of the hall proclaimed its being the domain of just the gods—totally beyond the reach of mortal man. But the presence of the torches was certain evidence of some human instrumentality, and I suddenly felt the creeping fingers of fear about my heart.

I took Ken's hand when I reached him, and together we approached the great statue of Osiris. We stood gazing up at the serene features on this father of the gods, neither of us willing to commit the sacrilege of climbing over his stony facade to reach the torches that blazed to either side of his head. Unless we did climb on him, though, there was no way we were going to get to them. Even if one of us stood on the other's shoulders, we would not be able to reach. That is how huge these statues were, Dr. Lawrence. The one of Osiris must have been at least twenty-five feet tall.

We were standing there, neither of us knowing just what to suggest, when a portion of the wall in back of the god slid open, and a reddish glow of light filtered into the chamber. A tall, slender old man in the very ornate, ceremonial robes of a High Priest came toward us. He was followed by a line of eight or nine completely shaved, completely naked young men. All of them were chanting some sort of cadence, and they moved with a stiff, almost mechanical precision.

We saw them before they saw us—not that it did us any good, because there wasn't any place to run. "That Nebnofer," whispered Ken. "He's the…"

The chanting ended abruptly, as Nebnofer stared at us in disbelief. "The outer door is locked," he said.

As Ken had told me happened to him, I was able to understand the priest's words. I think he spoke a variety of the ancient dialects I had studied in school, as I seemed to recognize the accented syllables. However, my perception involved more than the words themselves. Hearing a language spoken is much different from sounding out phonetics expressed by the drawings in a row of hieroglyphics.

The High Priest continued to stare at us, while his naked followers crowded behind him, not unlike a flock of chicks huddling behind their mother for protection. Indecision was plain on the old man's features, though he seemed awed by our presence…awed, and maybe a little afraid. "How did you come here?" he asked at length.

"You know some of the lingo," whispered Ken. "See if you can make him understand we aren't spies." With this, my friend moved slightly behind me, and from the corner of my eye I saw that he was pushing back his foreskin. "This is what got me in trouble the last time," he muttered.

"We are come…from a distant land," I managed to say. "We are…" I didn't know the word for "friends," and could only think of *nefer*, which means "beautiful," though in Dr. Summerfield's interpretation it implies more of the Spanish *simpatico* than just physical attractiveness.

Whatever I actually expressed, Nebnofer responded with a slow, sage nodding of his head. "You must truly be children of the gods," he said. "Else you could never have entered the sacred chamber." I seemed almost as if the power which permitted me to understand his spoken words was allowing me to sense the very fringe of his emotional projection as well, because there was still a note of suspicion behind the graciousness of what he actually said. This should have been a warning to us, but again there was little we could have done, regardless.

I tried to think, but I'm afraid my mind was boggled by everything that had happened. I still struggled against a basic urge to disbelieve what was passing before my eyes. I wanted to say something more, yet couldn't frame any reasonable thought into the limited range of my vocabulary. As a result, we just stood staring at them, and they at us. Then one of the young men behind the High Priest stood on tip-toe and whispered something into the old man's ear. Nebnofer smiled, and gestured for us to stand aside. It was a gentle motion, and implied an element of grudging respect.

"We must complete our rite," he explained apologetically. "The acolytes must dedicate themselves to Osiris before the orb of Re returns."

Pulling Ken with me, I stepped out of their way, and the procession—less perfectly in line, now, and with the boys obviously more interested in us than they were in completing their ritual—filed past. First, they grouped themselves in front of Osiris, the High Priest in the middle, and the others ranged in a semi-circle behind him. They bowed and went through a stiffly formal obeisance... asking the greater god's permission, as best I could understand it, before proceeding down the line of stone figures.

They next stopped in front of Thoth—the god with the head of a baboon. They prayed to him, asking that he grant them the knowledge to serve. "He's the moon god," I whispered to Ken. "It must be night, and I'd guess it's a full moon."

"As long as they don't all turn into werewolves," he mumbled grimly.

I laughed, in spite of my own fears. "That's the wrong culture... wrong century," I assured him.

"Well, I'm glad you find it so educational," replied my companion. "Now that you've seen it, and now that I've proved I'm not the only freak, why don't you figure how to get us the fuck outta here?"

When they finished their little session before the moon-god, they started back, making a short prayer to Anubis—or Seth—as they passed. It was a peculiar ritual, and as I listened to them I was reminded of some church prayer, where one asks a saint to intercede with God. Only here, they were praying that Anubis grant them favor in the eyes of his master. That would be Osiris.

"They obviously don't agree with you," I said to Ken. "They're calling him Anubis."

"They should know," he replied. "Only Paneb... that's the one who chained me up last time...Paneb says it's Seth, and he seemed to think it was funny as all shit..."

"If the children of the god will honor us," said Nebnofer, pausing in front of us, "we would like to make them comfortable."

"I'm hungry," whispered Ken. "Maybe we'll get a good meal out of it."

We followed the High Priest, and the flock of young acolytes clustered behind us. I didn't have the feeling we were prisoners, though I'm sure they would have stopped us if we had tried to get away. No one spoke again until we had passed through the doorway behind the idol of Osiris. The stone slab ground shut, after amends for whatever previous...misunderstanding there may have been."

The old priest conducted us to a wide chamber off the main hall.

Two of the boys brought a wide, low table, which they placed before our couches, positioned so each of us could reach it. Then a couple of others brought ewers and goblets, offering us large servings of an amber-colored wine. Very quickly, the table was loaded with an assortment of dried figs and plums, fresh grapes and a dish of some fruit that looked like apples, but with more of an orange-yellow color. There were sesame cakes covered with thick honey syrup, several kinds of nut-meats, and a platter of tiny roasted birds.

We both drank deeply of the wine, and Ken was soon munching away on something that looked a little like popcorn. The boys kept bringing it to him in quantities, once they saw he particularly liked it. Nebnofer joined us after a few minutes, and I moved over to allow him room on my couch. He seemed to accept this as a token of divine favor, and sat down with evident pleasure. He nodded at Ken, who was still tossing down handfuls of his unknown delicacy.

"What is that?" I managed to ask.

"Oh, it is my favorite, too," said the High Priest. He reached across me and picked up several of the small, crisp puffs. He popped a couple into my mouth, then a few into his own. "Locusts," he explained. "Fried in the finest fat and shelled by maidens in the Temple of Isis."

Since I'll eat about anything, the idea of devouring French-fried grasshoppers didn't bother me; but Ken turned green. I saw him looking about in desperation for a place to spit the mouthful he'd been chewing when Nebnofer spoke.

"Swallow it, baby," I told him. "Otherwise you'll offend the gods. Besides, you've had worse!"

Nebnofer was still sitting next to me, and as we spoke I could see puzzlement wrinkle his brow. All around us, the boys were joking together, a couple of them wrestling and others feeding themselves or their companions. Three young men had slipped into the room from the farther end. They began to play a weird, tinkling melody on a collection of ancient instruments. One had a tall lute that sounded much like a Japanese koto. Another had a smaller, harp-like lyre, while the third played a hollow, reedy flute.

"I must admit...to be perfectly honest," confessed the High Pries, "I do not know if you are truly children of the gods, or whether you may be innocent travelers as you claim. I know the ways of the gods are strange, and I know you..." he inclined his head toward Ken, "...were mistreated by Paneb several days ago. He was furious because you escaped his jailers."

"Paneb is not your...your..." Again I fumbled for a word meaning "friend."

Nebnofer shook his head. "Paneb enjoys the favor of Pharaoh," he said solemnly, "but we fear..." his hand moved in an arc that encompassed the entire group, "...we suspect he may be in league with Sethos."

"I don't get it," muttered Ken.

Nebnofer looked at us curiously. Quickly, I tried to explain the situation to Ken as best I could understand it. "If I've guessed right," I told him, "and assuming this isn't just one, big nightmare...we've somehow gotten ourselves into Egypt during the Seventeenth Dynasty. That's what historians call the Time of Troubles, when the Kingdom of Memphis had fallen to Semitic invaders—Syrians and the ancestors of what probably became the Hebrew tribes. The Egyptians called these people Hyksos, or desert people. Their kinds took the title of Pharaoh and tried to extend their power through both Upper and Lower Egypt. According to history they never made it, and the rulers of Thebes finally drove them out...but not for another hundred years."

"In other words, we're in the middle of a civil war," suggested Ken.

"Something like that," I said, "except the books don't record the Hyksos getting this far south. If we're in the area that later became Abu Simbel, then we're between the first and second cataract, near the city of Sebua..."

"Sebua?" said Nebnofer. "Yes, Pharaoh is in Sebua."

"See?" I said. "It's beginning to make some sense."

"But what about the gods and this Sethos character?"

"My guess is, both sides have spies," I said, "and this Sethos must be the opposition's James Bond. Whatever he's trying to pull off, it involves that grinning idol—Seth or Anubis, whichever it turns out to be."

"And these Hyksos, they worshipped Sethos?" asked Ken.

"Well, not Sethos," I laughed. "Sethos seems to be the chief spy...magician as they call him. Seth is the god, and this man would be his 'servant.'"

"And Paneb?"

I shrugged.

"I cannot understand your speech," said Nebnofer softly, "but I hear you mention the names of the gods. May I ask...whom you serve, and what you do here?"

I looked at him helplessly, spreading my hands in the universal gesture of indecision. Even if I could have spoken his language, how do you explain to a bronze-age priest that you've somehow traveled three millennia and half-way around a world he doesn't even know exists beyond his horizons? Christ, I can't even explain it to you, doctor! Neither of us said any more until Ken broke the silent impasse.

He was beginning to feel his wine, I guess, because he started to laugh, giggle really. "Ask him to take you to his leader," he suggested.

"Unfortunately," I replied, "He is the leader, or damned near it."

Now, Dr. Lawrence, I know I'm admitting I took this seriously, and I know I'm making myself sound more deluded and crazy by telling you about it. But to me...at the time...it was all very real. I decided Nebnofer must have been a priest of Osiris. This meant he worshipped the entire hierarchy of Theben gods, including Re, who had apparently not become as powerful as he would later on. I also remembered all the movies and stories about appeasing the witch-doctor, and saving your ass by not threatening him. So, in my broken Egyptian, I told him we were servants of Anubis. This made us followers of a lesser god, you see, and claiming this we made no pretense to a power greater than his.

It seemed to work, because Nebnofer patted my knee and personally refilled my goblet. He sat drinking with me for a long time, while the shaved, naked boys cavorted about us and the musicians played their clinking, increasingly lively tunes in the background. For the moment, at least, we were safe from Paneb, who did seem to be the villain of the whole piece.

I guess the boys had been holding back a little up to now, because when I finished speaking with the High Priest, he said something to them about our being "truly honored guest." Almost immediately after that, we had them swarming all over us. Several of the lamps had burned down, and no one bothered to refill them. The room was darker than it had been before, but it was comfortably warm and there was an odor of incense in the air. Except for Nebnofer and the three musicians, everyone was as naked as before...Ken and myself, as well as the troop of boys. The wine was deceptively mellow, and before I realized it I was more than a little drunk.

Both Ken and I had been eating the various foods, some of which were sticky—mostly with natural honey and the syrup that forms on dried fruits. The boys brought bowls of scented water and bathed our hands and faces, then continued to give us a more thorough going-over. Ken was especially intriguing to them, because of that damned foreskin. Circumcision was performed on all males at birth, I guess, both in Egypt and in the lands of the Hyksos. Even today, both Arabs and Jews do it, as you know, the custom stems from long before. The only people of that period who didn't do it were the Hittites—Egypt's arch enemies from what is now Turkey—and I think the Babylonians. During this particular period there must not have been much trade with an outside area, so I guess none of the boys had ever seen a natural cock before.

But Ken wasn't getting all the attention by any means. As I lay back, sipping the sweet, amber wine, I felt what seemed like dozens of hands laving my body with warm, moist towels. Through half-closed eyes I could see the boys working on Ken, who responded almost immediately—and obviously—to their treatment. Of course, I could feel my own energies rebuilding, and I wasn't very far behind him. Because we'd been...transported at the height of our sex, I'm sure Ken hadn't come. So if there was a whore in the crowd it was me! In just a few minutes I had a raging hard-on, and this attracted some very decided interest from the youngsters. I was also a curiosity to them, you see, because I'm blond and fair-skinned, much lighter than any Egyptian. I'm also a little over six feet, which made me a giant by their standards, and my cock... well, my cock is proportionate to the rest of me.

At some point, Nebnofer withdrew. I had my eyes closed, just enjoying what was happening to me, so I didn't see him leave. I just know he was beside me one minute, and when I looked again he was gone. It didn't seem to make any difference; by then the boys were keeping me more than entertained. This was their equivalent of a graduation party, I supposed, with Ken and myself forming their special, unexpected treat.

Our couches were covered with a soft, smooth leather that felt almost like human skin. It must have been impervious to most fluids...either that or the boys were unconcerned about damaging them, because after bathing us they began oiling our bodies. What they used was a viscous substance, like olive oil, heavily perfumed with a spicy, bitter-sweet fragrance. Warm, gentle hands began rubbing this into my skin, layer after layer, covering every inch of my body as they eased me from back to belly, and over again. I could see that the youngsters were taking turns, working in shifts, some on me and others on Ken...then changing off. At all times, though, I was surrounded by gleaming, slender bodies, dark skins reflecting the ruddy glow of guttering lamps. One of the boys was kneeling beside me on the couch, his hands stroking my upper chest and shoulders, his tight little belly arched across me and his well-formed cock dangling a tantalizing few inches above my hand.

Moving slowly, because in truth I was so intoxicated the whole scene was more like a dream than anything else, I slipped one arm around the kid's waist and grasped the nape of his neck with the other. I drew him down against me, until his slick, oil-coated chest slid on mine. I kissed him, gently at first, and then with greater force, driving his lips apart with my tongue and probing deep into the sweetness of his mouth. This surprised him, I think, as such total exchange may not have been common among them. He responded almost immediately, however, sliding his arms about me, while his friends chattered in gleeful pleasure behind him.

But the arts of physical love were not totally lacking among them, and while they may not have known to kiss as we do, they certainly were expert in other modes of expression. The boy I held against me was curled across my chest, so his loins were pressed to my hips, leaving my midsection and groin exposed. In moments, I felt cloying fingers lift my cock and balls, stroking softly along the risen shaft and hefting the balls, as if to test their weight. Then the moist warmth of lips encircled the crown, while at the same instant another mouth absorbed my nuts, drawing them in with an easy, sucking motion while the first descended along the shaft of my penis.

I could not see them, but the two who possessed me were curled against my legs and groin, while the boy whose lips joined with mine began a slow, sliding rhythm against my side. I could feel his hard little cock traveling across my skin and I tightened my grip about his body. Other hands were stroking me, and it seemed I was touched by a multitude of seeking fingers and caressing palms. I now encircled two young bodies in my arms, while the two who worked upon my cock and balls continued as they had before. Yet another was easing my thighs apart, stroking the inner curves of my ass.

Where I was and how I got there no longer mattered to me. I was blanketed in warm, living flesh...youth-hard bodies and willing, eager beauty. The coating of oil made the sensuous contacts extremely arousing, yet somehow more subtle and...I guess I'd call it "unified." When I closed my eyes it was as if a single entity enclosed me; the pressure against my torso, lips, midsection—all were like one. The dimly lighted chamber spun like a slowly accelerating merry-go-round, and the loving, tender movements drove me into such a state of euphoric arousal I was...I felt like I had once when some friends talked me into trying grass. Actually, I think there may have been something in the wine, because I felt a tingle—a tickle almost— pumping through my balls and all along the urethra.

I was getting dangerously close, so I wriggled free of the kid who was working on my cock. The other, the one who'd been sucking my nuts, had left off by then, and was tonguing the insides of my thighs. When I moved, my new position allowed me to catch another glimpse of Ken. I have to admit that for a minute I wasn't completely happy about it. I guess it was the realization I'd really fallen for the guy, because seeing him belly-down on top of a tall, slender boy, fucking the kid like there was no tomorrow, I felt a twinge of jealousy! Buried as I was in my own pile of sucking, loving boys...but love isn't supposed to be logical, especially when you've had more than you should to drink.

The irrational moment passed, and I was again involved with my personal vagaries. While Ken's behavior was not forgotten, the sensuous rise and fall of his ass, the flexing sinews beneath oiled and gleaming skin became a source of arousal rather than displeasure. His example was a good one, I decided, and I began taking stock of those who lay with me, wondering which boy would make the best object for a similar impalement.

I chose a delicate, slender lad, whose shaven head would barely have grazed my throat had we stood facing one another. His arms and chest were sleek and smooth, with an attractive, symmetrical outline of muscular development. While his shoulders were fairly broad for his height, his tiny waist could almost be spanned by the combined width of my hands. His little ass was round...perfect! It reflected a ruddy glow in the feeble light, and I thought of the poem where they called it a "rosy-cheeked beacon."

Amidst expressions of amusement from his companions, I made it clear I wanted him to lie beside me, and after this the other boys moved away. A couple of them seemed disappointed, which was flattering, I guess...but I soon forgot about them. I pulled the beautiful, unresisting kid against me, then slid myself on top of him. I felt his cock snap across mine as I aligned our bodies and shoved my mouth hard against his. Sensuously, his flesh moved in reciprocation to my mounting demands, until I maneuvered my iron between his thighs. He clamped against it, which created a firm, kind of possessing channel.

As a partner, he was outta sight! He seemed to merge with me, and his body fitted so comfortably with mine it almost seemed as if he conformed to my specific requirements...like we were supposed to meet and join, despite the miles and the centuries that had separated us. His mouth was sweet and warm and it didn't take him any time to acquire the art of kissing like a Westerner.

I still felt an occasional hand or sometimes an entire body brush across the oil-slick surface of my back. But these grew less as my concentration focused on the boy I'd selected. I held him prostrate, crushed between me and the leather-covered couch. I paid little attention to anyone else, now, though I was vaguely aware that several of our companions had paired off and were emulating us on the floor or the nearby benches.

By the time I finally raised myself and turned my young man onto his belly, only a couple of lamps were still burning. The dry, warm air had taken on a subtle fragrance and a cloying moisture from the bodies that twisted and acted out their rites of love around us. Both my companion and myself were sweating, our bodies seeming to melt into one another while a furnace heat surrounded us. My hardened cock had once again slipped between his thighs; only this time its gentle, plunging motion carried it near and past the desired opening. Finally, on one particularly high-risen, upward stroke. I felt my cockhead slip higher between his cheeks. Its tip brushed across the hidden recess, hanging there a moment until I pressed down, driving it toward the proper point. Volitionally unguided by his hand or mine, it penetrated the channel as I resettled my loins against the rounded curves of his ass.

Beneath me, my lithe, responding partner groaned deeply, acknowledging the demand of rigid flesh. For only a moment the muscular ring resisted me. Then, as if in answer to some deep, unspoken invitation, my cock sunk into the tight-stretched flesh. The waves of sensation rose like wisps of steamy bliss. It surrounded me and drove me into an oblivion.... [Long pause, followed by the patient's laughter.] I guess I got a little carried away, Dr. Lawrence. But he was a beautiful kid, even with every hair shaved off his body. He was delicate, but masculine—in that stage between being a boy and a man. Fucking him, with our bodies all slippery with oil...I've never felt anything like it!

Looking across, I could see Ken getting close to the end. His ass would draw tight, raise a bit, and slam down hard against the kid. The boy's legs were spread so wide apart, he'd actually hooked his knees around the edges of the couch. And Ken was giving it to him without any pause or holding back! Watching made me all the hotter, if that was possible. I started shoving my cock in and out, faster and harder, until I forced a rattling groan from the boy every time I connected with him. The way the cheeks of his ass fit up against me excited a feeling almost as intense as from the pressure of his muscle-ring about my dick.

I saw Ken slam one home, then arch his body, straining so he was all hard muscle and tight-stretched skin. I knew he was shooting his load, and though I hadn't been quite ready myself, that was all she wrote! Seeing him sent me spinning into that blind moment when you don't see or hear or know anything except the roar of your own blood in your ears and the fantastic surge of boiling jit— shooting up from between your legs, making your balls pull tight, and then the blast of sensation down your cock! I shoved myself all the way into the nameless kid beneath me, and felt him rear up against my loins while I hung on his back and gave him everything I had! And by then it was quite a bit.

After a long time, my body settled back to normal and I began to notice other items and people around me. We were down to one oil lamp; and that wasn't very bright. My boy had gotten up and was hunting for a towel to sponge me off. Ken was sitting on the edge of his couch.

"Man, what I wouldn't give for a cigarette, right now," he laughed. "Don't suppose you got one hidden...someplace, have you?"

"Just a big, limp cigar," I told him.

He came over and sat beside me while one of the boys brought us more wine. Because sex had made us thirsty, we both drank more than we should of it. Ken laid down beside me, and I closed my eyes. I don't know where the boys had gone...the boys we'd been with, I mean. There were several stretched out on the grass mats a few feet away from us, but I think my kid had gone over to the couch where Ken had been. Those last swigs of wine just about did me in. The room was spinning again, and it occurred to me that Nebnofer might have slipped us something. Probably not...probably just that we'd drunk too much.

Anyway, Ken was asleep, curled against me. My arm was around him, his head resting against my shoulder when I dozed off. The last I recall was the final lamp starting to sputter and go out, but I was gone before the room became completely dark. I remember a lyre playing in the background, but the other musicians had given up...joining the temple boys, I think, but even that I wasn't sure about...

The next I knew I was blinking against strong sunlight. Ken was still in my arms, but we were lying on the Persian rug in front of the idol…and it was morning. When I tried to sit up I awakened Ken. He stared blindly for a couple of seconds, then jumped to his feet and started hunting for his watch. "Seven-thirty," he said. "We've got about half an hour."

THE SLAVE PRINCE
Vince Gilman

"I want some of that slaveboy," said the first robber.

"Not till we have this fire lit," cautioned the second. "We'll all have plenty of time to use him."

"That faggot must think he's struck it rich," said the third. "He's sitting over there right now, dreaming about our cocks. I bet he never had three at once before."

A short distance away, Pasha sat propped up against a tree. The three robbers were setting up camp and had left him alone for a while. It mattered little; he was going nowhere. Pasha was still costumed in Dorabus's ingenious leather devices, his legs still spread uncomfortably by a wooden stick, chastity belt still secured, gigantic phallus still impaling his butt. He still wore his hood and remained blindfolded and gagged. His wrists were tied and secured over his head to a low branch of the tree.

They had been riding for hours, and Pasha was hungry. But he doubted that the robbers would be sharing any of their food with him, if they even had any.

Soon Pasha could hear the campfire popping and crackling as the robbers threw on more logs. He could feel the heat from where he sat, warming up his mostly naked flesh.

"Now, let's see what we have here," said the first robber.

"Hey, I have an idea," said the second. "Unfasten that wrist thong and grab his feet."

Pasha's wrists fell in front of him, still bound together but freed from the tree. Then the robbers picked him up by the wooden stick that spread his ankles, so that his legs were off the ground and he was merely resting on his buttocks.

They held him like that for a while, and Pasha could hear one of them messing with a rope—tying it around the wooden bar and securing it with several knots. The rope made a *whiff* sound whenever it was pulled taut.

"All right," said the third robber. "Let me do that."

Pasha heard the rope go high into the branches of the tree, then felt the end of the rope swing down and brush his thighs. One of the robbers fumbled for the rope and grabbed it. Then, the three robbers together let go of Pasha's ankles and started to pull on the rope.

Pasha's ass was lifted off the mossy earth. With another yank, he had risen another foot, and now all his weight rested on his shoulders. In the next moment, Pasha was pulled completely off the ground, hanging upside down from the bar, his legs spread wide. The robbers continued pulling on the rope until Pasha was several feet off the ground, slowly circling round and round. They grabbed the leather strap binding his wrists and tied it to something on the ground—a root, maybe, or a wooden stake—so that Pasha's body was pulled taut and he could hardly move.

"Mmmph!" Pasha said, struggling a little. He was suddenly worried that they might simply leave him there. The blood rushed to his head. Sweat dripped down his torso. A cool breeze brushed against his exposed armpits.

"Think that it's about the right height?" asked the second robber.

"Let's find out," said the first.

Pasha heard one of the men approach him. He smelled a cock somewhere very close to his nose. The man struggled with one of the buckles at the back of the hood. Neither the blindfold nor the gag were padlocked, so they could be removed with relative ease. The man unbuckled what turned out to be the gag, and pulled the leather plug from Pasha's mouth. Saliva drooled over Pasha's lips, trickling down onto his forehead.

"Open up, slave," said the first robber, prying Pasha's mouth open with his grimy fingers. Pasha licked the dirt off the digits. "Yeah, I would say that's about right."

With that, the first robber shoved his cock into Pasha's mouth. The head was huge. Pasha's tongue immediately went to work, laving it in circles and then working down the rest of the shaft as the cock made its way in deeper. It fairly filled Pasha's mouth; it was hard to tell exactly how big it was, but it was certainly almost as big as Korat's. Pasha loved the taste of it, and the pungent odor of the man's sweaty pubic hair.

"Yeah, fuck his face!" said the third robber.

"How much you think we'll get for him?" asked the second.

"I don't know," said the first. "He's an awfully well-trained cocksucker. A very accommodating mouth. Somebody must really prize this slave."

"He does have fine skin," said the second.

"Yes," agreed the third, "he is very well kept, for a stinking cockslave."

The first robber grabbed Pasha's head in both hands and rammed his cock in deeper and deeper. It was going straight up into Pasha's wide-open gullet. Pasha was just barely able to breathe between thrusts. His mouth was flooding with saliva, but he loved every minute of it. This was one of the tastiest cocks he had ever had the pleasure to suck. He only wished he could see it.

The robbers were right. Pasha was nothing more than a cocksucker, a slave destined only for others' pleasure. This was his true calling—not as a prince raised to rule over the Four Lands. His role was to be used by whomever had possession of him. He would rather that person were Korat, but if he never saw Korat again, he would have to make the best of it. He could ill afford to disappoint his new masters. He had to keep in mind that serving them well was all that mattered.

"There," said the first robber. "I've got him all slicked up for you guys."

He pulled out his cock, leaving Pasha hanging there with an empty, dripping mouth and a throat that needed filling. But that was soon remedied as another cock plunged in. This one wasted no time going the full length, so that Pasha's nose was pressed up against the robber's big hairy balls. This cock seemed slightly shorter than the first but was much thicker around the base. Pasha's lips had to stretch to get around it.

"Mmm, you lucky slave," said the third robber. "You love my cock, don't you?"

The third robber fucked him much more roughly than the first. He jammed the cock in and plugged Pasha's throat, holding it there until Pasha was gasping for air. Then he fucked Pasha rapidly, bucking his hips so that he was pounding against Pasha's face and driving his cock in deep.

"My turn," said the second robber. Pasha could recognize his voice the most easily, because it was deep and authoritative. The way the cock snapped out of Pasha's mouth, he would hardly be surprised if the second robber had merely pushed the third one out of the way.

The second robber's dick came in slowly, allowing Pasha's tongue to lick the head delicately. Pasha tasted a drop of pre-come at the tip, and did his best to give the cock a superb tongue bath. But the mushroomlike head was truly huge, and Pasha became uneasy as it slowly came in deeper, inch by inch filling his mouth. This one was at least as big as Korat's, if not bigger. The second robber was doing this deliberately, going slow so that Pasha would think he was never going to reach the base. Then the cock withdrew completely. Pasha's tongue reached out into the air, searching for it.

"Oh, look at him," said the second robber. "Where is that cock, boy? Where is that big ol' cock, you fucking slave? Where is that thing that belongs down your throat?"

Pasha began to moan loudly, then realized his mouth was no longer plugged by either gag or cock, so he said, "Please, sir! Please, my new master! Please give me your cock."

"Listen to him beg," said the second robber. He slapped his cock against Pasha's cheek. Pasha turned his head to try to catch it. The second robber then slapped his cock against the other cheek, causing Pasha's head to turn again.

"Uhnn!" Pasha cried. "Please, please, please!"

The second robber rammed it in deep. It was definitely the longest of all—perhaps as big as Korat's. Pasha realized he was comparing each cock by his new standard—that of the barbarian who had first claimed him. Korat had been his first master, and somewhere deep inside, Pasha knew Korat was also the best.

While the second robber fucked his throat furiously, the other two robbers rubbed their hands all over Pasha's body. One of them grabbed both of Pasha's nipples and pinched them harshly. The other was standing behind him, slapping Pasha's buttocks with a firm, unmerciful hand.

Within the chastity belt, Pasha's cock was growing. But it had met the restrictive cage of chain mail that was wrapped completely around his cock and balls. The more his cock tried to expand, the more painful it became. His ass muscles were squeezing the leather phallus rhythmically, tensing up each time he was slapped on the ass. He could feel his buns turning bright red; each slap stung more fiercely than the last.

The robber at Pasha's nipples was equally devious. His grip was strong, like a vise, and he would grab them and stretch them out, twist them around as far as he could, and flick his fingernails against them. Now he was bending over and biting them.

Pasha's cock was in great discomfort, straining against the ingenious cock cage that would not let him achieve his full length.

Finally, the second robber grabbed Pasha's head and held it there while he emptied his come into Pasha's gullet. Pasha could not breathe. The flood of warm juice spurted for what seemed forever before the cock finally pulled out. Pasha closed his lips around it so that he could get every drop of come, so that the robber's cock would emerge totally clean.

Now Pasha realized he was getting quite light-headed from hanging upside down so long.

As if reading his mind, the second robber said, "All right, let's take him down. He's had enough of this."

Slowly, they lowered the rope and allowed Pasha to fall gently onto the mossy earth. His legs had fallen asleep and now tingled as the blood came back in. His arms and back were so sore, he could hardly move. He simply lay there, swallowing the last drops of come that he could find still lingering in his mouth.

"Bezhdu," said the second robber, "where are those keys?"

"I gave them to Evgen," said Bezhdu, whose voice belonged to the first robber.

"Here, Horsk," said the third. Pasha heard the jangle of a large ring of keys.

"Thanks, Evgen," said Horsk, the second robber.

They untied the wooden stick separating Pasha's legs, then unbuckled the blindfold and allowed Pasha to see them. It was dark, but the fire gave off a great orange light, which flattered the terrific physiques of the three robbers with the light and shadows playing off their muscles. Pasha sat up.

"I am Horsk," said the tallest, who had a long mane of brown hair falling past his shoulders onto his pectoral muscles.

"This is Bezhdu," he said, pointing with his thumb at the short one next to him. Bezhdu was bald, with a stocky frame covered in black hair.

"And this is Evgen," said Horsk. Evgen was nearly as tall as Horsk, but leaner of build, with blond hair that was shaved off on the sides but sticking out two inches tall in a narrow strip down the middle of his scalp. Evgen's pale body was covered in nautical tattoos: mermaids, a ship's anchor, and on his left breast, the white-bearded god of the sea. Each of their cocks was still hard, jutting straight out from their bodies.

"I am going to take that belt off him," said Horsk, who was clearly the leader of the group. He tossed his hair back onto his shoulders and crouched down over Pasha with the key ring. He tried several skeleton keys in the lock of the chastity belt before he found the one that made it spring open. He unfastened all the various straps and unlaced the hard leather pouch, exposing Pasha's cock still in its chain mail cage.

"Will you look at that!" said Horsk, grabbing the steel-enmeshed cock in his fist and squeezing it roughly. "Your master didn't want not to take any chances, did he?"

The other two laughed, coming over to look at it.

"No, sir," Pasha croaked.

Horsk turned Pasha over and unfastened the leather strap that ran up his buttcrack.

"Hmm," said Horsk. "What have we here?" His finger looped itself into the ring of the phallus and gave it a small tug. Pasha's ass held it in firmly.

"Please," begged Pasha, "take it out, sir!"

Horsk laughed. "Evgen," he said, "Bezhdu."

But Pasha could not see what it was Horsk wanted of them. Evgen came around in front and grabbed Pasha's bound wrists, while Bezhdu pulled Pasha's ass up in the air, positioning Pasha's legs so that he was curled up resting on his knees, but with his knees spread apart. Pasha's cock in its heavy chain mail hung free in the air, while his ass was stuck up in Horsk's face.

"Do it, Horsk," said Evgen, pulling tightly on Pasha's wrists.

"Yeah, Horsk," said Bezhdu. "Pull it out."

Slowly, Horsk pulled on the phallus, and slowly, Pasha's ass muscles spread wider and wider, letting out the fat, blunt end of the thing.

"Oh, Gods!" cried Pasha. The phallus had been in so long, his ass had trouble letting it go. He tried pushing it out, as if he were taking a big crap.

"Come on, boy, push it out," said Horsk.

At last, the thick, bulbous end was free. Pasha was breathing heavily. The thing was stretching him wide open. The ring of his sphincter was crying out to him that this was as wide as it could ever get. Then, cruelly, Horsk thrust the phallus all the way back in.

"No, please!" cried Pasha, his eyes tearing.

Horsk slapped Pasha's butt hard, first one cheek, then the other.

"No one says 'no' to Horsk," he said. Then he yanked the entire base of the leather shaft out in one fell swoop—and again plunged it back in. "Hold him there," he directed his crew.

Evgen stared down at Pasha, grinning and laughing. Bezhdu remained crouched over Pasha's back, holding Pasha's knees underneath him so that he could not kick out his legs.

Pasha heard the thwack of leather as Horsk slapped something against his own palm. Then Pasha felt the sharp sting of a leather belt across his buttocks.

"I am going to tan your ass," said Horsk, "until you can spit that phallus out on your own."

"No!" cried Pasha. "Please!"

It was impossible; the thing was simply too big for Pasha to push out himself. He needed someone else to yank it out for him.

Pasha felt another lick of the belt across his ass. He could imagine how it looked, with two bright red marks already striping his pale butt. Horsk gave him another taste, striking a spot that had not been hit before. By the time he was finished, he was going to have the whole ass red as a radish.

"Ow!" Pasha cried. Tears streamed down his cheeks; the salty moisture combined with the leather smell of the hood, sending a heady odor up Pasha's nose. "Ouch! Please, sir!"

"Spit it out!" Horsk commanded, thrashing Pasha's ass mercilessly. He went from one side to the other, back and forth, hitting every spot he had not hit before, then going over the same red territory yet again.

Pasha tried to squeeze the thing out, but it was just too big. And the more he was whipped, the tighter his ass muscles grew. They did not want to let go of the phallus.

"I want to see that thing come flying out of your hole, you filthy fuckslave," said Horsk.

But the stronger the thrashing became, the larger Pasha's dick grew, until it was straining once more against the cock cage.

Relax, he told his butt. *Relax, you stupid ass. Go on, let it out!*

"If you do not do it soon, your ass is going to be one big mass of raw flesh," said Horsk, his belt strokes growing in strength.

Pasha was squirming now under the lashing, but he could not get away from Evgen who was holding his hands or from Bezhdu who was sitting on top of him. He pushed as hard as he could with his ass and finally felt it give a little.

"Come on, boy, you can do it."

"Yeah, slaveboy, push it out!"

"Give it up. Shoot it out your hole!"

Pasha moaned, gritting his teeth. It felt like it was beginning to come out, but he could not get past the wide part.

"It is coming, boy," said Horsk. "I will give you a little help."

Pasha thought Horsk was going to grab onto the ring and give it a tug, but instead, the tall, husky robber worked up an especially strong blow of his belt, which, instead of striking one of Pasha's asscheeks, was a bull's-eye direct hit of Pasha's straining butthole.

"Yeeow!" Pasha screamed, and in the same instant, his ass had a small convulsion, surrendering to his efforts and thrusting the giant phallus completely from his hole.

"All right!" shouted Evgen.

"Good job," said Bezhdu.

"By the Gods, will you look at the size of that thing?" said Horsk.

He brought it around and held it in front of Pasha's face. Pasha could not believe how big it was—truly monstrous, it looked even longer and fatter than a horse cock.

"You have been keeping this giant phallus inside you all this time?"

Pasha nodded his head. He was too spent to say a word.

"You must be your master's favorite," said Horsk, regarding the huge phallus, which was dripping with Pasha's warm ass juice.

"You might say that," said Pasha.

"Bezhdu," said Horsk. "Get underneath him. Let's show him something better than a fucking stuffed piece of cowhide."

"All right, boss," said Bezhdu, pumping up his cock with his fist. He squirmed underneath Pasha so that he was looking up into Pasha's eyes. With his blond strip of spiky hair and wide, hungry grin, Bezhdu was very charming for a bandit. He held Pasha up by his shoulders and set him down on his dick.

After the leather phallus, Bezhdu's fat dick entered with ease. Still, Pasha could feel it squirming its way deep inside him.

"See how you like this, fuckboy," said Horsk, crouching down behind Pasha. Then he stuck in his own dick, so that both Bezhdu's and his were fucking Pasha's ass. Combined, the two cocks easily equaled the thickness of the phallus, but they were warm, fleshy, living dicks.

Pasha loved the feeling. Even with all the slaveboys he had slept with at the Summer Palace, he had never thought of asking two of them to fuck him at the same time.

Bezhdu and Horsk worked up into a rhythm that felt good, one going in while the other came out, so that Pasha's hole was never empty. Then Evgen sat down in front and stuffed his own cock up Pasha's mouth. Now every one of his holes was filled. Evgen's cock was the fattest, stretching Pasha's lips to bursting. And together, Horsk's and Bezhdu's dicks were like having an arm up there.

Pasha had ceased to be a person with his own free will. He had become a toy for the use of these three robbers alone. His throat was filled, his ass was filled, and the cage around his cock kept him from getting fully hard, though his cock was straining against it with all its might.

"Fuck that slave's mouth," said Bezhdu, looking up at Evgen's cock from below. Saliva from Pasha's mouth was dripping onto Bezhdu's face, and he was licking it off ecstatically. "Ram it down his throat!"

"You like those dicks up your butt, don't you, slave?" said Evgen. "You like Horsk's rod reaming you out, and Bezhdu's stretching you wide open. You just wish you could come!"

Pasha did. He wished he could touch his dick. He wished he could jack himself off right now.

"That hole is so tight!" said Horsk. "Your ass is still red from my belt. It looks so hot. You are just a piece of meat for us to use, slave. Just a fucking hot piece of manmeat."

Suddenly, Evgen began shooting down Pasha's throat. Some of his come dribbled out of Pasha's lips and onto Bezhdu's face. Bezhdu's tongue came out to lick his buddy's come from around his lips, and just then Bezhdu and Horsk came together, both shooting off their warm loads into Pasha's battered butthole.

All three of them pulled out, leaving Pasha empty. He swallowed all he could of Evgen's come, but he could feel Horsk's and Bezhdu's come dribbling out of his loosened asshole. Horsk came over and picked up the phallus again.

"No," said Pasha. "Please, sir!"

"Did you hear something?" Horsk asked his comrades.

"Not me," said Evgen.

"I think it was an owl," said Bezhdu.

Horsk rammed the phallus back inside Pasha's butt. Then he fixed the chastity belt back around him, pulling the strap up his ass, stitching the leather pouch around the cock cage, buckling the whole thing up and fixing it with the padlock.

Pasha found the gag going back into his mouth and then the blindfold going back over his eyes. Both were buckled firmly in back. The hood remained padlocked around his neck. They had never even bothered to see what he looked like, which was good for Pasha, just in case the robbers happened to know what the runaway prince looked like.

The robbers fixed four stakes in the ground near the camp fire and tied Pasha spread-eagled to it. Each of his limbs was stretched as far as possible by ropes that pulled on his wrists and ankles.

"Good night, fuckslave," said Horsk, as the three robbers curled up in their separate blankets and fell asleep.

Pasha lay there in the darkness by the warmth of the fire and dreamed of Korat—his one and true master. His cock grew again within its cage, pressing against the hard leather pouch of the chastity belt. Pasha squeezed his ass muscles rhythmically around the phallus and dreamed that it was Korat's huge cock fucking him.

RITUALS
Kyle Stone

I took a cab to the park and arrived just as the chimes from the clock tower on Harding Avenue rang six. I handed the cabby my last ten-dollar bill, told him to keep the change, and walked into the park.

The winding paths were crowded at this hour, people taking a shortcut through the park on their way home from work; children rushing to the playground, eager to climb the amazing dinosaurlike jungle gyms; old men feeding pigeons or talking with their friends as they watched the world go by. And of course the joggers and people walking their dogs. It seemed a strange place for a slave to meet his master, but I was sure Tyler must have his reasons.

I wasn't very familiar with the place, but at last I found the pond. There was an outdoor restaurant there and it was crowded. Then I saw Tyler sitting at a table near the pond. At once I made my way to him and started to sit down in the one vacant chair.

"Don't sit down," he said. "Squat. Here, with your back against the fence."

I obeyed and at once he reached out to pull up my shirt with one hand. With the other, he took a pair of clips from his pocket and attached first one, then the other to my nipples. I gritted my teeth, afraid of drawing attention to what was going on if I protested. They were padded, but nevertheless, tiny sparks of pain radiated from my tits, jerking along the nerves of my body, connecting to my cock. There was a fine silver chain between the clamps. Tyler gave a tug, then pulled down my shirt again. I swallowed.

"Take off your shoes," Tyler said.

I obeyed at once, my breath harsh and short in my effort at control. My movements were awkward and without grace, squatting down, trying to keep my balance while pulling off the shoes. When I was finished, Tyler took my shoes from me and dropped them under the table. I had the feeling I wouldn't see them again.

"Now, go over there and stand under that tree until I want you. Put your hands behind your back, feet apart, and wait. Don't move until further orders."

"Yes, sir." As I stood up, the clamps on my tits moved too, the cotton of the tight shirt rubbing against them. Had he known I couldn't resist wearing a tight top that would show off my chest? Awkwardly, I moved back through the tables, my teeth gritted against the little shocks of pain that kept playing through me. My cock was already half-hard, emphasized by the small tight shorts.

The tree was back a ways from the path, directly opposite from where Tyler sat at the white table under the colorful red and white striped umbrella. I took up my position, legs apart, hands locked behind my back and waited.

It wasn't easy. I was painfully aware that everyone could see the tit clamps, plainly outlined against the white cotton. My state of arousal was also pretty obvious, and my face flamed crimson as I stood there, enduring the stares and snickers of the guys who noticed, and the teenaged girls who laughed and tittered behind their hands. My face streamed with sweat, which I was afraid to acknowledge, even though it stung my eyes.

Tyler was apparently not aware of my existence, but I knew he was watching every muscle spasm and twitch of pain I tried to suppress. Over the course of what seemed like several hours to me, he was joined in a drink by a series of men in expensive jogging suits or designer jeans, some carrying briefcases, one with a chauffeur in attendance. The chauffeur caught my eye and winked. His look said that he knew all too well exactly what I was going through.

As I stood there under the tree, tense with pain and awkward with anxiety, I had plenty of time to observe the man I was willing to trust with my life. The torment in my nipples acted like a direct link to him, and when he waved to an acquaintance or gestured as he talked, it was almost as if he tugged at the invisible chain attached to my tits and I winced. He was dressed all in black, the sleeves of his shirt rolled back to show his strong tanned forearms, and open at the neck, revealing the glint of chest hair. When our eyes met across the distance, I felt the shock all through me.

Finally Mason arrived and at last Tyler got up and left the restaurant. But if I thought my ordeal was over, I was dead wrong. Tyler came up to me and reached under the shirt to pull on the chain between my tits. I almost yelled in agony.

"Keep your hands behind your back and follow us," Tyler said, releasing me.

I felt tears in my eyes and prayed they wouldn't spill over, but as I followed the two men, the telltale moisture ran down my cheek. I looked straight ahead, making no move to brush the tears away.

Tyler and Mason turned off the more crowded walkways and went down a hill to a secluded area of bushes and trees and a tangle of footpaths. Occasionally, joggers passed at a steady pace, their breathing loud in the quiet warmth.

"Take off your shirt," Tyler said.

At once I obeyed, the stretching of my arms and the pulling of the shirt against my chest combining to make me groan in spite of myself.

Then Tyler produced the black leather collar and fastened it around my neck. "You have made the decision. You will wear this from now on. Always."

"Yes, sir."

"Why are you crying?" He sounded annoyed and I stiffened, afraid of his anger, but mostly because I longed to please him and was obviously far from doing so.

"I'm sorry, sir. I didn't mean—"

"Shut up." He started down one of the more private paths and I followed, feeling the air against my naked tortured nipples in an exquisite new way. It was as if the small area of the hard reddened tit had expanded, or had become capable of three times the feeling it had before.

Tyler pushed back some branches and pointed down the wooded hill for me to precede him. As I did, I saw the ivy-covered remains of an old gray stone building, one of the public washrooms that used to be in use around the park, apparently, before they had all been shut down.

"Lean against the wall with your hands above your head," Tyler said, pointing to the building.

I obeyed, taking deep breaths to steady the pounding of my heart.

"Cuff him, Mason."

Mason reached up and snapped black molded plastic handcuffs around each wrist. The chain between the two was hung over an iron hook high on the wall.

Suddenly strong hands grasped the latex material of my briefs and pulled them down in one motion, leaving me naked. I clamped my mouth shut to stifle the protest that rose in my throat.

"I want to see my mark on you," Tyler went on, his voice just the way it always was, casual and calm as if this were a perfectly normal thing to demand in a public park. I reminded myself that we were off the beaten track, but even so, we weren't that far from possible discovery. If I turned my head to the right, I could see the joggers' trail about ten feet away through a thin veil of leaves.

I felt his hand on my ass, his fingers probing the mark he had cut into me on our first meeting. "Looks pretty faint," he murmured. "I'll attend to that later. Right now, I have other marks to put on you."

I could hear the belt being pulled from his waist. Oh please, not here, I pleaded silently. How could I not cry out, as I had before when he whipped me? That had been bad enough, but the fear of being humiliated in public was even worse.

"Gag him," Tyler said.

Mason stepped up beside me and thrust a black lump of leather into my mouth. It was attached to straps that fastened the contraption firmly in place so that it was impossible to make a sound.

Tyler kicked my feet apart and then I heard the crack of the leather on the warm summer air. Pain cut through my ass in a narrow line, followed almost instantly by another strike, and another, always in a different place. I bit down hard on the leather, glad of the gag in my mouth. Tears spilled down my cheeks and I could smell my own sweat. My cock was getting hard.

My naked flesh was soon on fire from the beating. It was an eerie sensation, the quiet sun-filled afternoon, the panting of the occasional jogger so close to us on the path, the whistle and crack of the belt against my hot flesh. In my desperate struggles, my body ground itself against the rough bricks, gashing my chest and thighs. But soon I was aware of nothing but my pain and its connection to the man who administered it to me. When he stopped, my eyes were blinded with tears.

"Lock him to the ring," Tyler said, putting on the belt.

At once Mason produced a padlock from the gym bag over his shoulder and attached it through the chain on my handcuffs to an iron ring I had noticed beside the hook. Both looked quite new but had obviously been used before.

Tyler slid a finger down the crack in my burning ass. "Seems a pity to leave him for someone else's pleasure, doesn't it?" he remarked.

Mason chuckled as he removed the gag.

"Bring everything with you, Mason. I've got an appointment for dinner."

I turned my head in an agony of fear. "You're not going to leave me here like this!" I exclaimed in horror.

They paid no attention, but merely walked away, quickly swallowed up in the dense shrubbery.

I opened my mouth to yell at them to come back, then stopped myself. Anyone might hear me! I yanked at the cuffs in desperation. Shit! If the wrong person happened to come along, I could be arrested, charged with indecent exposure, probably a whole slew of things! Or worse, what if some skinhead came along and beat the shit out of me! I was helpless. There was no way I could defend myself. I didn't even have shoes on. I thought of the fag bashing I had undergone on Merton Lane and shivered with fear. My cock was limp; the drying sweat chilled my naked body.

Then I heard the crash and snap of branches breaking underfoot and muffled cursing. I had never wanted to disappear so much in my whole life! I felt the helpless rage of a small child whose secret rituals are discovered and knows punishment will be administered, no matter what. Naked and terrified, I hung against the rough bricks of the old building and prayed that whoever it was would walk right by and not see me.

I held my breath. Over my shoulder I caught a glimpse of two men in the striped shirts, knee socks, and short shorts of a soccer team, stepping out into the clearing. There was no way in hell they could miss a naked man handcuffed to a wall. I turned my head away, not able to look them in the eye. The noises stopped. I could hear their heavy breathing.

"What's this, then?" The voice was almost a whisper, ending in a stifled laugh.

"You okay, mate?" That was the other one. His voice was lighter, and they both had English accents of a type I had heard before but couldn't place.

They came closer. I gulped and turned back to face them, trying for a reassuring grin. "I'm okay," I said. "Really. It's just my friend's idea of a joke." But what if these were Tyler's men? I thought suddenly. What if this was part of the scene? It wouldn't do to sound too apologetic.

"Some friends." This one was short and stocky, with curly black hair and bright blue eyes. His companion was taller, with long blond hair, bleached by the sun, and eyes that reflected the sky.

"Bad luck for you, good luck for us." The blond one was carrying a soccer ball. He bounced it lightly against the wall beside me, a slow smile spreading across his tanned face. "Looks like his friends play pretty rough," he remarked. "Doesn't it look that way to you, Rog?"

Rog moved closer, catching the ball from his friend. "It does at that," he remarked. He tossed the ball against my back, caught it, threw it harder this time, lower, obviously aiming for the criss-cross of red welts on my ass. I winced. As my body jerked against the wall, the tit clamps bit into me. My cock reacted at once, an act that was not lost on my two observers.

"I think you're hurting him, Rog."

"He didn't complain. He'd say something if he wants me to stop, wouldn't he?"

They had stopped addressing me. I had become an interesting object to be explored, played with, used. I noted the shift and tensed. Rog grabbed my shoulder and swung me around. I stared at him, watching his face as he took in the tit clamps, the dog collar, the silver disk. Then he threw the ball very hard straight at my left tit. I bit my lip and tasted blood. The ball bounced across my chest to my right nipple, hitting the clamp at just the exact angle that would hurt the most but not dislodge it.

"His peter really likes that action, Rog," remarked the blond.

"Peter want to play?" The ball hit my cock. A hot burst of pain ricocheted through me and I couldn't stop the small scream it forced out of me. "Shut him up!"

The blond pulled my mouth open and crammed in a filthy hand towel that tasted of sweat and sex. I tried not to panic, not to fight back. I took a breath through my nose and nodded, trying to tell them I wouldn't scream.

"Keep a look out." That was Rog. "You, perv, turn around and move your feet up against the wall. There's a ledge about a foot off the ground." He slapped my cock. "Now!"

My face streaked with tears, I turned around and stepped up on the narrow ledge, my toes curled tightly against the wall. Rog grabbed my hips and pulled, so my legs were straight, my ass pushed high. I felt the air on my exposed hole and gritted my teeth. Was Tyler watching? Did he know these men? Or had he really abandoned me here to be raped? Then again, could that word apply in these circumstances? I wasn't sure about a lot of things anymore.

My arms stretched painfully in their sockets as most of my weight now pulled on them. I looked over my shoulder. The dark one, Rog, was pulling his cock out of an old jockstrap, his soiled white shorts down to his knees. His cock was long and thin, uncut, throbbing and eager to split my ass. He spat on his hands and lubed the cock with his saliva. Then, without any preamble, he shoved himself in me, right up to the hilt.

The screams that burst in my throat were smothered by the

gag as his pubic bone smashed into me over and over. In a few moments, he was finished. The men switched places. The blond's cock was small and thick. He didn't need any lube. He too slammed into me, shot his load, and pulled out.

"Let's get the hell out of here," he said, pushing his cock out of sight. Casually he reached up and pulled the towel out of my mouth, without even looking at me. I didn't exist for them any more.

I could hear them laughing as they rushed down the slope onto the jogging path, slapping each other on the back, leaving me alone and hurting in the sunny clearing.

Stiffly I moved my feet back onto the ground, my arms now stretched straight up to the ring. I could just manage to stand, and although I was almost on tiptoe, it was better than hanging from my arms as I had before. Come dripped down my legs from my battered asshole.

Time crawled past. The back of my calves ached, my shoulders hurt. Sweat smarted in the cuts and welts on my ass and back. Flies tormented me, making it impossible to sink into any sort of stupor. Mosquitoes, too, found my damp hot nakedness an unexpected treat and feasted on my wretched body in droves as I jerked about, helpless to escape. And every time I twisted from one side to the other, the small clamps tore at my tits, sending new jolts through my exhausted body. I had come several times by now, my cock continually excited by my own movements, the new extra-sensitivity of my raw burning nipples, and the rubbing of my cock against the wall.

For some time I had been aware of the need to urinate. Slowly that need became unendurable. At last, I realized there was only one thing to do. I turned away from the wall, trying to keep my space as free as possible from my own bodily waste, and tried to lean forward. It was impossible. Finally, I gave up and let the piss come, arcing hot and steaming into the moist earth at my feet. As my bladder emptied, my cock lowered. Piss dripped down my leg. Resigned, I turned back against the wall and found, to my surprise, that the familiar smell was oddly comforting.

The sun sank low in the sky, and shadows closed in round me. Although it was still warm, my joints were stiffening and a chill settled over me. I shivered. Although utterly miserable in one way, a strange torpor drifted down on my senses. In my mind, an image of Tyler floated steady and strong, my master whom I wanted to please more than anything else. For that reason, I hung silent and dutiful against the rough wall, enduring the pain and cold, the humiliation at the hands of strangers, the fear. Underneath it all was the knowledge that I had to trust my master, just as he trusted me not to cry out, not to bring the wrong kind of attention to myself that could reflect unfavorably on him. I tried hard to believe that he would not forget me; to remind myself that even if he did, it was his prerogative as my master. If I was to stay here all night, so be it. I shivered again and wiped the sweat and tears out of my eyes on my aching shoulder. This is what it is to be slave, I thought, and there was some comfort in that.

I must have slipped into some sort of half-sleep, finally, because I awoke with a start to feel a hand on my tender ass. I didn't need to turn my head to know it was Tyler. I could sense the man in his touch, inhale the distinctive masculine smell of him. I would never know if he had been close by, keeping an eye on things all along, or if he had trusted me to take whatever was handed out to me by strangers. All I cared about was that this ordeal was over. When he moved his hand to the chain joining my raw nipples and gave it a gentle tug, I rubbed my cheek against his hand. I didn't dare say a word as he removed the clamps. Pain burst through me as the blood rushed back. I swallowed my scream.

In silence, Tyler unlocked the cuffs and took them off. I rolled my shoulders, rubbed my wrists. Then I dropped to the ground in front of him, needing to express my joy at seeing him somehow, without words. He laid one hand on my hair and guided my head to his thigh. I remained like this for a few moments, basking in the first sign of real approval he had shown to me, but it was over all too soon. He threw the cuffs and lock in the bag Mason had been carrying, pulled out a T-shirt and handed it to me. It was not the one I had worn here. This one was old and stretched. It hung to my thighs when I stood up and put it on. Tyler pointed down to the jogging path and I realized with a shock I was expected to walk through the park with my ass bare. Granted the shirt was long, but not long enough to cover my cock, which ever since Tyler had arrived seemed to have a life of its own. I didn't move.

"Problem?" he asked. He lifted the shirt and touched my half-hard cock. I moaned softly. "I see. Hold the shirt up to your waist."

I did as I was told, feeling a warm flush spread over me. Tyler took off his belt and fastened it around my waist. Then he took a high-top canvas shoe out of the bag and ripped out the shoelace. Grasping my cock firmly, he tied one end of the lace around the tip, pulled my cock up against my stomach, and fastened it there by tying the rest of the other end to the belt.

"Drop your shirt," he said. "Your cock won't give you any trouble, now." He stepped ahead of me, leaving the bag on the ground.

I was still bare-assed and very nervous as the long shirt flapped about my thighs, but I knew any more hanging back on my part would lead to something far more painful than a tied cock. Without another word, I picked up the gym bag and followed him down the hill. The breeze tickled my balls. My stretched cock tugged against its restraints, making every step painful. Tyler strode briskly ahead of me, paying no attention to my possible discomfort.

When we came near the restaurant, there were more people about, but the atmosphere of the place had changed completely from earlier in the evening. I kept my eyes on Tyler's broad-shouldered back, following him at a respectful distance, which he seemed to expect. He never looked around to check if I was still there. It was cooler, now, but my skin still tingled with sexual warmth.

The limo was drawn up at the curb outside the park gates, the door held open by a tall man in uniform whom I hadn't seen before. Tyler got in and I followed, sinking at once to my knees on the plush floor. Tyler yanked my shirt off, pulled my head forward, and pressed my face against the back of the seat. In terror, I heard the sound of a zipper and gulped air. Could I take his great cock up my ass without screaming? I closed my eyes tight and clutched the soft upholstery with my hands. I felt cool ointment spread on my asscheeks, around my hole. His fingers greased me inside. Then I felt something hard, unyielding. It wasn't Tyler. It was a dildo, shaped like a large cock, and it was being pushed steadily up my ass until I thought I would burst. Then the cool ointment began to burn, deeper and deeper, hot and glowing like fire in my bowels.

I started to gasp, sputtering with fear and pain. "Please, oh please!"

"This is nothing, fucker. You have to be stretched, before you can take me. This is part of your training."

But why the burning? I thought. Was this to take away any pleasure? Or to associate pleasure and pain so closely that I would no longer be able to tell them apart? Tyler shifted and pulled me across his knee. He held my head down, my body sprawled awkwardly, held by his grasp of my wrist. He began to hit my bare ass with his hand, sharp stinging blows that left fire in the shape of his hand on my asscheeks. And each time he struck me, the phallus plugging my hole moved deeper, shifting inside me, releasing molten fire. As the great luxurious limo slid quietly through the evening traffic, the only sounds inside were my gulping cries and the sharp slap of his hand against my naked ass as I writhed head down across his knee.

Finally, he stopped and pushed me to the floor at his feet. He looked at me for a long minute as I tried to steady my heaving chest. My ass was on fire. It felt as if I had impaled myself on a burning sword. But when he touched my face and wiped the tears from my cheek, I thought I was in heaven.

"Sonny, you've made a good start," he said, and his voice now sounded as if we were having a business meeting and I was a new employee. "Go to work as usual until you hear to the contrary. I have a feeling that with you, it'll be soon. Any questions?"

"Sir, will I be…I mean, I thought I was going to live with you."

"Stop thinking. That's not your job." But then he smiled at me and touched my lips with his thumb. "You're still on probation, Sonny. No one moves in without a test period." His thumb pushed its way inside my mouth and stayed there. I sucked on it greedily, glad to have access to any part of him. Then he pulled me back over his knee and I tensed. But instead of another beating, he pulled out the dildo. Just as I was about to breath a sigh of relief, I felt another hard phallus shoved into me. This one was thicker, though not so long, and when it was all the way in, he threaded a narrow piece of leather through the flat handle and clipped one end to the belt at my back. Then he made me kneel, legs apart, while he pulled the narrow leather through my legs, over my tied cock and clipped the other end to the front of the belt. He wiped his hands with a small hand towel while he studied me. Then he handed me the old shirt to put on.

"Get some rest," he said.

"Yes, sir. Ah, what about tomorrow, sir?"

"I told you. Go to work as usual. Here's your key."

The car purred to a stop. I stumbled out, feeling almost drunk, and hurried inside my building, awkward and sore, what with the harness holding my cock and the butt plug tightly in place. At least I didn't have to worry about walking past a doorman, I thought irrelevantly, as I rode the empty elevator up to my floor. Inside my own apartment I was astonished to see it wasn't quite ten o'clock. I was exhausted. I pulled off the shirt and went into the bathroom to inspect my sore, bruised, and burning body. I looked a mess! My back was crisscrossed with long angry red marks, my ass burned crimson, the target scar even clearer than before. My tits were raw and bleeding. Carefully I rubbed antiseptic ointment on them, and even that made my cock twitch, as if a wire had been installed that ran from my tits to my cock. I undid the lace, pissed, and tied it up again. Then, utterly exhausted, I crawled into bed, still wearing the collar around my neck, my cock still tied to Tyler's black leather belt, my ass stuffed with the plug he had placed there. It was almost as if he was still with me.

The phone rang.

"I saw you come in," Polly said, in her usual abrupt phone manner. Her apartment was at the front of the building. "You looked pretty fucked up." She laughed low in her throat.

"Well, I guess you could say that."

"Lucky you. Just checking, love. Sleep tight."

"You too. Thanks for calling."

I hung up and was asleep almost at once, one hand at the collar around my neck, the large buckle of Tyler's belt pushed snug against my waist.

This page constitutes a continuation of the copyright page.

Hustling: A Gentleman's Guide to the Fine Art of Homosexual Prostitution, Copyright © by John Preston, 1994. *The Mission of Alex Kane: Golden Years*, Copyright © by John Preston, 1992. *Mr. Benson*, Copyright © by John Preston, 1992. "Elliott" by Sloan Ryder originally appeared in *Come Quickly: For Boys on the Go*, Copyright © by Julian Anthony Guerra, 1996. "Tour Guide" by Thom Spencer originally appeared in *Come Quickly: For Boys on the Go*, Copyright © by Julian Anthony Guerra, 1996. *The Initiation of PB 500*, Copyright © by Kyle Stone, 1993. *Rituals*, Copyright © by Kyle Stone, 1994. *Beware the God Who Smiles*, Copyright © by Larry Townsend, 1995. *Chains*, Copyright © by, Larry Townsend, 1994. *The Construction Worker*, Copyright © by Larry Townsend, 1981, 1995. *The Faustus Contract*, Copyright © by Larry Townsend, 1982, 1994. *The Gay Adventures of Captain Goose*, Copyright © by Larry Townsend, 1969, 1994. *Kiss of Leather*, Copyright © by Larry Townsend, 1994. *Leather Ad: S*, Copyright © by Larry Townsend, 1988, 1996. *The Leatherman's Handbook*, Copyright © by Larry Townsend, 1972, 1974, 1977, 1993, 1997. *Man Sword*, Copyright © by Larry Townsend, 1994. *Mind Master*, Copyright © by Larry Townsend, 1983, 1994. *Run No More*, Copyright © by Larry Townsend, 1993. *Solidly Built*, Copyright © by Matt Townsend, 1996.